Girl Afraid

By Ciarán West

One

The ringing had woken her, but it had stopped before she could grab the mobile from under her pillow. She looked at the screen: Withheld Number. She blinked, rubbing sleep from her eyes. It rang again.

'Hello?'

'Hello, Alice.' The reception was crackly, and there was an echo to the man's voice.

'Is that you, Tom?' She looked around the room, still waking up; nobody had her work number except him, or the people who worked for him.

'No, it isn't Tom. Are you by yourself?'

She swallowed, suddenly aware of her thirst. There was a bottle of water somewhere.

'Am I what? Who is this, please?' She found the Evian at the end of the bed, and twisted off the cap; it was lukewarm but welcome. Her head began to pound; the excesses of the night before, taking their toll.

'I said, are you by yourself? It's important that you don't lie to me, Alice. I can't help you if you lie to me.' Nothing about the voice rang familiar. She switched on the laptop that was on the side by her bed. Emails still needed to be checked, even on her day off.

'*Help* me? Look, I'm going to put the phone down now. This is a private number. I think you have the wrong person. Goodbye.' She had been trained in dealing with cranks and the mentally disturbed, because of Tom's job and the attention it brought. She wasn't supposed to engage them. She had never had one reach her on the work phone before, but nothing surprised her about Tom's fans and stalkers. They were nothing if not tenacious, she thought. She tapped her password into the entry screen, having paused to remember it first.

'I haven't got the wrong person, Alice... and you're not going to put the phone down, if you want to see Poppy again.'

Hearing him say the name hit her like a blow to the chest. She was overcome with a mixture of panic and dread. She caught sight of the clock on the laptop screen: it was almost three in the afternoon.

'What have you done with her? Where is she? If you've hurt her- if you've-' She scrolled frantically through the RSS feed that sent her the news headlines as they happened. There was nothing about Poppy. He was a crank, she told herself. *He's lying.*

'Forget the computer; just listen to me, okay? Alice? Are you listening?'

'How did you...' *He must have heard me typing.*

'I can see everything you do. You have a black t-shirt on; It says *Star Wars.* And grey trousers.' She knew he was right, but glanced over at herself in the mirrored wardrobe regardless. She felt violated; sick. Her eyes scanned the room, not sure what to look for. A film played her head of spies, from some TV show, opening a smoke alarm with screwdrivers.

'What have you done with her?'

There was silence at the other end.

'Answer me. Answer me!' Any remnants of drunkenness from the night before had vanished in the shock, but all the symptoms of a crippling hangover remained. Throbbing behind her eyes; an insane thirst. Finally, he spoke again.

'You need to calm down, Alice. I'm not the enemy. I need you to be calm. I want you to work with me.'

He doesn't sound like a kidnapper. The voice was quiet and soft. In different circumstances, she would have described it as non-threatening.

'Who are you?'

'I'm your friend.'

'My friend? I don't know you! I don't know who you are... What have you done with her? Please...' She noticed her hands were shaking.

'I haven't done anything with her, Alice. I don't have her; I promise you.'

'How... how did you get this number?' Her work mobile wasn't listed anywhere; she hadn't even been allowed to give it to her family.

'Pointless details, Alice. We don't have time for them. You need to listen to me, and you need to do it quickly.'

She took a breath. *Professional, that's what I need to be.* She was in the kitchen, running the cold tap into a tumbler. The Alka-Seltzers made a familiar plunk-fizz noise.

'Okay. What do you want me to do?' She drank it down, gagging at the bitterness; the fizz went up her nose, making her want to sneeze.

'I need you to get out of the house. And I need you to do it now.'

The room was pink. Poppy loved pink. The walls had been painted pink, the quilt and the pillows were pink; the curtains were pink too. She had gone over and opened them, but there was no window there- just lots of bricks. That's why she had put the lamp on. The lampshade was pink too.

It was a nice room, she thought. Not as big as her room at home, but hardly anyone had a bedroom as big as hers, Alice had said. Alice always told her she was lucky. She said most ten-year-old girls in the world would love to have a room as big as hers, a toy box as full as hers, or all the trips and holidays they went on. It was always Alice who came with her. Her father was usually working; making a film, and her mother didn't like most of the places she wanted to go. Her mother only liked holidays where she could sunbathe.

There was a toy box. It had a lot of things inside: My Little Pony, Barbie dolls, and a Nintendo console, with some games. She wasn't in the mood for playing. She couldn't remember how she had got there. She had been with Magda earlier; and then she remembered feeling sleepy and ill, but nothing more after that.

Magda was gone, but she couldn't remember her leaving. She needed the toilet. She would have to go and find someone to show her where it was. She pushed the handle down, but the door didn't move. She did it again, this time pushing out instead of pulling in. It didn't move either. It was stuck, like the the linen closet at her grandfather's house. For the first time since waking, she felt afraid.

She looked around the room, panicking. There was another door. She walked to it, but slowly. It mightn't be locked, but if it wasn't, she didn't know what was on the other side; or who. It opened easily, but not into a hallway. It was the door to a tiny bathroom, with the smallest shower she had ever seen.

'Are you outside, Alice?'

'Yes.'

'Where is outside, Alice? Were you at home?'

'Hackney. Yes. Yes, at home.'

'Right. Of course you are. Okay, I want you to get out of the square.'

'The square?'

'The square where your flat is, Alice. On Clarence Road, right?'

'Right, yes.' Another wave of sickness swept over her, which had nothing to do with her hangover.

'And Alice?'

'What?'

'There are two gates out of there, is that right?'

'Yes. Yes, that's right.' *He knows everything*, she thought, looking around the square. It was empty, save for a couple of boys kicking a ball in the centre.

'Okay, go out whichever one you use the least. And do it now. Fast.'

She took that as permission to take the phone away from her ear. She was running. *They've taken Poppy*. Someone had snatched her, just like they'd always feared. She needed to know more. He had given her hardly anything, and she had no idea who he was. She needed to call the police. Her head still thumped, but the painkillers were in her system. She tore through the gate on the far side, farthest away from her own front door. It could only be used by pedestrians. The big car gates were on the opposite side, near where her Nissan was parked. Alice looked down at the mobile in her hand. The display had two words on it:

Call Terminated.

The bathroom was white, not pink. There was toilet roll on the holder; Alice had taught her to always check first. She pulled down her pyjama bottoms. She didn't remember putting them on. The scared feeling came again, somewhere in her chest. Magda had put them in her own bag that morning before they'd left for school. That had been strange, but Poppy hadn't asked her why. They hadn't gone to school. Magda had said it was a special day, so they didn't have to. Poppy had asked her why it was so special, but she hadn't got an answer. They'd gone to the café for breakfast, instead of having cereal, or jam and toast, at home. Magda was nice to her, but she didn't always speak very good English. Sometimes Poppy found it hard to make her understand things. She was from Poland.

For years, Alice had been the only one who took her to school. Now Magda did it on Mondays. So Alice could go crazy on the weekend, Magda said. It must have been a joke, because Poppy didn't think Alice was crazy. She lived with them during the week, but she had a flat in London too. Poppy finished what she had to do, and washed her hands in the little sink. She stayed in the bathroom longer than she had to. There was something less frightening about it in there. She didn't know why.

Alice couldn't call him back. There was no number. She looked at the phone again, as if it would do something. Had she accidentally hit Call End, or had he hung up? She wasn't sure. She paused for breath at the traffic lights which led across the road to the Tesco Express, and the little deli next door where she bought most of her food.

Ring! I'm here now. Please! Ring...

The beeping tone which accompanied the green man jolted her from her thoughts, and she sprinted across to the other side, almost colliding with a Number 38 bus whose driver had been slow in braking. She didn't know if she was heading in the right direction; all he had said was for her to get out of the square. The mobile in her hand hadn't rung again. She wondered if she should forget him, and call the police. That would be the sensible thing to do, she thought. That would be what a sane person would do.

At the other side of the road, she had to decide on left or right, and chose the latter, for no particular reason. The people at the bus stop looked up in surprise at her as she ran past, one or two of them failing to get out of her way in time, and throwing muttered curses in her direction as she brushed against them. Another fifty yards down the street, she heard the phone ring and skidded to a halt, her heart pounding in her chest. She pressed the pick-up button in a frenzy and squeezed the handset hard against her face. Silence on the other end. It was still ringing, but not in her ear. In the old fashioned red phone box, a few feet to her left, a large black woman picked up the receiver, and began chatting and laughing in booming, musical tones.

Poppy came back out, slowly again. She looked at the locked door, but she didn't go over to it. Something in her head told her that it might not have been locked; she might have just been turning the handle incorrectly. And if it wasn't locked, then there was nothing to fear. And, if she didn't try the handle again, there was still a chance that everything was okay.

For no real reason, she thought about Jesus. One of the girls at school had told her that even if no one saw you doing a good thing, Jesus saw you, and rewarded you in Heaven. And that if you were in trouble, you could pray to him, and he would keep you safe. Poppy wasn't sure. They didn't have Jesus in their house; neither of her parents went to church, and Alice said if there was a God, he was a bad landlord. Poppy didn't know what that meant, but she wondered now if Jesus answered the prayers of children who didn't believe in him. She wasn't sure if she was ready to find out yet, though.

There was no one else in the room. Someone had been there though, because they'd left a tray. There was food and drink on it: a chicken salad; a glass of red juice with a straw, and a punnet of blueberries. Salads were her favourite type of food, because she was a quick and impatient eater, and hot foods burned her mouth. The juice was pomegranate, which was also a favourite of hers. It felt good, having the things she liked; but she knew there was something bad about everything that was happening. Food didn't just appear by magic. Someone had brought it, and she didn't know who. She looked at the door, and decided that she would eat before trying it again. Alice had always told her it was important not to miss a meal. Especially not breakfast. She said breakfast was the most important meal of the day.

She finished all the food; she was surprised at how hungry was. There was no way of telling the time, so she didn't know if it was because she had missed lunch, or even dinner. There was no clock in the room, pink or otherwise. The bad feeling in her chest had moved to her stomach now, and for a moment she panicked, thinking of the food. She shook her head and tutted to herself, thinking of all the times Alice or Tom had told her she had an over-active imagination. People got poisoned in the movies, but she wasn't in a movie. No one was trying to poison her, she told herself. She was probably somewhere perfectly safe. Magda had brought her there, and Magda was a good person. She would try the door again soon, and it would open. And later, Alice would laugh at her for being so silly.

There was a TV in the corner, with a remote control. She switched it on and went straight to Channel 71. She could watch something until someone came to collect her. She was used to entertaining herself at home. Channel 71 was nothing but snow. There was no Sky or Freeview; she couldn't see a box. She tried Channel 1, Channel 2, Channels 3, 4 and 5. None of those worked either. Poppy shrugged, and threw the remote onto the quilt. The television was useless. She stood up to examine it, furrowing her brow. At last, she found a small slot along the back of the top. A built-in DVD player.

Alice dropped down, feeling defeated. She tried controlling her breathing; a technique she had learned from hypnosis tapes she had used in the past to help her to quit smoking. She took a long breath in through her nose; held it, and then exhaled slowly out through her mouth. There was a noticeable wheezing sound, from the cigarettes she had never quite managed to give up. She only smoked at weekends anymore, and the night before had been no exception.

She looked at the phone and thought about the police. She should call them. That's what she always shouted at the screen when she saw these things on television: *Call the police! Call the bloody police, you idiot!*

They always said not to call the police though, in those programmes, she reminded herself: *Don't get the police involved. If you call the police, you'll never see her again!*

She pushed a nine, and then another. She paused; the breathing exercises had done something to slow her heartbeat. She was hot and clammy. As she looked at the two nines on the screen, her mobile rang.

'Yes! Hello? Hello?'

'Hello Alice.' It was him. She wasn't expecting it to be anyone else, but relief came anyway. She didn't want it to be Tom. Not when she had so much to feel bad about, and so little to make things right.

'Thank… oh, God. Why did you hang up? Where did you go, I was…'

'I didn't go anywhere. I'm still here.' His voice never changed in tone or pitch, she noted, not sure if it was a good thing or not. A car passed, blaring dubstep from its open windows.

'But…'

'Are you out? Of the square, I mean.'

'Yes. Yes, I am. Look, I don't know what you're saying to me. Poppy… what's going on? What have you done with her? Where's Magda? What-'

'Alice, be calm. Just… calm down, please. Where are you now?'

'I'm- I don't know. I'm just… down the road.' She couldn't remember the name of the street, nor did she think it was important. She wanted answers to her questions. He was giving her nothing, she thought.

'Which way down the road?'

'What? I don't know… right? I turned right. Look, what-'

'Are you heading towards town or away from it?'

'I'm, well, I can get there from here.'

'Good. How far away are you from the train station? How long?'

'The tra- which one?'

'Central.'

'I don't know. I mean… ten minutes- less than that if I-'

'Get there for me. As quick as you can, but don't run. Keep your head down, don't face the traffic. I'll call you in ten.'

The phone went dead again. She picked herself up and started towards the town centre, suddenly terrified for her own safety, but not sure why.

Poppy was exploring. There were board games under the bed. Scrabble, Monopoly, Cluedo, and some others. One called Go for Broke and one called Atmosfear. She liked board games. Alice had an old one called Ghost Castle. It had glow-in-the-dark skulls, and traps, and a coffin. It was one where she could play with all the pieces by herself, if there was no one around. Sometimes that was the best kind of playing, she thought; when you played with things in a different way than you were supposed to. She loved things like old watches; she would get Tom's special screwdrivers (which he used for fixing his glasses) and take an old watch apart, so she could play with all the parts inside. If you got up close to normal things, you could pretend they were other things, like missiles, or spaceships from another galaxy. She liked dolls too; she wasn't a tomboy.

She liked Scrabble because it was a game with words. Alice always wanted to play, because she was good at it, and because she said it was educational. Poppy had learned plenty of new words from watching Alice play. They always checked them in the dictionary, to make sure no one was cheating.

They were all good board games, in her opinion, but there were none she could play on her own. She would get Magda to play with her later, but not Scrabble. If your brain thought its thoughts in Polish, you probably couldn't play Scrabble in English, she thought. Magda had shown her some old Polish money once, in a frame. She said it was printed in the year she was born. She called it a *zwotty,* which had made Poppy laugh. Magda smoked cigarettes. She said to Poppy she had always wanted to come to London and see the Pall Mall, because that was what the cigarettes she smoked in Poland were called. Magda came from Warsaw in Poland, but she said it wasn't called Warsaw in Polish. It was something like *Wishy* or *Vishy.* Poppy couldn't remember exactly which. She pushed the boxes back under the bed; carefully, because they didn't belong to her.

Alice walked as quickly as she could without drawing suspicion to herself. She had crossed the road like he said to, so the cars closer to her were bringing up the rear. Every time she heard a car door shut or someone brake, her heart did somersaults. Her head was low and she let her hair fall in front of her face.

She had too many questions, with no hope of answers yet: *Where was Magda? What had they done with her? Why hadn't the school been in touch?*

Maybe they had. She had wasted most of the day in bed, recovering from Sunday night. For all she knew the police had been called; the news was all over the TV and Tom had rushed back from the North Sea rig where he had been filming. There had been nothing on the internet though, she reminded herself. It was twenty past three. Poppy finished school at a quarter past. Until they'd found Magda, it had been one of Alice's jobs to take the girl in the morning and pick her up in the afternoon. It still was, for the other four days. The first time Magda had taken over the Monday slot, Alice had felt like a mother on the first day of school. She had followed the Polish girl's car all the way to the school, taking care not to be seen. She felt awful about it afterwards, but also relieved.

The police would have come to her first, or maybe second, after calling at Tom's. The man on the phone knew more than anyone, she thought. That was if he was telling the truth. He could still be a crank. He might be something even worse. She had a sudden feeling that she might be voluntarily walking to her own death. She should stop, she thought. She shouldn't trust the word of some psychopath. Poppy was with Magda. She wasn't in any danger. This man, whoever he was, had somehow got a hold of her number, and was playing an elaborate hoax. She was suddenly overcome with relief.

She slowed down. She wasn't going to jump through hoops all afternoon for some sick prankster, she decided. She could call the police, just to make sure. They'd reassure her, and maybe they'd be able to trace the call to whoever the man was. *But then it'd be an official matter*, she thought, turning onto the main street. *Tom would find out about it, and I'd look like an idiot.* She didn't want that. His trust was important to her. A man sweeping the street outside a shop gave her a smile, but she was lost in her own thoughts. *Magda! Why didn't I think of that before? I can call Magda.* The number would be in the address book of her phone.

Poppy had a lot of questions. Alice always said that clever people were people who asked questions. She wanted to know where she was; why she was there, and where everyone else was. She wanted to know who had put her to bed; for how long had she slept, and why it was she couldn't remember things. She didn't know why the window had been covered up with bricks. Once, when she had been to Alice's flat in Hackney, they had walked past a building which had windows down low; underneath the pavement. Instead of glass, they had been filled with red bricks. She tried to remember what Alice had said about them; what the reason was for the bricks, but it wouldn't come. It made her feel bad, having no daylight; like she had been buried.

She had been left on her own before; they knew that she could entertain herself. Sometimes, if Alice had to visit a friend, Poppy would come along; and, if the friend had no children for her to play with, she would read a book, or watch TV. She was ten years old, and she could fix herself a drink, or make a sandwich. She didn't need looking after in the way a younger child would. It wouldn't be long before she was a teenager, her father often said. She always thought he looked sad when he said things like that, but she didn't know why. Being left alone while Alice or her father were in the next room was one thing; waking up somewhere strange, and not remembering how she had got there, wasn't the same. She had never felt frightened in those situations.

Whenever she had a bad dream or a nightmare, Alice would come and sit with her, and get her to sing a song. Not a pop song, or anything new; an old song, from when she was younger. A nursery rhyme song, like *Twinkle, Twinkle, Little Star*, or *Old McDonald*. No matter how silly it felt at first, or how babyish it seemed, it would always work. When she went back to sleep, the nightmares would be gone. She looked around the room again, and started to sing one of the old tunes; under her breath at first, but gradually getting louder. It was *Ten Green Bottles*, which was on Alice hated. She started off with fifty bottles, because she wanted the good feeling to last.

Magda's mobile was dead. All of Alice's relief, hope and optimism seemed to drop out of sight the second she heard the error tone, and a recorded voice:

The number you have dialled has not been recognised. Please hang up and try again.

She was on the street which led to Hackney Overground. She stopped walking and slid down the metal barriers to one side of the pavement, all her adrenaline seeming to have left in a matter of seconds. When the mobile in her hands rang, it took her some moments to register.

'Hello?'

'Alice.' It was him. She had wanted it to be Magda. She straightened herself up, although she was still on ground. One or two passers-by gave her a look, but most carried on without paying her any heed.

'Yes.'

'Are you at the station, yet?'

'No. No, not yet.'

'What? Okay, you have money? An Oyster card?'

'Yeah, I do. But-' She had taken her wallet and keys when she spotted them on the hall table. Her card was paid for by Tom's people. A yearly renewal, to all zones.

'Good. I need you to get on a train. As soon as possible.'

'No.' She wanted to say a lot of things to him, but 'no' was the most important one, she told herself. She helped herself up from the ground by leaning on the iron fence. Across from her, a homeless man was begging for change.

'No?'

'No. Look, this has gone on far enough already.'

'What? Look, Alice. I haven't got time for this. I don't know what you're trying to do, but it isn't helping you. It isn't helping Poppy.'

'Why should I believe you?'

'Why should you- What do you mean, believe me?' He didn't sound angry to her.

'You know exactly what I mean. I don't know how you got this number, or what your game is, but you don't have Poppy. Poppy went to school today, same as normal. No one else has called me, and there's nothing on the news; no police at my house. Why the hell should I believe that you have her? Who are you?'

'I've... I've already said I don't have her, Alice. You need to pay more attention.'

'Don't you tell me what I need to do. I don't know who you are, but this is bullshit. You're just some sad pathetic bastard who gets his kicks from trying to frighten people. Well, I'm not frightened. I'm-'

'You didn't get an answer when you called her, right?'

The words sent a chill through her.

'No. No, it said the number wasn't- it didn't work.'

'Of course. That phone is probably on its way to a landfill by now.'

'But, I-'

'Okay, Alice. You're right. I'm asking you to put a lot of faith in me, and I've given you no proof of anything. What if I was to tell you that Poppy has red Nike trainers on today? A blue ribbon in her hair? Would you believe me then?'

She couldn't speak.

'No? Okay. The Polish woman who takes her on a Monday- she drives a two-year-old Renault; it's blue.'

'I... yes.' Alice pressed the phone hard against her ear, not wanting to hear more, but at the same time, needing to.

'Okay, this Polish woman...'

'Magda'

'Magda, yes. That's what she's going by now. You found her where?'

'I... Tom interviewed some people. Then he had me interview the ones he thought were- why are you asking me this? How do you know so much about us?'

'Never mind any of that. So, you thought she was okay, I suppose?'

'She was perfect. We saw so many people before we picked her. I was just so... I didn't want anyone to- I needed to be sure she...' The words stopped coming. She wanted to cry, but she wasn't going to let herself.

'Right, well we all make mistakes, Alice.' He almost sounded kind.

'What the hell is happening? Where have they taken her? What have they done with Magda? What have they done with my little-' Her head was filled with possibilities, all of them morbid.

'Just... take your time. I'm going to help you. Poppy is safe, I promise you that.'

'How do you know that?' She wasn't going to rely on his promises. She didn't even know his name; let alone what his connection was to it all.

'I've seen her. Less than an hour ago. She's fine. Trust me, no one has hurt her.'

The song got to one green bottle much quicker than she would have liked. She had been sitting on the carpet, rocking back and forth, while she sang. The reason Alice didn't like it was because Poppy would deliberately start it with a big number, to delay her being left alone to go back to sleep. Eventually, it had been banned from their list of *Feel Better* songs, much to Poppy's annoyance.

The scared feeling came back as soon as the song was over. She didn't want to get up from the floor yet. She found that if she hugged herself tight, around her knees, everything felt a little better. She thought of another song to sing, wishing she had her old toddler books, from back at the house. Thinking about home made her feel sad. She started singing the one about the old lady who swallowed a fly. She wasn't sure if it had a name or not. She looked at the door again, and had an idea.

'Alice, are you still there?'

'Yes...' She wanted to know how he had seen her, if he wasn't the one who had taken her. It didn't make sense to her.

'Good. I need you get on the train for me.'

'Why?'

'It's not safe for you to stay there. You need to be on the move.'

'Why? Why isn't it safe? Who would-'

'They sent someone to your flat. We probably missed them by minutes. Once they see that you're gone, they'll come looking for you.'

'Who? Who is doing this? Why would they take her?' She didn't want an answer to the last question; either because she already knew, or because any alternative to her guess might be much worse.

'That's what I'm going to help you to find out, Alice. But you must get to the station. You need to get on the train.'

'You said you'd seen her. You've seen her today. How did you see her? Where?'

'I'm going to tell you all that, Alice. Soon, I promise. But you need to go.'

'Go where?'

'I'll tell you that too. Trust me; I'm the only person who can help either of you right now. You're just going to have to believe me.'

'And what if I don't? What if I don't want to go? What if I say no? I mean, shouldn't we be calling the police?'

'The police?'

'Yeah, the police. If you know so much, and you swear you have nothing to do with it, why are we having this conversation? Why aren't we telling it to them?'

'Because… if either of us do that, she's dead. Okay? We talk to the police, and we've as good as killed her ourselves.'

Alice felt her fingers dig into her palms, and a sense of dread washed over her. The world around her seemed to close in, crushing her. It was only the sudden pain of nails breaking skin, drawing blood, which jolted her back to reality.

Two

Dylan had poured roughly a third of the Diet Coke away to make room for the vodka. The ratio of soft drink to alcohol would be strong, but he couldn't spend all day topping one up with the other. He wasn't going to do that in public, where people could see. It was a case of filling it once, then taking it with him. He could pace himself, he thought. He could drink it slowly. He held the bigger bottle steady as he poured the neat liquor into its neck.

'Jesus!'

He had let some spill into the bowl, suddenly paranoid whoever was in the next cubicle would hear, and know he wasn't going to the toilet. He wasn't sure why that would matter, but it worried him, nonetheless. He often had paranoid thoughts in public lavatories. He hated the places, but he needed the privacy for what he was doing.

'Bollocks!'

He had spilled some more, this time onto his hand. He licked it off his fingers, baulking at the taste. The cola in the bigger bottle began to fizz and foam. A toilet flushed nearby; and, outside, he could hear someone using the automatic dryer. The bubbles went back down and he poured in the rest. His guess had been good; the liquid came right up to the neck. He took a taste.

'Jesus Christ…'

The mix was too strong, but he couldn't do anything about that. The fumes went up his nose and made him cough. The door of the other cubicle opened, and there was a sound of running water. He heard the dryer again, and then the sound of whomever it was, leaving through the main door. He opened his own stall and walked past the sinks, blinking at himself in the mirror. There was no need to wash his hands; he hadn't used the toilet.

Outside, it was bright and sunny. He opened the bottle and took another sip. Still strong, but easier the second time around. He wanted to be drunk quickly. He wasn't feeling social. He wanted to alter his state of mind, to the point where he didn't feel anymore. The drink gave him a shiver and relaxed the muscles in his shoulders.

Some teenage girls were standing outside HMV as a he passed. He couldn't put an age to them, but it didn't matter to him. She was the only thing on his mind. She could pass for a teenager, he thought. Her body was lithe and strong, from years of horse riding. Her face looked adult enough, but she was still asked to show

ID every once in a while. His brother had told him that she was far too good looking for him. *Punching above your weight*, was how he had put it. Sometimes he had wished that it wasn't true. He found it hard to relax in a situation like that. Sometimes it seemed like he was just counting down the days until she left him, for someone better.

He wanted to find somewhere that had a free Wi-Fi connection. He wandered into a coffee franchise and joined the queue. He didn't want anything. Coffee would sober him up.

'How may I help you?' The girl was Polish, or Lithuanian, maybe, he thought.

'Ahhh, I… Can I have… an orange juice?'

'Small medium or large?' She pronounced the word 'medium' peculiarly, he noticed.

'Medium.' He only chose it so he could correct her.

'Am, I am sorry, sir. Is no medium. Just small and large.' She had short hair and harsh, angular features.

'What? Okay, large.'

'Large juice, orange?'

'Yeah.'

'That is one pounds forty.' She smiled, but it looked insincere to him. He handed her a five pound note, and looked behind him to see if there was a free table.

Bob hadn't met this man before. He was large and imposing, and spoke with a foreign accent.

'You give her the food, yes? The Polish, she leave a tray for you?' It sounded German to Bob; definitely European, he thought.

'Yeah. Salad and that,' he replied, without looking up.

'And drink?'

'Yeah, some juice. Look, I ain't a bleeding idiot, mate. I know what I'm supposed to do. I ain't come down in the last shower.' He picked up his copy of The Sun again, and turned to the back.

'I don't think you are idiot. I'm just having to check this.'

'Yeah, well it's done now. You can wind your neck in.'

'Okay. Okay, this is good.'

'Yeah. Yeah, it's good.' Bob gave him a glance, and went back to reading about the weekend's games.

'I will be back soon. You will stay. Watch the light. Do not talk.'

He walked away, jangling his keys and whistling. Bob didn't say anything more to him.

From what he had heard earlier, when the other man was on the phone, it was a young girl in the room. There had been no names, or even any talk of a ransom, but that was a given, Bob thought. No one snatched a child unless there was something to gain from it.

Her profile page had nothing recent on it. That seemed suspicious to him. He could still see it, so he hadn't been blocked. She could still be stopping him from seeing some things though. You could do that. He had done it to her plenty of times, whenever he wanted to have a rant. He didn't like the idea of her hiding things from him. It fuelled his paranoia that there might be someone else.

He didn't want to know. He would have preferred if he never knew anything about her again. It would have been better if she just disappeared into thin air. Better still, if she just never existed. That would have been the easiest way. There would be someone else eventually, even if there wasn't already. He closed his eyes and groaned. He hated the feelings he was having; the jealousy, the suspicion. He had to stop torturing himself. People were already telling him the usual things: that there were plenty of fish in the sea, or that time was a great healer. Both were true, he knew, but he was still grieving. He didn't care how many other women there were. He wanted her.

He had cried in front of her. That had felt like a mistake. It hadn't made a difference. In his experience, women weren't moved by crying or by declarations of undying love, once they'd decided that the relationship was over. No amount of emotional blackmail would sway them.

He scrolled down through her friends lists, stopping every so often to view the profile of any male he didn't know. *Any of them could be him*, he told himself. He took another swig; it tasted chocolaty to him. Overly sweet, and beginning to go flat already.

'Juice is not okay, no?' The girl who had served him was at the table opposite, spraying and wiping.

'Am, no it's fine. I'm, ah, not thirsty.'

'Why do you buy drink then?'

'Um, cos… What?'

'I see you drink this other. This *dee-it cock*. You are thirsty, no?' Her face had no expression.

'Dee what?'

'*Dee-it cock*. In this bottle. Here.' She pointed at his bag.

'Huh?'

'The *dee-it cock*; it is, how do you say, like *cock*, but no *shoo-ger*. You make a *dee-it*, yes?' She put her hands around her waist and did a cinching movement.

'Oh. Diet Coke. I getcha.'

'Yes. Like I say, *dee-it cock*. Why you drink this and not juice? You are not liking juice? There is something wrong?'

Bob lit up a cigarette. There wasn't an ashtray; he had been flicking them into an old peanut packet he found in his coat. It wasn't the sort of place you could put ash on the floor, he thought. It was a beautiful house, and immaculately clean. He hadn't seen the outside. He had been working for their outfit for almost a year, but he knew little about who they were. He had never met the boss, or heard a name mentioned.

A van had picked him up at eleven from outside The Crown. The text had said to get in the back when it came. He hadn't talked to the driver. No windows either, so he had no idea where they'd taken him. He was sure that that had been a deliberate thing. They were professional and discreet. He hadn't made many friends, but the money had been good.

He had spoken to a Polish woman when he arrived. She had told him what to do. He was to sit outside the room at the table and watch the blue light. They'd given him a tray with some food and drink on it. When the blue light came on, he was supposed to unlock the door and bring it into the room. He wasn't to let the child see or hear him, and he shouldn't engage her in any way. He was in and out in quickly, when the time came. He heard her singing to herself in the toilet. *Baa, Baa, Black Sheep*, or something with a similar tune. He felt a pang of guilt as he let himself out. He was fond of kids, and always had been.

They'd driven the van straight into a big garage, and the woman had taken him to the room herself. He hadn't met the German until well into the afternoon. They hadn't told him not to wander around the building; but he guessed that it wouldn't go down well with them if he did. The less he knew, the less he could tell, should anything go wrong. They would have no worries in that respect with him; he had never been one to talk to the police about anything, if he could help it. Bob was from the Old School, as he liked to call it. He had been in his line of work since the Sixties. He had known the Krays and the Richardsons, and had done jobs for both, although not at the same time. He was godfather to one of Frankie Frazer's girls.

He had done some prison time, but mostly been lucky enough to avoid it. He had never turned a job down, unless it involved harming women or children. They hadn't told him what the latest thing was until he had stepped out of the van, but the girl didn't seem to be in any danger. She was being fed and kept warm, and his role was little more than a glorified babysitter's job. The money would have been too difficult to turn down, regardless; especially in his financial situation. The five thousand pounds would be enough to clear his debts with the loan sharks who had been harassing him for the last few months. And there would be some left over, which he was planning to spend on his grandson. Sheila, his daughter, had miscarried five times before George had come along. It was such a relief to everyone involved, that it didn't seem to matter that the boy had been born with Down's Syndrome. Everyone loved him just as much, and probably more, Bob thought. He doted on the child, even if it was sometimes hard to do normal things with him, or even to communicate. He wouldn't be with them for long, even with the advances in modern medicine. Their time with him was precious; they all knew it.

The little girl in the room didn't know how lucky she was, Bob thought. *A rich Daddy, no doubt, and probably everything she's ever wanted.* Bob hadn't had anything, growing up. There had been six of them at home, with just his mother to look after them. His father had been killed in the war; he died instantly, the letter had said. No suffering, other than the suffering he left behind him in England. That was how his mother had put it.

Dylan said goodbye to the café girl, and headed outside again. Her boss had come over to them while they were chatting, and told her to get on with her work. She had probably been glad, he thought. She probably hadn't wanted to hear his drunken ramblings about heartbreak, and a girl she had never met.

He threw his Android tablet into the backpack. His head felt light; it had been a while since he had his first drink. Took about a half hour before the alcohol got into the bloodstream, he had read somewhere. He wondered where she was. She had answered his first few texts the night before, but she had stopped replying at about eleven. He didn't know if it was because he annoyed her by being too needy, or if it was because she was busy doing something else. His stomach knotted with jealousy, thinking about it.

He had thought things were getting better between them. No fights; or not as many as before. He had finally started to relax around her, and feel comfortable. She had said she wasn't happy. He didn't understand it. He never understood women or relationships, and it wasn't due to a lack of experience. He didn't seem to be able to learn. He was always in the dark when it came to how his girlfriends were feeling, or what he should do to make things better. She had said they were stagnating; that she wanted to do things with her life, and that he didn't seem to feel the same. He had tried to argue with her about it, but arguing never led to anything other than her feeling even more unhappy, and him feeling more helpless.

He missed her. It was a feeling he was familiar with; because, even when they were together, she would need a lot of space. He seemed to be the opposite, although he was never sure if it was his nature, or just a reaction to how she seemed to push him away. Equally, he didn't know if her pushing stemmed from his being so needy and smothering all the time. It was difficult to gauge where one thing ended and the other began. It seemed like a vicious circle with no end, to him.

He had tried to back off; to give her the space that she craved. And, when he remembered to do it, it paid huge dividends. Her mood changed; she began to text and call him more often, and she would tell him that she loved him almost every day that they spoke. After a while of doing that though, he would forget himself, and go back to the old habits of neediness and self-pity. And, when that happened, she would go back to pushing him away, and needing space.

He loved her, that was never in question. And she loved him too, he was sure of it. He wasn't going to walk away without a fight, he told himself. Alice was still his girl, even if, officially, they were *taking a break.*

The smell of pipe tobacco hit her as she passed the pub at the end of the street. She could see the station up ahead, about twenty feet above ground. A freight train, laden with containers, rushed through without stopping. She had no idea what time the regular trains ran, or how much time there was until the next one.

She felt completely responsible for what was happening. It might have been her day off, but what had happened was still her fault. She had been the one who vetted Magda, and she had been the one who had given her the all clear. Tom wouldn't blame her, and the police would certainly not hold her accountable, but she would hold herself accountable, she knew. If anything happened to the child, there would be no living with herself. *Something has already happened*, she reminded herself, crossing the road before the green man had time to appear.

She ran up the gangway to the turnstiles at Hackney Central. She touched in without any trouble; her card was paid up until the following December. There were two platforms. One went to Stratford, the other one into King's Cross and towards West London. He hadn't said where she should go. She caught her breath half way up the steps. A Turkish-looking man gave her a friendly look. She carried on.

Magda had given nothing away to suggest that her intentions had been less than honourable, Alice thought. She had watched her with the child; sometimes when the woman knew she was being watched, other times when she didn't. There had been nothing amiss, ever. Poppy had taken to her immediately; Alice had too. There had been countless nights when the two of them had sat up at the house, drinking Chablis and talking about life and love and about the child. Alice was a good judge of character, everyone told her so. There was nothing about Magda which sounded alarm bells. Tom thought so too, although he wasn't around her as much. He had been impressed with what he saw, however. She had a pay rise long before the end of her three months' probation.

She was on Platform 2. The next train was the 3.43, the board said; in five minutes. Her head had stopped pounding, but she was thirsty again. There was no vending machine on either platform, nor a kiosk. It was more of a rest than a proper station. She wished she had brought her other phone. She could use the work mobile to call out, it didn't have any other numbers stored in it that weren't work-related. Not even Dylan's.

He had been in touch the night before. His usual routine; starting off sweet, spiralling into guilt-tripping. He was taking the whole thing hard, but she didn't want to indulge him. It just led to them going around in circles and never getting anywhere. She loved him, and she wanted it to work out between them. It just seemed less and less likely, the more they went on.

The phone buzzed in her hand. She picked up before it could finish the first ring.

'Yes?'

'Alice?'

'Yes. I'm at the train station.' She kept an eye on the digital sign. There were two minutes left, it said.

'Which platform are you on?'

'Um, 2. Yeah, Platform 2.'

'Platform 2, for the 15.43 service to, Richmond', came the lady's voice over the PA. The orange coloured Overground carriages slowed to a halt in front of Alice and the other commuters. Someone pushed behind her. She put a hand out to press the door button.

'Get on it.' He hung up again.

Bob had heard a voice. They had been proper words this time; not the sing-song humming which had been going on for some time. He put the paper down and leaned closer to the door. Nothing, then:

'Hello?'

It was her: the child. She was on the other side of the door. He didn't know what to do. They had told him not to engage her in any way. He thought about Sheila, when she was young, years ago. She had been so helpless for such a long time, he remembered. His wife had died a few hours after giving birth, so Sheila had always been a Daddy's Girl. His sisters had helped of course. In truth, they'd done all the hard work. Bob had been busy working.

'Hello, Treacle. You all right in there?' There seemed a long pause before any answer, then:

'I, I think so…' She sounded old enough. Ten or eleven maybe.

'Listen, love. Everything's gonna be fine, all right? You take it from me now, won't you? Everything'll be okay, in a little while. We'll have you back home with Mummy and Daddy in no time. You'll be right as rain.' He needed a drink. They'd stuck a fridge out in the hall next to him, so he didn't have to leave the door. It was full of soft drinks and fruit juice, for her, he supposed. He took out a can of 7up.

'Excuse me. Where's Magda?'

'Magda? Who's Magda, sweetheart?' The can hissed when he opened it, and the fizz bubbled up, wetting his fingers.

'The lady who looks after me, when Alice isn't here.'

'I dunno, darling'. Tell us, what's she look like? What's Magda look like?' It sounded to him like she meant the Polish girl.

'Aaaaaaaaam, she's small, and she has brown hair, and she has curls, and she sometimes has glasses, but she hasn't got them today.' His guess had been correct.

'Ah, Magda's gone down the shops, sweetheart. Gone to do a bit of shopping, yeah? She'll be back in a bit. No worries.' It struck him as odd that the little girl knew one of her kidnappers personally. He hadn't been told any of the details; nor had he asked.

'Where's Alice?'

'Who's Alice, love?' He knew he was doing the wrong thing, talking to her. If the others knew, there might be some trouble. He kept his voice low, looking over his shoulder for anyone who might be coming down the hall.

'She takes care of me the rest of the time.' The girl sounded slightly cross with him, he thought; like she was annoyed he didn't know these things.

'Oh right, yeah. Gotcha. Well, I dunno where Alice is, sweetheart. I'm sure she'll be back soon though. Don't you worry.'

'Oh. Okay then.' Footsteps, away from the door.

Sweet little thing, Bob thought. He took out another cigarette. Something wasn't right. He thought of the five thousand, and little George. George had been his own father's name, and his grandfather before him. He wasn't the eldest, so they'd called him Robert. His older brother had died aged four months. Cot Death, they'd said at the time. His mother had been floored by it. *No therapy or counselling in those days*, Bob thought, leaning back in the chair. *You just got over it. And if you couldn't get over it, you got on with it.*

'The next station is Dalston Kingsland...'

He wanted her to go west. It was the same train she took to work; seven or eight stops to Hampstead Heath, depending on how you counted it. It was almost empty; there were a lot of free seats. Alice stayed standing, leaning against a cushioned side next to the doors. She looked around her; no one looked back. There were five or six people, most of them lost in books. E-readers had replaced paperbacks as the preferred method of ignoring everyone else on London's public transport. Next to her, a handsome black man in a suit was nodding his head with his eyes shut; the fashionable oversized speakers keeping in everything except for the drumbeat. Down the end, a greying business type was squinting at the screen of his phone. Pink patches of scalp showing through in places near the crown and temples. The train pulled into Dalston, but no one got off or on. The beeps went after a minute and they were off to Canonbury. Still there'd been no word. He was getting her to use the Overground so he could stay in touch by phone; she had figured that part out. She was still kicking herself for leaving without the Samsung.

'Scuse me...' The handsome black man pushed past her to get to the button on the doors. A sporty teenage boy in board shorts got on, carrying a modern, carbon fibre bike.

'The next station is Highbury & Islington, change here for Victoria line and National Rail services...'

The teenager gave her a grin. He had good hair and golden skin, and was probably used to getting a smile back. She ignored him and stared at the screen of the phone, willing it to ring. It did.

'Hello!?'

Three

'Who is this man? This... this Cockney. I don't like him. He is your friend?' The Austrian spat the words down the phone line at him.

'Reinhart, didn't I tell you I was busy this afternoon?' Harry took one of the Cubans from the inside pocket of his jacket.

'Yes. I am sorry, boss. But this new man; I do not trust him. Who is he? Where has he come from?' His accent was still strong, but his English was almost perfect.

'His name is Bob, and I trust him completely, Reinhart. I've used him plenty before, don't you worry about him.'

'When? When have you used him? I have not met this man before. I would know.'

'Some jobs, here and there; you weren't involved, I don't think. How is the girl?' The cigar end came off easily with the cutter.

'The girl is fine. This man is not fine. I don't think he is-'

'-Reinhart?'

'Yes...'

'Do you know what 'HR' is?' He nodded at the table boy to bring him a light.

'HR? No. What is this?' His Austrian tones made the two letters almost unrecognisable when sounded aloud.

'Well, it's a position, or a department, that deals with personnel. Hiring, firing, employee-employer relations, that sort of thing. You understand now?' The boy flicked open a Zippo he pulled from his own pocket.

'Yes. I think so.'

'Well now, Reinhart. Do I employ you in my HR Department?' He pulled the first drag of smoke into this mouth; it rolled over his tongue, to the back of his throat.

'Ah, no Herr Goldman, I...'

'Well, then. Keep a bleeding lid on it. Now, the girl?' He settled back into the leather of the chair.

'Yes, Herr Goldman. The girl, she is good. Happy. She has breakfast in the morning and now another meal, here.'

'And the dose?'

'In the drinks, like you said.'

'Good, good. And the woman?'

'The Polish? She is… well, she is Polish.'

'No, no. Not her. The other one. The PA. Riley's girl.'

'Ah, yes. I see now. I have sent someone to get her. He doesn't tell me anything yet.'

'Right. When was this?'

'Last time he calls is half before four.'

'Right. Okay. Yeah, well keep me posted, all right? Important stuff only, though. I don't want to hear about Bob again.'

'Okay, yes. Sorry, Herr Goldman.'

Not a problem.'

Harry put the phone down and took another long smoke of the imported cigar. Neither Bob nor the Austrian were exactly the friendly type, he thought. *I should have known the bloody sparks were gonna fly with them two.*

It was all wrong. The door to the room shouldn't have been locked. You didn't lock a bedroom door; she had seen it in the adverts for the Fire Brigade. And you didn't lock a child in anywhere on her own. Magda wasn't there, or Alice. There was a man outside the door. He sounded like the people in Eastenders, which she wasn't supposed to watch, but Alice always let her. The window shouldn't have been made of bricks, and meals didn't just appear out of thin air. Something was going on, she thought. It scared her. There was nothing genuinely frightening happening; not like in a horror movie, or one of her Goosebumps books. But things didn't seem right to her.

She had been asleep, but she didn't remember going to bed. She was in her pyjamas, but she didn't remember getting undressed. It didn't feel like night time either. The café had only been in the morning, when she had breakfast. Then she had woken up in the pink room.

If I woke up, I must have gone to sleep, she thought. Then she had more food, and a drink, and it hadn't been a whole day and night. It was still the same day, she was sure of it. She must have had a nap in the morning, after she had her food. She didn't remember getting back in Magda's car, or coming to a strange house. There was a lot of the day that she didn't recall.

She wanted Alice. She had stopped wanting Magda to come back so much. She hadn't answered any of Poppy's questions in the morning, about why they weren't going to school; or, if they weren't going to school, why they hadn't just stayed at home. She hadn't answered anything, she had just drunk coffee, and sent text messages, with an odd look on her face. Alice wasn't ever like that with her. She answered all Poppy's questions, even the ones about grown-up things which her father wouldn't.

There was a wardrobe. It was brown and varnished, unlike the pink-painted children's furniture in the rest of the room. Poppy pulled the doors open and looked inside. There were no clothes, only hangers. She was disappointed. Then she spotted something: it was black, and looked like a fur coat. It had fallen from its hanger and it was lying at the bottom of the wardrobe, on top of a big box. Poppy tried to pick it up, but it was either too heavy, or it was stuck. She held on tight to it, and leaned back on her feet, trying to use her weight to make it budge. It reminded her of a book she read when she was little, a Ladybird book. It was about this enormous turnip, and everyone in the village was trying to pull it out of the ground. One person pulled the turnip, then someone pulled them, then another person pulled them, and so on. She hadn't read it in years, but she still remembered. The coat came off suddenly, and Poppy fell back and landed on her back. It wasn't a coat at all; it a piece of carpet, or rug, she guessed. It didn't have sleeves or a neck, it wasn't *clothes*.

The box underneath was big and wooden. Poppy's mother had boxes in her wardrobe too, for all her shoes. Hers was a walk-in one; she had a lot of clothes. The box was probably for shoes too, she thought; although it was probably empty, like the wardrobe. She looked to see if it had a lid, and if there was a special way to open it. She felt around the front and the back. It was a normal lid. She found two hinges at the back. There was dust everywhere. It made her sneeze when she wiped it off, and then the sneeze made her sneeze again. She tried lifting it; it was heavy. She gave a loud groan and the box opened. The hinges made a squeaking noise, and the lid banged loudly against the back of the wardrobe when she managed to push it over. There were a lot of things inside. Poppy picked up a long white tube of what looked like toothpaste.

Dylan hated love songs. *Nothing Compares 2 U* had caught him by surprise, when it came on the radio in the shopping centre. There had almost been tears. It was supposed to be cathartic to cry; it was even supposed to be unhealthy not to. He wasn't going to cry. The next song was *Walking on Sunshine*, and he felt the gloom lift, momentarily.

Mondays were Alice's day off. She would be up and about by now, he thought; it was after four. It wouldn't hurt to just send her one text. Just to touch base. She might be worrying about him; he hadn't sent her one since the night before. He had sent a lot, thinking back, and she hadn't replied to most; especially not the ones at the end of the night. The more he sent and the more she had ignored him, the more he convinced himself she had met someone else; or gone home with some new man. In quieter, saner times, he would never think something like that of her. But being ignored made him feel isolated, and isolation led to paranoia. When he was paranoid, he would always think the worst.

He was in the McDonald's upstairs in the mall; sitting at a table, with some fries he had no intention of eating. They had been the cheapest thing on the menu, and he had needed somewhere to sit. The place was full of loud teenagers in school uniform. He never went there of his own volition; it was usually with Alice and Poppy, so that the child could get one of the meals which came with a toy. He hated the smell of the oil, and the general lethargy of the clientele and staff alike. He was sitting at a table which was meant for four, by himself. His back was to the wall, which suited him. He did the same on buses. It made him feel easier, having nobody behind him in those situations. Nothing made him feel more paranoid than the sound of laughter coming from somewhere he couldn't see. It was a hangover from his school days, when he seemed to be a magnet for pranks and negative attention. Nothing like that had happened to him in years, but he still had an innate fear of it.

Across from him, a pretty black girl made an annoying slurping noise with the straw in her milkshake. He looked at his phone and went to the text messages. As he touched the icon for *Write New*, the sound coming through the overhead speakers changed from loud pop to quiet, almost lullaby music. He glanced at the counter, where a large queue had gathered, with just two servers on the tills. They changed the music to diffuse the customers' stress at having to wait, he noticed. *Psychological warfare with your Big Mac and fries...*

'Alice, thank you for trusting me. I know it's been a lot to take.' His voice was educated but by no means upper class. He didn't sound old; probably early thirties, she thought. She didn't answer him, because she didn't trust him.

'Alice? Are you there?'

'Yeah. Look, you've got me this far, but *trust* you?' She looked around the carriage. The silver haired man was still there, and the smiling teenager. A few others had got on at Caledonian Road. No one was paying her any attention.

'I know, I know. I'm going to try to explain everything; well, everything I can explain anyway. Just listen to me, and then I'll answer your questions.' He left a space for her to reply, but she just nodded.

'Right, I'm not going to tell you what my name is; call me Frank. I have not got Poppy, but I think I can find out who does.'

'But, if you don't have her, then…'

'Alice, I need you to not ask questions now. Not yet. Please.'

'But, I…'

'I just heard the doors- where are you now?'

'Ah, ah…' She looked at the map above her head, 'Camden Road.' Another glance round the carriage to see was anyone listening, but no.

'Okay. Can you hear me okay there?'

'Yeah. Yeah, I can.'

'Okay. Poppy has been taken. The men who arranged it are extremely precise and careful, and they've been planning this for months. These people are no amateurs.'

Her heart sank, followed quickly by a feeling of nausea.

'But, why? What do they…'

'Please, just let me finish Alice.'

'All- All right.'

'The Polish girl: she was the key. No matter how much you or Poppy's father may have convinced yourselves you chose this woman, the truth is she chose you. If, by some chance, you hadn't ended up offering the job to her, another girl would have been sent to replace her.'

'But how? That doesn't make sense. What if we'd already hired someone? They couldn't just make us fire her and hire someone else. We're not-'

'Who said anything about firing her? People die every day, Alice. Accidents happen.'

'Jesus…'

'They took their time, these people. They were in no hurry, I know that for sure. They knew you were the key.'

'Me?'

'Yes. With Tom not around and the mother, well… They knew it was you that the woman had to impress.'

'This is all my fault. I should never-'

'You can't think like that, Alice. You did what you thought was right. You didn't know.'

'This is too much. I can't-'

'I know. The first day you let her take Poppy to school, where were you?'

'I was- I was driving…'

'You followed them.'

'How did you… how do you know these things about me? Who are you?'

'I know these things because they know them.'

'Did you know they were going to take her? Why didn't you do something to stop it?'

Silence on the other end. Some people in the carriage were looking at her, but she didn't care. They were at Gospel Oak. The doors slid open and a throng of commuters swarmed through.

The box was full of clothes, and other things which were unfamiliar to Poppy: a small wooden paddle with three holes in it; a long silver object which she thought resembled a bullet, and the toothpaste tube which didn't say 'toothpaste' anywhere on it. Poppy held the silver thing in her fingers; it was big for a bullet. She thought it might be a tank bullet. She twisted the cap to see if she could look inside, but instead of coming off, it made a buzzing sound and began to shake. She dropped it in the box and it rolled around in there, making a noise against the wood like her father's phone did when he got a call. She picked it up and twisted it again to turn it off. This time the lid came away, and inside she saw some batteries; one on top of the other, like in a flashlight. She put the lid back on carefully and put the thing away.

It was mostly clothes in the box. Bras, knickers, tights; and a few things she recognised, but didn't know the names for. They looked like adult clothes to her, but they were so small, a child might have fit them. She held one of the bras up against her and giggled. She wondered would it be okay to try them on. She liked costumes and dressing up. And having something to do might take away her frightened feelings, the same way it took away bored ones. She sorted through the silky pants and stockings, choosing what to try on first. They felt nice to touch, so they'd probably feel even nicer when you had them on, she thought.

Bob looked up at the blue light. It hadn't come on in a while. She was okay though; because he had spoken to her. Part of him wished he knew more about the plan. At least then, some of the things he said to reassure her might have been true. If he knew when they planned to give her back, he could use it to calm her down. *That's if they're going to give her back at all*, he reminded himself, feeling a chill as he considered the possibility. It had crossed his mind more than once already they might be going to hurt her. He hoped not; he wanted no part in something like that. It didn't matter how much they were paying him. If he knew that any harm was going to come to her, he would walk. They could keep their five thousand pounds. He didn't have many principles, but the ones he had were important to him.

She had stopped the singing after they had had their chat. He didn't know if it was a good sign or not. He hadn't heard any crying from her, or shouting for someone to come and let her out. No screaming for her Mummy or her Daddy, and no banging on the door. He had never been involved in taking a child before; he didn't know if her behaviour was normal. If it had been him in there, he thought, he might have kicked the place down and screamed bloody murder; even the ten or eleven-year-old him. He had never liked confined spaces, or locked doors. He always took the stairs and never used the lift. Not everyone was like him though, he told himself. Some birds didn't mind the cage.

'I knew, yes.'

She felt herself sway on her feet, and had to steady herself against the carriage wall.

'Why- why did you just let them? Why couldn't you have-'

'It isn't that simple, Alice. I couldn't just-'

'You said you saw her. You said you saw her an hour ago. How? How did you see her, if you didn't take her? What is this? What are you trying to do to me?'

'I... I saw her, yes. I promise you I'm not lying. She's safe. She's-'

'Safe? How can she be safe? Where is she?'

'I don't know yet.'

'Then how did you see her? I don't-'

'It's complicated. I'd rather not tell you on the phone. I don't want you to- I don't want to frighten you...'

'Jesus Christ! It's a bit late for that. I want to know where she is. You tell me now, or I swear, I'll call the police. I'm serious.' She didn't know how serious she was, in truth. A few people in the carriage had looked at her, then away again.

'Alice, please. You know you can't do that. I've told you-'

'Why should I believe anything you say?'

'Because-'

'Please.... Don't hurt her. I mean, don't let them hurt her. I can't take it. It's all my fault. I should have been there. I should have-' She was almost crying. Instead of inquiring as to what was wrong, the other commuters looked the other way, ignoring her.

'There wasn't anything you could have done to stop this, I promise you that. Don't blame yourself; keep it together. Please.' His voice was different, almost kinder.

'I... I just want to make it right... I need to fix it.'

'I know, I know. And we will. I just need a little more time. Please, stay with me.'

'Okay. All right, what do we do now?' She felt thirsty again, and suddenly tired.

'Get off at the next stop.'

Four

PervDad54: Any dad on cam with dau? Message me.

The person posting the message was police, or FBI. No one was that obvious or stupid, Bill thought to himself, scrolling past it. Or it could have been genuine; he could never tell for sure. He had done a few stupid, risky things himself in the past, when overtaken by one compulsion or another. The website, *xtaboo*, had changed a lot over the years, as the internet became less esoteric, and more accessible to the masses. Before 2000, it would have existed in secret; the address passed around on private bulletin boards. There would have been no way to find it via search engines.

He was in the 'Incest' room, which was heavily moderated these days. They even monitored private chat windows, if rumours were to be believed. There was seldom any incest related chat in the room. Just men posting links to young looking girls, and other men congratulating them on their taste. There were clear guidelines as to what was considered acceptable, and punishments for those who flouted them. Five years before, the galleries on the main site were full of illegal content. The management would delete anything if it was reported, and more than likely claim ignorance if the law got involved, he guessed. The instances of content being reported had been few and far between, however; most of the site's visitors sharing a common interest, and a high tolerance for obscenity. When a report did happen, the owners deleted the material immediately, assuming that the reporter was working for the authorities.

He clicked on a link posted by someone called 'Dad4fun'. It was pretty tame; a girl of around ten in her underwear, posing. But it was still out of bounds under the new rules.

Bill was sure the administrators and their moderators had no real issue with the more controversial material. The problem for them was, the more popular it had become, the more visitors it attracted. And the more visitors downloading pictures or watching videos, the more bandwidth it consumed. To pay the bills, the people who ran the site had to sell advertising; even though the only potential clients who would touch the place were pornographers; ones who owned porn sites which featured extremely young looking girls, legal of course, but who would have withdrawn their funding on principle, had the site not cleaned up its act and lost the reputation for being a place to find child pornography. Bill was amused at the idea of someone who owned websites called *Exploited Teens*, *Teen Throat Abuse*, or *Young Pussy* could object anything on moral grounds.

The chat rooms were labelled things like *Incest* or *Jailbait*. The jailbait room was for those who liked their girls post-pubescent but not quite legal. Incest was for people who liked them even younger. Those were the unwritten rules, and most users paid them more heed than the official ones.

In the Incest room, Daddy4u was still posting, with no sign of a ban. The girls were getting younger, the clothes getting skimpier. The mob in the room bayed for more from him. Bill looked at each picture without saving it. He had seen better, in his opinion. He had chosen the username 'billhanson'. It was only one letter different from his real name. No one was going to think the billhanson chatting about jailbait and incest on xtaboo was the Bill Hansen who presented America's Dumbest Home Movies or who had won Celebrity Jungle on the UK networks two years before. He had chosen it for that reason. Someone once said if you want to hide your drugs from the police, you should hide them in a box marked 'drugs'. Bill never hid his drugs anywhere; there were never any left to hide.

There was a long mirror in the pink room. It was perfect for what Poppy wanted to do. It wasn't a mirror in a stand, like the one Alice had in her bedroom. It was on the wall. She pulled her pyjama bottoms down and stepped out of them. Then she took the rest of her things off, except her knickers. The miniature corset was the right size for her, and did up with Velcro instead of traditional fasteners. It didn't have cups on the front like the one Alice had, but it didn't matter, because she didn't have anything to put in them, she told herself.

She stood up tall and looked at herself in the mirror. She thought it looked good on her. She felt pretty, like someone in a music video. She looked down and saw that she was still wearing her own knickers; pink ones, with the Hello Kitty cat on them. She pushed the elastic down over her hips and the pants fell down to her ankles. She didn't like having her parts on show, even if there was no one to see, so she pulled on the other knickers as fast as she could. They fit perfectly, and she did a little twirl in the mirror. She had chosen some sheer hold-ups to go with the rests, and those seemed also to have been specially made for a child. They were much shorter than the ones Alice had let her try on before the Christmas party a few months before.

She couldn't stand up on one leg and put the stocking on the other; it was harder than it looked. She sat down instead. They felt good against her skin, cool and warm at the same time. She was careful not to snag them on her toenails. Alice was forever getting *ladders* just before they were supposed to go somewhere, and it would always make her swear.

She stood up in front of the mirror and did some poses and pouts. She looked grown up, she thought. She wished Alice could see. She wiggled her hips and hummed a Shakira song. She and Alice always danced to Shakira songs on Fridays after school, before Alice went home. Sometimes Alice would drink too much wine and try to sing as well. There were shoes in the box, all of them size two, which was her size. She picked a pair with had clear plastic platform soles, because they looked like glass, and it reminded her of Cinderella's slippers. The heels weren't that big, but she still felt incredibly high up. She almost fell over a couple of times, and then she had to take them off. *Health and Safety,* Alice would have said. It was when she was bending over to untie them, with her back to the mirror, that she heard it. A sound; like a cough or a grunt. It had come from behind her, but there was no one there except the reflection of her, in her new costume. It had come from inside the mirror itself.

'Where am I going now? What do you want me to do?' Alice looked around the platform at Finchley Road and shivered from cold for the first time that day. *No such thing as bad weather, just the wrong clothes*, her father used to say to her.

'Nothing. There's another train in the same direction in nine minutes. Jump on it. I have to make sure no one is following you. Did anyone get off with you?'

'What? No.'

'I don't just mean from your carriage. The whole train. Did anyone get off at the same time as you did?' She heard a noise in the background on his end, like a car horn, and it occurred to her he might also be travelling.

'Well, I… I'm sure someone did. I mean…'

'Look around you on the platform.'

'Okay, I…'

'Don't be too obvious. Just tell me, is there anyone on the platform with you now?'

'No.' She looked around, but there was no one. Not even the people arriving for the next train, in nine minutes time. She hugged herself from the cold.

'Good. I have to let you go now. I'll call you in ten.'

'Hang on a-' He was gone. There was a bench behind her; cold, hard metal, but it felt as good as soft leather when she sank into it. The sound of his voice in her ear was replaced immediately the thumping of her heartbeat.

Her thoughts returned to Poppy. She wanted to know that the girl was all right. She couldn't take his word for it. There were bad people in the world; she read about them all the time in the newspapers. There seemed to her to be even more of them these days; every other day there would be a story about something happening to a child, or someone arrested for having disgusting things on their computer. The world scared her a lot more than it had when she was growing up. It was possible that Poppy would come to no harm; that there would be a ransom demand, Tom's people would pay it, and she would be returned to them, safe and unharmed. But if that were the case, she asked herself, why was this man calling her? What was his part in all of it, and how much more did he know?

Somersby couldn't believe what was happening. He had seen her rooting around in the wardrobe and going into the wooden chest. He hadn't known the clothes were in it. She couldn't have known what the lube was; she had put it back in the box without opening it. The vibrator had frightened the life out of her. She was so pretty; even more so in person, he thought. He had seen her many in the celebrity magazines; being carted around by her mother, or on the set of one of Tom's movies. Everyone knew Poppy Riley; especially in their community. Some of them had been into her for years, since she was old enough to walk. Not him. He liked them this age- right before everything developed. He shifted in his chair as she stepped out of her pyjamas. The show was starting early for him.

He met Harry Goldman at a showbiz party; for one of the AIDS charities. All the important people had been there. He was looking for backers for a new film, and Harry was the sort of man who liked to be seen to support the arts. The Jewish community had always been big players in his business. He was having a cigarette outside when the big man had come over, cigar in hand.

'Can I trouble you for a light?' He was much taller, close up, Somersby had noted.

'Of course; here.'

'Thanks. Say, you're the director, yeah?' He blew the smoke out slowly, and gave a cough.

'Yup, that's me.' It was surprising to him that Goldman knew who he was, but his last picture had done some business, especially in London.

'Summers- Summer-'

'Somersby. Ian Somersby. Pleasure to meet you.'

'I guess you already know who I am then?' He was as confident as one would expect from a man so notorious and feared. Everyone in London knew who Harry Goldman was.

'Yes, Mr Goldman.'

'Please... It's Harry. Well, unless you end up in my bad books. Then you can call me whatever you like. It ain't gonna help ya.' Goldman laughed, and slapped him on the back.

'Harry it is, then. So... you've seen my films?' Somersby didn't care if he had, or if he enjoyed them. He wanted his money, not his thumbs up.

'Oh, yes. I've seen them all. I loved the one with the young girl and the chap... which was it?'

'*Nobokovia*?'

'That's the one, yes. She was very... sweet, that girl. Couldn't have liked her more.'

Nobokovia had been his most daring film, in a career of daring films. The underage nudity and child sexualisation had been virtually ignored by the censors. There seemed to be different rules for art-house films. It had passed with a fifteens certificate, uncut. Someone up there liked him, he thought at the time; or liked underage girls. From the impression Somersby was getting, so did Goldman.

'Suzy? Oh yeah, she was something else all right; a real find.' He supped his drink, the ice long melted, and gave Goldman a knowing look. Harry gave him a smile, took a good hard pull on the fat Cuban, and said:

'She looked like a girl who knew how to make a man happy. No wonder that old bastard couldn't resist.' He gave another laugh, and took a gulp of champagne.

That was how their relationship had begun. A few more tentative questions back and forth and they were in no doubt their special interests were of the same nature. The words were never voiced, but it had been clear to both of them. Goldman had promised him there and then he would become a major investor in his films. It wasn't until more than a year later that Harry had come to him with the idea to shoot a different sort of picture. One where the male actors would pay millions to be a part of the production, and where copies of the finished article would change hands for six figures on the underground market. One where the star would be the most photographed child in the world.

He kept his trousers on, in case Reinhart came back. He wasn't sure about the Austrian. He didn't seem like their type, but some people kept it better hidden than others. On the opposite side of the glass, Poppy danced in her tiny Brazilian-cut knickers and custom made basque. She turned around again, and bent down to untie her shoes. He looked at the flesh at the tops of her thighs, and felt his face flush.

He had come to terms with his sexual desires over the years. He had felt the worst sort of guilt when he first realised he was attracted to young girls. He had attempted to ignore it, or to deny it. He had tried to stop it and forget it. Nothing had worked. His mind would always return to the same place, and he would always have to satisfy the urge. He had never touched a child, not like that. He didn't know if it was because of morals, or the fear of being caught. That was all going to change soon.

She stood up again and swung round to face him. She was looking straight at him now. He knew she couldn't see him, but he still felt like she was looking at him. She squatted down and leaned into the mirror, squinting at him. He was close. Nothing was as good as when he allowed himself to indulge those desires; not sex with Karen, or even when he slept with his new P.A, who had been barely seventeen. It wasn't the same; nothing could compare to it. That was why he always came back to it, in spite of himself

When he was done, he looked at the one way glass again; she looked innocuous. Childish and clumsy. His open belt jangled against his leg as he felt around in the coat for the pack of tissues. He looked away from her, overcome with a guilt which he knew wouldn't last.

The brandy was finished. Dylan hadn't touched the chips. He wasn't drunk yet, in his opinion. Someone else might have had a different view. He got up to leave, hitting his thigh on the table as he manoeuvred his way past the buggies and their owners. He needed more drink. There was a supermarket next door.

The man on the security desk gave him a disapproving look as he went past. He needed the toilet. There were two cubicles; one was free. He went in, just in case he needed to do anything more. His stomach gurgled. He hated when there was someone in the stall next to him; especially the stalls where there were gaps at the bottom. He didn't like seeing someone else's shoes, it felt like he was intruding on someone, or they on him. Down in the mall toilets, they had granite walls between each cubicle and they went right down to the floor, same as the doors.

Someone who cleaned the place was a bit too fond of lemon scented toilet cleaner, but it was better than smelling what it was blocking out, he thought. There was half-washed off graffiti in permanent marker pen on the white wooden walls. *Eight inches, hairy, for bottom*; *Curious bi, nine inches, call for suck*. He needed to go; it was curdling inside him. He hadn't eaten much all day, if anything. He couldn't let himself go while there was someone so near. He heard a faint jangling sound. He looked down at the foot under the gap in the stalls, and saw the hem of the man's trouser leg shaking a little. Dylan held his breath and listened hard. More jangling, more shaking. Shallow, fast breathing. A slap of skin on skin.

Dylan let out a laugh and forgot about stopping himself from going. The wet, porridge-like faeces sprayed out of him and into the bowl underneath. The water splashed back onto him, and he instinctively pushed the flush handle, without standing up first. Cold, cleaner water replaced the filthy and he shivered with the horribleness and the niceness of it. The man in the other stall hadn't been put off by Dylan, or by the smell; he kept going, increasing in speed; he could see the man's toes pointing in that familiar way which said he was almost done. Dylan bunched up some paper and stood to wipe himself. It took several attempts, which was no surprise, all things considered. The other man finished with a satisfactory grunt, then quickly gathered his things and left. Dylan didn't hear him stop to wash his hands. There was too much paper in the bowl, and he didn't want to risk flushing it.

The cubicle beside him became occupied again; someone in clean white Nikes. He opened his own door; there was a man there, waiting to go in. Dylan looked at him, and then behind at the bowl full of paper.

'Sorry mate, I think it's out of order.'

The next train to Richmond had been delayed by two minutes. That was another thought: had he meant for Alice to get on the next one going to Richmond, or the next one in general? They went to Clapham Junction too, splitting when they passed Willesden. In the end it hadn't mattered, because the next train and the next train to Richmond turned out to be one and the same.

She thought about Dylan. Amongst all the guilt-tripping and over-analysis, he was right about one thing: they loved each other. It wasn't enough reason by itself for them to stay together, but it was a fact. She missed him, more than she had in a while. The phone rang.

'Hi.'

'Hello, Alice. You're on the train?'

'Yes. Just got on, it was-'

'Richmond, right? Not Clapham.'

'Yes, Richmond. Where am I going?'

'I'll tell you when you get there. I'm not trying to mess you around, Alice. You'll have to trust me. The less you know about what we do, the safer you'll be.' She had feeling he meant the less she knew, the safer *he* would be.

'Is there something new?' She was afraid to ask, because it only took one answer in the negative, and her world would come apart. Ignorance wasn't bliss, but it was better than devastation.

'Yes. I've got a better handle on the whole thing now…'

'What? Where is she? Can we get her? What do they want? Is it money?'

'You can get money?'

'I can try.'

'Wouldn't you need to tell Riley?'

'Tom is away. I haven't spoken to him since last week. He's not- there was a problem, with the phones.'

'Okay...'

'I can get them the money; if we need to.'

'How much?'

'Enough. A lot, actually. But how can we- shouldn't we wait until they ask?'

The doors at West Hampstead opened to cacophony of chatter and whistles, and she wasn't able to hear what he said to her. She waited until they'd shut, and tried again.

'What was that?'

'I said the money won't be for them. It'll be for me.'

Her blood went cold.

'What the hell do you mean? You said you were going to help me. You said-'

'I am going to help you. And you're going to help me. I'll take you to where she is, I promise.'

'You promise? How do I know that you're not the one who took her in the first place? How do I know that you're not just stalling me, so that I don't call the police? How am I supposed to know anything, if you won't-'

'You don't. Okay? You don't know anything, and you're going to have to trust me when I say that if you call the police, it'll all be over for Poppy. I know it's not easy, Alice.'

'Trust you? How can calling the police make things worse for her? That's their job, isn't it? I should be talking to them, not you. You think I'm going to hand over money to you, just because you-'

'I'm not playing games with you, Alice. Everything I've told you is true. What does it matter who the money goes to, if you get her back? Do you honestly care?'

'Yes. No, I mean I don't know.'

'Look, I'm sorry. Maybe I should have been upfront with you about the cash… maybe that was my mistake. I just didn't want you to think I had something to do with it, like you're doing now. I wanted you to trust me.'

'I don't trust you!' The doors opened again, they were at Brondesbury.

'Well you're going to need to. Oh, and get off the train at the next stop. I've sent a car for you. It'll be a black Bentley. You can't miss it.'

Five

'Telephone call for you, Sir. It's a Mister Hansen…'

'I'll take it in the office, Maura.' He flicked his cigar into the ashtray and walked around to the other side of the desk. Terry had driven him back from the club. He had needed to check a few things before heading to the charity lunch.

'Hello, Bill.'

'Harry! How's things?'

'Things are, eh, fine, Bill.'

'Good good good! Everything set for the main event?'

'What?' Harry would have thought it went without saying they would never speak about something like that on his company telephone.

'The big shoot, man. The main attraction, heheh. You know!' Something was different about his voice. Different, but not unfamiliar. Harry had been here before with him. It was drugs.

'Ah, Bill. I'm not quite sure what you mean. I have a rather pressing engagement now, so if you don't mind, I'd sooner…'

'Hey, man. Don't fucking blow me off here. That ain't cool…' He was definitely high on something, Harry thought.

'Bill, I think…'

'Listen man, I paid you a lotta Samoans, you dig? I'm just lookin' to protect my investment, capice? I just need to know everything's going to go to plan. Yuh-huh?'

Harry stubbed out the cigar and cleared his throat.

'I hear you, Bill. Loud and clear. You have nothing to worry about. Package has been delivered, the show will start without a delay. I personally guarantee it.' The expression on Goldman's face was miles from the tone of his voice.

'All right! Thanks, Harry. I really appreciate it. And hey… sorry about being an asshole just now… it's just…'

'Don't worry about it, Bill. No offence taken. I'm a man of the world! I understand…' He said it with a big smile which wouldn't be seen, but he was sure could be felt on the other end of the phone.

'Awesome. Okay, Mr G. See you on the flipside. You're good people!'

'See you then, Bill. God bless.'

'You too, Harry.'

Goldman took a sip from his glass. Once this thing was over, maybe he would get Reinhart to pay Bill a little visit, he thought. They could make it look like a sex game which had gone wrong. Upload some photographs and videos to his hard drive: animals, children, rape, snuff. The press would enjoy that. Killing someone wasn't satisfying enough by itself sometimes. He switched on the early evening news; nothing about the girl yet. And there wouldn't be either, if all went to plan.

The drink aisle in ASDA was always full of unfortunate looking people, Dylan thought. He didn't count himself among them, of course. He turned around to the spirits. There were small cans of premixed drinks, in all the popular brands and combinations. He grabbed some Southern Comfort, lime and lemonade. It was near enough to brandy for him to believe he wasn't mixing his drinks. On his way out of the aisle, he bumped into a dishevelled man, smelling of cigarettes and vomit.

'Washer yer goon, pal!'

'Um, yeah. Sorry, mate.' He gave a smile, to disperse the tension. The Scottish man didn't smile back.

'Am no yer mate, friend.' His teeth were almost green with plaque. Dylan kept walking.

The girl at the checkout looked about fourteen to him.

'Would you like any help with your packing?' He looked at the four small cans and shrugged.

'That's five pounds, please!' She seemed overly happy to him; especially for someone who had to do that for a living.

'Cool.' He took out a card; he had used the last of his cash in McDonald's.

'Enter your PIN number, please.'

'PIN.'

'Yeah, your PIN number; put it-'

'No, I mean it's just PIN. The N in PIN stands for Number; so you don't have to say it again.'

'Yeah. Thank you. Here's your receipt.' She either didn't understand what he had just said, or she didn't care.

'Thank you.' Dylan took his bag with a sigh.

'Have a nice day.' She was already looking past him, at the next customer.

Rick caught sight of his self in the mirror on the other side of the bathroom and smirked. The shower was too distracting for what he wanted to do. He preferred to fill up the bath, have a thorough soak, and then stand up to finish the job. The razor was one of the older kinds, with the triple blade. He hadn't got on with the newer models. He squeezed some gel into his hand and wet his other one with water from the bath. A lather on the hands first, then over what was left of the hair down there. He had already done as much as he could with the scissors. The soap felt pleasurable on him; he felt himself twitch. He tried thinking of something else, but it was impossible. He gave himself a few short strokes, and then dragged the blades over the rough between his navel and the base of his penis.

He had been quite a ladies man when he was younger. Rock stars were always studs, that was the reputation; they could have whomever they wanted, and they could last all night too. That was the myth, anyway. Everyone wanted to sleep with you when you were in the band; especially a band as big as his. It had been a long time since they'd been considered important or relevant by the music press, and the crowds had got older and older. The groupies still came though. Some of the girls couldn't even have been born when he had written his first Number One. Groupies didn't care about albums or song writing or what new direction your music was taking. They just wanted to sleep with someone famous. You didn't need to be in a band to have sex with a groupie. You just needed to be someone, was what he had found.

He didn't sleep with them anymore. He had cleaned up his act; found Jesus. All the vices had gone, along with most of the band. He was the only original member left; everyone else had been hired in. The others had been gone for years. They'd either jumped or they'd been pushed, by him. It was mainly the latter.

'Screw 'em,' he had said to his management at the time. 'It's my band.'

The hair came off easily on the flat areas. Down below was more tricky. He almost nicked himself a couple of times. There were a few stray hairs growing up the side too; he needed to get them, and be careful doing it. He wanted to look good. He should have gone back to the gym, he told himself, looking down at his torso. The six pack had gone, even with the cleaner lifestyle. It got harder to maintain, the older he got. His official age flattered him somewhat. As did his hair colour, and the clever way his hairdresser styled it to cover the pink patches on his crown. He lifted himself up to shave underneath.

Harry Goldman wasn't playing around; the text had come in the morning. They had her; there had been no hiccups. He took the showerhead down and turned the tap on to rinse himself. A little too hot, then the cold evened it out. He looked down at himself, without any hair. It looked good. He thought of Poppy Riley, with her angelic face, and golden skin. He squirted some more shower gel into his hand and, in an odd moment of shyness, pulled the screen across.

He had been right. She couldn't have missed it. Not quite a limousine in the traditional sense, it was still a very big, very black luxury car. All the windows were blacked out. As she approached the back, the central locking popped open. As she was wondering if she was supposed to go in the front passenger side or the back seat, the door nearest to her opened automatically. The phone rang.

'Okay, you're there? Get in the back.' It sounded quieter than before, wherever he was. He must have been indoors again, she thought. She ducked down and slid across on the leather seats. There was no one but her in the back. The space between passengers and driver had been blocked up like in a stretch limo. There was a small slit, she assumed for talking to the driver.

'Okay. What now?' She felt an odd calm, in spite of herself. The seats were comfortable, and reminded her of how tired she was.

'Now I'm going to tell you everything.' The car rolled out of the station car park. It was smooth and silent. The windows were blacked on the inside as well as outside; she assumed this was for a reason. They had put strip lights on roof and down the sides, which gave everything a slightly green tint. She looked down at her bare arms; they looked sickly.

'Did you find her?'

'Not yet. We're going to though. Now listen to me.' He was travelling again; she could hear noise which sounded like traffic or a city. She was on speakerphone; she could hear the echo.

'Okay. What about me?' She ran her finger over the ashtray, wishing she had a cigarette.

'What do you mean?' A car horn in the background; he was definitely going somewhere, she thought; perhaps coming to her.

'Do I need to watch what I say? Will your driver be listening?'

'No. You can talk. Nobody will hear you except me.'

'Okay, where am I going?' Her fingers found a button on the ashtray. She pressed it and a small silver shelf slid out from underneath. It was full of loose cigarettes.

'You don't need to know until you get there. I don't even know yet. It might change.'

'Fine. I... I don't care anymore. I just want her back.' She put one of the cigarettes in her mouth. She wondered if she should ask. No, she had earned it, she thought. There was a book of matches in the silver tray. It took a couple of tries, but she got one of them to light.

'You found the cigarettes then?'

'What?' She looked around for cameras, despite knowing that any camera he had put there would have been well hidden. She remembered what he had said when she was in her flat, and shuddered.

'Hey, it's fine. Help yourself. I just didn't know you smoked.'

'I don't, usually. Just in-'

'...times of stress. Yeah.'

'Hello?' It was her again, the child.

'All right sweetheart? You okay?' He looked over his shoulder to check that the German wasn't anywhere near.

'Yes. I think so. Why is this door locked?'

'Er, that's so's to keep you safe, Treacle.' He hadn't been prepared to answer her questions; he hoped she wouldn't have many more.

'Safe? Safe from what?'

'Ah, it's nothing really, darling. It's just... complicated. It's grown up stuff.'

'Oh. Do you know when I can go home?' He heard a yawn in her voice which made him want to yawn too.

'I dunno, darling'. Soon, I think. Not long anyway. That's what Maggie told me anyways.' Just keep her calm and she'll be fine, he told himself. There was no need to panic her, even if it meant he had to tell her a few white lies.

'Who's Maggie?'

'The Polish bird, innit? Looks after you, like.'

'That's Magda, silly!'

'Eh? Oh, yeah. Yeah, that's it. Magda. Sorry, Treacle. I'm no good with names. Never forget a face though, eh?'

'Poppy.'

'Eh?'

'My name's Poppy, not Treacle. I thought you said you didn't know Magda?'

'Eh, what? Course I do, Tre- Poppy. Me and Magda go way back, innit. Thick as thieves, we is. I just- like I said, bloody terrible with names.'

'I don't remember her saying anything about you. I think I'd know if Magda had a man friend! Especially an English one.'

'Eh, I'm her little secret, Poppet.'

'Poppy.'

'Poppy! Yeah. We're keeping the whole thing under wraps for now, yeah. Grown up stuff, in't it? Don't you worry about it.'

'Oh, okay. What is your name?'

'My name? My name's… George.'

'Nice to meet you, George. When you see Magda, can you tell her I want to go home?'

'Course, Dar- Poppy. Course I will.'

Harry was at his desk, using the calculator on his phone. The singer had paid two million, Hansen the same. The footballer had been a surprise; Harry never would have had him down for being into it, but appearances were deceiving. He had paid two million as well. Don was getting it free, for obvious reasons. The director was paying half, because he was shooting and editing it, as well as being in the film himself. Harry had considered letting him off, but a million was what Somersby had suggested first, and Harry wasn't going to turn down that sort of money.

That was what was going to make it special; Somersby's talent. They all enjoyed his films, and if there had been anything about the Milly Frazer affair which Harry had regretted, it had been the fact that their recording of the thing had been so poor. One camera, on a tripod. Everything came out too dark and grainy. Without prior knowledge, it would have been hard to tell who the girl was from watching the tape; it didn't matter how many times the Tribune had plastered her face all over the front page for seven years, Harry thought. The Tribune was Monty's paper. He had been in the Milly film too. He had gone third.

Harry would be the only one who had been involved in both films. Not that the first one could be considered a real film. The Somersby one was going to be a masterpiece, in his opinion. He would spend a month or two editing the thing, and then Harry would begin selling it. That was where the real money was going to come from.. There was definitely a market for it, he knew. As well as the private collectors, the people who ran the VIP sites would buy a copy, and then sell clips from it for a smaller price to their members. It was easier to charge money for content now Bitcoin, the digital currency, had come about. No need to use a credit card which could be traced back.

There were a lot of wealthy people into the scene. It was almost as if having so much money and power made people bored of their own excesses; made them look for new sins to commit, and bigger risks to take. There were at least two types, as far as Harry was concerned. The type who just had the sickness in their heads; couldn't get aroused at the thought of a grown woman or even a grown man. Their brains were wired the wrong way; they had no choice in the matter. Apart from choosing to do nothing about it, he supposed; to ignore the urges, to stay away from children, or to stop masturbating to illegal images. The Church used to say it to homosexuals: Just don't indulge, and you'll be allowed into Heaven. It was easier said than done, Harry knew. If you asked a heterosexual man to deny this natural urges, he wouldn't last long. That had been the trouble with the priests.

The other sort was more like him. He liked adult women too, although the ones his age were out of the question now. A woman in her sixties seemed a vile suggestion to him. He had money; he could still attract the good time girls in their twenties and thirties. They weren't in it for anything other than the money of course, but that didn't bother him. All women were whores in one respect or another; that was his thinking.

He became interested in the younger ones when he was young himself. Back when things were easier, and more acceptable. As a young man, he had his time messing around with girls who were still in school. A lot of men did it. The girls were young and silly, and easy to impress with a few drinks and a ride in a nice car. Fourteen and thirteen year olds had been his usual fare. After a while, he started to want more; he found himself looking at the younger ones, and wondering. It wasn't something that he was proud of, and if anyone had known, he would have been dealt with in the appropriate manner. Men like that were feared and hated, and they existed. He heard stories about them, and what happened when they were caught. It rarely came to a trial. Street justice was always quicker and more satisfying. He was careful for a long while; just looking and not touching. Opportunities would arise, but he wasn't a fool. In the circles he moved, there were plenty of men who'd be more than happy to castrate a man who interfered with children. So he kept those worse desires bottled up, and satisfied himself with girls who were closer to the legal age. When the time came that he could hold it back no longer, he had been careful. The girls had practically fallen into his lap. A rival gang member had been ordered dead by Harry's bosses. When the deed had been done, Harry found himself alone with the man's daughters, in their house. While their father lay dead in the kitchen, he took the seven and ten year old girls into a bedroom upstairs. After building something resembling a rapport with them, he was overcome by his compulsion, and by the notion that he could do the thing and it not have any consequences for him. He asked them to undress for him, so that they could play a game. Knowing no better, they did as they were told. After all, he had said he was a 'friend of Daddy's'. Everything had happened so fast, looking back on it later, he found it hard to remember details. Even now, he couldn't be sure what he had planned to do with them after it was done. In the end, the decision had been taken from him. He winced at the memory of it, silently thanking whatever God had smiled on him that day. After that close call, the compulsion to act on his impulses faded away, for many years.

In the eighties he went to Denmark on business and happened to pick up some magazines from a sex shop, of which there were many. *Lolita Love* and *Color Climax*, among others. There was no law against it back then. It was almost innocent. The magazines showed everything. There was no censorship; not in Denmark. The girls were mostly teenaged, but there were some even younger. It was like opening a vault of forgotten wants and needs. The guilt festered still, but the excitement and arousal was so intense as to be narcotic.

He made a lot more excuses to visit Copenhagen after that, until the censorship laws began to change. Then it was all underground, and dangerous to pursue. He kept his old magazines, and the internet arrived, bringing with it the ability to contact others anonymously, and share material without ever having to meet in person. When he needed something more real, he would travel to the Far East; Thailand and Vietnam, where laws were ostensibly strict, but enforcement was corrupt and easy to manipulate, if you had money. Then he found out about the Albanians, under his nose in London. They could get you anything, or anyone, for a price.

The Milly Frazer film had opened the floodgates for him, when it came to shooting his own child porn for profit. In the years since, he used the pink room to make scores of films, using girls who he acquired from child prostitution rackets, personal vendettas against rivals who happened to have children, or occasionally he would have a girl snatched to order. There was an incredible amount of money in it, as well as a similar amount of risk. That didn't bother Harry. He had stopped caring about the police a long time ago.

Alice took another drag as she listened to Frank talk. He had a strange, lulling, bedtime story quality to his voice. The content of what he was telling her was less reassuring.

'...and so I set up a website; more of a message board or a chatroom, on the deep web. Then I spammed all the image boards and chans where I knew people like them hung out.'

'Wait, what's the deep web?' She stubbed out the cigarette and reached for another one, immediately.

'The deep web is the real internet. If you picture it like an iceberg: the Googles, the Yahoos, the social networks, the video tubes- those are the www, right?'

'The world wide web…'

'Yeah. The world wide web. That's the tip, and then the underneath of the iceberg…'

'The biggest bit.'

'Exactly, is the deep web. Or the dark web, or whatever they're calling it these days.'

'And there are what, paedophile rings, down there? Don't the police know about this? Or… the people who run the internet?'

'No one runs the internet… it's just a bunch of computers, connected to each other. I'm simplifying, obviously.'

'Okay, yeah.'

'Anyway, the deep web isn't like the world wide web. It's a lot slower for one thing.'

'I thought no one knew about it?'

'Not a lot of people do, no.'

'But I thought the internet was slower when there were too many people on it at once? Like at peak time? Or when you have lots of people in an internet café- no?'

'It's not… it's not as simple as that. It's not about how many users in this case. It's about how many hosts. Do you understand?'

'I guess so, yeah.' She didn't, but it wasn't important that she should. It wasn't getting her any closer to finding Poppy. There was another button, in the seat under her. She pushed it. Another shelf slid out; this one had a silver flask in it.

'Anyway, it's not just paedophiles. I mean, yes, the anonymity certainly helps with the… things they get up to; but there's a lot more happening down there.'

'Like what?' She couldn't help it. She was intrigued. The flask had neat brandy in it, from the smell of it. She took a drink.

'Drugs. Gangland hits. Counterfeiting. That sort of thing.'

'Jesus! Really? On the internet?'

'It's the way we communicate now, Alice. People used normal phone lines and the post to arrange those sorts of things in the past. This is just progress.'

'But, the police; they must know about this, right?' She took a long drag on the cigarette. She didn't recognise the brand, but they were expensive; she could taste it.

'They do, but it's not that simple. Some of them don't take it seriously; they're Luddites, being left behind by 21st Century crime.' She could still hear traffic in the background.

'What about the others?'

'Well, some of the others are on the payroll. That's always been the case. Until we start paying policemen what they're worth, there'll always be ones on the take.'

'I see.' She remembered, growing up, there had been a big scandal in the neighbourhood; Sally Braun's father had been sacked from the police for taking bribes from some massage place in town. She had only been ten, so she didn't understand it until years later.

'You do have some actual police officers or federal agents down there, it's just it's such a big place to police, and the sorts of people who use it aren't idiots.'

'How so?'

'Well, just using the browser to go down there takes a fair bit of learning, and there are tricks to change your IP every few minutes, by bouncing it off other IPs.'

'I see.' She thought about Poppy again, and hoped his story was going somewhere.

Six

Paul looked at himself in the mirror. He was in good shape, he thought. All the time off injured had done him good; given him time to get down the gym more and work on his upper body. The thing was going to be soon; the next day. He opened the folder of pictures Harry had sent by private message on the site. It was her: Poppy. He swallowed drily.

He wasn't a paedophile. He hated those people; especially the ones who touched young boys. He had seen some disgusting things on the internet, when he hadn't known his way around the websites properly. Some of them were Japanese or Russian, so he didn't know what he was clicking on until it was too late. Anything with boys tore him to pieces. He didn't have much time for gay people anyway, but the things he saw left him horrified. Then there were the other types; the bondage and the torture. That sort of thing made him sick and angry. Some of them were even into infants; one and two year olds, in nappies. He wasn't one of them; he wasn't like that. Sometimes he hated himself for looking at things, but he wasn't like those people. They were monsters, as far as he was concerned.

He just liked girls; all sorts of girls. He had always loved porn. When they were apprentices at West Ham, they'd never had much to do, or the money to do it. Even if they had, the club had been strict about curfews and about stopping them from going out drinking. If they were caught by the wrong person in the wrong mood, they could say goodbye to their careers. So they'd end up staying in, drinking cans and looking at skin magazines and videos; the same as any other teenagers. Sometimes, if everyone had had a lot to drink, they'd play games. They weren't gay, any of them, so it was fine. They'd all seen each other in the showers every day, so no one was shy about it.

He liked the younger porn back then; teen girls, all overage, of course. Magazines like Barely Legal and Hawk. He had only been that age himself. The girls they used were natural looking; no breast implants, hardly any make-up. The older women looked terrible to him; he wasn't interested in looking at a thirty five year old who'd been on the scene for ten years. Tam had been twenty when he married her, but she looked even younger.

One day, while surfing the internet, he found a website with girls even younger; fourteen and fifteen year olds, taking pictures of themselves in the mirror. That was before people had camera phones. He closed it down immediately the first time, out of paranoia. The papers were full of people being arrested for having things on their computers. Some of them were famous people. You didn't know who was spying on you. But he went back looking for it the next time, with a few drinks in him. Most of them were just in their underwear, with the odd topless photo. But he found himself enjoying those pictures more than any of the hardcore content on the legal sites. It was the thrill of looking at something he wasn't supposed to see; he had always been someone who liked breaking the rules.

There was nothing wrong with it, he told himself. The girls had taken the photographs themselves; no one had held a gun to their heads. They were only a little younger than the sixteen year olds walking around town, and it was legal to have sex with any of them. A few years before, he would have been able to take one of them out to see a film down the multiplex. They weren't children. They had bodies like grown women, most of them. Some of them were smaller or less developed, but he wasn't looking at those ones. The girls he was attracted to would have been able to get into a pub or a club, in his opinion. There had been nothing to feel guilty about.

Of course, after a while, those ones had got boring to look at. He started taking an interest in the ones who looked a little younger. There was no harm in it. He was just looking. They weren't little children, he would assure himself. They knew what they were doing.

'You will go now, into the room. She needs to see a face she knows, yes? You don't leave yet. You must help first, please.'

'No! I am finish. This is deal I make: Bring girl here in morning, then I go.' She sucked hard on the end of the cigarette and slurped her coffee.

'The deal is changed. There is a different deal now. You will go now into this room with the girl. You will tell her all is good.' He didn't speak any Polish, and she didn't speak his language either. It had to be English.

'I no go. I want to see boss.' Her eyes were wild, and full of anger.

'The boss is busy today. You do not talk to the boss. You talk to me. You will see the girl now.' He cracked his knuckles. He had weathered, Indian Ink-stained hands; souvenirs of worse times.

'I tell him. And I tell him you are bastard.'

'Yes, you can tell him later. You go see the girl now.' He gave her a look which said there was no choice to make. She muttered something under breath in Polish, and walked down the corridor.

'…that was when I realised there was a gap in the market, so to speak.' He had been talking for a while. Some of it she understood; some she had to ask him to explain; other parts she just let pass because she didn't think they were important.

'I don't… I'm finding this hard, sorry.'

'What? To follow? I'm sorry, I get a bit…'

'No, I can follow you all right. It's just… these people. I can't believe that they exist, or so many of them do- I just thought…'

'It's not a lot. We're talking about a place where people like that are much more likely to be. If you went to Wembley Stadium on F.A. Cup day, everyone you met would be a football fan. It wouldn't surprise you. But if you were just walking down the high street and everyone you met was into, say, the Lord Of The Rings, that would be strange…' They'd been driving for a while; she didn't know where to. In films, the kidnapped girl would be tied up in the boot and still be able to figure out where she was going by how many speed bumps they'd gone over; or the noise of screaming children as they passed a playground. She wouldn't have had a chance to do that. And anyway, she wasn't the kidnapped girl in this story.

'I see what you're saying, but it still seems like a lot.'

'Oh, there are a lot. But as a percentage of the population, it's almost nothing; despite what the papers want you to believe.'

'But, you don't approve of what these people are, surely?' She had had too much brandy, without a mixer. She capped the flask.

'I have no opinion either way.'

'Bullshit. Everyone has an opinion.'

'It's not. These people are who they are; they are what they are. I don't judge. I just take their money.'

'You don't have children.'

'No. Neither do you.'

'I know, but… still. You don't care because it doesn't affect you.' She felt disappointed in him, in a strange way. He was being obtuse.

'I don't let it affect me, Alice. It's business.'

'But how, anyway?'

'How what?'

'How do you set up a… a secret website, where these… people can come and do whatever it is they do. How did you find them?'

'I just found them on sex chat sites; on the normal internet… it was pretty easy.'

'Sex chat?' She wondered if she could manage another cigarette. She had already smoked three.

'Yeah. Well some were sex chat rooms; some were just normal chat rooms, for teens and children usually.'

'Oh.' She felt ill, and it wasn't the brandy.

'Yeah. I went in under some name like HotGal12, or SexyBabe11; something to bait them.'

'And people messaged you? Grown men?'

'Sometimes they'd say they were grown men. Sometimes they'd pretend they were teen boys. Try and get you to send pictures; or to go on webcam. Of course, they'd be fine with sending you pictures of them. But their video cam was never working…'

'Because they weren't young boys…' She lit the cigarette. She needed it.

'Exactly. Or sometimes their cam would magically start working, but all you'd see was a view of their genitals. It got predictable…' The driver slammed on the brakes and she was flung forward.

'Jesus!' She held onto the seat to steady herself. A seatbelt hadn't even occurred to her. The car was too limo-like for that.

'Are you okay?'

'Yeah. I'm fine. The car just… anyway; but, how do you go from that to getting them on board? Did you just stop being the little girl, and talk to them straight?'

'No, I kept two browsers open. So on one I was the horny little teen, and on the other, I was another person. I'd find the men who were chatting to my girl, and message them with the second account.'

'Ah…' She wanted to ask him lots, but she felt like they were getting further and further away from Poppy.

'Yeah, so after I had a chat with them to make sure they weren't LEA, I dropped them a link they could follow, to a landing page which told them all about accessing the deep web, what they'd need, etc. And an email address for them to contact me at once they were in.'

'Did it cost them money?'

'Yes. A grand.'

'A thousand pounds???'

'I wanted them to show me they were serious; serious and rich.'

'Did they all give the money?'

'God, no. There are plenty of rich perverts, but not all perverts are rich.'

'What happened to those ones?'

'Well, by clicking the link, they automatically downloaded a Trojan Horse to their computers.'

'I think I can guess what that does.'

'Yeah, well it let me in and gave me enough info to scare them. Those were my first hustles. I showed them things like their email passwords, their bank balances- all simple to get. I made it look like I had them by the short and curlies, though. I made them sweat.'

'And what then?'

'A simple direct debit. So much a month to an untraceable bank account. It paid for itself. It's still rolling in, every month.'

'Jesus. What about the ones who actually paid?'

'Well, they got access to what they believed was the most secure website on earth. And fast, too. Nothing like the normal deep web.'

'I thought the deep web was always slow?' He was contradicting himself.

'Not always. I have ways. Anyway, these men paid for the privilege of being able to discuss anything they wanted, swap all the videos and pictures they liked, and have access to the archive.'

'I thought you said you didn't deal in that stuff?' He had, earlier. He said he was just a provider of a service, and what people chose to do with it was on their own consciences. Or some other similar bull. She hadn't believed him.

'Oh, I don't. The thing is, the people who run most of the other sites have no real idea about security. They think they do, with their guides and disclaimers and whatever; but in reality, their servers are extremely easy to break into. Well, for someone like me.' He sounded proud of himself.

'But it's still… child porn.' She wanted to spit.

'It is, but I don't host it on my site. I just give them links to the archives of all the other webmasters; without the other men having a clue someone is rooting through their toy boxes. Like I said, I don't do anything illegal.'

'Apart from the blackmail…' She opened the flask again and took another shot.

'Well, yes.' He laughed a little then.

'Please… what has this all to do with today, and are you going to get Poppy back for me?'

'Oh, yeah. Alice, do you remember Milly Frazer?'

'Oh my God.' She remembered; how could anyone forget?

'I need to go do some work, Marie. Don't bother me for a couple of hours, yeah?' He kissed her on the top of her head as he passed the armchair. She looked up at him over the top of her reading glasses.

'Work? Oh, Don; you need to go look up the meaning of 'sick leave'!' There was a tone of mock exasperation to her voice, but she smiled when she said it.

'You need to go look up the meaning of 'shush'…' He smiled back at her. He loved her very much.

Upstairs in the attic, he switched the computer on. It was brand new; a present from the son-in-law. It was expensive too, top of the range. It had been for his Sixtieth. Don knew a fair bit about computers; he spent most of his work time sifting through them, trying to find incriminating evidence. He opened the desk drawer with the tiny key which hung on a string around his neck. Inside was a small USB thumb drive; there wasn't much on it, apart from the browser software. There was no need to install it; it just ran from the folder on the device, then it disappeared when you took the hardware away.

The blue bar on screen filled up slowly while it tried to find the network. He opened the text inbox on his phone and looked for today's link. It was a smart system. They paid their money into a dummy account every month, using their mobile numbers as the payee reference. The man who ran the site changed the web address every twenty four hours, and texted them all the new one every morning. It didn't even look like a website address; there was no .com and the rest of it just looked like random numbers and letters. No one looking in his phone would have a clue what they were, or what to do with them. He tapped the new one into the address bar. It took a while to connect. The site itself was fast, but this deep web thing was incredibly slow by modern internet standards.

A cheesy 'success' noise came through the speakers when the browser finally connected. He had been allowed to use his own username, but the password changed once a week. Every Tuesday morning, a letter arrived from a random junk mail company, the names changed all the time, but the envelope always had a blue ink blot on the back, with a number in it. This week's had been twenty-eight. That meant that the password was the twenty-eight word of the letter inside. Once he jotted it down somewhere, he was supposed to destroy the letter. It had become a ritual. He usually did it outside, in the back yard, using a Zippo lighter that someone had bought him years ago, when he still smoked.

On the right hand side there was a list of who was online. No one he wanted, so far. The gallery was flashing pink, which meant one of the members had uploaded some new pictures or videos. He stood up and double checked the door was locked. He settled down and undid the top button on his trousers. Nice navy ones his wife had got him from BHS. He could never feel comfortable in tracksuit bottoms or even in jeans. He had been a policeman for too long.

The new pictures were disappointing. They were always too young for him. In his time on the force, he had seen tens of thousands of photos and videos like that. That was what his department dealt with, exclusively. He was the head of it now. They were usually this age or younger. The ones with girls from twelve to sixteen were like gold dust. The older they got, the smarter they got. The younger ones were easier to fool, someone had told him once. They didn't run away and tell as much either, as long as they had been trained well.

He had no interest in this sort of thing before he was promoted to the division. It hadn't felt like a promotion at the time. The Chief Superintendent had told him in no uncertain terms he was joining an uphill battle. They were understaffed, overwhelmed and up against it. He started at the same time as another man; Briggsy had been his name. They both had the same baptism of fire, on the same day. Sitting in front of a haul of pictures; shown exactly the sort of thing the men in the division had to go through every day, and told if they weren't up to the job, to speak up and there would be no hard feelings.

Briggsy had lasted twenty minutes before he had to go and vomit. Don had held out for longer. He hadn't needed to be sick at all, but after an hour and a bit, he felt like he should make some sort of gesture. He sat in the cubicle, killing the time. His feelings hadn't been of disgust or horror. He felt like someone had shone a torch in his eyes; woke him from a deep sleep. He felt alive; and ashamed for it. He went back in and joined the others, so as to carry on the charade.

The girl in the new pictures was brown haired, curly, with a pretty smile. Some of the children looked bemused, and with good reason. How were they supposed to know what was going on? Or why their Daddy was doing those things? That's why he preferred the older ones. If there was older one in action, he knew she had been doing it a while. She was used to it; she had been shown how to make all the right noises. She probably wasn't enjoying it- at work they'd seen plenty to suggest none of them ever enjoyed it. He had seen children ripped apart; horror stories. He liked to forget them though, and tell himself maybe some of them enjoyed it. He thought about the Riley girl, who always looked much older than her years when you saw her on the red carpet for one of her father's films; or when she was on TV, advertising child's shampoo or the fast food place which gave out the toys with their children's meals. She had a look about her, Don thought. One which said she understood it; she wanted it; she needed it. He closed his eyes. He felt his toes curl, and then the pleasure wash over him. He reached under the desk for some tissues.

The door was opening. The man was coming in to let her go home, Poppy thought, excitedly. The person who came in was not a man, though.

'Magda!' She ran over and gave her the tightest of hugs.

'Small One! How you are doing?'

'Fine. I didn't know where you'd got to!'

'Ah yes, sorry, I busy. I do work, for your father, yes?'

'Oh. Okay. Magda?'

'Yes my love?'

'I don't remember coming here. Where are we?'

'Oh. This is friend's house. Friend of Alice. We come here in car; when you sleep.'

'Ah.' She remembered being asleep, sort of. She didn't remember the car journey.

'Yes. Now, I sorry again, I must little more work, then I come get, yes?'

'Oh, Magda!' She did a sad face and a pretend sniffle.

'I know, I know. I'm sorry, Small One. I come back, I promise.'

'Okay...' Poppy rubbed the sole of her shoe on the ground, like she was wiping something invisible off it.

'You are hungry? I bring the sandwich for you?'

'Eh... I'm not hungry for a sandwich...' She looked at the floor and then back up at Magda. A small smile.

'Ah, I see. You are a different hungry, yes? Like hunger for the sugar.' She opened her handbag and brought out a triple chocolate muffin, still wrapped in plastic, which she had bought in the coffee shop in the morning. Poppy's eyes lit up, and she bounced up and down on the spot.

'Ooh! Yes please!' She grabbed it from her hands and tore open the wrapper.

'You are welcome,' said Magda, already turning to leave.

'Sorry, thank you!' She had forgotten her manners again. Alice would have been cross.

'I see you later, Small One. Be good.' Then she was gone.

'Okay, Reinhart. How about Bob. Is he okay?' Harry was on his new mobile. The reception was pitiful.

'The Cockney? He is a prick, but he is okay, fine.'

'Bob's all right. How is the child?'

'The Polish, she says the child is good. I send her into the room. She says the girl is okay. She is not happy though; she wants to go home.'

'Who, the child?'

'No, no, no no. Not the girl, the Polish. She went a little crazy. Wanted to talk to you. I tell her-'

'Tell her to bugger off.'

'I did. Do not worry.'

'Great stuff. And the staff at Riley's house, they think the child is still with the Magda, right?'

'Yes. She talked to her man, in security. The one she is- she told him she is taking the girl to Alex house.'

'Alice.'

'What?'

'It's Alice. Riley's P.A. Her name is Alice.'

'Yes. Alice, sorry.'

'Well it… never mind. Right, I'm going across London for lunch.'

'Lunch? It is half before five!'

'It's a late lunch. Might be a liquid lunch. Charity thing. It doesn't matter. Don't call me; I might have to turn off the mobile. You know what it's like. You know what you have to do, so just do it.'

'Yes, Herr Goldman, and what if there is an emergency?'

'Well then the emergency can wait until I've had my bloody lunch.' He hung up. He had ordered some good food and drink for later. Somersby was already at the house. Hansen would probably show up later, coked or not. Sykes was coming in the morning, Don the same. The singer was coming in the evening. That was all of them. His one Maybe had dithered too long, which had been a shame, in his opinion. He poured himself a Scotch from the decanter in the back of the Rolls. It was going to be a chore, but he had to make an appearance at the lunch. It was a children's charity. Doing things like that helped his public image, and kept up the charade of his being a legitimate businessman, he thought.

'And a packet of crisps, please; cheese and onion...' He should have eaten the fries, he told himself. The pint of Foster's looked great; the barmaid not so much. He wondered if the Wetherspoon's 'no frills' approach also applied to the staff. Dylan made his way over to an empty table in the corner. The place was half full. Drinks were cheap on Mondays, even more so than usual. There was some football on later, but not in there. They only ever had Sky Sports News on their TVs, with the sound down.

You were supposed to shift the focus, was what they said, he reminded himself. If you wanted to get over someone, you had to stop thinking about them; or about you as a couple. Stop thinking about the past or the future, if either of those had you both in it. If you were the one dumped, you had to avoid contacting her; make sure not to fill her answerphone with pathetic messages; act like you didn't care, even though you did. Advice columns were always telling you to pretend you were something you were not, if you wanted to get what you wanted. Lie to the people you love, if you want them to love you back. He had no idea anymore about anything; especially not women or relationships. He wanted her back. He wanted her to love him. She said she loved him, but it wasn't enough, according to her. He wanted it to be enough. He wanted her to call him and say 'I was wrong. Forgive me. Let's get back together.' He didn't want to get over her; he wanted to get back with her. These were the things he wanted, and he was going to have to get good at pretending he didn't want them, if he had any chance of getting her back. It was madness, but it was hardly unique to their situation. Relationships were a minefield, he always thought.

He had a sip of the lager; it was refreshing and cold. The crisps were good too. Pub crisps always tasted great, he didn't know why. The front of the pub was made of sliding French doors, which were half-open now. The smell of cigarettes was drifting though, and he had to stop himself from wanting one. Not that again. He didn't need that on top of everything else.

She had given up on him. They had chemistry; amazing sex; real love. Movie Love, he called it. Like Harvey and Sabrina, she said. But she still thought it was the right decision to throw it away. He was going to hate her for it. That's why he wanted her back quickly; so he wouldn't end up hating her. Although it would be easier to get over her if he hated her. But he didn't want to get over her. He wanted her back. He wanted to be in her living room, watching trashy TV on a Tuesday night; or in her kitchen, eating something she had cooked for them. He wanted all the normal and the mundane things, as well as the exciting ones. It hadn't been enough for her. All of those things together weren't good enough, when she weighed them up against the things she didn't like about him. Things he never thought about before.

Any other time he had been dumped, his ego had taken the biggest battering. He felt unattractive, useless, and terrible in bed. There was none of that this time. The last day they'd talked, the sex had been mind-blowing. His ego was fine this time. He was licking different sorts of wounds. According to her, he was terrible with money; he had too little ambition; he was never in any great hurry to dig himself out of a financial scrape; he give her the feeling she was responsible for him. Those were the things she couldn't live with. And they were all true. It hurt more to be accused of things which were true than things which weren't. At least when they weren't true, there was righteous indignation, he thought. The cigarette smoke smelt delicious. He wasn't going to buy any. He could have just one though. *Just the one; one won't hurt.*

Alice sat, slightly detached, as he told her the story of Milly Frazer. She read all the news articles seven years before, and all the ones since. The Tribune had never let it go. They were either extremely optimistic about the possible return of the five year old who'd been snatched from a holiday villa in Crete, or they were exploiting her tragedy to sell papers. Most people held the latter opinion. The story the public had heard was that Milly's mother and father had left the window in her bedroom ajar because of the extreme heat, and because the child had a fever. An opportunist abductor had snatched her right out of bed while the parents slept. An absolute tragedy of course and everyone in the country sent their prayers and wishes to them at first. Then people grew tired of the constant coverage. The Tribune and its sister papers plastered Milly's face everywhere. You couldn't escape her blue eyes and curly brown hair. People started to turn against the parents, asking if leaving the window open like that should be considered neglect. The red tops questioned the motives of the Tribune, suggesting bias and favouritism because Milly's parents were both middle class barristers. Some people even began to suggest the parents' involvement was even more sinister. They started pointing fingers. The press themselves flirted with conspiracy theories, but eventually all but the Tribune forgot about poor little Milly. She was never found.

Frank's version of the tale was different.

'She was abducted to order.'

'I'm sorry?' Alice pushed took another cigarette from the tray.

'It was an organised job. It happens all the time.'

'You mean someone… asked for her, specifically?' The lighter clicked and the first hit of nicotine found the back of her throat.

'Not her specifically. Someone with her stats.'

'Stats?'

'Age, race, hair colour; those sorts of things. There would have been a list.'

'Jesus. But… who? Who does this stuff?'

'Well, the people who do the dirty work are just your normal thugs. Although this man was pretty skilled.'

'How so?'

'He stalked the family. Took a job in the restaurant near where they were staying. He made sure he served them on that last day, and when Milly had a drink, he put something in it which would give her the symptoms of a fever. He was good.'

'None of this was in the paper…'

'I should think not. Especially not the Trib.' He laughed, then stopped himself.

'But how do you know? Who are you?' She dragged so hard on the cigarette the heat burned the back of her mouth and throat, but it didn't give her any satisfaction. The brandy hadn't calmed her either.

'I told you. I give these people the feeling they have somewhere completely anonymous and safe to talk.'

'You saw them plan this? And you did nothing?'

'Good God no, Alice. I'm not... I just… I just found out about it after.'

'After what?'

'After it happened…' He made a sound like he was about to say something else, then didn't.

'The kidnapping?'

'Uh, yes.'

'There's something else though? Something you're not telling me? And it has something to do with Poppy, because otherwise why would you be telling me about this? Where is she? What are they going to do with her?' She almost screamed it at him.

'Hang on. Hang on. We're here.' The car slowed to a halt.

'We're where? What do you mean "we"? Where are you?' As she spoke, the locks on the doors either side opened with a pop. She heard the driver's door open and felt the car get lighter as he stepped out. The door on her left swung open, and the driver said:

'Hello, Alice,' in a voice which sounded impossibly familiar. He had driven her there himself.

Seven

It wasn't going to happen. Bill tugged at himself while clicking through the pictures on the site. The cocaine had numbed him too much; it was an exercise in futility, but he persisted regardless. The pictures were soft-core; a Japanese website. None of the girls were Japanese though. Eastern European he guessed. It didn't say, but it was going to be more likely they took them from some impoverished place on the other side of the Iron Curtain than it was that they came from his country. It would take a lot less money to sway parents in Romania or Bulgaria, he thought.

The girls were anything from six to fourteen years old. He liked the older end of the curve, but it depended. A good looking thirteen year old with some curves was great, but some days, for him, a nine year old with a real pretty face would be just as good. Besides, the more wrong it felt, the better it felt to him. There would be shame after he had finished, obviously. But he didn't think about that.

He flicked through some more. He liked the look of the next girl. She was about eleven; long blonde hair, shapely legs. She was dressed in a PVC cat suit. The Japanese loved that sort of thing, if the picture sets on the site were anything to go by. It was more like a leotard; sleeveless and high cut on the legs. She had long PVC gloves too, and PVC high heel boots which went up to the tops of her thighs, and clung to her skin like they were stockings. They could only have been custom made. He imagined a bunch of Japanese dressmakers working away on little sex costumes for children, thinking it was the most natural thing in the world. The country was bizarre. His Grandfather had been captured by them in the War. They'd done things to him which he was never able to speak about; he kept it with him until he died.

He opened another tab. Email. He had got the web address off them by email before, but he wasn't sure which email account. He searched the inbox for 'candy'. There were no matches. He searched for 'Candylove'; still nothing. He took the rolled up note and railed another line of coke. There was MDMA somewhere as well, he remembered. He tried 'LoveCandy', and got a match.

Dear Customer.

Thank you for inquiry and deposit. Please follow link to site and choose your service. Login and password have been sent to your phone. Please do not share this information.

Management

LoveCandy

He opened the link, then immediately closed the new tab before it had time to load. He clicked on the programs menu and found the IP Hiding software. One click and he was safe. He held down Ctrl, Shift and T to open the page again. There was nothing outwardly illegal; it just looked like another child modelling site. The girls were Ukrainian, Hungarian or Albanian. Clicking on a picture opened up a gallery. The clothing was all of an adult nature: miniskirts, heels, stockings and suspenders. They wore too much make up on their faces, and their eyes looked dead to him. He went to the member login page and tapped in his details. His username was billhanson again for this one, but he had to get the password out of his mobile. It was numbers, letters, uppercase and lower, impossible for him to memorise, so he had to write it down. Once you were logged in, the site changed. The girls had extra galleries, with more revealing pictures. There were videos too.

They were mostly aged from thirteen to fifteen. The last girl he ordered had turned up looking a lot less attractive than her Photoshopped snaps, in his opinion. She had some teenage acne under the caked-on makeup. She had known what she was doing, however. He had booked her for two hours, but he finished almost as soon as she got him in her mouth. He kept her around while he tried to get hard again. He wanted to get his money's worth; she wasn't cheap. He took some Viagra and made her touch herself. He got her to put things inside herself. The handle of a hairbrush, the TV remote; anything he could find lying around. He took her into the shower and got her to get on her hands and knees for him. He couldn't get hard for her, so he urinated on her back, then he turned her around and did the same in her mouth. She made trained noises like she was enjoying it, but her eyes were dead. With about half an hour to go, the Viagra had kicked in, and he leapt on her. By the time he finished she was crying and bleeding. She whispered 'Thank you…' when he sent her out the door with an extra hundred in her hand. He had no idea much of her fee the Albanians let her keep. He had looked at her on the bed; covered in his mess, and almost cried. If he had had more than a hundred on him, he would have given it to her too.

There was a new girl. She was bleached blonde, with brown eyes. Petite, flat chested, with a prettier face than the usual fare. It didn't say her age, but she couldn't have been more than twelve. He groaned. *She's fucking hot*, he thought, clicking through her gallery. *Hot, and new.* She was available, it said. He clicked the button which said 'Book Some Time With This Model' and chose the Two Hour option.

-Pay Now With Visa/MasterCard/Amex?

-Yes

-Are You Sure?

-Yes

-Payment Received

The computer they'd installed was brand new. Somersby had been thrown by it at first, because there was no mouse or keyboard or hard drive tower. It was touchscreen. There were cameras all over the pink room, in the mirrors and the light fittings. He could control them all from the console, and all of them would record at once. That way, he could edit them, post-shooting, and even make different versions of the same film. It was the most ambitious project of his career. Most of the famous videos on the circuit had one thing in common: the people who had made them were now in jail. Fame came with a price. One man had made a series of films of him abusing his own daughter which looked nothing like the usual fare. They were well lit, the sound was clear, and the daughter seemed to be enjoying what she was doing, rather than being forced in any way.

It was videos like that which made him feel less like a monster or a pervert. They showed it was perfectly natural to feel like he did. The man had gone to prison for twenty years. Someone had recognised the bedside table, and called the FBI. It had been a chance in a million. What the helpful neighbour was doing watching the video in the first place, no one ever found out; it was an anonymous call.

His job wasn't just to shoot the picture; it was to make sure everyone stayed unrecognisable. With so many of them participating, it was going to be impossible to just shoot everyone from below the neck; especially not with these robot cameras. He would have to shoot it all as it happened, and then cut it in post. It was that or they'd use masks, like they'd done in the past, Harry hadn't decided yet.

The girl was lying on the bed, yawning. The Polish woman had been into see her, which had surprised him. From what he had overheard between Reinhart and Harry on the phone, he thought she was going to be out of there already; one way or another. He had learned a lot about Goldman in the last couple of years, but the number one thing he garnered was how ruthless the man was. He killed people or had people killed all the time. He had no scruples about it, and no fear of reprisals or police action. He owned most of the police in London; the ones which mattered anyway. Somersby was pretty sure one of the people who were going to be in the movie was police. And not some Detective Sergeant either. From what Harry had been hinting, this man was some sort of high-up. He zoomed in on Poppy's face using the camera hidden in the ceiling light. The definition was incredible, he noted. She had chocolate stains around her mouth.

'Take a right here,' Harry said into the driver's intercom. There was no need; the sat-nav had already let Terry know they were there. A small huddle of press was camped next to the entrance. Paparazzi mostly, looking to snap some minor celebrities.

Inside, the usher showed him to his table and pulled the chair out for him. He immediately wanted a smoke. There were five places at the table. They'd all paid five thousand pounds a head, the same as him. The redhead ran one of the biggest PR companies in London. He had known her father. The old fellow beside her used to produce comedies with Sid James and Hattie Jacques in them. He must have been close to a hundred by now. The other two places were empty. Harry got up and headed for the door. The woman raised an eyebrow at him, and he acknowledged her with a nod, and then held up the cigarette lighter by way of explanation. Her smile showed off some expensive veneers, and she got up to join him.

Outside there was a special area reserved for smokers.

'Mr Goldman, isn't it?'

'Ah, yes. You're... You're Henry Nelson's girl, aren't you?' Her name escaped him. It might have been Betty.

'Yes. It's Beth, Beth Nelson.' She smiled again.

'Nice to meet you, Beth. And it's Harry. Mr Goldman was my old man's name. God rest his soul.' He smiled back at her, but his own teeth were closer to ivory than to hers.

'Well, Harry. I hope now we're acquainted, you'll be a gentleman and save me from that horrid bloody letch in there...'

'What, old man Jones? Have some respect, Beth. He practically invented the double entendre.'

'There wasn't any ambiguity in what he was suggesting before you arrived, Harry.' She had a great figure; a genuine hourglass. He liked her already.

'Oh well, can't be helped. He's a national institution. Have you not seen any of his films?'

'Can't say I have. Was one of them called *Carry On Raping*?'

He let out a belly laugh.

'Oh, Beth. I'm glad I came now.'

'You came? Oh. That was quick.' She stubbed out the butt with the sole of some expensive looking shoes. They were the ones with red soles. He had no idea what they were called.

'Careful now; Jonesy'll think you're after his job.' He put his hand on the small of her back and walked her back to the table.

He was handsome. Alice hadn't expected that. It hadn't been an issue. He was just a voice on the phone telling her terrifying things in a calm voice. He was who had Poppy, except he wasn't at all. He knew who did have her though. At least that was what she understood.

'Why?'

'What do you mean, Why?'

'Why didn't you tell me you were driving the car? What the hell is going on?' She stepped out of the back door, and he stood aside to let her pass.

'I don't bring just anyone here. It's bad enough that you have to be here. I couldn't have some driver involved in this. I don't even have a driver.'

'Why do you have this car then?'

'It was a present.' His smile was handsome, she thought; but there was no warmth to it.

'A present or a payoff?' Everything he had told her in the car made her think he wasn't to be trusted. He had no morals; he wasn't going to play fair with her either. The deceit with the driving had been the straw.

'A little from Column A; a little from Column B. Come and sit down.' The same smile. He had beautiful eyes- hazel with gold flecks. She made herself look away.

The door out of the garage led into a short corridor with a door at either end. He took her through the nearest one, into the main house.

'This is where all the action happens,' he said. It was a big room, with minimalist décor, and one wall completely covered in computer monitors of varying sizes.

'Bloody hell!'

'What. Oh, the Battle Station? Yes. Totally impressive. Especially to the ladies.' He was wearing a suit of sorts- expensive looking, but with no shirt, just a white tee underneath. Hard to pull off, but it looked good on him. Again, she had to stop herself looking. The brandy had gone to her head. Frank made a waving movement with his hand which was picked up by some infra-red device, and all of the computer monitors flickered into life. Alice's hands felt clammy now; possibly from the alcohol, maybe from the fear of what was to come.

'Coffee? Tea? More brandy?' The suit jacket hung well on his frame. He didn't look like a computer nerd, but maybe this was what computer nerds looked like these days. She wouldn't have known. Poppy knew more about computers and the internet than she did.

'Coffee, please. Have you got a cigarette?' She saw an ashtray on the coffee table in front of her. There weren't any butts in it, but maybe he was just clean, she told herself. The rest of the room was fairly spotless.

'Latte all right? I don't smoke, but there's a pack of Marlboro Lights over there, in the second drawer.'

'Thanks.' The word felt wrong in her mouth. She didn't want to thank him for anything yet. She didn't feel safe; she didn't know where she was. As a teenager she never felt okay at a house party or a pub unless she knew how to get home easily from there. The box was almost full. She wondered whom they had belonged to, and shivered a little.

'Poppy. I need to know more, Frank.' She lit up, not bothering to ask if it was all right to do indoors. She had a feeling he wasn't going to be okay with her going outside; and besides, there was the ashtray.

'I'm going to show you something in a minute. Then you'll know she's okay.' He sounded sincere. The noise of the espresso pod machine ate up any silence between them for a few seconds. She sat down on his leather couch and pulled the big glass ashtray over toward her. She looked up at all of his screens. Some of them were basically flat screen TVs, plugged into a computer. She couldn't see it at first, and then she spotted it underneath the desk. It was shaped like an alien's face. All the screens had different things on them. There was an email inbox, an open documents folder, and several websites which she didn't recognise. There were social networking pages as well, both of the ones she was on herself.

'They're not planning anything for tonight.' His voice startled her, as he put her drink down on a metal coaster next to the ashtray.

'Tonight?'

'No. Poppy is going to be okay tonight.'

'How do you know?' The coffee was the perfect temperature.

'I told you, I watch them speak.' He was still standing, talking down at her.

'In your... in your chatroom.' She said it in an almost derisory way.

'Not just in there. I just use that as a springboard.' He walked away from the couch, toward his keyboard.

'What do you mean?' She sipped the latte. It tasted good.

'I just start by eavesdropping on them in there. Then I'll start to bait them myself. Go into the room under an alias, get them to chat with me outside. On MSN or Yahoo maybe.'

'Why?'

'Well, because it's the real internet. Once they're out of the Deep Web, I can find out who they are in minutes…' He was talking at her over his shoulder while tapping on the keys.

'Why would they be so stupid?' She stubbed out the fag.

'Men can be very stupid when they have their dicks in their hands, Alice.'

It was the nearest she had heard him come to swearing.

Eight

They'd met on an internet dating site. He had joined it to have a laugh. No intention of going on any dates. He had never been on a date in his life. A date to him just involved going out and getting drunk at club, meeting up with a girl, and then if you could still stand the sight of her in the morning, you started going out together. That had worked fine up until then. She said her friends had made the profile for her, to give her a little push back into the dating world. She had gone along with it reluctantly, she said.

They'd chatted for two weeks on email, and he became more and more interested. She had looked okay in her pictures, although there weren't many of them. They got on from the beginning. Emailing through the whole day and sometimes into the night. They didn't have much in common; they just both liked writing and English and words, so communicating like that was perfect for them both. After a fortnight of mails, they were both in love; not that anyone sane would admit that before meeting in person.

On the day, they went to the nearest pretentious, overpriced London coffee shop and got to know each other all over again. She told him he talked too much and he kept on talking anyway because he liked talking. She wore black skinny jeans and he couldn't quite figure out if she had a good body, but he thought she probably did. He didn't ask if he could kiss her, he told her he was going to, and she liked that. It was perfect, at the first time of asking. They went to her place, because it was nearest.

They'd been talking and joking about sex in their emails, and they'd decided they weren't going to have sex straight away. They hadn't bargained on the chemistry. He was intoxicated by her- the scent of her made him feel like an animal. When they kissed and touched, it had all the poetry and romance of love songs, and all the urgency and dirt of pornography. He was aggressive and she was submissive; quite unlike who they were outside the bedroom. He pulled and pushed at her, he bashed and bruised her, and she begged him to do it more. Everything he did with his mouth or his hands turned out to be the right thing.

'Everything okay?' The glasses in the barman's hands clinked as he added Dylan's empty to the bunch.
'Yeah, mate. Safe.'

'Pass Daddy the ketchup will you, munchkin?'
'I'm not a munchkin!' said Charmaine, with a little sulk.
'Yes you is! Munchkin, munchkin, munchkin!' said her sister Colleen, who was the older.
'Yes you are, dear' corrected their mother.

'Mum!' Charmaine banged her fork on the table.

'Yes, honey?'

'You're supposed to be on my side!' She gave her mother an icy glare, and had another handful of chips.

'I am on your side, munch- Charmaine. And use a fork, please. We're not animals.'

'Listen to yer Mum, you two.' Paul didn't say it in too much of a Dad voice; he wasn't cross with them. Tamara was a bit too strict sometimes. Sometimes he would have preferred they eat their food off their laps in front of the telly; like he did when he was growing up. It probably wouldn't have been worth the stress though. If one of the children had spilt sauce on their twenty thousand pound sofa, there would have been hell to pay. He smiled at this wife across the table. She gave him a wink. She was extraordinarily beautiful; he was lucky.

'Daddy, do you think I could get a pony?' asked the older girl. Her mother's face narrowed and all of them turned to see what his answer was going to be.

'Well, erm. Do you think you'd look after it, Col? That's the question, really. I still remember all them goldfish, sweetheart.' She could have whatever he wanted; he could afford it. He loved spoiling her, and Charmaine. That's what money was for. You couldn't take it with you, his Grandfather had always said.

'What do you mean, "look after it?" The people at the stables would look after it, wouldn't they? And ponies aren't fish, Dad. They eat hay, and sugar cubes.'

'The people at the stables, eh? What stables is this then? Found 'em already, have ya?' He was trying to keep a straight face, but it was hard. They were too cute sometimes; like their mother.

'Well, no; but you can just Google it, and-'

'I can just Google it, eh?' He gave a snort, between mouthfuls of vinegary chips. Tam couldn't cook, but she knew how to order in. Any other night, they'd go out to eat. Sometimes with the children in tow.

'Well, yeah. I mean, you or Mum can. I really would like one, Dad. Tilly at school has one, and we went...'

'Oh! Tilly has one? Why didn't ya say before? Hang on, lemme get out me credit card...' He went into his trouser pocket to give the full effect.

'Dad!'

'What? Col, if Tilly from school jumped off a cliff, would you jump off one too?' He sometimes thought sending her to the private school caused more trouble than it was worth. Tamara was in charge of those decisions though.

'You mean like Bungee Jumping?'

'Jesus H Christ... why do I bother, eh?' He slapped his forehead and rolled his eyes at the ceiling. He would get her the pony. Tam would have to deal with it though. He had things to do.

'Listen, before I forget, Tam...'

'Yes?' She looked at him over her dinner plate of salad leaves and giant couscous; models didn't eat chips.

'I have a thing tomorrow. Mightn't be home until late.'

'Oh, Paul. You know I wanted to go to Covent Garden tomorrow!'

'Covent Garden? For what?' Probably another opera.

'For the opera! You said you'd come. Really, Paul... sometimes I...'

'I'm sorry, gorgeous. I'll make it up to you. Promise.' He was in love with her. Trophy wife or no trophy wife; he was as fond of her now as he had been the night they'd met. He hadn't even been playing for a big team then. She hadn't known the difference. She didn't follow football, not even now.

'Daddy?' The younger girl spoke now.

'Yes, Char? What can I get you? A dog? A rabbit? One of them unicorns?'

'Mummy said to give you this...' She handed him the bottle of Heinz.

'Oh! Thanks, Char. Just what the doctor ordered.' He turned it upside down and sprayed the rest of his dinner with it.

'Can you really get me a unicorn?'

'Probably wouldn't be enough room in the stable, Char. Not with Colleen's bloody pony in there.'

The blue light was on again. Bob opened the fridge and took out the big glass pitcher full of orange squash. He opened the door with his key, and went over to the small bedside table. From a little zip lock bag he had in his pocket, he took out a couple of gel caps, and snapped each one open over the neck of the jug. The powder inside made the liquid foam for a few seconds, then it settled again. Behind him, he heard the handle on the bathroom door turn. And turn again. It was locked from the inside still; it was automatic. The mechanism would release once he closed the main door behind him on leaving.

He hadn't been given many instructions, but the ones he had were clear. He was never to let the person in the room see him, and he wasn't to communicate with the person in any way. He had already broken the second one. The first one had been stressed a lot more though. The man on the phone had made it pretty clear if he saw the occupant (their words, not his) or the occupant saw him, things would get complicated quickly. He felt slighted by that. It didn't matter who the little girl was; he wasn't going to tell anybody. That's how he built his reputation in the first place. It was common knowledge Bob Carter would do serious prison time before he would give anything or anyone up in a police interview. The police knew it too. That was how he managed to make a living from doing what he did, even at his age. He was reliable, and that sort of thing was in short supply these days.

He had been wary the first time he worked for the firm. They didn't have a name or a reputation, and no one spoke to him face to face. It could well have been a police operation. The money had been good; easily enough to take a risk. It'd been a simple job: Go to a Church hall in Peckham, pick up a bag from a couple of West Indian men and drive it to Greenhithe. He didn't even have to take it by force. It felt like DVDs in the bag. It was open, but he didn't look inside. None of his business; it never was. They'd given him two thousand pounds for it. The next one was a driving job as well. Get the train to Dover, pick up a white van and drive it back to Southwark. There had been at least twenty Chinese men and women in the back. Migrant workers; probably smuggled in illegally on a freighter. Bob never asked why or how; he kept his mouth shut and did the job. Another two thousand. After that, he did a job every few months for them. It wasn't always the same number they called him from; not always the same voice. But he knew them by the M.O.

He went out and closed the door behind him. They must have been planning on moving her, if they were drugging her. He was sure that was all it was; putting her to sleep for a while. She wasn't in any danger. She belonged to someone important and rich; they'd pay whatever it took to get her back, and soon. He just had to stick to the plan, and he would be out of there soon too, with five thousand pounds in his pocket.

Don cleaned himself up with the tissue and opened up a regular internet browser to check his emails. Nothing from Harry. That meant it was still going ahead. There were going to be others there; paying punters. Two million, as far as he gathered. Obviously, Harry was waiving Don's fee. The others wouldn't know though. His contribution would be worth more than two million to Harry if any of it ever got out. He would be the one to kill it before it had a chance to get going. That was what had happened with the other business- the Milly thing. Harry had come to him for help; for a tidy fee, of course. That was one of the ways Harry Goldman did business. He had the right people on his payroll to destroy someone's life entirely, in a matter of hours. He could use policemen to plant drugs or child pornography on someone, and then get his friends in the newspaper business to pronounce them guilty in public before anyone had even suggested a trial, or even before anyone was charged with anything. Most of the time it didn't even get that far. Just knowing Harry could ruin his life in a heartbeat was usually enough to make someone behave themselves. Only the brave or the stupid tried to resist. Framing someone with planted drugs or a gun was how they'd done it in the past. Since the internet and the new Sexual Offences Bill, it had become a lot easier. Someone who wouldn't bat an eyelid about people thinking he was a heroin dealer usually felt a bit different when you told him you were going to make sure everyone in the country thought he was a child sex predator. There was no innocent until proven guilty with that sort of thing. People had been dragged out of their houses by mobs; beaten, castrated, or worse. And with the papers and the police both in his pocket, Harry didn't need to make threats. He could make promises.

Don made a good living out of clearing things up for people like Harry. A tax-free second income. He didn't have any scruples about it either. The job didn't pay a fair wage, and it never had. Even a man in his position; head of one of the most overworked departments on the force, barely took home enough to cover the mortgage and keep up the payments on the car. It was only right he skimmed a bit off the top for himself. There was nothing uncommon about it either in the force. Just because someone wanted to be a policeman, it didn't mean they were inherently honest.

'What am I looking at?' Frank had put it on the biggest screen for her, in the middle. It was just an empty room, with a wardrobe on one side, and a bed on the other.

'Wait.' He tapped some keys and the view on the screen changed; same room, from different angles. A door on the left opened, and a little girl came out.

'Poppy! Oh, Jesus God… Poppy!' She leaned closer to the screen, as if it would bring her nearer to the little girl.

'Yes. That's her. Safe and sound.' He went back to the original camera angle; the one which showed most of the room.

'Where is she? How do you have this? Is it a tape? Is she okay?' She picked up the stubbed out half cigarette from the ashtray and lit it again. The taste was much stronger than lighting a fresh one, and she coughed.

'It's a live feed. She's completely okay. I promise you.' On screen, the little girl walked over to a jug of orange liquid on the bedside table and eyed it suspiciously. She looked around her, then leaned forward and gave it a sniff.

'Oh, Poppy... Frank, we have to do something. We have to get her! Can't you... trace this? How are you able to see it?' Her mouth was dry again. The latte hadn't lasted long, and she usually had water on the side when she drank coffee.

'No, I can't trace it... things aren't like they are in the movies. The reason I can see it because they can see it. They're using an extremely secure channel to send the feed to their own computers. Well, they think it's extremely secure anyway.' On the screen, the girl poured some of the orange liquid into a beaker.

'How come it isn't? Do you think the police can see what we see? Or the FBI, or... whoever?' She didn't know the right questions to ask.

'Oh, no- nobody can see this, except a handful of people. It's being piped directly into their computers or their laptops. No one can intercept it; it's not like your home Wi-Fi or-'

'But you can intercept it!'

'Well, I'm not intercepting it. I wrote the software; I write lots of software like this. It's another one of my... side lines. I put malware in all of my programs. To collect names, credit card details, bank accounts...' He was definitely not to be trusted. Her throat felt dry again.

'So you can trace this!'

'No. The malware in this makes the program send the feed to my computer, as well as to wherever they're sending it.'

'But you'll know where it's being sent from?'

'No. At the most it'll tell me who the laptop or computer belongs to.'

'Isn't that a start? Jesus! If we know who they are, then we can-'

'I already know who they are, Alice. It's not the-'

'You know who they are? Why aren't we talking to the police then? Come on, Frank! Look at her! They have her and they're going to do God knows what to her, and you're just sitting there...' Poppy was drinking from the beaker now. She was wearing her pyjamas.

'I'm not sitting.'

'Standing there, then. You're just going to do nothing? How can you be like this?'

'I'm not doing nothing, Alice. That's why you're here. I'm doing something. I'm doing all I can. Knowing who these people are doesn't actually give us much-'

'How can you say that?' Poppy was looking through what looked like a book at first, but Alice recognised it as a wallet for DVDs. They had some of them at Tom's.

'Because, if we went to the police; well… we'd be dead by the morning. Probably sooner.'

'That's ridiculous! The police are there to help us. Yeah, there are a few bad apples, but they're not all like that. If you know who-'

'One of the men who took her is a policeman.'

'What? How could-'

'He's not only a policeman; he works with the Child Protection Agency. And he has friends in even higher places.'

'I don't believe you. I don't trust you. I think-'

'I'll prove it to you, soon. What I'm saying is, unless you personally know a police officer that we could go to; one you trust 100%, the police are not an option. One phone call from us, making accusations against the people who are involved in this, and we'd both end up on the missing list with Poppy. Or there'd be some sort of accident on the station steps. Or we'd be overcome with depression and hang ourselves before the squad cars pulled into the drive.'

'Oh for God's sake. You're just doing the tinfoil hat thing now… I suppose you're going to tell me now that all of this has something to do with Millie as well? That the whole country is in on one big conspiracy?' Poppy had taken out one of the DVDs and was swapping it with a disc which was already in the tray of the TV's built-in player.

'I don't believe in conspiracy theories, Alice. I could tell you right now the identities of all of the men involved in this… thing.'

'Go on then.'

'No.'

'Hah! Why not?'

'If I did, I might as well just kill you.'

'Oh, for Heaven's sake. I've had just about enough of this crap, Frank. I want to go home. I want to get Poppy and I want to go home.' On the screen, Poppy yawned dramatically, and stretched out her arms.

'I want that as well, Alice. I need some more time though, to find her. I need to listen in on these people- find out when it's going to happen.'

'When what's going to happen? What are you not telling me?' Poppy got up from her spot on the floor and went to sit on the bed. She yawned again. Alice did too, not sure if it was just mimicry or her own tiredness.

'I… I'm hoping nothing is going to happen. That's my plan. There's been nothing on the news, by the way. They've been good at this.'

'What do you mean?'

'Well, the people at the Riley house haven't raised any alarms, so I'm guessing your Polish girl has been calling them and telling them that the girl is with her. Because the only other person who'd have the clearance to keep her off the premises that long-'

'…would be me. Yeah.' On the screen, Poppy was sinking back into her pillows. Her eyelids started to flutter. He was looking at her as well.

'Looks like an afternoon nap; probably for the best.' Poppy was zonked. There was no sound, but Alice imagined cartoon Zs coming out of her. She was so precious.

Listen, I need to show you something.'

'What is it?'

'Remember Milly? This isn't going to be a pleasant experience. I want you to tell me when you've seen enough.' He opened a folder on screen and double clicked on an orange traffic cone icon.

It was French food. Not frog's legs or snails or anything quite so clichéd. It was just smoked salmon; but it had a pretentious French name, and it tasted of garlic butter. Harry couldn't stand garlic. Beth seemed to be enjoying hers. She liked her food, for such a slim girl. There'd been soup to start with. He hadn't been able to pronounce what it was called. It tasted of broccoli, but there were bacon pieces floating in it, like in a Japanese noodle soup. No one served you a normal soup any more in a restaurant, Harry mused; a tomato one, or cream of mushroom. He had made his fortune, and he liked all the finer things in life these days; but, when it came to food, he preferred it simple. His mother had never been strict with kosher, so he had grown up eating traditional East End fare. If he had to eat out now, a steakhouse was usually the choice. He ate the salmon up though; he didn't want to look like a Philistine in front of her.

'Nice, isn't it? I love French cuisine.' She held her fork delicately.

'Ah, yeah. Lovely stuff. I love a bit of fish myself.' He gulped down a big piece and tried not to let the disgust show in his face.

'Yes. Food for the brain, they tell me.' Her eyes flashed with mischief.

'Who tells you?'

'Imbeciles, mainly.' She looked down at the napkin on her lap and he took the chance to glance at her cleavage.

'Harry, is this the right thing to do?'

'What's that then?' He was still chewing the salmon. He thought he felt a bone in it.

'The napkin. Do I put it on my lap?'

'Where else?' He would have called it a serviette.

'Well, I could…' She took the cloth off her thighs and tucked it into her diamond choker, making it look like a lobster bib.

'Very nice.' Good looking, smart, funny, willing to put up with an old fool like him. She had to be after something, he thought. He hoped it was something he had. Otherwise, he might have to go and get it for her.

'I think I might just wear it like this for the rest of the evening.'

'I think at £5,000 a table; you should be allowed to wear your knickers as a hat, to be honest.' He had finished his drink; there was a waiter at the other table, he tried to catch his eye.

'That would be a great idea, if I were wearing any…'

'Jesus Christ, Beth… Here, boy! Can I get some more, yes? Remy, it was. And whatever the lady is having.' He gave her a wink. He couldn't risk taking her back to the house tonight, but she was bound to have her own place. If not, the hotel would have rooms upstairs. He wasn't going to take no for answer.

'You will go lunch.' The German was big, up close. His breath stank.

'What?' Bob took a cigarette out and lit it, keeping eye contact throughout.

'You can go now. I can take over for an hour maybe, yes? There is a room.' He pointed down the corridor to an open door.

'I ain't hungry, mate.' He took a long, calming drag on the Benson.

'It is not a request… Bob. Boss says I will take over now. Give you a break.' He smelled of onions, or garlic. That was what they ate on the continent. *And pickled cabbage too.*

'I weren't told nothing about breaks.' He didn't need a break; he had been sitting down all morning, smoking.

'Is no need to tell. Boss has said. You will go to other room now. I come for you when the break is over.' He had a tattoo on his neck, of a bird. Not a military symbol; just a pretty looking songbird. A nightingale, or a lark.

'Well, I ain't-' Bob stopped himself; there wasn't any point in arguing. He could sit at the table or sit in the room on the other side of the hall; he was still getting paid. He didn't like letting the German think he had got the better of him, but five thousand pounds was five thousand pounds. He needed it more than he needed to cause a fuss.

'Okay?' Reinhart looked straight at him; without blinking. He had a menace to him which was never overstated, but undeniably present.

'Yeah, cheers. See you later.' Bob was already halfway down the hall, tipping ash into the palm of his hand, so as not to drop any on the carpet.

Nine

It took him a while to realise it was one of his own songs on the radio, there was so much over-production on the remix; when he did, he turned it straight over. He was sick of it by now; he was sick of all of their songs. He couldn't do a tour with just new material though; the record company would never let it happen. They liked to let him feel like he was the boss, because he was the talent. They employed several people, each whose job was to stroke his ego, but he wasn't fooled. He might be the talent, but he was also the product. They were the ones who distributed it. Without them, he would be playing hundred-seater bar rooms and village halls. The music industry was evil, but it was a necessary one, he knew.

It was happening the next day; it was that soon. He had nothing else planned. The tour was finished, and he had written everything for the new record while he was on the road. It was easier now he had his own bus. The other men slummed it together in another, but that was only fair. He was Rick Jarvis; and Rick Jarvis *was* Reprobate. All the other founding members were gone. It was great to have his own space; with his own refrigerator, his own big screen TV. He missed the boys though; even the ones he hated. Not so much individually; it was more that he missed the vibe of them being together. There was too much boredom now; too much time on his hands. He had given up the drinking and the pills and pretty much everything illicit, so there was no risk there. Being clean and sober made the boredom worse however; and he hadn't been able to quit the other thing.

When at the height (or the depth) of his addictions, the other thing seemed sort of excusable. When he was out of his brain on every intoxicating substance known to man, debauchery was an occupational hazard. The books about Motley Crue and Led Zeppelin and The Who were full of depraved sexual tales. They'd never mentioned anything about little girls, but their lawyers would have been all over it if they had. Besides, back then things were different. It was an accepted thing to sleep with some thirteen or fourteen year old girl who was hanging around by the stage door. Children weren't children for as long back then; a girl who had a woman's body was treated like a woman. People today had a warped view of sexuality, Rick thought. Too much tabloid TV and paranoia.

He was downloading some picture sets and videos. He must have done it a thousand times. He never held on to anything. The fear set in. He would download sets and sets of whatever girl was his favourite, and would look through all the pictures, getting more and more aroused. He would tell himself *this time* he was going to save them on a memory card or flash drive; that it was less risky than erasing them and having to download new ones the next time; that someone was bound to catch him in the act some day. He told himself he might as well be hanged for a sheep if he was hanged for a lamb, but none of the reasoning or logic mattered in the end. When he finished with them; when he was cleaning himself up and the sexual high was evaporating, the guilt would always set in. And the guilty him would always offer just one solution: wipe the drive; erase everything. Never do it again. He wasn't sincerely telling himself this would be the last time or that he would be able to resist the temptation again. He didn't believe it for a second. It had just become a ritual, and he had become accustomed to it.

Dylan was on his second or third pint. They gave him a card at the bar with a password for the Wi-Fi. There was no one in the pub. Well, no one young, or his age. If his age could still be described as young. He was thirty one. It didn't feel young when he was sitting next to a table of seventeen year olds, but there was no chance of that at the moment. It was just old men. Supping cut-price Guinness and huddling in the doorway while they chain-smoked roll-up cigarettes. The tables out front were always taken, from morning til night. They usually had the roughest looking customers sitting at them; shaved heads and facial tattoos, West Ham shirts and pregnant girlfriends. Just walking past there at any time of day was dangerous. Those sorts of people looked for trouble; eye contact was to be avoided.

There was nothing happening on the internet. His inbox was full of spam about accidents and Payment Protection Insurance refunds. His newsfeed was full of new mums talking about their babies. *So many baby pictures*, he thought. Alice wanted children. He hadn't ever thought about it before he met her. He wanted them because she wanted them though. Especially now; now she was gone.

'She is out'. Reinhart felt the pulse on Poppy's neck to make sure she was still alive. The dose had been high enough to knock her out for about an hour, but these things could go wrong. His face was covered with a woollen balaclava, as was Somersby's.

'When do you want me to-'

'In a minute. First help with this.' He started to roll Poppy's pyjama bottoms down, and motioned to Somersby to take the top half off. She had Hello Kitty underwear on- a vest and some knickers.

'Okay.' Somersby's heart was pounding in his chest. The girl was so near to him; she felt so warm. He could smell her hair. The Austrian removed the lower half of her night clothes. Her thighs weren't too white; she had probably been on a beach holiday over the summer break.

'Quick, now; get it done.' Reinhart turned the girl over onto her front. He had already taken off her vest.

'Okay, okay.' He zoomed out and in, trying to find the best composition. The shots needed to be good. They needed to be enticing, he told himself. Above all though, they needed to look like her- unmistakably. He got down low and filled the frame with her legs and bottom. He could smell the detergent from her cotton underwear. He thought he saw her stir, and almost dived for cover.

'It is fine. She will not wake. The drug is strong. Keep going.' Reinhart put her on her side with her back to the director, and moved her knees up to her chest. Somersby clicked and snapped and changed his position to get a better view.

'I need some where we see her face.'

'Yes. It is difficult. She looks like she sleeps, but for the photograph, she will maybe look like she is dead...' He squinted at her. Her chest was rising and falling; she looked peaceful.

'Okay, lie her back. No, no- on her back. Yeah, that's it. Now... spread the hair out. Okay, now let me get up.' He climbed onto the bed, and loomed over her. His knees on either side of her little frame. She was topless, still in the Hello Kitty panties. This was the shot, he told himself. This was the one they'd use to prove the authenticity of the tape; the one which would sell the clips. This was the link which a million paedophiles would click.

'You have enough?' The big Austrian was on the other side of the room, by the mirror. Somersby watched him lift it carefully from its moorings, and reveal the control centre behind.

'Yeah. I have my face shots anyway. You want me to do more though, right?' They had to get something else to draw the punters in. Something a bit more risqué.

'Naturally. I will turn the cameras off.'

'My cameras?'

'All cameras.'

'There's no need.'

'Why there is no need?'

'I switched it before we came in. It's playing a loop of the last few minutes. Just her sleeping.' Harry had told him to fake the feed when they took the photos, or if they had to come into the room. He had done it for the times Bob had come in. The people with access just saw a still of the room, with Poppy in the bathroom. When the man had finished in there, Ian restarted the live footage. Only someone paying close attention would notice the food or drink appearing out of nowhere. It was an insurance policy, in case the tapes were seized before the shoot. Or after.

'Ah. Ah, yes. This is clever.'

'Yeah. Not just a pretty face, and all that.'

'Alles gut. Now, like this?' He put the little girl on her front again, then lifted up her hips so her bottom was in the air; the cotton pulled tight, accentuating every line and crease. Somersby felt a little dizzy. He took two wide shots, then zoomed in for the close up.

'Okay. Okay. And now, this…' said Reinhart. His tattooed fingers took hold of the elastic on Poppy's kickers, and gently slipped them down towards the backs of her bended knees. Somersby swallowed drily, and listened to the whirr as the autofocus found a new target. Reinhart walked across the room to the wardrobe where the big chest was.

The new video window had opened on the same screen as the video of Poppy, which worried Alice at first. She had seen her fall asleep though; nothing much was going to happen to her in the next few minutes. She needed to stop thinking of worst case scenarios. Frank maximised the new window, so it covered the one of Poppy completely.

'Sorry. This is the best monitor. Better to watch it on this.' He did something with the keyboard, and a brightness gauge appeared at the bottom of the screen. He slid it up to almost the highest setting.

'Okay.' She felt a nervous excitement, but it wasn't a pleasant one.

'She'll be fine, trust me.'

The tape Frank had put on was grainy and wobbly. Lower quality camera maybe, or just an old camera, from when digital videos were starting out, she thought. The first one her father had bought had been terrible compared to his old VHS one.

The camera was pointed at a bed in a room. It wasn't anywhere she recognised; the walls were white and the bed was dressed in yellow sheets and a duvet with an orange cover. Someone must have picked the camera up, because everything moved backwards and then it went black, and then when the camera came back, it was the same scene, but from further back, so you saw more of the room.

'Wider angle…' said Frank, not to anyone in particular. Alice took another one of the Marlboros and lit it up. The scene stayed the same, but now she could hear muffled voices; deep, men's voices. No one was on screen yet. A feeling of dread came over her; she knew something awful was coming, and she wasn't going to watch it. She would just see what was going on first, and then tell him to turn it off. Someone walked across the screen for a second. They were naked.

'Christ.' The bad feeling inside her grew. There were more voices; a laugh- deep, booming, nasty. The body passed in front of the lens again- or it might have been a different one. Naked, and it was a man. He was older, out of shape. He had a sagging paunch, and his penis was almost invisible through a forest of black pubic hair. She couldn't see a face; the camera wasn't tilted enough. She supposed it might be deliberate. Someone joined the man now, another naked male. This one was younger, and shaved. He was pulling and pinching his foreskin while talking to the older man. She couldn't make out what they were saying; it was muffled. The whole thing was reminding her of something, but she couldn't quite put her finger on it.

A third man came into view. Naked as well, but he was in the background, so she got to see more of him. She could see above his neck, but he wasn't facing her. He was quite dramatically ginger, and seemed to have some sort of string or elastic stretched across the back of his hair, from ear to ear. *Turn around. Turn around.* He stayed facing the bed though, and the younger man turned to look at him, possibly to say something. She still couldn't hear much.

'What is this?' she asked. Frank was coming across with a tray in his hands.

'Keep watching.' He handed her a crystal tumbler with a dark looking spirit in it. Brandy again; or maybe cognac. She wasn't going to say no. Being a little drunk might have been hindering her judgement, but it was also numbing the reality of the situation. The younger man walked towards the third man. She found herself absent-mindedly admiring his physique, and then detesting herself for it. They weren't good people; she knew that much. The dread swelled in her again. Younger man tapped the red haired man on the shoulder. *That's it; here we go.* He turned around, but there was no face. She wasn't afraid of clowns, but the Halloween mask was particularly sinister in this context. As if he knew what she was thinking, the younger man turned back to face her; his face was covered by a smiling Donald Duck. She knocked the brandy back in one.

Bob peeled the thin red strip away from around the new ten-pack of Benson & Hedges and slipped the top of the plastic sleeve off. The table was an old one, probably worth something, he thought. The room looked like it had only been recently furnished; the bed looked comfortable and there was another fridge, a coffee machine, and a kettle for making tea. He took out a cigarette and tapped the butt of it on the wood. The filter coffee was ready; he poured out a large black one. He hated milk.

The German couldn't have got rid of him any quicker; he was in some sort of hurry, it seemed. Bob wasn't swallowing the story about a lunch break. They wanted him out of the way for a reason. There was something happening they didn't want him to see. Bob didn't want to think about it too much. It was probably nothing. No one was going to harm the little girl. Bob hadn't got that sort of vibe from Reinhart. He could usually tell if there was something amiss with a person, in that sort of way. People who liked to mess around with children; they had a look to them. You could sense it from them. That was what Bob thought anyway.

When he was a teenager there had been an incident on their estate. He was about thirteen or fourteen; a bit naive, but strong as an ox and already known to the Police for some minor things. It was the youngest girl of the Murphys; a beautiful little thing, eight or nine years old. She had been playing the swings in the early evening; a bit too late for her to be out on her own, but it was to be expected. The father was a desperate alcoholic, and the mother had a reputation for promiscuity. Rumour had it she didn't do it for free either. Children like that didn't have a chance. She had been on her own in the play area which the council had built. People had come forward later to say they'd passed her on their way home from work, or to the shops. No one had tried to take her back to her parents, because the general feeling had been she was probably safer where she was. Little Bridget Murphy, trying to push herself on the swings, with legs which didn't quite reach the ground.

Then, out of nowhere, there was pandemonium. Screaming and shouting; wailing and screeching. Everyone on the estate had heard it. She came running home to the house, tears streaming down her face. Her mother was with someone in the bedroom, and ran down the stairs when she heard the commotion. The father was passed out drunk on the couch and didn't even stir. Bridget wasn't able to get the words out through the sobbing and the sniffling. The mother picked her up to give a cuddle, and realised the child didn't have any underwear on. And that wasn't all. Her whole lower half was saturated with fresh blood; all down her thighs and into her school socks she was still wearing on a Sunday, because her mother was behind on washing the clothes. Now Mrs Murphy was the one wailing and screeching, and this time everyone heard; even her husband.

Every man or boy on the estate, including Bob, went out looking for whoever it was that had done it. They didn't have a name, but Bridget had given them a good description- what he was wearing, what colour hair, that he was wearing glasses. Right from the beginning, Bob had a sickening feeling he already knew who it was; and, as it turned out, he was right.

They found him in the woods, not far from the playground. He still had the blood on his hands. He didn't try to run. They let Bob have the first go at him; seeing as it was his best friend. He broke the nose with the first swing; Bob was already the best in his weight class in South London. Jonno didn't stand a chance. It wasn't in Bob's character as a fighter or a person to kick someone when they were on the floor, but this was different. He kicked and kicked at his best friend's head while the boy lay on the ground. He took long run-ups, like he was taking a penalty kick. The rage in him was uncontrollable. He kept going, until the face was a wet, red mess; until it didn't look like Jonno anymore; until it just looked like raw meat. The less it looked like him, the easier it was. Bob wasn't even the one who did the most damage that night. The gypsies from the halting site on the moor, with their iron bars, made sure the lad never walked again. If the police hadn't arrived in the middle of it to stop them, they would have been digging a grave. As it was, Jonno got off lightly.

No, the German wasn't one of those, he thought. He was just another hard man, in it for the money; the same as Bob. He finished the cigarette and opened up one of the magazines they'd left on the table for him. Penthouse Forum. The clock on the wall had hardly moved since he had sat down.

'What are you doing after this, Harry?' She wasn't backwards in coming forward, he thought.

'Ah, well I should probably get home.' He caught the eye of the waiter, and showed him his empty brandy glass.

'Home? Bit soon for home, isn't it? I hadn't figured you for an early bird.' She was rubbing her wet finger over the lip of the glass in a way which affected him more than it should have.

'Oh, I'm far from that. I just have… some business.'

'I'm sure you have plenty of people who can take care of it for you, Harry. Otherwise, what's the point of being fabulously wealthy?'

'Who said I was fabulously wealthy?'

'People talk. I've seen you on a few lists, Harry.'

'Heh. I've got a few bob squirreled away, yes. For-'

'- for a rainy day? Why do people say that anyway?' She had great eyes, he thought. They came to life whenever she smiled.

'Say what?' He wanted another cigar, but going outside was a pain.

'Saving money for a rainy day? Is there something special about rainy days that makes people think they'll need money to get through them?'

'Maybe they're thinking about the cost of umbrellas?'

'Well surely it'd be cheaper to buy the umbrellas when it's sunny out? Supply and demand and all that?'

'Too true. Maybe you should go into business.' The waiter brought over the bottle of Remy Martin.

'I'm already in business, Harry.' She winked at the lad pouring Harry's cognac, and he smiled nervously back.

'Is PR a business?' He palmed a folded up twenty pound note into the boy's hand without looking.

'It's the business of keeping people in business; or, more importantly, it's the business of making people who are out of business look like they're still in business; like they still do business, and they still mean business.' She was sharp as a tack, even with all that liquor in her, he thought. He stopped counting her drinks after the fifth one.

'What did you have in mind?'

'For?'

'For after this?'

'Oh, I know a little place. Better food than this place; better music; and if you come, better company.' She gave him another filthy look, to leave him in no doubt about where all of this was going.

'Is this place… is it your place?' *You don't ask, you don't get.* That was what Mama Goldman used to say.

'Oh, Harry. I'm not that kind of girl.'

'We'll see.'

Frank was beside her on the couch. He was a virtual stranger and she didn't trust him, but he was the nearest thing to moral support. She wanted Dylan to be there. She needed to talk to him. She had to get a moment away from Frank so she could call him or text him. She didn't have his number though. She could try to remember it. It was 07815… something. She should have brought her own phone too, she thought, cursing herself.

There was a fourth man now. He was sitting on the edge of the bed, looking at his mobile phone. The casual nature of everyone was almost as unsettling as the rest of it. He had a mask on too; it was a cartoon pig.

They weren't normal Halloween masks; they were the more sinister type, where most of the plastic is almost transparent and colourless. The fourth man was paunchy and middle aged. His nipples were dark and surrounded by hair. His legs were crossed in an almost feminine way. The redhead in the clown mask was still talking to the fitter, younger man in the duck mask, but the other old one had walked away without her seeing his face. Someone said something off camera which must have been important, because the men all turned and took positions around the bed. Someone moved the camera from behind; tilting it so you saw less roof and more of the floor.

'I'm going to shut this off the second you've seen enough, okay?' He was drinking something which looked like lemonade or Seven Up, but he could have put something in it; she hadn't been paying attention.

'What's going to happen?' She knew what was going to happen. Part of her thought if she asked him though, there would still be a chance she was wrong. He didn't reply; his look told her everything.

On the big screen, the other man came back. He had a mask on too; it was the canary from the old cartoons where the cat is always trying to open her cage and eat her. The 'tawd I taw a puddy cat' ones. Her mind was blank. He went over to the cartoon pig man- *Porky the pig*- and remonstrated with him, taking his mobile phone and walking off screen with it. The others looked at each other and shrugged their shoulders. They were pulling and pinching their penises now, and rubbing oil or lube on themselves. She remembered why it was familiar now- she had seen a documentary about a porn star called Annabel Chong. It was about a woman's attempt to break the world record for an on-screen gang-bang. Alice swallowed hard but there was no moisture in her throat. The canary man came back, and he wasn't by himself. There, dressed in what must have been tailor-made lingerie and stockings, was who she assumed to be five year old Milly Frazer. Her hair had been styled into romantic curls, and she was wearing the sort of blindfold you might buy in one of London's more high class sex shops. It was double tied, as her head was so little.

Ten

The vomiting came easy; a lot of drink on an empty stomach. There was nothing of substance; just brandy and stomach acid. He was outside the toilet door- she could sense him there, cupping his ear to the door. She didn't know why he needed to be there, because there wasn't a window, and her phone was on the table. Maybe he was just genuinely concerned for her, she thought. *No*, she couldn't start thinking he was on her side.

She had hardly watched any of it; she couldn't. She knew what was going to happen. Her heart ached for the little girl on the tape. She thought of the Frazers, who knew nothing about the tape, still putting up posters and spending money on computer aging simulations to try and see what their little Milly would look like now. *All that hope, wasted*. Milly was gone. Frank had told her as much. They'd had their way with her- all of them. Used her little body in ways it was never meant to be used, until there was nothing left of her innocence; nothing left of her soul. And then someone had disposed of her. Because that was all she was to them- a toy, to be played with until they broke her. Alice vomited again, no liquid; just dry heaves.

'Are you okay in there?'

'Of... of course I'm not okay...' She flushed the toilet again and tried to stand up.

'I... I'm sorry. I just meant-'

'I know. I know...' She opened the door without warning, making him fall into her. The awkwardness of them touching each other helped diffuse the tension for a few much needed seconds. He helped her to get steady on her feet, and then stepped away.

'Sorry. I'm sorry you had to see that, but-'

'- but I had to see it. I know.' She sat down on the couch again and looked up at the big screen, which was now off completely. Her thoughts returned to the present.

'Poppy! Turn it on!' She needed to know the girl was okay, after watching what they'd watched. Her mind began to imagine the possibilities of what would happen if they didn't manage to get her out. She wanted to be sick again.

'She's still there. She's still okay.' He pushed the standby button on the monitor and then maximised the window with the live feed. Poppy was still asleep on the bed, but she had pulled the duvet up over her. She looked incredibly peaceful; nevertheless Alice found herself glued to the screen until she was certain she saw the girl's chest rise and fall at least once.

'Frank, we need to get her out. We need to make her safe. We can't let them- I can get you the money…'

'Good. I'm going to need a lot though, Alice. Once I do this, they're going to know it was me. They're going to come after me. They're going to kill me. I'll need to start a new life, somewhere else. I know it's a cliché, but-'

'There's five million.' She looked at the floor when she said it.

'Cash?' His eyes widened.

'No! God, no. There's a bomb shelter under the house. There's a safe down there, with a quarter of a million pounds in cash; and there are keys.'

'Keys?'

'Yeah. To safety deposit boxes. Gold, diamonds, cashier's cheques. It's five million altogether. We've talked about it lots of times, me and Tom.'

'And he has this in case someone kidnaps Poppy?'

'Well, yeah; and for a few other things. His dad… his dad was awful with money; ended up completely bankrupt, with four children. Their mum had to take them to a homeless shelter for nearly a year.'

'Christ.'

'Yeah; Tom was only four, but he says he can remember pretty much all of it.' She thought of his tears when he had told her the story. She saw sides to him which cinema audiences never would.

'I can imagine…' Frank poured another brandy for her, and she picked it up without hesitation. There was plenty of room for it now.

'Tom says you never know what might happen in the future. He always wanted some sort of nest egg. Bloody ridiculous, really; he makes eight million quid a film. I don't know how he thinks he'll end up squandering that much… maybe it's in his blood though. Anyway-.'

'And the safe; you have the combination?'

'Yeah; because of the whole kidnap thing. He was shooting some action film thingy in the Dominican Republic, and he wanted Pop and me to come out and see him on set.'

'The Vietnam film?'

'Yeah. 'Brothers Of Hanoi', it was called. Terrible load of crap. Anyway, he asked me to book the tickets and I was doing some Googling, when I read this article on the kidnapping problem over there.'

'I think I've read about it too. It's a big thing; Columbia as well, and Venezuela.'

'Yeah. Anyway, I mentioned it to him on the phone, and he talked to some people there. Long story short, we didn't end up getting suntans.'

'And then?'

'Well, when he came home he had a meeting with me and we talked about someone trying to take Poppy, and what if he was out of the country and couldn't be reached…'

'And you ended up with the keys to five million pounds…'

'Pretty much; yeah.'

'And you've never been tempted to just-'

'Well, obviously… I have some morals though, and a conscience. Don't judge everyone by your standards…'

'Touché. He was still drinking the lemonade.

'What happens then? I mean, after I get you the money?' She didn't trust him; not even one bit, but she didn't have a lot of options. It was Tom's money, and Tom would have paid twice as much to see Poppy safe- she was sure of that. She would need to go there, to Hampstead Heath, to get it; and she couldn't go alone. He wasn't going call her a cab and wait until she came back. They both had vested interests here which meant neither could let the other out of their sight.

'You'll want some guarantees, I suppose.' He picked his car keys up from the coffee table.

'Yes.' She looked down at the glass in her hands and twirled it in her fingers.

'What did you have in mind?' He walked over to the bank of computer screens as he spoke.

'The people who have her, Frank… do you know their names?'

'I have a good idea of most of them.' She saw him tap something on the keyboard, and the screens began dimming and shutting down, one by one.

'Tell me. Tell me one of their names. Tell me any of their names.'

'Why?' The whole wall of screens went black.

'Because I don't know if this whole thing is going to work, Frank. I don't know what you're planning to do, or if you're able to do it. I don't know if they are going to kill you before you can get Poppy out, or if you're going to get her out at all. I need something… something as a backup plan, is all.'

'And you think if you know who they are, you can just… what? Go to the police?'

'Well, yeah, I-'

'Alice, some of these men *are* the police. And a couple of the others have friends inside the force. If you went to the police with this, or to the newspapers, they would kill you.'

'Who would? How?'

'It doesn't matter who; they just would. You don't know how powerful these men are. You go shouting your mouth off about any of this and you've as good as signed Poppy's death warrant. You saw the video, Alice-'

'Yes, I did see it! And I want to get my Poppy back before anything like that… happens. How can you be so bloody calm? It's a little girl. It's a little girl and they're going to… to rape her, just like they did to poor little Milly.'

'The people who have Poppy aren't the people in that tape.'

'What?'

'It's different people this time. Well, nearly all of them are different. The same guy is running the show.'

'You mean there's more of them? Jesus Christ, Frank; how many other videos are there?'

'This… this one is the only one I've ever seen.'

'You're lying!'

'Okay, it's the only one I've seen… on this scale. The only one like that. This organised- with such high profile people- there's been nothing like it before.'

'But… how do you know they want to do this with Poppy, Frank? That Milly girl was different; she was just someone's daughter. Tom is worth millions. How do you know they're not still going to ask for a ransom? What else do you know, Frank? Tell me!'

The buzzer went and Bill jumped. His nerves were shot; too much cocaine. He had no idea of the time. He dragged himself over to the intercom, looking down into the street below. There were two girls there; not one. He had to check with himself that he hadn't booked them both. The young one was there all right. She had a chaperone though.

'Hey! Just send her up, yeah? She'll be okay.' The older girl below shook her head and gave him a scowl.

'What? Come on, bitch. I fuckin' paid. Fuck off, and send her up.' She shook her head again, and mouthed 'no'. The younger girl didn't look up. He kicked at the wall in anger. He felt nothing, but there would be a bruise later or the next day.

'Okay, bitch. Here's how it is. Either you put her in the elevator and you fuck off, or I call your boss. Yeah, understand "Boss"? Comprende? I call your boss, and tell him his fucking whore has been giving me a bunch of bullshit, after I paid two fucking grand to-' He stopped. The older girl gave an exasperated look at the window, then pecked her friend on the cheek, before walking away. Then she re-appeared for a second, to give him the finger. He let out a giggle which lasted far too long. When he stopped, his eyes darted nervously around, the paranoia taking over momentarily.

He turned around and looked at the room, as if he was expecting genuine company and should tidy up, then stifled another giggle. There was a sugar bowl full of white powder on the glass coffee table. There was a soft knock on the apartment door. He stood up and brushed himself down; an odd sensation of nervous excitement crossed him, as if he was about to go on a first date.

She looked like Madonna in her Like a Virgin days, only much younger. The Eighties seemed to never have gone away for Eastern Bloc girls. He looked her up and down as she stood in the doorway, then he took her hand and brought her through.

'Well now. Well now. Look at you. Here, have a seat.' He pointed at the couch, rather than the chair. He wasn't going to sit on opposite sides of the room; he had paid his money. She was wearing fishnets and jewellery and a lot of lipstick. Her eye make-up made her face look much older than the rest of her. He touched her on her bare shoulder, and she didn't flinch. He wondered how many men had already been inside her, and was overcome with a mix of arousal and hate.

'A drink? Beer? Wine? What's your name, sweetie?' He pulled open the mini-fridge. She pointed to a premixed can of vodka and ginger ale.

'Goska.' Her voice was tiny and musical.

'Pardon me?' He looked at her again. She had no visible bust, but they'd put her in a corset regardless. He didn't care; he hadn't bought her because she looked like a woman. He rubbed himself through his trousers, making sure she saw him do it.

'Goska. This is my name. For you, is Margaret.' She didn't smile, but most of the Eastern European girls didn't, in his experience. Not the whores anyway.

'Go-Sha. Cool name. What about Margaret?' He hated the name Margaret. It was his ex-wife's mother's name.

'Ah, is the same. Goska is Margaret.' She fiddled with her necklace- an oversized, seventies style pearl one; looped three times around her little neck. Her accent was strange. Not thick at all. She must have come to England a while back; enough to pick up some British undertones to the Polish lilt.

'Oh. Oh! Oh, I see now. Okay, well I'm gonna just call you Go Sher, okay?'

'Goska...' Her eyes were enormous and blue.

'Go Sha! Yes, my bad. Okay Goska honey, how about you show me what ya got there, yuhuh?' He licked his lips and swallowed. The back of this throat was numb from the phlegm he had swallowed. The girl stood up, robotic and with faraway eyes. She started to undo the clasps on the corset, in a way which said to him she had done it far too many times before.

'Whoa! Hold it there, Go Sher, sweetness. Take your time, baby. Leave the clothes on... just- just turn around for me there.' He made a twirling motion with his fingers. She turned, still silent. There was nothing there; he was pretty sure she hadn't hit puberty. She wasn't far off it. It would happen soon. She was maybe twelve, going on thirteen. She didn't have any of the roundness yet. He was hard; so much so that he had to undo the top button on his trousers.

'Oh, honey; aren't you the pretty one? Okay, pull up the skirt a little now. Show me those pantyhose.' She lifted the elasticated hem and he saw the fishnets were not tights, but stockings. The clasps on her suspenders shone gold under his harsh, shadeless room lights.

'Wow, a garter belt! Daddy likes...'

Dylan needed to get something to eat. They did food there, but he had never tried it. There was something about pub food which made him lose his appetite. He had seen someone earlier behind the bar in chef's trousers, but it was a safe bet most of the food on the menu would be microwaved. He was in the cubicle; he hated standing at the urinals. He liked the privacy; no chance of someone starting a conversation. He couldn't go if someone was talking to him. He went back out into the lounge.

His glass was gone, and there was someone in his seat. An old man, nursing a glass of bitter. He was reading a newspaper which had some story about a man who used to be on the television in the Eighties. He died the year before, and then stories had started to come out about him molesting children. Teenagers, in truth;

but it was still a big scandal. He got away with it for years too; because he was famous, he was rich, and he had some powerful friends. Dylan looked at the picture of him on the front page and shuddered.

He went outside, past the smoking tables. The place next door was more of a gastro pub, but he didn't want to go in there. There was another McDonald's by the station; he walked past it as well. He turned the corner onto Victoria Road and walked down to Dixy Chicken. It was quiet. All the loud school children were gone, and it was too early for the fallout from the pubs and clubs. The two men behind the counter were talking in Arabic. He knew one of their faces.

'Yes please?'

'Ah, yeah. Can I have this?' He pointed at a poster on the wall.

'Six hot wing and chip?' There were two baskets in the chip fryer. One of them had half cooked chips in it; he dropped it into the oil. The other one was empty.

'Yes please.' Dylan fiddled around in his jeans pocket for some change or a scrunched up note.

'Two fifty, mate.' He said 'mate' like it was 'might'. He pulled open a bag of frozen chips and poured the whole lot into the empty fryer basket.

'Yeah. Hang on.' He dug deep, the skinny fit of the jeans not helping him. At last, he found something which felt like money. He opened it out; it was a ten. The man gave him back the change.

'And seven fifty, mate.' He didn't go back talking to the other man; he just stood there, looking at Dylan. It was moments like these when he wondered what he did before mobile phones. It was the same when he was walking down the street past the charity people with clipboards. He would have whole conversations, both sides, rather than have to tell them he wasn't interested. He went to a book launch once, on his own. Alice had cancelled at the last minute. He didn't know anyone. Spent the first half hour talking into a turned off mobile and knocking back free wine. No one talked to him. Every minute felt like a year. Eventually he spoke to some woman who looked like she was on her own too. She just sort of tolerated him for a while, then made an excuse and left the room. He sank some more free wine and went back to talking to no one on his phone. Alice had had to come pick him up from Covent Garden tube station; he had fallen asleep drunk on a bench and missed the last train.

'Six wing and chip. Drink, mate?' He had a baseball cap on which said '49ers'.

'What?'

'Drink! What drink you want, my friend?' He waved his hand over the front of the fridge.

'Oh, right. Water.' He watched how many salt sachets the man put in the box. He liked salt; if he put less than three in there, Dylan would have to ask for extra. He put four. They knew him by now.

'Water, my friend?' He took a bottle out of the fridge.

'Please.' It was good he didn't have to ask for extra salt. They always thought he said "extra sauce", and tried to give him ketchup. There must have been something peculiar about the way he pronounced "salt".

'Carrier bag, mate?' 49ers man had a Chicago Bulls shirt on.

'Please, yes.' He had to find somewhere to eat it. That was the thing with buying food in Dixy; it was cheap, but you had to eat it somewhere else. They had tables there, but they were usually full of people who he didn't want to be around. He went back to the Liberty mall. If there was space on the benches outside BHS, they had free Wi-Fi. He took a hot wing out of the box. Alice wasn't a fan of spicy wings. He wondered where she was now, and if she was thinking about him.

She hadn't been lying. They weren't going to her place. Terry dropped them off in Soho, outside some little jazz place, a basement bar. Beth had given him the address for the Sat Nav. She let Harry pay the cover price, after he insisted. He still wasn't sure if she was sincere or just a tease. He doubted he was being taken for a ride. She wasn't some stupid child, and she had plenty of money herself. Anyway, even if she had tried to pay for anything, there was no way he would have let her. He was from the old school; women didn't pay for things on a night out. Well, the pretty ones didn't anyway. And they were the only ones who mattered to him. She was more than pretty though; she was smart too, and successful. He would have called her a catch if he wasn't already sure a girl like her was far too hard to handle. The smart ones were trouble in the long run. He had learned that.

'Drink?'

'I'll have a Moet.' She had come without a jacket, or left it back at the other place. The skin on her shoulders was soft and milky.

'Oh yeah? Are we celebrating?'

'Always.' The odd coloured lighting made her hair look more blonde than auburn.

'Well in that case, I'll join you. Two Moets, son.' He waved a wad of notes to get the barkeeper's attention. The place wasn't a dive, but someone had paid a lot of money to make it look like one, he thought. The band was almost an afterthought; pushed over into the corner. They were all white, and dressed in skinny fit suits. He handed the barman a twenty and walked away without discussing change. It was the sort of place which had tip trays they pushed toward you when you paid for the drinks. There was more than likely an African man in the toilets, spraying people with scents or handing out paper towels. He would have a tip tray too.

'Where d'you wanna sit?' He looked around; it was busy. He scanned the people in the room; there was money about, but it was New Money; young money. He looked at her again, and tried to put an age on her. It was hard to tell. He spotted a table by the wall, with a couple who were getting up to leave. The woman had an unimpressed look on her face, and the man looked sheepish.

'There.' She was looking at the same table as he was. They walked over, her in front; him carrying the drinks. He took the opportunity to enjoy the shape of her from behind. It was as impressive as the front. He wondered how long she was going to make him wait tonight. She wanted something from him, definitely. He was no Brad Pitt; women usually wanted something from him. That suited him fine; he usually had it to give. Not all women were whores; just the ones worth sleeping with; his Uncle had said that at some drunken family occasion when he was younger, and it had stuck with him.

'Whores' was a strong word, but sex was still a business transaction, as far as he was concerned. The women who had nothing to bargain with didn't interest him. A woman should be attractive and glamorous. It was good she was smart and funny too, of course; but that wouldn't have been worth anything to him if she had been fat and ugly. He ended up paying for sex in the end; one way or another, he thought. He might as well get something worth the asking price. He pulled her chair out and waited until she had sat down before taking his own seat. The fizz in their glasses had gone down.

'Cheers,' she said, clinking her glass to his.

'Mazel tov,' he said, taking her in. Her lips looked even better when they were wet.

'Oh yeah? Are we celebrating?'

'Always'

Eleven

There were websites with pictures; message boards, anonymous chat rooms. It wasn't necessary to provide a real email to join. Someone could just write any made-up address, and they'd be given a login. Rick was using a proxy, just to be safe. He didn't think there were police on there; there was nothing illegal going on. Just some people sharing picture sets from the websites of underage models; nothing nude, nothing hard core. Nothing anyone could be arrested for. The worst they could get in trouble for was copyright, but the men who ran those modelling sites were hardly going to take someone to court for stealing intellectual property… They might have disclaimers on their front pages about everything being legal and above board; how there was no nudity or child pornography on their sites, and how they existed 'solely for the promotion of young models', but that didn't fool anyone. No one from casting agencies was paying thirty dollars a month for memberships to these things; no seven year old aspiring model was joining to look at pictures of her peers. They only had one key demographic, and they were well aware of it.

The men on the sites were obsessive, almost to the point of OCD or Asperger's. If they liked a girl, they wanted to collect everything she had ever done, from the earliest age to the latest. If a set was missing some numbers, they'd start a forum post about it, looking for the others. There were the regular posters, the site admins, the mods and the trolls. The forums were heavily moderated, with the owners banning anyone who made suggestive comments about the girls, or posted any links to illegal content. It was a glorious hypocrisy, the idea of 'appreciating beauty', Rick thought. Everyone using the site was collecting pictures to masturbate to. The admins knew being open about it would mean the FBI intervening to close the site down, or the people who owned the servers terminating their contracts. So they stayed in a grey area between the laws, continuing to exist under the noses of the authorities. Rick had no doubt the law knew about these places, or that they probably collected IP addresses and info about the people visiting them. He was also sure the whole thing would be considered 'small fish' by LEA, and that none of the members would ever end up having their doors kicked down at 6am. As long as they kept their noses relatively clean, that was.

He hadn't always. He met a lot of people on there, through the private messaging system. That was how he got the harder material. Everyone seemed to have some of that, hidden away. Every new conversation he had with someone from those sites was just a little game; an 'I'll show you mine if you show me yours' that usually ended in him downloading the sort of pictures and videos that would land him with a long spell in prison if anyone ever found them on his computer. He had every cleaner and history kill program available, but he knew that the police had more sophisticated tools which could find anything on a hard drive, regardless of how thoroughly it had been deleted. If the day ever came when he did get the knock at 6am, there would be nothing he could do to stop them finding everything. It was the chance they all took, every day.

He didn't care. It was a compulsion, the collecting. He started off with a few sample pictures from sites that specialised in them; sites that made affiliate money from any click-through to the model's individual pages. Then he went on the message boards, and start downloading whole sets. Before he knew it, it would be two in the morning and he would have four different instant messenger windows open, swapping pictures of girls in thongs and bikinis first, then nudes from Russian pay sites, and finally hard core photos and videos of real abuse. That was the only thing he could get off to now. That was the end which justified the means. And then, when it was all over, the deleting would start again, fuelled by the paranoia that someone somewhere had been looking in on what he was doing; or worse, that one of the faceless men he had been trading with had been a policeman, or an FBI agent. It did happen; he was sure of it. That was how they caught people. He could never sleep afterwards. Part of him was always expecting the knock. Part of him stayed awake, imagining vivid scenarios of him being interrogated by angry policemen in a dark room, and tabloid headlines screaming about the depraved child sex lusts of one of Britain's best known rock stars. The light coming through the curtains would pump the anxiety up several notches, and the real waiting would begin. It was only when the seven on his bedside clock changed to an eight that he allowed himself some peace and sank into sleep until the afternoon.

'Fuck. Fuck, Jesus fuck…' He had laid her down in the bathtub; it was the only place he could put her. She was bleeding too much and the suite was full of expensive carpets. Bill hadn't meant to hurt her. It had been a mistake; a stupid mistake. He was too high; it was too easy to keep bumping. At least with MDMA he knew when he had enough. It was easy to time, and it stopped working after a few hours. Cocaine was different. He could keep going for two or three days straight. He had lost count of when it was that he had started. He was in trouble, he knew that. The Albanians were going to cut his throat. He needed a plan. He could ring and ask to keep her for the night. That would give him some time to figure it out. It'd all be clearer in the morning, he thought.

He hadn't meant to do it. He was happy with her. She was beautiful. He had wanted to do things with her; to her, but he hadn't meant to hurt her. He had asked her to dance for him. He sat there, watching, touching himself through his trousers. He made her take the skirt off, so she was in her underwear and stockings. He asked her to take off the corset too, but he didn't like looking at her chest; it was so pre-pubescent. She gyrated for him like a pole dancer; moved closer to him, rubbed against him, licked her lips. He thought about all the things he was going to do to her later, ignoring the faraway look in her eyes. He had her on his lap, grinding against him. He put his hands on either side of the chair and didn't touch her. When he couldn't stand it any longer, he undid his trouser buttons and got her to kneel in front of him.

She didn't touch him. He put his hand on her head; felt his fingers slide into the mess of curls, and a shudder went through his lower half. He bit his lip and looked down at her, but she had already closed her eyes in anticipation of what he was going to make her do. She opened her mouth, and he saw her tongue- pink and wet. A massive involuntary spasm jolted through him, and he felt his face flush. Her eyes opened- big and confused- as his ejaculate sprayed onto the chair behind her. He looked at her in shock, struggling to catch his breath. And then she had laughed at him.

He opened the browser and clicked on Recently Closed. The site had logged him out. He grabbed his phone and found the password again. There was a number on the home page. It was a mobile. He wanted more cocaine; it would help him to think, he thought. The chair was covered in his semen and her blood. He dialled the number, let it ring once or twice and hung up. He didn't want to speak to them. He didn't even know if it would be possible to ask them for a few more hours, or to keep her overnight. But he knew he had to call; otherwise the other girl would be back in- he looked at the clock on the bedside locker- half an hour, and the game would be up.

He had lost control; beaten her badly. He could see it in his mind's eye, the look changing on her face- from amusement to terror. She shouldn't have laughed at him, he told himself. It wasn't his fault. *People shouldn't do that; make fun of you- when you're feeling... vulnerable.* He kept on punching, even though she had stopped laughing. He could still hear the laugh inside his head. She had been laughing at him; at his virility; at his worth as a man, it had seemed to him. *A little child, laughing at ME- Bill Hansen.* He had to show her what was what. He had to teach her a lesson. No one laughed at him, he told himself. No one disrespected him like that. He stopped punching when she hit the floor; and started kicking; her stomach, her ribs, her already broken face. The rage was uncontrollable. She screamed first, but eventually it was just whimpering. After a while, she made no noise at all.

It didn't matter to him if she was still alive. He concentrated his blows on the lower stomach; where he thought her womb would be. He wanted to ruin her, to destroy her chance of ever having a child of her own. He kicked her between the legs. He had got no pleasure out of it, so no one else was going to either, he told himself.

By the time he had run out of energy, she was unrecognisable. Her face looked like bruised fruit; her hair was matted and sticky. He dragged her into the bathroom, the effort draining the last of his energy.

He stared at the phone, then at the website, and back at the phone. He needed to call someone else. Harry would be no good; he had already sensed annoyance in the man's voice earlier, even if his words had been less hostile. The mobile rang, the high pitched tone jarring him back to the present moment. He looked at the display, confused. It was the same number he had just dialled. The Albanians were ringing him back.

Poppy woke up from strange dreams. Her father had been there, in their old kitchen. They had been getting ready to go to Ireland, on the plane. It was early in the morning. They were waiting for the taxi to arrive. He made her some toast out of the bread she liked; the one with seeds. He had some toast too. That felt odd to her, because he never ate breakfast; he just drank coffee and smoked cigarettes. Before, he had given them up, but he had started again, and he hadn't told her. He would disappear for five minutes and then come back to her. She never smelled them. He must have had mints.

In the dream, they were talking about Sesame Street- Bert and Ernie and Big Bird. Her father was saying he didn't like Big Bird, and she was telling him to be quiet, because Big Bird was her favourite. And then he turned into her mother, and it didn't even seem strange to her. They just carried on talking, even though it wasn't about Sesame Street anymore. She couldn't remember what they talked about. *Nothing too interesting then*, Alice would have said.

She was still in the pink room, but it felt colder. She looked under the duvet. She wasn't wearing pyjamas anymore; she must have taken them off before she went to sleep, she told herself. She didn't remember doing it, but sometimes she didn't remember things, especially things she did just before bed. She was glad she had dreamt about Tom; it seemed like a long time since she had seen him. She wondered what the time was. Magda had said she would be back in a while. She looked down again. She was wearing her vest, but not the same pants. There were strange knickers on which rode up her. They were made of skinny material, and they were black. She didn't remember ever seeing them before. Some people walked around when they were asleep. Maybe she had started getting undressed and dressed again when she was asleep. Because there was no one else around who could be doing it.

She was hungry again, and she could smell something nice. She wrapped the duvet around her like a towel after swimming, and she scooched down to the end of the bed to look for her PJs. There was a chair there, with a little outfit on it. Her eyes widened- it was a Tinkerbelle set. A cute vest and little shorts, with a big drawing of Tink on the top, and on the bum of the shorts it said 'Tinkerbelle' in sparkly writing.

'Cool!' She took the weird knickers off- under the duvet, even though no one was looking at her- because they were making her sore. She had no pants to put on under the Tink shorts, but it wouldn't matter. Grown-ups weren't going to tell her off for wearing no knickers when there were no knickers to wear. She didn't think any of the ones in the strange trunk were comfortable enough to wear all the time. She hopped down from the bed and went over to the big mirror again. She did a twirl and a kissy face, like Alice used to do in the mirror at home when she was getting ready to go out. They fit perfectly. Then she saw the food.

'Om nom!' There was a tray on the table, with a glass and some plates. Orange juice- smooth, no bits- a chocolate chip cookie for pudding, and- best of all- a vegetarian pasty, like the ones from the café. Poppy wasn't a vegetarian, although sometimes she wanted to be. Emma from school was a vegetarian; her whole family were. Poppy had had dinner over at hers a few times- it was usually cheesy pasta. They didn't have a turkey at Christmas, or a ham. That was very strange, she thought. There was always a turkey at Christmas. The pasty was delicious, and the juice was even better. She gulped it down. She wished she had proper telly. She wanted to watch Horrible Histories. She needed the toilet again.

Alice sat in the back again. He insisted that she did. She guessed it was because he wanted where he lived to stay a secret. It seemed ridiculous now she had seen his face and spent so much time with him. She went along with it anyway; she didn't want to know what happened when he didn't get his way. Something told her that the cool, calm person she had been dealing with all day was only one side of him. She had no desire to see the others, if she could help it.

They were going to Tom's place; to the safe, and the five million. She still had the work phone with her, and she made a note of the time when they left, so she would know roughly how long it had taken to get there. That way, the police would be able to estimate where Frank's place was, or at least draw a radius on a map. It might never come to that of course. If they got Poppy back, she would leave it at that. Tom would want to as well. Five million would be nothing to him, compared with the alternative. Going after the man who called himself Frank would be pointless; he hadn't taken her. It was in case he took the money and ran. She was acutely aware of the possibility.

'Do you need a postcode?' Frank had turned on the microphone and speaker in the middle of the car's privacy screen. She could speak to him and hear him through it.

'No. I know where we're going, Alice.'

Of course you do.

She needed answers from him. And for the next ten minutes or so, she got them. He told her more about the things he learned from eavesdropping on the chats he hosted. Most of it was hard to take. Poppy was apparently very popular among the users of his website. Alice cringed when he heard of how her 'fans' obsessed about her. She had been present at many of those magazine shoots, and had signed the consent forms in loco parentis. She never dreamed they were contributing to the scrapbooks of paedophiles. Frank made it sound normal; like teen girls having crushes on pop stars. That was one of the things he kept stressing to her; the way, once one came to terms with the nature of their association, these people behaved in normal ways. The chat rooms and message boards were the same as any others on the web. There were flame wars and Grammar Nazis and clever nicknames and a sense of community. As Frank put it, the only difference was these people were sexually attracted to children. She couldn't be as obtuse as he was about it; not while Poppy was still in that room. Not until she was safe. She didn't want to think about it any deeper. She needed to keep herself together.

'How did you see me, by the way?' She lit a cigarette.

'How did I see you?' Another car blasted its horn outside.

'When you called me. You could see I was using my laptop. You told me I was wearing a Star Wars T-shirt...' She got a chill, remembering it.

'Oh, right. Just a little trick.' He didn't laugh, but she could hear a smile in his voice.

'You have cameras in my home?'

'No. Well, yes. Kind of.'

'What do you mean, kind of?' The car took a sharp right and she had to hold on to her seat.

'You want to know?'

'Wouldn't you want to know if someone was watching you twenty-four seven? How long have you been doing it? What have you seen?' Her stomach did cartwheels as she imagined the possibilities.

'Today was the first time.'

'That's a lie.' She pressed the button for the ashtray, just in time to tip the cigarette.

'I'm telling the truth.'

'But how did you-'

'There's a program. A service that a company do. Your laptop is a work one, right?'

'Mmm, yeah.' Tom's people had given it to her a few months before.

'They signed you up to a company who put software on your computer which lets them turn your webcam on remotely.'

'Why the hell would they do that?' She picked up the brandy from the shelf.

'Well, so when someone steals the thing-'

'-they can take his picture!' She drank straight from the hip flask. It tasted strong but good.

'Bingo.'

'But, how-'

'I just broke into their website and looked for you.'

'As simple as that?' Talking to him made her regret everything she had ever done online, especially anything involving her credit card.

'As relatively simple as that. Okay. We're here.'

'We're at Tom's?' Already? They couldn't have driven far, she thought. She looked at the phone. It had been fourteen minutes.

Bob looked at his watch. It hadn't been an hour yet. He couldn't remember if the German had said an hour or a half hour. He was staying where he was; if they wanted him they would tell him. He was getting paid regardless.

There was a stereo there, he turned on the radio. BBC2 was his station. All of the rest were either young people's music or they had too much talk on them. He liked the old tunes; Springsteen, Billy Joel, and Elton John. 'Saturday Night's Alright for Fighting' came on when the tuner reached 89. It was one of his favourites; reminded him of being young, going out in London. He had some great friends back then, and some terrible ones. Some of them were still around; plenty of them had ended up in early graves. Such was the nature of the business. He had few legitimate jobs, and most of the time he just took them to get the DSS off his back for a while. In the end, he registered as self-employed, as a store detective. He rarely did any shifts, but he was paying enough contributions every year to keep the taxman and the Social out of his affairs, and that was all he wanted: The quiet life. He lit another cigarette and leaned back in his chair so he could see out the door. There was no one outside; the German must have been in there with the girl. He hoped that there was nothing sinister happening, but even if there had been, it wouldn't be his place to interfere. No matter how much he might want to.

His mobile rang. He still had an old Nokia; he liked the way they worked. He could understand how to send text on it, and the battery lasted at least a week. He didn't need a phone to be a satnav or a video camera. He just needed it to be a phone.

'Yeah? Who's this?'

'You can go back now. The girl. *Ja?*'

'Yeah.' He took one of the magazines with him as he left. The girl on the front reminded him of someone; he couldn't remember whom.

'Whatcha doin?'

Paul hadn't heard her come in; she was light on her feet. He quickly scanned the laptop screen for anything that might have been unsuitable for her, but it was just the sports news.

'Oh, 'ello Col. I'm just reading me emails, innit.' He ruffled her hair and she pulled away with a grimace. She was getting to an age where she thought she was too old for babyish things.

'Sounds boring.' She had her mother's eyes, and her long legs. Both the girls did. Someone had said they were both probably going to be models. He was annoyed by that. He wanted something better for them.

'Yeah, boring Dad stuff. What you up to?'

'Nothing…' She was ten years old. Tamara dressed her like she was a teenager sometimes. Not provocatively or anything, in his opinion; just a bit too old. It made him feel more protective of her; as if the day when she wasn't his little girl anymore was getting closer, somehow. Having to deal with boyfriends, and everything that went with it, seemed like it was still years away, but he didn't know. She was his first daughter; he had nothing to measure against.

'You want me to tell you a story?' Paul raised an eyebrow at her.

'What? Noooooooooo! I'm not a baby, Dad!' She rolled her eyes and exhaled dramatically.

'You sure? You used to love my stories, Col. What happened?'

'Pfffft. I'm ten, Daddy. Stories are for children.'

'Oh, right. What age do *children* stop liking stories then?' He shut down the laptop and turned on the swivel chair to face her.

'Uh, about nine I'd say.'

'Oh right. I didn't know. I had a good one and all for you. Never mind, eh?'

'Oh? What was it about?' She had big brown eyes, and long lashes; like something from a Disney cartoon, his sister had once said.

'What was it about? Oh, it don't matter now, eh? Stories is for children, like. You just told me.'

'Aw, Daddy!'

'What? What've I done, eh? You don't want none of me stories. You ain't a baby no more, Colleen.'

'Daddy!' She grabbed him around the waist and shook him, still giggling.

'What? Bleeding hell, Col. Make up yer mind, wouldn'tcha? I ain't got all day.'

She hopped up onto his lap, and he made up a story for her on the spot. It was a mixture between the three little pigs and Goldilocks, and she laughed until she cried and he hugged her until he thought he might burst. They always had the best of times together. He was close to her, and so good with her, everyone said. He would never do anything to harm her, and would murder anyone who did.

But the person holding her and telling her stories was the same person who stayed up til the early hours some nights, watching videos of girls her age and younger. Girls who were someone else's child. The same person who looked at her friends in the playground after school and imagined the things he would like to do to them, even though he hated himself for it afterwards. The same person who'd paid two million pounds to Harry Goldman to do those same things to Tom Riley's daughter.

All of those things existed in him at the same time, and he tried to avoid thinking about it as much as he could. Those were the thoughts that kept him awake so much he needed a prescription for Valium. The thoughts which made him a little less careful crossing the road some days. There'd been times when he had sat at the table with a bottle of pills, and asked himself to come up with a good reason not to swallow them all; times when he sat in the bath and started to run a blade across the skin on his wrist, to see how easy it would be. Times when he stood on the platform at Liverpool Street station, waiting for the announcement to stand back, because the train coming through would not be stopping. In the end, he didn't have it in him. He would be leaving the girls behind without a father, and he couldn't do that to them.

'So, how are we going to do this?' Frank had dropped the privacy screen completely now and was looking straight at her.

'What do you mean?'

'Well, I don't really know you. And I don't think you trust me. That's understandable, considering everything that's happened today.' They were parked outside the big gates. There was a barrier, which was down, and a small cabin to the right of it.

'I… I don't know what to think.' She blinked a few too many times, and then rubbed her eyes; drowsy from alcohol and stress.

'Well I need you to think, Alice. Please.'

'I can get you the money; well, some of it, and I can get the keys too, I just-'

'I know. But, I mean if I was in your position, there would be things going through my mind.' He looked at her like he wanted confirmation, but she had nothing for him.

'I… like what?'

'Well. I mean, if you walk in there, there's going to be a part of you that will want to tell them everything.'

'Tell who everything?' She was trying to sound innocent, but he was right.

'Doesn't matter. The first person you see. No matter what you tell me, there's part of you that'll want to scream for them to call the police; to tell them I'm some madman who's kidnapped Riley's daughter. Get them to hold me down until the cavalry arrive.'

'I…' She couldn't think of anything to say.

'It's okay. It's natural. I'd feel the same.' She couldn't picture him screaming, or panicking. She couldn't imagine anything other than the calm, careful way in which he was speaking to her now. He didn't seem to have another gear.

'I don't… I don't have to talk to anyone in there. The door to the place isn't in the house. I don't have to go through the front door…' The shelter was under the drive rather than the house.

'I still can't let you go in by yourself, Alice. You understand that, right?'

'But what if someone sees you?'

'Why would that matter?'

'I just thought you wouldn't want to get-'

'I'm not committing a crime, Alice. And even when I have the money, it won't be stealing.' He started the engine.

'I suppose so, I-'

'And it won't be ransom money either; I didn't kidnap her.' He had thought it all through, she noted. She heard him start the engine again.

'Wait.' She grabbed his shoulder, instinctively. Time stopped for a few seconds. She let go again.

'What's wrong?'

'I need to be the one driving.'

Bob lit another cigarette. He had brought the ashtray back with him from the room. He wondered who would guard the door when he was asleep, or if they were going to let him have any sleep at all. He wouldn't mind; he had done all night jobs before. The room they'd given him had a bed though, so it seemed like he would be allowed to sleep. They might have someone else to take over the night shift, he thought. The girl was locked in anyway; there was no way for her to get out. They probably just needed him to be there when she was awake; to take the food and drink in, or to tell the German if she started screaming, or banging on the door. It was a job anyone could have done. He couldn't think of a solid reason why they had chosen him, but he wasn't going to turn down the money.

He hadn't ever met the boss, or even spoken to him on the phone. He didn't need to; he had learned over the years that curiosity wasn't something these people looked for in an employee. He didn't care, as long as they were paying him. He would have liked to know more, of course, but wasn't going to ask. Epping Forest was full of holes with men in them who had asked too many questions. He knew when to keep his mouth shut. The text to his phone had said two days, but if it was a kidnapping, they might end keeping her for longer than they had planned. It happened; people said they could get the money, but not all at once. That was usually the police's idea. People who were told not to involve the police usually called them regardless. They thought that life was like television; that the good guys always won in the end.

Real life was a different, Bob knew. Things were messier. Everything didn't always get tied up in nice neat bundles. People made mistakes, things went wrong. In his experience, there were few criminal masterminds. It was fear or muscle that got someone to the top of an outfit, rather than brains. Prisons were full of bosses who hadn't planned things properly, or the thugs who hadn't executed their plans well enough. This arrangement felt more professional though, the same as any of the other jobs he had done for them. Whoever the little girl was; whatever family she belonged to, she was going to make them a lot of money. Something still felt wrong about it, however. Something was still nagging at him inside. He just hadn't figured out what it was yet. He crushed the cigarette end into the ashtray and went back to flicking through the magazine.

Bill slid down the couch and onto the carpet, head in hands. It hadn't been easy to get them off his back. The Albanian wasn't just ringing back because he had got a call from Bill's number. It turned out the second girl, the older one, had complained about him not letting her come up to the room. Apparently it was the part of the deal if someone wanted to hire Goska- her 'sister' had to come along and wait around while she did her business. Bill tried to play it cool; to pretend that it had all being a misunderstanding. He hadn't used them enough to pull the whole 'I'm a valued customer' shtick. He just told the man that he had only asked for one girl, and he didn't want to have to pay for two, if the other girl tried to con him out of some money for her being there. The man had laughed and called the sister something derogatory. Bill didn't need to be fluent in Albanian to understand the sentiment. Then he asked for her to be put on the line, so he could check she was okay. Bill managed to bluff his way through, saying she was tied up and gagged in his bedroom- that he was into bondage. The man had believed him, after a fashion.

Getting them to let him have her for until the morning was harder. They did offer an overnight service, but they'd never had anyone ask for it with her. She was their youngest girl, and the man was acting protective. It was almost sweet. When Bill had offered money though, the Albanian had dropped the fatherly act quickly. It had turned into haggling almost immediately. They'd settled for six thousand. Bill would have agreed to ten or twenty if the man on the other end had pushed him. It was time he was buying, and some space in which to think of a plan.

The sister was going to pick her up in the morning, if she even was her real sister. He hadn't seen much resemblance. He had no idea what he was going to do then. He could check out of the hotel, but he couldn't leave a dead child prostitute in the bath. Housekeeping would be there at eleven to give the room a tidy, although he could tell them to go away. He had checked in using his real name, with his own credit card. Things would get messy for him quickly. He chopped up another line of cocaine. The bump took him back up to a place where he could think clearly again. He needed to get her down to the car.

'Oh, I don't know. I'm pretty open minded.' She had been matching him drink for drink. The band was playing something he didn't recognise, but he never recognised modern jazz.

'Oh yeah? Tell me.' He slid his hand into his trousers to adjust himself. He was wondering how they were getting on back at the house, but Reinhart would have it under control.

'Telling's for wimps.'

'Oh, so you're going to show me then?' He looked her up and down in a way that made sure she knew it. Her legs were as impressive as the rest of her. A woman in that sort of shape didn't come cheap, or without complications, in his experience.

'We'll see. More drinks?' Her glass was empty again.

'I'm all right with this one. Where is it you're living then? In town?'

'I have a couple of places, yeah.'

'A couple? Blimey, business must be good.'

'You can talk.' She nodded at the signet ring on his wedding finger. An immense diamond on a thick gold band.

'That? That's my insurance policy. Like the gyppos.' He remembered being a child at Christmas, when his uncle Saul would come around to see them. Saul had a mouth full of gold teeth, and a plenty of large, heavy rings. His eight year old self had asked about all the shiny things, and the Uncle had told him that he didn't trust the banks, so he kept a bit of gold on his fingers and in his mouth, to pay for his funeral if the rest of his business interests ever failed. His mother had made some joke about that being how the Romanies did it. Saul was long gone now. Harry had looked at him in the coffin, still wearing his ring. He wondered to himself if the teeth were still there too.

'I'm with Scottish Widows myself,' she giggled.

'Sensible girl.' He finished the rest of his drink and got up to get them some more. The jazz seemed like it was getting quieter.

Twelve

Paddy at the gate had barely given her a glance, he just nodded as the barrier went up. No one questioned anything she did. Tom trusted her completely, so his staff did too.

'I'm taking us around the back; that's where it is,' she said; ostensibly to Frank, but half to herself. She was concentrating on her driving. There had been a lot of brandy and no food to soak it up. She parked up as close as she could, and popped the driver's side door open. Frank came out of the back and followed her.

The house was a lot older than the shelter. Tom had paid more than three million pounds for it and the land around it, if the newspapers were to be believed. She loved the place and so did Poppy. Her stomach lurched a bit and she wasn't sure if it was fear or hunger.

'What's the situation with surveillance here?' Frank was wearing sunglasses and a hat with the peak pulled right down. He didn't look up at any point. She felt like he had done this sort of thing before.

'There are cameras everywhere, but I don't think they're much good.'

'How so?' He was chewing gum; it made him seem even more detached and emotionless to her.

'Well, we had an incident last Christmas. Some crazy bitch, a fan of Tom's…'

'She broke into the grounds, yes? I remember reading about it.'

'Yeah. Real bunny boiler. Anyway, I was on site when it happened, and Paddy- the man that let us in just now- called me, and told me to come down and have a look at the monitors.'

'There's a security room?' His eyebrows lifted behind the mirrored lenses.

'It's a big place.'

'Yes.'

'Anyway, he showed me a tape of her, walking around the gardens, looking in the ground floor windows.'

'Wow.'

'Yeah. She was completely tapped. She was just wearing a t-shirt and jogging bottoms-'

'In December…'

'Yeah. The men in the control room were pissing themselves at her. They didn't really think she was capable of much, but-'

'But Poppy was there.'

'Exactly. It was Christmas Holidays. Tom wasn't even home that day; he was shooting in Pinewood. Anyway, the point is, on the tapes, I couldn't make out her face; there was no real detail. It's an old set-up, they cameras only record a few frames a minute. It's black and white, and fuzzy.'

'Is it digital?'

'Well, it's not VHS. The 'tapes' are more like CD roms. But, the cameras themselves are pretty old.'

'Well that's something at least.' He looked over at the bracket mounted camera that was whirring on the wall.

'Yeah. Oh, and those just move by themselves. There's probably no one watching us now. Or if it's Geraint, he's probably asleep.' She smiled briefly, but it was mainly to herself.

'Will someone think it odd that you're going inside the cellar, uh, bunker, and with me?' He chewed slowly, like he was savouring it. She looked at herself in the reflection from his aviators.

'Oh, no one knows about this place at all; just Tom and me, and the firm who built it. He's told me that a few times.' They were standing at a small, old-looking door now. She picked a long gold key from the bunch clipped to her belt loop, and the door opened without a creak or a groan.

Bill snorted the too-fat line up the left nostril, because the right one was stinging. He winced with the pain of it- too lumpy, he hadn't bothered to crush it up enough. It was good, but there must have been damp in the room, because it was clumped together in the bag. It was that, or his fingers had been wet the times he had dipped a finger in to gum some earlier.

Cocaine was his poison. He had tried other drugs, but nothing suited quite like coke. It helped him to lose control, and losing control was good. It was a release from the tedium of being pampered and handled by studio people. Sometimes they would send him a fresh faced intern, always a girl, always pretty. That would break the monotony after a while, but he always let them go once he had his way. They got clingy; thought they were special, just because he invited them into his bed.

Those girls were a distraction at best, but he couldn't ever get wild with them. Not like with working girls. He had been too wild this time though. He needed the situation to go away, quickly. He had to deal with it himself, and not call anyone. He had used up all his chances with Harry. He could do it himself. It would be easy. He was capable of anything, he felt.

He could roll her in a rug and take her downstairs to his car. It would be risky, but the hotel was quiet. He hadn't met anyone in the corridors since he checked in. Or he could cut her up. There weren't any real tools there, but there was a block of expensive knives on the kitchen counter. There were ones there that were made for boning chicken; it couldn't be much different. He looked at her lifeless body. She could have been sleeping, if he ignored the blood around her nose. She looked peaceful and beautiful. He wondered what her actual age might be; not that it mattered anymore. He pinched her cheek; the skin was still hot. Foundation and blusher came off onto his fingers; reminded him of something from long ago. He had been six years old, living in Queens. There had been a light in the stairwell outside the apartment his mother rented. When it got dark, there would be moths; great big things. Massive, furry eyes, and wings that made the most horrible fluttering noise. He had been terrified of them. One night, his brother had caught one, in a butterfly net. He forced Bill to hold it inside his closed hands, despite the younger boy screaming in protest. When their mother came out to investigate the noise, she found Bill standing stock still on the steps under the buzzing light. He had wet himself from sheer terror, although it didn't seem like he knew. The moth was gone, but Bill could still remember the coloured dust all over his hands. Pink and red, like the colours on his fingers now. Bill touched her lips, pushing them open with his fingers, so he could see her teeth. Her jaws came apart with little effort and he held her mouth open for a few seconds. He saw her pink tongue, still wet. Arousal stirred somewhere in him, from a dark place. Some people had limits to their depravity. He had yet to find his. She wouldn't feel it, of course; she couldn't feel anything anymore. That was no good. He liked it when it hurt them. He needed to hear them choke. He took a long drink from the bottle of bourbon and tried to focus.

It was one of her favourite episodes. She had a lot of favourite episodes. 'Blink' was one of them, so was the one had just put on. She had seen it plenty of times before, but that didn't matter. It was a two-part story, continued in the next one. The Doctor and his friend Donna went to a new planet, with a library on it. There was danger in the shadows there; things living in them. The dark could kill. Magda hadn't come back. There had been no Alice either. It was the first episode with the woman called River. Poppy didn't like her to begin with, but she had grown to be her favourite. She was funny and she knew things that the doctor didn't, because she was from his future. Poppy's father had been asked to appear in an episode of Doctor Who once, but he couldn't, because he was busy making a film.

There hadn't been a lot of toilet paper left in the little toilet the last time she had been. She hadn't seen any spare ones around, like they had at home. She would need to ask someone, but she didn't know who to ask, because she was on her own. She had got to the part where pretty girl was eaten by the shadows. She still jumped when the skull fell forward inside the space visor, even though she knew it was going to happen. She wished Alice was there, because it was good to have someone to be with during the frightening bits. She heard someone move a chair or a table outside the door. It was probably the man. She might be able to ask him for some toilet roll, when she ran out. He had been nice to her, but she didn't know him. He was still a stranger, and strangers could sometimes mean danger. They'd told her that in school, and Alice had said it too. She didn't know what time it was. There was no clock, and the TV channels weren't on, so she couldn't look for the time on one of the news channels. She climbed up on her bed and took the remote control with her, letting out a yawn, and then another. She felt like she had only woken up a few minutes before, but she was tired again already. She slipped her feet and then all of her legs under the duvet. She wasn't cold, but it was more comfortable under there, and it made her feel safe. There was something not right about the room, about not being at home, about the way Magda had been. She turned down the volume on the TV, because it was getting too loud for her ears.

There were some benches in the area between the market and the steps up to ASDA. The chips were underdone, but he chomped them down regardless. The wings were delicious. The bench was wet from the rain, but he didn't care. An old homeless man was sitting on the other one; Dylan recognised him from around. Spending a lot of time around town in the day time like he did, one got to know their faces. This one used to push everything he owned around in an old shopping trolley, but not in the last few months; must have got a place from the council. He still wandered around town all day. Some of them just liked the life, Dylan supposed..

He was drunk. The brandy was still going through his system when he started on the cans. He hadn't been concerned with pacing himself. He was drinking to numb things. There was something about his thought processes when he had a few drinks that made it easier to cope. He finished the last wing and put the bone into the carrier bag, then shovelled down another handful of chips. The tramp was reading a newspaper and smoking a dirty looking cigarette. His fingers were yellow and his hair looked like a dog that had been rolling in something unpleasant. Dylan's eyes closed for a few seconds, then he jerked awake again. He couldn't fall asleep on a bench. He wasn't a tramp. He didn't even have enough possessions to fill a trolley; a couple of baskets maybe, he thought. He needed the toilet again. He didn't want to wake up in four hours having wet himself in the street. ASDA was two minutes away. He got up, and when he passed, the homeless man gave him a nod of recognition.

'Talk to me, Reinhart.' Harry had stepped out into the corridor to make the call while she was in the toilet. He was sure the Austrian had everything under control, but it was best to check, since it looked like his plans for the night were about to change.

'Everything is alles- everything is good, Harry. The baby girl is fine. She had a small sleep, after her medicine.'

'Good, did you get the pictures?'

'Yes. She is awake now. The medicine does not last long…'

'Yeah. It's not supposed to' He had specified that they only use small doses on her. Later, when they needed her to sleep through the night, they could give her something stronger.

And what about, uh, Magda?'

'What about her?' Harry thought he heard some derision in the Austrian's voice.

'Has she covered her tracks with Riley's people?' It had been amazing how quickly the Polish woman had become familiar to the staff there and gained their trust, Harry thought. She had been a good choice, definitely.

'Ja. She told them that the girl is with her after the school; to visit the other- how do you say- babysitter?'

'Good. And what about her- the other one, Alice?'

'What do you mean?' Harry heard the other man flick open a lighter and then snap it shut.

'Have we sorted her, in case they call her to confirm?' They mightn't call her at all, since she was on her day off. But he couldn't leave something like that to chance.

'I send Max this morning.' His voice was slightly wheezy, Harry noticed. He smoked strong French cigarettes; at least thirty a day.

'And?' Harry ran his tongue over a cavity in one of his back teeth. He would need to make an appointment soon, before it got worse.

'I do not hear from him, but he is good. The best. She will be no trouble.'

'Good, good. Yeah, Max is a diamond. But try to get hold of him anyway; to make sure.' He looked at his watch.

'Ja, Harry. It is understood.'

'I don't want any cops on this yet. Don can't do us any favours on something like this. It's not his patch. I want us to be all done and dusted before the coppers get a sniff of this. Or the press. I want it nice and tidy.'

'Ja, ja. Same as last time.'

'Same as last time. Okay, Reinhart. Let me know as soon as our boy checks in.'

'Yes. And you don't want him to… take care of her?'

'There isn't any need. If he's as good as you say, he can keep her quiet for a couple of days without having to resort to-'

'But if there is complication?'

'Well, if there's complications, it can't be helped.'

'Understanden- understood. Is there something else?'

'Yeah. How long more will we need the Polish girl for?'

'Her? Hah! She wants to go now. I tell her no.'

'You think she'll stay until tomorrow at least? If we give her some cash?' He needed the woman around, he thought. She kept the child happy. He needed her happy, not panicked or upset.

'I think yes if money. Women, they all are whores, you know?' There was a booming laugh on the other end of the line.

'Okay. Have a word. If she's not going to play ball, then…'

'Get rid of her?'

'Well, yeah. It ain't ideal, but it's not like we aren't going to do it tomorrow anyway…' She knew too much already. She wasn't worth the risk. A woman like that was the type who wasn't above blackmail. Not that he would pay her. He would just have her taken care of.

'Understood. I will take care of.'

'Cheers, Reinhart.' He snapped the phone shut and went back into the lounge.

The first time Tom had taken her in there, she had marvelled privately at the stupidity of his keeping all that money behind a lock that any half-experienced burglar would have been able to pick or force, and a door that someone could kick right off its hinges, given enough time and strength. Once they had got inside, she had changed her tune. She was there again now with Frank, in front of the enormous twenty inch thick steel inner doors, and she wondered if his mind had just gone through the same process.

'Wow.' He gave a long, quiet whistle.

'Yeah, that's what I thought too, first time I saw it.' She pressed her thumb against the digital print reader on the right hand door, and a panel slid away, exposing a keypad. As well as the usual digits, from zero to nine, there were other keys- Egyptian or Babylonian hieroglyphics of reeds, eyes and cat's faces. The code was more complicated than a conventional PIN. She had to memorise a twenty four character sequence; a new one every six months. She had resisted the urge to write any of them down. She squinted at the keys and concentrated on remembering. It would give her three attempts before locking her out, sealing them inside the vault and sending an alert to Tom's phone, and the firm which had installed the security.

'When was the last time you had to do this?'

'I have to inventory everything once every three months. We're in the third month now.' She tapped in the last few numbers, and then groaned as the display read negative.

'What's wrong?' He didn't look worried, but he never did.

'I... I got mixed up. I put in an older code, or part of one.'

'Right. Take your time. There's no hurry.' He said that, but for her there was. Poppy was still in that place, and no matter what this man reassured her, she wasn't safe. She wouldn't be safe until they had her back.

'How do I know that what you're planning is going to work, if you won't even tell me the details?'

'The less you know, the better, Alice.'

'Oh don't give me that. We're here, aren't we? I'm getting your money. I need some guarantees. I can't just hand this over in blind faith...' She had put in the code, but was hesitating over whether to push Enter. One more wrong code and it would be all down to the last one. She didn't want that pressure.

'Yes, you're right. Let's just get the money and the keys, and I will tell you on the way back.'

'That's not good enough. I want to know now.' She didn't have anything to bargain with, except that she was the only one who could open the door. If she could even do that. She pressed Enter, finally.

'Okay, I'll-' He stopped as the doors separated with the sound of metal scraping on metal.

'Thank Christ for that,' she said, looking at the keypad. Her hands were clammy and she could feel sweat trickling down her chest and her back.

'Was that the only lock?' He followed her into a room that was floor to ceiling with large steel drawers; like in a mortuary, only smaller. There was nothing else in there, and no sign of a safe.

'There are more locks, just carry on talking, please.' She walked over to the left hand wall, and crouched in front of one of the drawers. He stayed where he was, still taking the room in.

'Okay. The girl is somewhere, but I don't know where yet…'

'Well that's no good, is it? What am-'

'I don't know where she is, but I know who it is that has her.'

'What? But you said that you-' She had the drawer open; there was a conventional looking safe inside, with a digital keypad on it.

'I said- it doesn't matter what I said. The point it, I can find out where she is if I try hard enough.'

'Who is it? Who has her?' The keypad made a positive bleeping noise after she entered her code, and she wrenched the manual lock to the left.

'You don't need to know the name. You won't be meeting him.'

'But why? How? How will we get her out?' She swung the safe door back and took out a canvas bag. It was filled with cash.

'I'm the only one who'll be able to do it. He knows me. He knows my face. I have to make sure that he's keeping her where I think he is, though. Otherwise I'll just be risking everything for nothing.'

'But how does he know you? I thought you weren't one of them? I thought you blackmailed them, ripped them off; how do you end up meeting some- someone like that?' She moved on to another drawer, dragging the sack of money behind her. The drawer had the same sort of safe in it.

'I designed software for him, showed him how to trace IP addresses, all that sort of thing. But I must have been sloppy somewhere…'

'What do you mean? What happened?' She had opened the second safe; all that was in it was an envelope.

'One day I came home to find two East End gangster types in my living room, and the boss man himself.'

'Jesus.' She was on the third safe.

'Yeah. We had a nice chat over some tea. I was told in no uncertain terms what kind of a man he was, and what would happen if I crossed him.'

'But why did he need to do that? Were you blackmailing him?' Another envelope, the same as the last.

'No! It was just… paranoia. He got it into his head that while I was installing software for him and showing him how to find the identities of the other pervs he was chatting with on my site, that I must have been tracing him too. So he thought he would get in first and make sure I was aware of who I was dealing with, I guess.'

'Jesus. Who is he? The Prime Minister or something?' She hadn't tapped the code into the fourth safe. They all had their own separate PIN, but in a sequence that was easy to remember. Or at least it had been.

'No. No, just a very wealthy man, most of whose money comes from, well, crime.'

'And you'd been tracing him?' She remembered the code and punched it in; allowing herself a small smile of relief.

'No, not at all. I didn't have any need. He was a paying customer, same as his friends. I never blackmailed those guys. There was enough money just from having them on the site. And like I said, this other bloke was paying me for extra things.'

'So he got it wrong and showed you who he was? That's crazy; it doesn't make any sense. Why didn't he just send the heavies round on their own?' She was in front of the last drawer now. It was high up, past her chest. All the drawers in the room could be opened, but only five of them had safes inside. The sequence of where they were also had to be memorised; it was based on the letters of Poppy's name.

'This man … he's a one off. He's literally afraid of no one. I know you hear that all the time about people, but trust me, in this case it's true. There is no one alive who would think it was wise to shop this guy to the police. I've heard stories of people who considered it. They ended up in Epping Forest, or washing up on the banks of the Thames, in several different bin bags.'

'So coming over to your house and showing his face wasn't him being stupid?' The last safe was done; she had the bag and four keys.

'No. That was just him being him. Let's get back to the car.'

Thirteen

She wasn't dead. Bill had started cutting, on the arm. He got a few inches in when he heard the shriek. He looked down into the bath and saw her eyes snap open, terrified, and heard her gasp, sucking the air into her lungs. Bill stepped backwards, trying to comprehend. She thrashed about in the bath, the expensive boning knife still stuck in the flesh of her upper arm. She was alive. It was going to all be okay. He just need to calm her down. There was Valium somewhere. She leapt out of the bath and made a run for the door. He was wasn't quick enough to grab her.

'No! Gosh-er! Come back! I can explain! I'm sorry! Come-' She was through the doorway into the main room. He couldn't remember if he had locked the front door. He heard a crash, and the girl screamed. He ran into the next room, and saw her on the ground, covered in fresh blood. She had run into the table coffee table, smashing it. There was no safety glass in the thing, it was an antique. Long, terrifying-looking slivers were all over the ground, several of them on her naked back. She looked so much younger than earlier, he thought; she was just a baby. He edged toward her, suddenly feeling like he wanted to pick her up and cradle her; to make everything all right. The kitchen knife was still swinging like a pendulum from the hole in her arm, she was bleeding heavily.

She seemed to sense him over her, and darted out from his grasp, quick as a cat. She was at the hall door now, but he was fast too. Before she could push the handle down, he was against her back, pushing her into the wood. She screamed and screamed and tried to squirm out, but he was strong. He cupped her mouth from behind.

'Shush now. Shhhhhhhh. Come on, honey. I'm sorry. I'm sorry. It's gonna be okay. Okay? It's gonna be fine. It was just a mistake, yeah? We're gonna fix it. We're gonna fix you up too, okay? But you gotta calm down first. You gotta calm the fuck down, okay?'

She bit down hard on his fingers. Through the skin and flesh and right into the bone. Even with all the cocaine he still felt it. He let go of her, immediately regretting it. She ducked and swerved, pulling the hall door open and disappearing around the other side.

'Fuck! No! You can't! Come back!'

In the hallway she tore away from him; she was fast. Her feet were red raw from splinters and broken glass. She reached the lift and pushed the button. He had almost not followed her out, in case someone else opened their door and saw him. But he couldn't let her go. It didn't bear thinking what the Albanians would do to him if she went back to them like that. The dial above the doors said the carriage was on the next floor up, and moving down. She hammered on the door with such force that the knife fell out of her arm and onto the carpet below. The doors opened with a pinging sound. It was empty.

'You can put it in the boot.' He unlocked it with the key fob and opened his own door.

'Hmm, I think I'll just hold on to it myself…' She opened the back door and threw the bag onto the seat.

'Okay. Suit yourself.' He started the engine. Alice took a quick look around before climbing in. There was no one around. They'd been in an out in minutes. Her heart was still pounding.

'You remember where you're going?'

'Yes. Out through the same gate, right. Wait, don't we need to swap again?'

'Oh, yeah. Sorry.' She had too much alcohol in her system. She needed to be careful; the last thing they needed was to get in an accident. She got out and switched with him. She thought she saw a hint of a smirk as they passed each other, then it was gone.

Paddy was still at the gate. He didn't raise the barrier when he saw her coming this time. Her heart sank.

'Damn it…'

'What's wrong?' Frank's voice came from the back seat.

'Ah, nothing, I think. I think he might want to talk to me. It'll be nothing, don't worry.' She wasn't sure if she was reassuring herself or him.

'How'rya, Alice?' He had been in England for years, but still had an accent.

'I'm okay, Paddy. What's up?' Her own voice sounded peculiar to her. Hoarse and off key.

'Well ah, nothing, really. It's just, yer one, the Polish girl.'

'Magda?' Her hands tightened on the steering wheel. Whatever he was going to say next, it wasn't going to be good.

'Yeah. Well the lads inside said for me to ask ye…'

'Oh yeah, what about?' The words seem to sober her in an instant.

'Well, she rang earlier, yeah. Said she wasn't bringing the youngone back after school. She said himself knew, but he's not in today.'

'Uh huh?' She heard a noise from the back. Frank, shifting about. Her heart was speeding. Her forehead felt hot and cold at the same time.

'Yeah. Did ye know anything about that then? Cos-'

'Yeah, of course.' That was it. She had lied now, she thought, feeling a pang of guilt hit her in the chest. There was no taking it back.

'Oh right so. Cos she said she was takin' the little one over to your place, like. She said you knew all about it, shur. I was just-'

'Yes. That's right. They came straight over after school.' The lie stuck in her throat, but there was no other choice. If she told the truth, it would be the police, and she might never see Poppy alive again. She couldn't look him in the eye.

'Ah, I see. Well, that's grand then. T'was just when I saw ye comin' in there, I thought-'

'Heh, yeah. No, I just needed to pick something up. Something for Poppy. I thought I had it at mine, but I'd left it here. Forget my own head if it wasn't screwed on; you know me. Yeah, Magda's at my place, making some food for us. I should really-'

'No, right ye are. Nice aul motor there, by the way. New is it? Jaysus I wouldn't mind being on the wages you're on, girl. I'd say ye're doin' all right, all the same.' He smiled, showing off a yellow tooth on one side, and a gap on the other where the other should have been.

'Heh, no… this is a friend's. I'm looking after it.' *Lie after lie after lie.*

'Sure ye are. I believe ye. Thousands wouldn't. Go on with ye.' The barrier lifted up, and he turned back to his newspaper, tipping his fingers to his temple as a goodbye. Alice put her foot down a little too heavily, and the Bentley screeched as it went through the gates.

'Damn it, anyway.' She said it to herself as much to anyone else.

'You're fine. You did the right thing. Don't worry.' His voice was as calm as ever.

Don's team had been tracking a number of different people over the past few months. They were understaffed and expected to get results, so the majority of little fish they caught, they were generally advised to throw back. The Crown Prosecution Service was after the big shots; the abusers, the makers, the website owners. Don's favourite type of collar was when they caught a celebrity. There had been an operation a few years back where they'd set up a fake website as bait, and had caught some extremely high profile names. An actor in a TV comedy, the bass player from a world-famous band, several politicians. The first two had been opportunities they couldn't pass up. For one thing, both were watertight. They had used their own credit cards to pay. It seemed impossibly foolish. Commenters had said at the time that it was because celebrities like that thought they were above the law, or just that their over-inflated confidence fooled them into thinking that they were invincible. Don thought it was simpler than that- they'd just been thinking with their genitals. Men did peculiar things, took stupid risks, when it came to sex. That's why politicians and priests got found with rent boys, or famous, handsome actors with downmarket prostitutes on the Sunset Strip. It was a kind of temporary insanity, in his opinion.

The politicians had got away with it that time. Some people were too connected, even for Scotland Yard. There had been backhanders, of course, for Don and his men. Anything to make it all go away. A few on the squad had tried to refuse, but Don had made it clear that it was all of them or none of them, and that anyone known to have turned down a bribe like that would find it hard to fit in anywhere else on the force, if they thought a transfer request would be a way out.

Don had no scruples about taking cash. If these people didn't want to do the time, they'd better make it worth his while, that was his view. Head office were supposed to have the final say on whether or not Don's team pursued each case, but they generally left it up to him. He had a good, trustworthy group working with him, which made it easier for him to keep a suspect from being common knowledge around the Met until he had a chance to see if they were the sort to pay up, or if it would have to be squad cars at six in the morning and a smashed-in front door.

It was always a dawn raid. They'd been the most successful type, going on past form. They usually stayed up all night, and once they'd been doing it a while, they got lazy about erasing their internet history, or wiping their drives. Most of them didn't bother wiping. Sometimes they kept everything on a separate drive, hidden away. Nine times out of ten it was a loose floorboard, under a bit of carpet that wasn't tacked down.

He wasn't officially in for a few days, but he still had them text him if anything serious was going down. They'd been keeping him up to date for the past few days about a new one. A minor celebrity, they'd said. They'd found him on a routine sweep of chat rooms, and had been building up a rapport with him via instant messenger. The chat rooms were a goldmine for his division. Often the meetings happened in what was ostensibly a children's website. It wasn't too surprising to find paedophiles somewhere they had anonymity, and where children were online, unsupervised. When they weren't trying to chat to children though, they'd chat to one another.

They'd make themselves known by using code in their usernames, or in messages posted in the open chat area. Don's men had become good at spotting the covert (and sometimes not so covert) language and terminology used. Once two of them found each other, they'd take the conversation to private chat. Then they'd swap instant messenger IDs (Yahoo or MSN, usually) and carry on off site, thinking they were safe. Don's men would intercept the private chats (with the help of the site owners) and eavesdrop when they were exchanging contact details. They couldn't get into those off-site messenger conversations, for obvious reasons. But they could keep the contact details on record, and then add them to one of their own dummy messenger accounts. Then all it would take was a simple 'All right, mate? What u into?' message to their address when they were showing as online, and most of them would answer. They were so desperate to have someone likeminded to interact with, that they didn't care that it was a stranger who wasn't on their contact list. They didn't question it. If they did decide to ask, the officer would say something like 'Oh, I think know you from such and such chatroom', and they'd usually comply. It wasn't too far-fetched, and they weren't likely to remember every anonymous person they'd chatted with in their lives. They took stupid risks, and it was his division's job to punish them for it.

This man wasn't a big shot when it came to child porn. He wasn't creating it, just trading, the notes said. And he was mostly into non-nude, quasi-legal material; he only occasionally talked about or swapped the harder content. He was a small fish, unless one was judging him by the sheer volume that he got through. They rarely did. The figures meant nothing, in real terms. It was the severity of the images that mattered; not the quantity. Of course, those rules changed when someone was famous. A celebrity could be made an example of; or exploited, if they were rich enough. They found out who he was by back-tracing the email from his instant messenger; it turned out he had the address for years, and had used it to sign up for some mailing list a few years back, with his real name. It was sometimes as simple as that. Not every criminal was a mastermind, Don could testify to that.

From the chats they'd logged, he appeared to be a Deleter- they were the paranoid types who'd spend hours in one session downloading material, only to delete it all when guilt or panic set in. Others were Collectors or Cataloguers- storing everything they saved, usually on a removable drive or memory stick. The Cataloguers were a distinct subset of the Collectors. Their drives would be full of alphabetically filed folders, often tagged and cross referenced for convenience. A lot of the people Don arrested showed signs of Obsessive Compulsive Disorder when sent for psych evaluation. No one was quite sure what the connection was, although their obsessions and compulsions would definitely have been a factor in them taking the risks which had brought about their respective downfalls.

Whenever it was reported in the press that someone was found with a hundred thousand images on his hard drive, unless that person had been a collector/cataloguer, the real figure was probably in the hundreds, if any. Don's squad and the CPS counted every picture viewed on a computer as being one possessed, as most of their finds came from reversing the deletion process. When it came to charging the offenders, there was often so much evidence that it was more logical to give them a set of sample charges to plead. Their lives were ruined at that point anyway; it didn't matter if people thought they'd looked at five pictures or five thousand. No one was going to hate them any less or any more.

'Making an indecent image of a child' was another misleading one that they could use to their advantage. It didn't always mean taking a picture or making a video. Just saving something from a website to a hard drive could count as 'making an image'. The Sexual Offences Bill of 2003 had made the law even vaguer, and with that had made Don and his boys' jobs much easier. The press had made people everywhere disproportionately terrified of paedophiles and child sex predators. Big cases like the Soham murders and Sarah Payne had made everyone even more paranoid. Exploiting people's fears to sell newspapers was nothing new. It had been around since Whitechapel. Don had watched something about it recently on one of the history channels.

They wanted to go the next morning. They had to wait until they were sure he was online, and that he was home. They had about ten dummy messenger accounts, waiting for him to make contact. They weren't supposed to do anything to bait him, or to contact him. They had to let the suspect do all the running. It was cleaner that way. Of course, if it didn't happen like that, they could go in the dirty way. Sticking to procedure didn't matter when they were after these people. They'd have enough evidence to make any charge of entrapment seem pointless. The public would have passed sentence long before any trial regardless, because of what they'd read in the tabloids. Even when they walked, the mud tended to stick. The idiom of 'no smoke without fire' was almost as popular as 'an eye for an eye', among readers of the popular papers.

The name wasn't familiar to Don, but that was irrelevant. In a couple of days, everyone in Britain with access to a newspaper or the internet would know it. Unless he was willing to play ball, that was. He looked at the text again. *'Rick Jarvis'*.

Dylan hadn't even got to ASDA. There was a certain confidence that came with being drunk that made it seem acceptable to urinate in public. He would never have considered it if he was sober. There wasn't an alley nearby; the doorway of a block of flats would have to do. People walked past behind him and tutted, but he paid them no notice. The relief was immense. He finished up, shook himself, and did up the buttons. It was dark already. Under the streetlamps, he noticed that his aim had been way off; the left leg of his jeans was peppered with warm liquid.

He sat down on the kerb and unzipped his bag. There was still a can in there. He didn't think, he just opened it and took a gulp. He wasn't in control anymore. Stopping wasn't an option. He wanted to see her. It wasn't a good idea, he knew that. Alice drank, quite a lot; but she could control it. She understood moderation. She drank with friends, socially, as an accompaniment to the rest of an evening. He drank by himself, anti-socially, as the focus of the evening. She would think he was pathetic, turning up at her door in such a state. He looked down and saw the liquid snake its way around the corner toward his feet, like an arrow pointing to the perpetrator. He got up quickly, and immediately regretted it, his head spinning. He was glad he hadn't smoked. It had been nearly two years. He missed them sometimes.

Having one wasn't an option though. He was an addict, and he had to keep the chain unbroken. That was what Alan Carr had said, in the book. Just one cigarette starts the chain again, and then you're hooked. It would be the stupidest thing in the world to be finished with them for so long and just smoke one out of the blue. But then ever taking up smoking to begin with had been stupid too. And he had done that. Along with millions of other people. He wanted one now. Just one. He was staggering towards the bus stop now, the incriminating trail of urine following him as he went on his way.

'That wasn't good.' She was in the back seat again. They'd switched just outside the grounds of the Rileys' place. She might have felt sober, but she wasn't, and they couldn't have her getting pulled over and breathalysed. Besides, she didn't know the way back to his place.

'We're fine, Alice.'

'We're not fine. I just lied to him. I just made myself look guilty; like I'm in on this thing, with Magda and whoever else, I-'

'You did what you had to do. Come on, Alice. What other way was there?'

'I don't know. I just… I'm-'

'We have more important things to worry about. What you did was buy us some time, and time is what we need to get Poppy out of there. When this is all over, you can explain-'

'Explain to who? The police? Tom? What if when this is all over it's because Poppy is dead, Frank. Who will I explain to then? Who will-'

'You need to calm down.'

'I AM CALM.' She thumped her fists against the roof of the car in frustration, fighting back long overdue tears.

'You're not, and you need to be. Here's what I don't understand; why didn't they phone you when Magda told them that she wasn't bringing Poppy home?'

It was a good question. She took out her mobile, looking for a Missed Call notification. There was nothing.

'Eh, I don't know. Maybe they did, but I was on the phone to you? Or maybe I was out of range…'

'You'd have a voicemail then, right?'

'Yeah.'

'Well, do you?'

'No. I mean, I don't think so.' She looked again, this time for the cassette tape symbol, but there wasn't one.

'Landline?'

'Yes. I mean, I have one, but I don't think Work has the number.'

'Why?'

'They just contact me on this.' She held the mobile up where he could see it in his mirror.

'Trust me, they have it.'

'What do you mean?'

'I'm pretty sure I saw it when I got your mobile number from the database.'

'Oh.' She felt a little sick again, although there was nothing in her stomach apart from brandy.

'We need to get you something to eat.'

'Yeah. Is there somewhere we can stop off?' The thought of eating a nice meal while Poppy was still holed up in the other place made her feel bad, but she needed to eat something, otherwise she would be no use to anyone.

'No, I'll cook.' They were on a busy road again, going fast.

'Oh yeah?' It surprised her. He seemed privileged, and she always imagined privileged people had other people to cook for them. Tom certainly had.

'Yes. Do you like Chinese food?'

'Doesn't everyone?' She lit up a cigarette; it would stave off the hunger for a bit. She had smoked more in half a day then she had in a month. Dylan would have been cross.

'I've never met anyone who didn't.'

'Me neither.' She suddenly remembered Poppy, who loved Special Fried Rice, but not the prawns. She took a long drag on the cigarette and then tipped the ash into the tray. Her face must have betrayed her; she caught his eye in the rear view mirror.

'She'll be fine,' he said. They had stopped in traffic, and he turned back to look at her. It wasn't a smile, but there was some kindness in his eyes at least.

'I hope so. I'm trusting you, although it's not as if I have a choice.'

'You always have a choice, Alice. You're trusting me because it's what's right. I'm on your side, believe me.'

She eyed the bag on the seat beside her, reminding herself why he was on her side. He was no friend. He was there for the payday. The engine stopped with a thud. They were there. Or they were somewhere at least. She could see nothing through the windows.

She had jumped through the lift doors and landed on her knees inside the carriage. She got up to push a button, any button, but he was too quick. In a second he was on her, grabbing her by her hair and digging his nails into her flesh. She was strong for her age, and for her size. He needed to keep her quiet, or someone was going to hear them. He wasn't worried about someone coming out of their suite; people didn't do that anymore: no one interfered in a domestic. Whatever they thought was going on in the hall, they'd either be too scared to come out, or just think it was none of their business. He thanked God for people's cowardice and their apathy. They might call security though, or the police. Then it would all be over for him.

She screamed. It cut through the air around them, chilling him. It was the sound of someone in fear for their life. He held onto the fistful of hair at the back of her neck, and then tried to cover her mouth with his other hand. They were on the floor together; her squirming, him trying to keep her still. She got her mouth free from him and screamed again. It was only a matter of time before someone heard her and made that call, if it hadn't already happened. He had to get her back in the room. He found the cut in her arm, and dug his thumb into the wound. Her eyes widened in panic, then she convulsed a little, before vomiting a thin pink sludge over herself. The smell was appalling, and Bill gagged before pulling himself together.

'Okay now you listen here. We are going back in the room-' He watched as she shook her head at him, eyes filled with terror.

'Yes. Yes we are. And you're going to shut the hell up, or else-' he dug the thumb further in, and this time she let out another scream, more blood curdling than the last.

'Jesus. Shut the fuck up. Come. Now.' He took a deep breath, and lifted her whole weight; one hand on her arm, the other still in her hair. She went limp in an attempt to stop him, but he had at least two grammes of pharmaceutical grade cocaine in his blood, which seemed to give him the strength of someone two or three times his size. He moved quickly along the hall carpet, dragging her with him- her screams having dropped to a whimper. It was as if she needed all of her strength to deal with the pain he was inflicting. Behind them, someone must have called the lift from another floor, and it pinged shut and started moving. He almost reached the room door when he remembered the knife that she had dropped.

'Fuck'. He stood for a moment, looking back and forth between his suite door and the lift; like a cartoon tennis spectator. Finally, he opened the door and flung the girl through into the room. Then he turned on his heel and sprinted back. The dial above told him that the car was on its way back up already. The doors opened just as he reached the blade. A proper looking old British couple emerged, just in time to see a wild-eyed Bill Hansen pick himself up off the carpet (the knife quickly hidden under his sweater) and dash back to the open room door. He thought he heard the woman 'tut' and say something under her breath about 'people today'.

He came in expecting to see her prone on the ground, but there was nothing. Straight away, he scanned the room to see if there was a window open. No. He shut the door behind him without looking. He should have looked, because the girl was behind it, with another kitchen knife.

Rick had been online for a while. First, he used the private browser to check if it was all going to plan. There was a message from Harry. He hadn't been bluffing them. A link took him to a video stream of a pink room. The girl was in there. When he saw her, his chest surged, like it used to do when he had that first bump of coke or speed, back when he still indulged. He was supposed to go there tonight sometime; that's what he had told Harry. He had been nervous about it; figuring something was going to go wrong. He didn't trust Harry, although he didn't have any real reason. The man had after all revealed his identity to him, and probably to the others, as a show of good faith. Rick wouldn't have parted with the cash otherwise. If it all had been a scam, he could hardly have gone to the police and told them that someone had conned him out of two million pounds, unless he could tell them what it was he was supposed to have paid for. It was hardly a risk for Goldman to show his face; he was someone who was genuinely afraid of no one, whereas anyone with an ounce of sense was terrified of him. The one time the CPS had managed to bring a case against him, the papers had reported that more than three hundred potential jurors had handed in doctor's notes to excuse them from duty. He had walked regardless; no doubt because he had managed to pay off the judge. By all accounts he had half of the Met in his pocket. Harry Goldman wasn't ever going to prison.

Rick always created a new folder on the computer to save the pictures and the sets in. Not on the desktop. There would be a folder called something innocuous, then another inside of that, called something equally vague. In that folder he would make another, and call it 'Stuff'. Then he would fill that with a bunch of random folders. Finally, he would make one more subfolder, and call it something beginning with Z, so that it went right down to the bottom. That way, even if someone had innocently clicked through one, two and three folders, they wouldn't see the final folder at the top of the list when they opened it. It was paranoid in the extreme, but he was an extremely paranoid person. Some nights went through all the possibilities of what could happen- the worst case scenarios. Perhaps he had been drunk and forgotten to erase everything? And then the next day he just carried on with his life, completely unaware that there was a time bomb of illegal material somewhere on his computer, just waiting to be discovered by some nosy parker, or the staff in the computer repair shop? The 'recent files' link had been a godsend when he first read about it. He always gave it a check the next day, to see if he had left a folder called 'Zilla' or 'Zebra' on the computer. There was also a command to delete the recent files. He did it every day, as a ritual.

No one on his messenger contacts had been biting. It was still early in the day, relatively speaking; especially if they were across the Atlantic, or farther. Rick had no idea about who any of them were, and he struggled to remember what they were into. He could waste a lot of time swapping with someone who was interested in different things. When he found one like that, he usually blocked or deleted.

Most of the instant messengers had a photoshare option, to add pictures to the conversation, and save the ones the other person added. He had wasted hours swapping pictures of his type of girl with people who only sent back things in which he had no interest. Toddlers or nineteen year olds; or little boys. None of that was for him. The pictures of boys made him want to vomit. It was an occupational hazard that he had to associate with these people. He hated the ones who wanted to chat while the pictures went back and forth. He wasn't there to chat.

There were leechers too. People who just looked but never shared anything of their own. Who wanted to get straight into the nude photos or the hardcore ones, when he hadn't ever spoken to them before. Strangers who wanted to know his age/sex/location, like they were teenagers on a chat site. Those people got blocked immediately. The paranoid side of him convinced they were police. *Who would give their real age or location to someone in those circumstances?* The whole business was rife with terrible risks, without a doubt; but he never considered that until he finished. It would be only then he considered the stupidity of some of the things he had just done. Only then did he feel anything approaching moral guilt either, although that got less and less over the years.

The compulsion to keep doing it was so strong that it always pushed his doubts and worries to one side. Addiction was like that- it wore a person like a glove, and took risks with his safety, just so it could get its fix. He had been the same with drugs and drink in the past. He was certain that he was one of those people with an addictive personality. Every time he gave up, swore off, pledged to turn over a new leaf, something in the back of his mind told him he would be back again soon enough.

'So, you like this sort of shit?' asked Harry, motioning towards the jazz band in the corner.

'It's not shit, Harry; you old curmudgeon.' She smiled at him. She didn't seem to get any drunker with each drink, but he supposed that was because he was getting drunk along with her. It was like how he didn't notice people his own age getting any older, he thought, looking at her again.

'Oi! I listen to jazz. Coltrane, Charlie Parker, all the greats.' Some of the men in the group playing couldn't have been more than twenty. He had forgotten more than they knew about jazz, several times over, he thought.

'I suppose everything was better back in your day, eh?' She touched his forearm, and let her fingers stay there a little longer than was necessary.

'Well, now that you mention it, it was. Yeah.' He gave her cleavage another quick glance, then back up to the eyes again.

'Oh, I bet it was. Bet the women were better too, right? 1950s housewives, always ready to please their men. Washing, Ironing, Cooking-'

'Hey! I'm not that old!' He was near enough it though; much nearer than she was.

'Awww. Someone's a little sensitive…' She said it in a baby voice, like Marilyn Monroe, or Betty Boop.

'Actually, people tell me all the time that I look good for my age.' He wanted another smoke. The time between them was always much shorter when he had a few drinks in him. He cursed the day when they banned smoking in bars and restaurants.

'Are they people whose wages you pay, Harry?'

'Bugger off.'

'Awww. Poor Harry. Well I think you look very good for your age, sweetie. What are you again, eighty?'

'I'm old enough to teach you a few things, Darling.'

'Promises, promises.'

'Yep. And if you ask anyone about Harry Goldman, they'll tell you, he-'

'-always keeps his promises?'

'Got it in one.'

'Will we get out of here?'

'What, another bar? No more jazz please, Beth. I don't want to have to kill someone tonight.' He gave her a pretend 'Hard Man' stare; it didn't take much reaching for him. She giggled and touched his wrist.

'Oh, I think we can find something to listen to that you'd like, where we're going.' She got up from her seat, every part of her looking as immaculate as they had three hours before.

'Oh yeah?' He was sure she meant they were going to her place this time.

'Yeah. I might even have some Coltrane for you, old man.' She finished up her drink and gave him a wink.

'I'll get the coats.'

Fourteen

Somersby slotted the SD card into the slot on the side of the touchscreen monitor and opened up the photo editing suite. Reinhart had told him what Harry wanted, in some detail, and the cameras had all been set up, so there was nothing else to do. The beer was terrible- a supermarket version of one of the more popular European lagers. Pretty cheap of Harry, he thought. At home, he only drank imported beer. His rule was: if he could see any English words on the label, it wasn't worth drinking. Snobbery, perhaps. But he made enough money that he could afford to be a snob. German, Belgian, Indian, Japanese: they all could make a clean lager, with no sore heads the next morning. The British brewers put chemicals in theirs; they tasted foul, and gave him hangovers, without fail.

They had got some good shots, he thought. The room was already perfectly lit, which had been down to him. *Perfectionist* was a word that critics and fans threw about whenever Ian Somersby's name was mentioned. It was a sort of trademark, along with his penchant for beautiful, young-looking leading ladies. The pictures were still in RAW format; he wouldn't have been caught dead shooting Jpegs. The first thing he needed to do was junk the shots that hadn't worked- overexposure from the flash; camera movement; blurs. There would be no blinks, for obvious reasons.

Harry had probably told him more about who was going to be in the thing than anyone else. He didn't know whether to feel honoured or scared by that; only time would tell. When they'd watched the video of the Milly girl, he noticed everyone had been wearing masks, although they still spoke as if they knew each other. Harry hadn't said anything about who those people were. The video had been terrible to look at, and it hadn't ended pleasantly. The girl had been in a lot of pain at the end, and incredibly distressed. That wasn't Somersby's thing, although there were some who preferred it.

Harry had wanted it to be different. As well as the footballer, there was going to be someone from TV. From little things Harry had let slip, he was almost certain it was Bill Hansen. Mainly because he had met the man a few times- an obnoxious cocaine addict with no discretion whatsoever, and apparently another big fan of Somersby's films. He could always tell the difference between someone who enjoyed them for the acting and cinematography, and someone who liked them for other reasons. He opened up a shot that looked great to him in the thumbnail, but once it was enlarged, was slightly out of focus. The sort of detail that wouldn't matter to Harry or Reinhart, but he was different, and this is what they were paying him for; although it was more a discount than a wage, depending on how one looked at it. The shots were for sending to webmasters, when they were going to sell the tape. They would end up on clickable banners. The whole business was getting more and more professional. The next picture was perfect. He adjusted the brightness and the contrast, and then opened up the colour balance toolbox.

One of them was a policeman, and there was some sort of musician; a singer. He didn't know any more about those two. He wasn't entirely comfortable with being privy to it all. He had heard Harry use the phrase 'bloke knew too much' about other people, and although no one ever said anything specifically, Somersby knew he had been talking about people he killed, or had someone kill. It was more than likely the latter. He had no doubt the man was capable of killing; he just reckoned that, nowadays at least, he could afford to get someone to do the dirty work for him. *Someone like Reinhart.* Somersby had no idea what their connection was, or how they'd come to know one another. He just knew that Harry trusted the man enough to let him in on this plan. And he had been, from the start. The first real meeting he had with Harry about doing the film, the big Austrian had been there. 'You can talk in front of Reinhart. He's okay,' Harry had said. And that had been that. No one argued with Harry.

They hadn't discussed who the star of the show was going to be, in those early days. He didn't know if that had been because they didn't trust him yet, or if they just hadn't known yet themselves. She was perfect for it. No other celebrity child was as popular on the net, in their communities. There were appreciation threads about her every day on the more legitimate sites, like 4chan or Reddit; to the point where the admins of those places had had to ban the making of topics concerning her. There was big money in the internet, and sites which had been previously notorious for unseemly content and subversive material had eventually tried to distance themselves from it, so as not to put off potential investors and advertisers. Mark Zuckerberg's almost overnight rise to power and riches had changed the game for the internet. Of course, on the underground web, things were different. There, anonymity still reigned, and there were no sponsors to upset.

Another great shot appeared on his screen. There were too many to choose from. She was sublimely beautiful; even someone with no sexual interest in her couldn't deny it, he thought. It was a shame they hadn't got any shots of her awake, with her eyes open. But there were thousands of those all over the web already. He had seen grown men fall in love with her on message boards and chans; she was the real deal. Faceless paedophiles, writing sonnets to her beauty, and obsessing over every photo and news story. Obsession and compulsion seemed to be synonymous with their 'condition'.

Every so often, a young actress or pop star would appear who caught the eye of the collective, and there would be online crazes about them that were as crazy as only the internet can be. There were always rivalries and competition though; each little girl (or boy) with their own legion of devotees- all claiming their girl to be the one and only; proclaiming their undying love for her, and spitting hate at anyone who proposed an alternative candidate. It was like the teenagers in the legitimate world, with their boy bands and their vampire novel heroes.

Poppy was different though. She polarised no one. Everyone seemed to agree that she was the most beautiful thing in existence. He guessed that was why Harry had decided to get her. Probably not even because he wanted to have her; it was more likely that he saw her as the ultimate meal ticket. Everyone was going to want to see it. It would probably make more money than all of Somersby's actual films put together. It was a sort of pity that he would never get the credit, he told himself, saving the edited photo to the USB drive.

'Jesus fucking Christ, you fucking bitch.' The blade sliced through the skin, long but not deep. He could see blood, but he felt nothing. The cocaine seemed to have anaesthetised him. That, or he was in shock. The look on the girl's face was somewhere between disbelief and terror. She had probably to get the blade all the way in, and take him down. Instead, he stood there, looking at her incredulously. She didn't have time to decide what to do next; he already had his hands around her throat and was pushing her across the room. He slammed her head against the concrete of the supporting wall, and she fell down. He dropped to the floor and gripped her around the neck again. She was still conscious, despite the bang. He held her down, staring into her terrified eyes as the breath started to leave her body. He had a knee on her thigh and he pressed down hard, pinning her to the ground.

'Fucking whore! Why did you do that? I just wanted to talk, Go Sher. I just wanted to make things right.'

He felt her arms flailing and then scrabbling underneath them, probably looking for the knife. He tightened his grip even more. She couldn't have much more strength left. The little whore had tried to stab him to death, he thought, squeezing harder. What did she expect him to do now? Let her go?

Her eyes were bulging, like something from a cartoon. He was shipping blood from his side, superficial wound or not; it was all over her skin, and pooling on the floor underneath them. He still felt no pain.

He couldn't squeeze any more, he was losing strength. He took a hand away, and like lightning, she rolled out from under him and got up. He tried to get to his feet, but the blood was everywhere, and he slipped, almost comically, landing on his face. He looked up and saw her make her way towards the door again. She was almost naked and covered in his blood and hers. He was only half surprised to find that he had an erection. Bill got up and bolted towards her. He was too quick for her, slamming her against the door. This time, the fight seemed to have gone from her. Her eyes had closed. He grabbed one of the knives from the floor; he wasn't taking any chances this time. With blood-stained fingers, he searched her for a pulse; on the neck, wrist, everywhere. He couldn't find one. He looked down at her tiny form, in just some panties, a garter belt and some stockings. She had cost him a lot, with more to come, once the Albanians found out. He should get something for his trouble, it was only fair. Checking one more time for a pulse or some breath, he pulled her underwear down and over her knees and ankles.

'Right then. It's someone's bedtime, innit?' Paul looked over at his two daughters who were both sitting far too close to the fifty inch flat screen.

'Aw, Dad! I don't have to go until eight! Mum said!' The elder of the girls sprung up in protest. He couldn't decide whether she got the quick temper from him or from Tamara. Several Premiership referees might have wondered what the debate was.

'Not you, Col. I know all about you and eight o clock, love. Don't you worry.' He gave her a smile, and got one back.

'Aw, Dad!' The littler one, Charmaine, was up now too. DVD forgotten.

'Aw Dad, nothing, sweetheart. It's time for your bed now, come on love.' He tried to do an angry voice, but he could never manage it to make it convincing when it came to those two.

'Boo!' said Charmaine, but she gathered up her things and headed towards the door regardless. She was much better behaved than her sister, despite being the younger.

'Haha!' said Colleen, and then blew a raspberry.

'Oi! Watch it you!' He shook his fist at her, trying to keep a straight face. From out in the hallway, Charmaine shouted back:

'Daaaaaad! Tell her!'

'I did, sweetheart!' He got up from the chair and threw the remote over to Colleen. She caught it with two hands. He might make a cricketer out of her yet, he thought.

'What did you tell her?' She was incredibly cute, in so many ways; she never failed to put a smile on his face.

'I told her to f--- I told her to mind her own business, Princess.' He tried not to swear in front of them. Nothing worse than a child saying 'shit' or 'fuck' because they've heard their mother or father say it. Families like that had no class, Paul thought.

'I didn't hear you tell her that, Daddy.'

'Well... erm. Go brush your teeth now, there's a good girl.' He walked out after her, giving Colleen a playful smack on the bottom before he went. He had never hit them properly. His father used to give his brothers and him a lash of his belt, and it hadn't stopped him turning into a tearaway as a teenager. Football had been the only thing that had straightened him out. Tamara wouldn't have approved either. Her parents had been extremely left wing; practically hippies, apart from all the money they had.

He sat on the bed in the girls' room, waiting for his younger daughter to finish in the bathroom. The house was a mansion, but Tam had insisted that the girls share a room for the early years. It was important to have your sister be close, she had said. He wasn't sure about that. Most sisters he knew growing up had hated each other. Girls could be cruel, even to their own blood. But it seemed to work for his two. Colleen was going to have her own room next year. She had been promised. Charmaine came through the door, beaming.

'All right love? Where's yer pyjamas then?' She hadn't taken off her school uniform; they were supposed to do it every day after they came home, but they were supposed to do a lot of things. He hated telling them off. He didn't want to turn into his father.

'Here!' She had a backpack in her hands, shaped like a teddy bear.

'That's not pyjamas, love. That's... a bag. Or is it a teddy, eh?' He knew what was inside it, but he liked to tease her.

'Daddy! The pyjamas are inside the bear bag, silly.'

'Oh! I see!'

'You are silly sometimes, Daddy. Even Mummy said so.' She took her jumper off, then her shirt. He found himself looking away for some reason. He felt peculiar, seeing her like that. He wasn't usually the one who tucked them in. He probably hadn't seen Charmaine without her clothes for more than a year; maybe longer than that.

'Mummy said so, did she? Well, then. I'll have to have word with Mummy, won't I?' The feeling persisted. He looked at the skin in her back, and found himself thinking how smooth it looked. He looked at how her little bottom had started to stick out; it had been flat as a pancake not so long ago. She was growing up.

'Ooh! What will you say?' She undid her school trousers and let them fall to the floor. She was wearing the Daisy Duck knickers she had got for Christmas. He caught himself staring for too long, and looked away again.

'I'll uh, I don't think I'll say anything, sweetheart. I, ah, I think I might just have to put her over my knee.' She turned around and bent down to get her pyjamas out of the bag. He looked at her again, and tried to exorcise the thoughts that were creeping into his mind, without much success.

'You'll spank her?' She pulled on the pyjama bottoms quickly, and then the top. He didn't look at her again until she was fully dressed. He could feel his fingernails digging into the palms of his hands, and had to stop himself before he broke the skin.

'Mmm, ah, yeah. I suppose I'll have to.' His eyes were starting glaze over. He could feel his hands shaking now.

'Naughty Mummy!'

'Yep. Naughty mummy...'

Alice was in his toilet again. He was in the kitchen, preparing dinner; surreal didn't even begin to describe it. She had gone for what seemed like five minutes. Normally, when she was drinking, she would go to the toilet every half hour; she had a terrible bladder, people told her. There was something about today that was different though. She had taken MDMA the night before; just a few dabs. It sometimes stopped her from going, but that was more the pills. She didn't touch those since she discovered crystals. Dylan introduced her to them. He liked them because pills made it impossible for him to have sex, so he would be stuck with a very aroused girlfriend and nothing he could do to remedy the situation.

She made a face. She hated thinking about him with his exes, or with anyone else at all. She was a jealous woman; there was no doubt about that. Today had been the first day in a long time- since their break up, that she hadn't had to deal with his constant texts and emails, mainly because she had left her phone in the flat. He didn't have her work number. No one had. She sort of wished he did now. She could have done with some of his lovesick pestering today; just because it would have kept her in touch with reality. This wasn't reality, what was happening- watching Poppy asleep in some makeshift dungeon, knowing that if they don't get her out in time, she was going to be gang raped on film for the enjoyment of a bunch of rich paedophiles. And in the meantime, some man who ran an underground website for child rapists was cooking Kung Pao Chicken for her. She would have found it funny if it wasn't so distressing.

Poppy had been snuggled up in her duvet, watching television, when they'd come in from the car. Alice had sat and watched her for a bit, noticing the familiar fidgetiness and restless moving around that happened just before the little girl fell asleep; she had seen it hundreds of times before. It couldn't have been more than a couple of hours since they'd last seen her sleep, but it was getting late. In the time it had taken for Alice to go to the toilet and come back, the temptation of sleep had got the better of the little girl, because she was comatose now; the remote control still in one of her hands.

'She's asleep again,' Frank called from in the kitchen. He must have come in to check on her while Alice had been in the toilet.

'Yeah. Do you think she's okay?' Alice didn't take her eyes off the screen; she was looking again for the breathing; any sign that it was just sleep, and not–

'She's fine. I think they might be giving her something.' She could hardly hear him over the sound of the food frying.

'Giving her something? Like what?' A feeling of dread hit her in the chest like someone had punched her.

'Some sort of sedative. A weak one though. They'll know what they are doing, trust me.' She didn't trust him; she had to keep reminding herself of it.

'But what if something goes wrong?' She saw Poppy stir a bit, then roll over in the duvet.

'It won't. These men have too much to lose. They won't leave anything to chance.'

'I hope you're right.' She didn't want to think why they were sedating the child. In her head, drugging a child in those circumstances went hand in hand with abusing her. That's how it happened in the stories in terrible magazines she bought at supermarket checkouts, in spite of her better judgement. It didn't matter that he had said nothing was going to happen for another day. He didn't know for certain. He wasn't one of their gang. What was to stop one of them just going in there now? They were monsters; monsters don't have rules or plans. He came into the room with two bowls and a handful of chopsticks.

'Okay, I'm hoping you're hungry, and even if you're not, you should still eat as much as you can. We don't know what's going to happen; we might need to pull an all-nighter. You'll need the energy. Unless you want to sleep.' He was almost parental in the way he said it. The food looked amazing; she hadn't realised how hungry she was until the moment she saw the steaming bowls.

'I don't think I'll be able to sleep. Listen… Poppy; what if one of them decides–'

'I don't think any of them are going to touch her, Alice. See that thing that we can see?' He pointed at the monitor.

'Yeah.' She stuffed a heap of chicken and rice into her mouth. The taste was delicious. *Hunger is a great sauce*, her father used to say.

'Well, we're not the only ones watching. The man who organised this whole thing can see it, so can... so can all the others. That's sort of the point of it.' He was good with the chopsticks.

'How do you mean?' The sauce on the chicken was not too sweet and not too hot. She winced a little as she bit down on a piece of chilli.

'Hot, isn't it? That's the bird eyes. Chillies, I mean. Not actual bird eyes. Anyway, this feed; I think I said this earlier, but the live video is there so that all the participants... the people, can see that she's okay, that she's the girl who they... who they were told she was going to be, and above all, so they can see that no one has... messed around with her.' She noticed how he was choosing his words carefully for her, so as not to upset her. But now she was trying to think of the word he replaced, which probably made it worse. He was mistaking her for someone a little more fragile. It was almost sweet, his concern.

'Okay. Well, I guess that's something at least.' She ate some more rice to cancel out the heat of the dish.

'You like it?' He nodded at her bowl with a smile.

'Yeah, it's delicious. Where did you learn to cook like that?' She felt guilty, talking about Chinese cuisine when Poppy's life was in such danger, but on the other hand she needed to take her focus away from the horror. It was a defence mechanism, she told herself.

'Oh, I practically grew up in Hong Kong. My father was there on business a lot, before the handover to the other lot.' That explained the expertise with the chopsticks as well, she thought.

'What was he, a diplomat or something?' She noticed his eyelashes for the first time. Long and slightly curly. Almost feminine.

'Uh, yeah- something like that.' He was clamming up. He had obviously said too much already. She felt she should change the subject, but the only subject to change back to would be Poppy.

'It's fine. You don't have to say. It's not important anyway.' She felt a strange urge to comfort him, before remembering herself.

'It wouldn't have been that interesting anyway. What about you? Grow up anywhere exciting or strange?' He balanced some rice, chicken and cashew nuts expertly between the points of the sticks, before depositing the lot in his mouth, without dropping a single grain.

'Uh, no. My dad was from Ireland, so we used to go over once a year to see his folks. It was hardly the Far East though.'

'It's more to the west, I think.'

'Well, I kno- Oh right, yes. Very good.' Her Kung Pao was almost finished; he had given her a small helping.

'Will you have some more?' He stood up and reached down for her bowl.

'Oh, I- is there more?' She could have eaten the same size portion again, twice.

'Plenty more. And did you want some wine? Or are we keeping you on the cognac?' She would have found him charming in another situation. As it was, his personable manner was making her feel a slight unease. There was something wrong about all of it. She wasn't going to drop her guard for him, no matter how much he tried to make her.

'Um, I'll have some wine, please. No more cognac. Is there white?'

'I can open some.' His clothes hung perfectly on his frame; although she was in no doubt they had been tailored to fit him.

'Thank you.' She watched him make his way to the kitchen and wondered how many other versions of him there were, and would she get to meet all of them before this thing was done.

'Woman trouble is it?' Dylan looked confusedly at where the voice had come from, wondering was the tramp talking to him.

'Eh?' He took a slurp of his can, then put his other hand around it, to cover the label. It was as much to hide it from the old homeless man as it was to hide it from anyone passing; especially the police.

'A girl. It's always a girl.' He smelled bad- somewhere between excrement and vomit, with some fish thrown in for good measure. There was some stale sweat in there too, and, somewhat ironically, a hint of cheap deodorant.

'What is?' Talking to tramps was like urinating in the street, Dylan thought. He only did it when he was inebriated.

'You. Drunk as a lord, drinking booze in the middle of town. Got to be a woman involved, am I right?' He gave a smile that was a mixture of tobacco-stained yellow, wide gaps and brown stumps. Dylan felt queasy.

'Ah, yeah. It's a woman all right, mate.' Some pretty teenagers walked past and looked at them, then collapsed into giggles. Dylan felt hurt, but he wasn't sure if it was on his own behalf or the homeless man's.

'Gave you the shove, did she? Ah, never mind, fella.'

'Well, sort of. It was mutual.' That was a lie.

'Mutual, was it? Hahaha! A bit more mutual on her side than if was on yours, am I right? Hahaha.' He had a nice laugh. Like a grandfather might have, Dylan thought.

'Er, yeah. I mean, she didn't- she doesn't-' He couldn't find the right way to phrase it.

'She wasn't happy, was it?'

'Yes! That's exactly it, mate.'

'Yep. That's what most of them say, pal. Never met a bloody woman who was happy. What's your name, son?' He reached into the inside pocket of his coat and took out a handful of cigarette butts. They were all different brands, he could tell from the sizes of the filters. He must have fished them out of ashtrays or off the ground. Dylan's stomach lurched a little.

'It's Dylan, mate.' He thought of offering a hand to shake, then thought again.

'Dylan? After Bob Dylan, is it? Or are you a bleedin' Taff?' He gave another big laugh, followed by a violent, hacking cough, and a phlegmy wheeze. More people passed, but this time they just acted like he and the old man didn't exist.

'Well, my mum's from Swansea originally. But my dad was a bit of a fan, yeah.'

'Overrated, he is.' He took out a disposable cigarette lighter and tried to light one of the filthy stubs. The flint was working, but it didn't look like there was any gas in it.

'Oh yeah?' Dylan watched him struggle to light it, and wondered should he volunteer to shield the flame from the wind. Not that there was a flame.

'Yeah. Couldn't hold a bleedin' note. Apart from Lay Lady Lay. No, Simon and Garfunkel though; them pricks could play you a tune. Saw them live once. In America. Detroit Michigan it was, early seventies. Blew me away.' He managed to get it lit. The cigarette end smelt better than it looked, to Dylan anyway.

'Yeah? America? Wicked.'

'Yeah. I used to live over there, with the missus. Well, she used to be the missus. Mind if I?' He nodded at the can.

'Oh, yeah. Go ahead.' He handed it over. The old fella took a long drink, spilling some down his chin and the front of his dirty coat.

'Cheers, Dylan. I'm Del, by the way. Del to me friends, Derek to the magistrates. Hahahaha.' He went to pass the can back, but Dylan pushed it away, shaking his head.

'No, no, man. I mean, Del. You have the rest of it.' He suddenly felt ill, thinking about the man's personal hygiene, or lack of it.

'What? You don't want to drink it after me? Is there something wrong with me, kid? Have I got some sort of disease?' Dylan couldn't tell if he was being serious or not.

'Naw, mate, naw. I'm just… pissed. Had way too much today. Way too much. You keep it. Seriously.' It was an excuse, but it also more than half true.

'You sure, pal?' He was already emptying it down his throat, regardless.

'Hundred per cent, Del. No worries.'

'Cheers, mate. And you're right. I'm probably bleedin' riddled, hahahahaha. Am I right?' He stubbed out the cigarette end with a shoe that seemed to have more holes in it than bits that weren't holes.

It was a beautiful apartment; the girl had class, he thought. Harry's driver had dropped them off in Covent Garden. The traffic had been atrocious. He hated the area- the tourist trap side of London. It was always full of foreign children in backpacks, watching jugglers and street theatre and all the other artistic things that kids with trust funds seemed to end up doing with their lives. None of that said *London* to him. He was from the real London, even if he didn't live there any more.

She had told him in the lift that it was the smaller of her two flats, but, sitting on the expensive-looking leather couch, it didn't look small to him. The walls were covered in modern art- peculiar looking paintings which made no sense to someone like him, but he didn't hate any of them. She was a woman of taste, even if they didn't share the same in everything. She had gone to the bathroom, to 'powder her nose'. There was an ashtray on the coffee table. He heard the bathroom door open, the noise of a fan coming from inside.

'Beth, love? Beth?'

'Yes?'

'It okay if I smoke?'

'One of those smelly cigars?' He wasn't sure of her tone, without being able to see her face.

'Well, yeah. I suppose.' Some people hated them, though he didn't think there was much difference between a cigar and cigarette. A smell was a smell.

'Hmmmm. If you must...'

'I can go outside if you like, love. No bother.'

'No, no. It's fine. I smoke in here all the time. Knock yourself out, Harry. Honestly.' Her voice wasn't getting nearer. He expected her to be back by now. She must have been fixing them some drinks, he thought.

'Well if you're sure it's no trouble...' He lifted his coat off the arm the sofa and took out one of the Cubans. A present from a business associate. It always paid to keep each other sweet in their line of work.

'No trouble at all. Now, was it a coffee you wanted, or are you going to join me in a Scotch?' She was a serious drinker. They'd been knocking back shorts for hours. She seemed no worse than slightly merry.

'Depends on what's on offer. You got some of the good stuff?'

'What's the good stuff?'

'You know. Laphoraig, Glen Fiddich. Single malt, twelve year old.'

'Nothing like a nice twelve year old on your tongue, eh Harry? Or do you prefer the younger sort?' She was back in the room again. She had made an effort for him. Stockings, suspenders, and an expensive looking corset.

'Well, I- I like me a real woman, Beth. With all the lumps and bumps in the right places.' He did, sometimes. Times like this, specifically.

'Oh? How vanilla. I thought you were a bit more open-mined. Harry...' She put the tray with the decanter and glasses down on the table, deliberately nice and slow, so he could get a good look. She stood back up again just as slow, so he could take it all in.

'Bloody hell, Beth...' He took a puff of the cigar and blew the smoke out slowly over his tongue. It tasted as good as she looked.

'What? Oh, this old thing?' She gave a smile and then did a little wiggle, followed by a twirl. The back view was as impressive as the front. She came over and sat beside him on the couch.

'Very nice. Very nice.' He reached for one of the glasses; she had already taken the liberty of filling them.

'Glad you approve. Although... you look a little uncomfortable there, Harry.'

'What? No, I'm good, love. I'm comfortable, thanks.' He took a sip of his drink. It tasted good, which was almost a miracle, considering the amount he had already consumed.

'Doesn't look like it from where I'm sitting,' she said, nodding at the bulge between his legs.

'What, oh. Heheha. You're not backwards in coming forwards, I'll give you that.'

'Mmmm, yes. I like coming forwards. Well, I like any sort of coming, really.' She rubbed her hand along his thigh, stopping just before she got to his crotch. He took a sharp intake of breath, and looked over her shoulder for the ashtray.

'Oh no, you're okay. Carry on smoking. I don't mind. Gives it the more executive feel, am I right?' She moved over onto the carpet between his thighs, and started to unbuckle his belt. He shifted back in his seat to make it easier for her.

'Yep. All we need now is the private jet.' He took another pull on the Cuban and looked down at her pretty face, and exceptional cleavage. She undid his belt.

'Someone's a big boy, aren't they?' He loved it when women said things like that, regardless of if it was true or not. When a woman said something like that, they made you feel like it was true.

'So I've been told, yeah.' He leaned back and looked at the ceiling, as her hand found its way inside his boxers. The first touch of her fingers on him was like electricity.

'They were telling you the truth, trust me.' She rolled back the elastic waistband of the Calvins. He was already hard. It looked almost as big as she insisted it to be. It always felt bigger when he was with someone, than when he was on his own.

'Do you want me to-'

'Shhhhh, shush. Let me take care of it.' She pulled the whole lot down, trousers and all, down his ankles. He felt like he should kick the shoes off, but she wanted to be in charge here. He wasn't one to argue. Not when he was on a promise.

Fifteen

The man had good taste. He had all Rick's favourite models- *Janie, Saskia, Olive-* and hundreds of their pictures. All the same age, roughly, all professionally shot. They'd been swapping for more than an hour. He loved those long sessions, trading photos with a stranger, while they both enjoyed themselves. Slow and long, building up, waiting for the perfect picture or video. And if it came along too early, he would just save it and keep it for later, until he was ready to finish. He sometimes thought it was better than sex. It was definitely different. It was always another male, but there was nothing homosexual about the experience, as far as he was concerned. There was just more of a thrill in it.

They'd moved onto nudes then, the other man shared his tastes too, in that respect. Professional models, in full make up, shot under proper lighting, in a studio. Rick was into top quality material, and so was this other man.

They hadn't chatted much. He had been in the Jailbait room on xtaboo, and another member had been sticking up links to pictures. Rick had a clicked on a few, and they'd all been exactly the sort of thing he liked. He sent him a friend request, and they'd continued talking on messenger. It was as easy as that to make a new contact. His username was the same on there as it had been on xtaboo: Renz26

The nudes he had were good. He didn't waste time with the boring shots or poses either. He could see that he had gone through the sets, selecting the best ones. Rick was the same. The other man liked a similar age range as him, and the same sort of look in a girl. Rick had been online for a few hours beforehand, downloading photosets, so he had plenty to share. Technically the nudes were legal; it was classed as Art Photography, and done with the permission of the models' parents. He had read that somewhere. It still wouldn't look good to the police if they found it on his hard drive, but it wasn't likely to get someone the sort of jail time the hardcore images would. Jail time or not though, his life would still be ruined. The tabloids were never overly cautious when it came to suspected paedophiles; especially when they were celebrities.

>Renz26: So, you like so far?

>Jrocker: Yeah, mate. Bloody sweet as.

>Renz26: Haha, glad you approve. You like Olive, yeah?

>Jrocker: Fucking hell, yeah. What an arse.

>Renz26: Heh. Yeah, she pretty. What else you into?

>Jrocker: Lots

>Renz26: Such as…

>Jrocker: What've you got?

>Renz26: Hmmm, lots of stuff, lol. You jerking?

>Jrocker: Yeah. You?

>Renz26: Lol. You have some good taste, man.

>Jrocker: Cheers ☺

>Renz26: So?

>Jrocker: So what?

>Renz26: So what else you into? Boys?

>Jrocker: Eh, no.

>Renz26: All right, cool. Just girls then?

>Jrocker: Yep. Pretty much what you're into, mate.

>Renz26: You do vids?

>Jrocker: Yeah, a few. Just models though. No hard. You?

>Renz26: Yeah, me too.

>Jrocker: What, just models?

>Renz26: Ummmm, ☺

>Jrocker: Lol, you have some hard?

>Renz26: Ummmm.

>Jrocker: Nice one. Share the wealth?

>Renz26: I dunno, man… you haven't sent me any videos, or hard stuff. So I'm a little bit…

>Jrocker: Sorry, just have some Olive ones and a Saskia one. That one's really good though. She's dancing. In some little knickers. Very fucking hot, honest.

>Renz26: Sounds cute. What do you want from me?

>Jrocker: I dunno. What have you got?

>Renz26: Well, okay Officer, I'll just get my list out…

>Jrocker: LOL!

>Jrocker: I'm not a cop, trust me.

>Jrocker: Hello? You still there?

>Jrocker: ... ☹

>Renz26: Hey! Yeah, sorry. I was just looking for some vids. What did you want?

>Jrocker: Hard, please.

>Renz26: You sure? It's very illegal, you know...

>Jrocker: Haha! Yes, officer. I suppose it is. What ages are they?

>Renz26: Who?

>Jrocker: The girls, in the vids.

>Renz26: Hmmmm, I dunno. Let's see. Eight, nine, seven as well?

>Jrocker: Any a little bit older?

>Renz26: Nope, soz. I have younger though.

>Jrocker: Jesus. No thanks, that one will do. Cheers.

>Renz26: No probs ☺

Renz26 is asking you to accept a file transfer '8yroldanddaddy.mpg' Do you want to accept?

Bill hadn't lasted long. It didn't matter now, less than ever. When he was paying for it, it wasn't an issue how he performed, or for how long. They weren't his girlfriends. They didn't have to be satisfied. And this one, even less. He couldn't look at her when it was over. He pulled a throw off the sofa and put it over her face. He had to move her. The plan to cut her up, before she decided to come back to life, that had been the right one. He no longer had the stomach for it though. The fight had taken his strength, and what he had just done with her; with her body- it wasn't her anymore- had taken the desire from him. He had to get her downstairs and into the car. Then he could decide where to put her. He couldn't stay at the hotel another night; they knew where he was, and they'd be back in the morning for the girl, if not before.

He looked at the rug on the floor again. It was that or nothing. The lift would be too risky. There was another way though. The door at the opposite end of the corridor led outside onto a fire escape. It said so on a safety diagram in the bathroom. It wouldn't be that far to his car once he got her down the bottom of the stairs. He had to rely on blind luck not to run into anyone who might ask any questions. The trick would be to act like he was doing nothing wrong. A body rolled up in a rug just looked like a rug to anyone with no grounds for suspicion. That was what he told himself anyway. He got up from the floor and did up his flies. Just a couple of more lines, to give him a bit of momentum.

It was the first time they'd talked about anything except Poppy and kidnapping and all of that other business, and she was almost enjoying it, even if 'enjoying' wasn't quite the right word. She needed the relief; she couldn't just constantly think about bad things, no matter how important they were. She wasn't an overly sensitive or fragile person; Dylan always teased her about being more of a man than he was. It wasn't that far from the truth.

Even today, she had managed not to cry even once, despite everything. Her father had taught her from an early age that crying only made things worse. If ever she fell over and hurt herself as a child, he would always pick her up and tell her to smile and it would make the pain go away. And he was right, it did. Eventually, she would pick herself up and smile, without having to be told. And later, she didn't even need to do the smiling bit. There were some times later when she silently cursed him for making her so hard, and there were other times, the worst times, when she thanked him for it.

'So how do you get into a job like yours? I don't even know what it is you are; A PA, is it? They call you all different sorts of things in the press.' He had taken off his suit jacket, and she could see from what was underneath that she had been right- his shape wasn't just down to good tailoring. The wine tasted expensive.

'I just sort of fell into it.' It was a cliché, but it was true.

'Really? How do you "fall into" being the right hand, uh, woman of a world famous movie star then? I doubt you found an advert on Gumtree…' He was well spoken. He had probably gone to an expensive private school; or a few of them, if his father had genuinely been in the diplomatic service, she thought.

'I met him at a party. A big swanky New Year's thing, in the Dorchester. Don't ask me what I was doing there- I used to know some people who could sort of get you in to that sort of thing. This was years ago now.' The people she had known had been able to get into that sort of thing because they were the ones who had supplied the pharmaceuticals. She used to dabble in it herself too- the retail side of it, when money was tight at college. It seemed light years away from what she did now. He didn't need to know any of that.

'The Dorchester? It's nice.' He filled her glass up without her asking and she made no objection.

'Oh, you've been?' They were from different worlds. Even now, with her association with Tom, and her comfortable salary, she would always be leagues below people like him. People were born into a life like that, she knew. It wasn't earned. She wondered what the rest of the house was like, or even how the outside looked.

'A few times, yes. Lunch, mainly. They do a good shrimp salad, although they call it something else on the menu. As you do. Anyway, please go on.'

'Oh, there's not much to tell. He came over to the bar when I was trying to get served, and got the barman to come right over. I knew who he was, obviously. Thought he was doing the whole I'm A Big Deal thing to impress me, but it wasn't like that at all. He was just… friendly. We spent the rest of the night sitting together; talking about stuff and taking the piss out of all the twats that were at the party. I liked him straight away.'

'And there was never anything more to it?'

'How do you mean?'

'Well, you're a very attractive girl…' Her heart leapt a little when he said it, and she half-hated herself for caring what he thought. She couldn't help it. She never thought of herself as pretty, so anyone who suggested it either got gratitude or scorn, depending on how much she believed them.

'Er, no; it was never like that. I mean yeah, when he pulled that stuff at the bar, part of me thought he might be trying it on, but then I thought, nah. He could've had his pick of that room. I was just-'

'You're beautiful.' He said it like it was a matter of fact, not a reassurance.

'Heh. From the neck down, maybe.' She had always had a figure. Somehow, that made it worse. She had been getting the wrong type of attention from men since she was thirteen. She would have taken a more modest body if it meant she could have had a prettier face.

'No. From head to toe. Believe me.' The slightest fingertip touch to her knee as he said it.

'Well, um, thank you, I suppose.' She avoided his eyes.

'You're welcome.' Another smile. He joined her in drinking the wine; he mustn't have been planning on doing any more driving, she told herself.

'Okay, where will I put this?' She nodded at the empty bowl, changing the subject.

'I'll take it, here. Was it okay?'

'It was great, yeah. Thank you.' The words felt wrong. She wasn't on a date. This man wasn't doing her a kindness. Or maybe he was. He was going to get Poppy back, he said. He stood up and put his glass on a coaster. He leaned in to take the bowl from her, and there was a hint of a scent. Expensive, like the suit and the car. She watched him leave and tried to think about Dylan. On the big screen, Poppy was still dead to the world.

'There was any blue light again?' The German had come of nowhere; light on his feet for such a big man. He was inches away from Bob before he noticed there was anyone there.

'What? Oh, naw. She ain't moved in ages. Probably asleep or something.' He noticed something in the man's hand- it was a six pack of Beck's.

'Good, good. You want a beer?' Reinhart pulled out the other chair and sat down next to him at the small table.

'Well, yeah. Cheers.' Bob eyed the man with suspicion. This was too sudden; there must have been more to it.

'Good, good. Here. I think me and you, we should make some peace. Sorry if they are a little warm; they were not in the cooler.' He popped the cap off one of the bottles and put in down in front of Bob.

'Yeah. Well, I-'

'I talk to the boss, yeah. He says you are a good man. He says he has used you before, for other job.' Bob nodded. It was the same outfit as last time then, and the other times. That was confirmation.

'The Boss. And who's he when he's at home, if you don't mind me asking?' He took a sip. It was more room temperature than warm. They made good beer though, the Germans, he thought. Good beer and good cars.

'Hah. Well, I think he likes to keep his, how do you say- identity, for a secret.' He chuckled, and opened the door to the little fridge.

'Fair enough. Better safe than sorry, yeah?' Bob didn't care, long as he got his money.

'Yes. Safer maybe for you.'

'Bloody hell. Sounds a bit dodgy. What is he? Some sort of criminal?' Bob's laugh was loud and dirty; like Sid James. That's who people always said he reminded them of, mostly because of the laugh.

'Heheh. Yeah, something like this. No, I would say that it is better not to know. Sometimes, with this boss, if he is seeing you with his face to your face, you are probably in trouble.' That sounded familiar to Bob. In the Sixties, when he worked in the East End, the lower-downs would never get to meet Ronnie or Reggie, unless they'd done something very wrong. So wrong that the bosses wanted to mete out the punishment themselves, or at least be present while someone else did it. When someone got that call, his first thought was usually to hop on the train to Dover.

'Yeah, well; the money's always good, so I ain't complaining.' He took a cigarette out and offered the box to Reinhart.

'No thanks. Yeah, the money it is always good. This job is all right for you, yes?' He looked less frightening when sitting down. Half of his menace was in his height.

'Well, yeah- from what I can tell so far. What's the story now though, mate? Do I sit here all night or what?' He tipped the cigarette into the ashtray, and wondered for a second if it had been all right for him to take it out of the other room. Some people were peculiar when it came to their homes.

'Ah, no. This other room you are in for the break? You are sleeping in this room. When it is morning, I will come to you and wake.'

'Fair enough. And how about tomorrow? All day again is it? I ain't complaining mind, just wondering.' He had almost finished his beer. The bottles were small: 275ml, which Bob guessed was probably half a pint. He had never got the hang of the metric system.

'Am, I must think... I think tomorrow it is not all day. I think we are finished this not late. Early, but not morning. How do you say, afternoon. The plan is for afternoon. I will speak to the boss later; he will say.' He took out his own cigarettes. Coloured ones, the kind they had in France.

'Right you are. But, tell me...'

'Yeah?'

'Dunno if it's my place to be asking, mate; but why'd you need me here?'

'How do you mean by this?' He looked slightly perplexed.

'Well, this whole thing- sitting outside, watching the light, popping in with some grub and that- why does he need me for it? I mean, the room's locked, little 'un ain't going nowhere. Why ain't it just you who's sitting here, instead of me? If you don't mind me asking.'

'Ah, I see. If this was normal day, you are right. I am doing this job then. Today I must do other things. Other man I would use, he is not here. And the boss is not here until... later. This is why he ask you, I'm thinking.' He took two more bottles out of the fridge.

'Cheers, Geez. Don't mind if I do. So, will I meet him?'

'Who will you meet?' Reinhart belched loudly, without covering his mouth or apologising.

'The gaffer. Er, the boss.' The second beer was colder, from the fridge.

'No one meets the boss. Is easier like this.'

'How d'you mean, mate?'

'The boss has a lot of... interests. He uses many people. Sometimes, the people get in trouble with the police...'

'And what they don't know, they can't tell?'

'Exactly, yes. It is easier like this. For everyone.

'Oh, right. But he'll be here tomorrow? How's that gonna work then? Me not meeting him and that?'

'Erm. I don't know how exactly. But we will see.'

'Um, yeah. We'll see. Cheers for the beers, by the way, geez.'

'Keine problem.'

'You what?'

'Ah, I mean, no problem.'

'Oh! Fucking hell.' Harry felt her tongue run up and down the length of him, then light, tickling licks and kisses everywhere else. The obvious places and the less common; the latter feeling even more arousing, for some reason.

'Mmmm, Harry likes?' She looked up at him with green eyes which looked even more beautiful than they had when he had first set eyes on her, earlier in the evening.

'Harry fucking- uh! Harry fucking loves.' He moved her hair out of the way so he could watch her as she took all of him in. He felt himself at the back of her throat, as she pushed her face as close to his body as was possible; breathing through her nose, fighting the urge to gag. She knew what she was doing all right, he thought, as she brought him back out with a gasp, then spat on him, rubbing it into him with her hand.

'Harry's a big boy.' She smiled at him, then swallowed him down again.

'Fucking hell. Fucking Jesus Christ.' He looked down at her. She let him drop out of her mouth again, then held him to the side and ran her closed mouth back and forward along his length; her teeth touching his skin whenever the pressure parted her lips.

'Mmmmm, such a big boy…' She put her spit-covered hand on him, and slid it up and down, while looking into his eyes. She repeated the same action over and over, until he was almost ready to finish there and then.

'Jesus! Slow down, okay? Just… slow down a little. I don't want to-'

'Oh, I'm not going to let you, don't worry. I've got plans for you.' She took her hand off it for a second, still holding him in her mouth. Her fingers went down the front of her knickers, rubbing herself, while she carried on pleasuring him with just her mouth.

'Jesus Christ… where did I find you?' He pushed his hips toward her face, trying to get more of himself inside her. She took the hand out of her pants and held it out to him.

'Here, open wide.' He felt her fingers on his tongue, the taste and smell of her making him harder. She spat on him some more; lubricating him, so she could take him farther back into her throat. He had seen that sort of thing often in pornography, but never in real life. He started to thrust; meeting the bobbing of her head, until they had a rhythm. She took all of him in there, letting him dominate and control her. He pushed himself in farther and farther, ignoring the sound of her gagging on him. Finally, with a guttural noise, she ejected him from her throat, long strings of thick saliva hanging between her mouth and him.

'Ungh, wow. You like that, baby?' She smiled at him, the spit running down her chin, her mascara starting to run. She was out of breath, but didn't look anywhere near being ready to stop.

'Too fucking right I do, yeah. Jesus Christ.' He hadn't felt like this with a woman in years, probably decades. She rubbed more of her saliva over him, her touch not to firm or too light.

'You like these, Harry?' She looked down at her cleavage, then back at him.

'Jesus Christ, yeah.'

'Well then, let's see what we can do…' She pulled down the top, and lifted herself out of the cups. Without missing a beat, she pushed herself together and leaned into him.

'You'll- you'll have to help me here, Harry. I haven't got a free hand…'

'What? Oh.' In a daze, he slid himself off the couch and onto his knees.

'That's it. There now.' She manoeuvred herself nearer to him, sliding him between her breasts, adding even more spit. His first thrust slipped through entirely and caught her on the chin, making her let out a giggle. He looked down at her, almost confused.

'Oops! Told you you were a big boy… Here, let me.' She angled her face downward and opened her mouth a little, letting her tongue rest on her bottom lip. It took some repositioning, but eventually she was in the right place to meet him each time that he slid out from between. Harry groaned with pleasure. With the strength of someone half his age, he grabbed her shoulders and pushed her back onto the floor, straddling her, but without putting the full weight of himself onto her.

'Mmmm, the rough stuff, eh?' She moved her neck a little again, and started giving him little flicks with her tongue each time he came up to meet her mouth.

'That's it. That's it, you fucking… You… Unnngh.' It was hot and wet, and he liked how his skin felt against hers. He would have to stop soon, before he finished on her like that, without even getting to the sex. At his age, he wouldn't be able to manage it more than once. He had pills at home to help out- Cialis, even stronger than Viagra. He wasn't at home though. She squirmed on the ground underneath him.

'I've lived here and there, I guess. Like I said before, I spent a lot of time in Asia when I was younger.' Frank was at the keyboard, tapping. His back was to her now.

'Yes. The diplomat's son.' Alice was watching the screens above him. He was doing things on two or three of them at once. She couldn't quite work out what though.

'I never said that.' The main screen was showing the feed from Poppy's 'bedroom'. The camera angle changed each time he tapped a different key. Different views, but all of them with the bed as their focal point. Alice shuddered, remembering the Milly tape. She wondered what he had to hide, then stopped herself. He had so much to hide. What his father did for a living was probably the most innocuous thing she could uncover about him; accidentally or otherwise.

'Jesus Christ.'

'What?' She wondered if she had offended him. He didn't seem the sensitive type.

'I just… why didn't I see that before?' He was looking up at the screen where Poppy was still sleeping; tossing and turning a little, but looking unharmed.

'See what? What's wrong, Frank? Is it Poppy? Tell me?'

'Oh, no. Poppy's fine. In fact, she's never been more fine. I think I know where she is!' He spun the office chair to face her, stopping it with his foot.

'What? Where? How?'

'It's so simple. I was banging my head against a brick wall with all of these programmes here-' He gestured to the other smaller screens above his head.

'Okay…' She drank the last of her wine. It had a bit of an aftertaste this time. She wasn't sure if it was from the same bottle. He had poured it in the kitchen, out of her sight. Paranoia gripped her. She had been too trusting of him. He could have slipped something into her drink. She looked at him, but he was lost in his own spiel. There was no reason for him to drug her, she thought. She didn't know a thing about him, though. He might have reasons for anything.

'I was getting nowhere, see? Trying to hack a program that I'd designed to be unhackable, even by me. And then… this.' He pointed back at the screen with the video stream.

'What? What is it?' She licked her lips, trying to figure out the taste. It was almost chemical. It could have been her imagination. Or maybe some stray MDMA in her teeth or gums, from the night before. It was hard to think straight. Her eyes focussed and unfocussed without any input from her. She held onto her seat, overcome by a feeling that she was going to fall.

'This. Do you see the little white box there? Up in the top corner. On the right hand side?'

'Uh, yeah. What is it? Burglar alarm?' That was her first thought; it reminded her of one of the security devices in Tom's. She thought of Tom, out in the North Sea, unaware of any of what was happening. Her head was swimming; it didn't feel like drunkenness; it was different.

'No, no, no. It's a silent ringer.' He was beaming now. It made her feel calmer.

'A what?' She considered the box of cigarettes, wondering if another one would help.

'Silent ringer. They put them in quiet rooms, studies, libraries. I've seen them plenty of times.' He was excited, and she felt like she was getting excited too, just watching him. There was something distinctly artificial about her feelings, however.

'So… it's a doorbell?' He was losing her now. She felt the warm fuzzy feeling again; so out of place in the circumstances. Her mind felt like it was racing, but not with any thoughts in particular. She decided to have the cigarette. It might calm her, she hoped.

'No, no, no! It's the phone. If the phone rings, that little box flashes red. Do you see?'

'Um, not really.' A warm feeling moved across her stomach, and down to her crotch. The feeling was one almost of arousal. Her chest felt fluttery, her blood warm. She took a long drag on the cigarette.

'I have their numbers. All of their home numbers. All we have to do is call, and watch the screen.'

'And…' She was trying to concentrate on what he was saying, but everything going on with her body made it extremely difficult.

'And when the light flashes on that box, we have our guy.' He looked delighted with himself. She still wasn't sure what he meant, and she wondered a little why he would have the home numbers of these men. It must have been without their knowledge, she concluded. Her head throbbed for a second, and then stopped again.

'That's- that's amazing. And then we go get her?' She stood up from the couch and made her way across the room, but not to him.

'Well, there are some things we'll need to do first, but yes. In a nutshell. We can get her. Are you- are you okay?' He looked at her face, then down to her hand, which was inside the waistband of her trousers.

'Me? Oh yeah, I'm fine. I just- I just need the loo.' She felt a blush cover her entire body before she pulled the door to behind her.

>Renz26: You still there?

>Jrocker: Yup. Yeah, still waiting.

>Renz26: Huh?

>Jrocker: The video. Not downloaded yet. Is it good?

>Renz26: Yeah, man. Good stuff, definitely. You still swapping?

>Jrocker: What?

>Renz26: Pics. You stopped putting pics up. Thought we were still swapping.

>Jrocker: Oh, right, yeah. You still want to?

>Renz26: Well…

>Jrocker: Okay, I'll see what I have. What you want?

>Renz26: Pics

>Jrocker: Heh, I know. What kind of pics?

>Renz26: Dunno, surprise me. Cute girls, yeah. You choose.

>Jrocker: You hard?

>Renz26: lol

>Jrocker: You stroking it?

>Renz26: Lol, did the video come through yet?

>Jrocker: Are you a fucking copper?

>Renz26: lol, am I a policeman? You're crazy, bro.

>Jrocker: Are you or aren't you, yes or no?

>Renz26: Hey man, I'm just sharing some pics and vids. Same as you. No need to get heavy, yeah? Chill.

Jrocker has cancelled the file transfer

'What's her name then?' The tramp took out a blue glass bottle from inside his jacket. It looked like wine.

'Huh? What's whose name?' Dylan felt slightly drunk; maybe more than slightly.

'The Princess, mate. The one whose got your head in a shed. What's she called?' He took the cap off, it smelt a bit like wine too.

'Oh. Oh, her. Yeah, it's Alice.'

'Alice? Alice in wonderland, hah? Hahahaha.' He leaned his head back and poured the wine down his throat. Dylan was almost impressed, watching him.

'Yeah. Yeah, something like that.'

'Want some-a me sherry? Harvey's Bristol Cream that is, mate. Only the best for me, am I right? Hahahaha.' He passed it over.

'Cheers. Yeah, her name's Alice.' He took a mouthful. It tasted disgusting, like vinegar.

'Alice through the looking glass, eh? Good books, them. He were off his tits on drugs, him.'

'Who was? Thanks.' Dylan passed the bottle back.

'Lewis Carroll, mate. They all were, back then. All the good ones anyway. Hahahaha.' He took another drink, then handed it to Dylan again.

'Really?'

'Oh yeah. Well, apart from that lion in the wardrobe tosser. He were just high on Jesus, hahahaha.' He took another dirty stub out of his pocket and squeezed it to get the flatness out.

'Yeah? Crazy, man.' He seemed to know a lot about books for someone who was homeless, Dylan thought. But then people weren't born homeless. Everyone had their story.

'Yep. You gotta be a bit crazy, I suppose; to come up with all that shit. Well, you gotta be a bit crazy to believe in all that Jesus and God claptrap too.'

'True.' He took another swig of the vinegary liquid, wincing at the taste.

'So it's swings and roundabouts, innit. So, tell me; what went wrong with Alice and Dylan?' He passed it back.

'Well, I mean; where do I bloody start, eh? You know women…'

'I've known a few of them, yep. Hahahahaha.' He lit the half cigarette and took a long pull. It burned fast up on one side, and stayed unlit on the part that had been wet.

'Well, she doesn't think I'm good enough for her, Del. That's the bottom line.'

'Yeah? Why not, mate? Is it them bleedin' jeans? Hahahaha.'

'Hah. No, I just… I don't have enough drive, apparently. No ambition.'

'No money, you mean?'

'That's what I said!'

'Too bleedin' right, Dyl. They're all the same, women. They'll tell you they want romance; hearts and flowers and all that shit. And they do, let's be fair. But if it don't come with some sponds, you ain't getting none of that fanny. Am I right?'

'Yeah! I mean, she's right, I suppose.'

'They're always bleedin' right, mate. Hahahaha.'

'No, I mean she is right… about me, and the drive thing. I'm not good at… motivating myself. You know what I mean?'

'Look who you're talking to, mate. It's just the way things is these days. I see it all the time. People who'd rather just do bugger all. In the old days, it were different.'

'How so?'

'Well, there weren't no dole, or no housing benefit. Yeah, in them days if you didn't get yourself a job after you left school, well, you'd starve to death, wouldn't you?'

'I suppose so, yeah…'

'You would, Dyl. Why d'you think you can go in Primark and buy a T-shirt for what, two quid? D'you think them up in Primark Towers is selling you something and not making no profit? Are they bollocks. They're making a profit because them shirts is made by little children in bleedin' sweat shops in the Philippines, for five bob a week. And you know why them children is working for that money?'

'Why?'

'Cos their parents is at home with no jobs themselves, and there ain't no dole in the Philippines, mate. So they're popping out sprogs and sending them to the factories. So you can have your Rolling Stones t-shirts and them- whatever them things you're wearing is called.'

'Skinny jeans.'

'Skinny jeans, right. They ain't nothing new, by the way. Oh no, the Ramones was wearing them in the seventies. Of course, they were real men, eh? You didn't see Joey Ramone crying into his beer about no bird called Alice. Joey'd just go out and get himself a new one.'

'Hey!'

'Sorry, Dylan mate. No offence. I've been there meself, trust me. Listen, birds has always been the same; don't you believe nothing you read about no women's lib or no feminism. A bird today still wants the same thing as she did fifty years ago, mate. She wants a bloke to look after her. Plain and simple. Yeah, she'll have a job now, and she'll make her own money. But don't think that that means she's all right with you sitting on your jacksie doing sweet F.A. Jesus, a woman with a job is even worse about that sort of shit. She don't want no bleedin' Jimmy Giro lying on the couch scratching his balls when she comes in from a hard day's slog.'

'Well, yeah. I sort of see what you mean, but-'

'No sort of about it, mate. And no buts either. That's the way it is. Now, your Alice, she might wrap it up in fancy words like ambition or drive and whatnot, but the bottom line is, she wants you to be earning. Cos a man who don't do nothing for a living ain't a man at all as far as she's concerned. It's bred into them. That's how they all think.'

'Well, yeah. But I mean, if I was a millionaire or something, or even if I like just had a job, I'd be fine with her not working. I wouldn't care. It's not fair that-'

'Listen to yourself, mate. It's not fair, it's not fair. Life ain't bleedin' fair, Dylan. I got used to that a long time ago. You ain't no millionaire, and you probably ain't never gonna be. A woman needs a man to be someone, or to have a plan to be someone. What's your plan, mate?'

'Well, I- I want to be a writer. Screenplays, films and that.'

'That's great. And what have you done about it?'

'What do you mean?'

'What have you written? Who've you talked to about it? How is it going to make you money?'

'Well, I'm working on a few things. I don't know. It's hard to get into the business. You sort of need a big break, you know? It's not that simple.'

'I hear you, pal. So, what are you doing in the meantime?'

'What?'

'To make money now, until you get that big break?'

'Well, nothing. I'm trying to concentrate on-'

'There's your problem right there. You're doing nothing. And that's all she sees.'

'Mate, you're living on the street. No offence, but I don't think you're the best-'

'Well, I ain't the one trying to get into Princess Alice's knickers, am I? And anyway, maybe I am the best one to give you advice about it. You think I'm here cos I wanted to be?'

'No. No, sorry Del. Sorry.' There had been no need for rudeness. Dylan felt bad, but it was the drink talking, not him.

'No need, mate. I've heard worse. Listen, I weren't always like this. I were young once, like you. Had better taste in trousers of course, but each to their own am I right? Hahahaha. I made a few bad choices is all. Some of them was to do with birds, same as you. So maybe I'm the best bloke for you to be listening to…'

'Yeah. Honestly Del, I'm sorry. So… what did happen?'

'With me? Jesus, that's going back a long while. Well, me and you, we ain't so different. I were a bit creative meself, me.'

'Yeah? You used to write?'

'Yeah, I suppose I did. Not bloody screenplays though, mate.'

'What then?'

'Songs, man. Yeah, I was gonna be Dagenham's answer to Lennon and McCartney, me.' He took another long drag on the cigarette end and washed it down with some more alcohol.

Sixteen

Don put the name 'Rick Jarvis' into Google and poured himself a sherry. It was the good brand that he usually only bought at Christmas time, but one of the officers at the station had given it to him. They'd stopped a lorry with a container full of stolen wines and spirits coming out of the docks the other day; while performing searches related to another case. It wasn't uncommon in that sort of situation for the men to cream something off the top for themselves. The higher-ups usually looked the other way, when it wasn't hard drugs.

Jarvis was famous, or at least he had been a few years back. He didn't particularly look like a man who was sexually interested in children, but the majority of them didn't. The News of the World's archetypical paedophile- unkempt, socially stunted, haunting stare, etc- was more the exception than the norm. The people his division brought in were usually just average looking men, sometimes women. The papers weren't interested in a handsome looking paedophile, or one with any degree of charm. There was a sort of unwritten rule about running those stories. Monty from the Tribune had told him as much some drinks one night. He said that the punters were only interested when pretty, white children went missing, and when the man who did it looked like a monster. It was the right fit for their agenda. People wanted life to be like a movie. Also, they didn't want to end up being responsible for starting any bizarre cults or followings. People worshipped celebrity, even if it was the notorious kind. Don remembered when they had caught Sutcliffe, the Yorkshire Ripper. He was only a young constable on the beat then, but he had friends in the force who had been working up north back then and they'd told him that the Ripper got love letters every day. Proposals of marriage even. It was the same with Bundy in America. People didn't want that sort of thing on their consciences, if tabloid editors had consciences. There weren't any sacks of Valentine's cards for Ian Huntley or Roy Whiting.

Jarvis was rich, without a doubt. Another man with too much money, too much power and too much spare time. It happened a lot. He was going to meet a few of them tomorrow. He was sure that Harry wouldn't have told them he was police, let alone the area in which he worked. He tried to imagine the look on their faces. He had another sip of sherry while scrolling down Jarvis' Wikipedia entry. He was a bit of a character, by most accounts. Over the years, he had fallen out with everyone in the band; sacking them all, one after another. An egomaniac, the testimonies said. The last few albums had done badly, commercially and critically, but he still made money on the touring circuit; playing the back catalogue for die-hard fans. Don was more a lover of classical music than rock and roll. J.S. Bach in particular.

The page said Jarvis was a reformed hell raiser- he became Born Again a few years back. He was a Mormon now, who didn't have any vices. Don sniggered at that. It was usually the most straight laced people in society who ended up on his team's radar. Clergymen especially. Catholics more often than not, but they'd picked up holy men from every denomination over the years. They were always the ones most in denial too. He didn't know if their arrogance came from feeling that they were above normal people, or if they just assumed that their god was going to save them, but they were all pretty vehement, right until the judge passed the sentence. Then would come the tears and the regrets.

For a sex offender, the idea of a spell in prison was much more terrifying than it would be for any 'normal' criminal. Everyone knew what happened to rapists and child molesters away from the eyes of the guards. Also, a paedophile's sentence was more than likely the first time he would have ever been inside. Don had never arrested a career criminal who also happened to dabble in that sort of thing. The two didn't seem to go together. Harry definitely wasn't going to do any prison time for it. He knew how to pick his friends.

Harry Goldman was a familiar name in the corridors of the Met and Scotland Yard. They knew he was a major player, and they'd have given anything to be able to bring him down. To have something on him which would stick. Much to their frustration, they knew he had plenty of their own men on his payroll, and more than a few judges. The other thing that made him so elusive was the way his organisation was run. Don once compared it to the way the Americans ran their intelligence agencies. There was a director at the top, and he spoke only to a few deputies. They were the only ones who ever saw him in person. Each of them would have a few men below, to whom they passed orders. Each of those would have a handful of lackeys themselves, and at the lowest levels, none of the men committing the crimes had any clue who they were working for. Plausible Deniability, he had heard someone call it once. Whenever Scotland Yard picked one of them up, for robbing a post office or turning over a G4 van, they could have given them the thumbscrews and they still wouldn't have told who was running things. Because they had no idea themselves. The police of course knew exactly who was behind all of it, but with the CPS it wasn't what they knew that counted. It was what they could prove. And no one could prove anything when it came to Harry Goldman.

She was heavier than she had looked. The rug too, it must have weighed enough by itself, even without her in it. He got down the hall easily enough, no unfortunate meetings with any of the other guests. That had been another reason to get out fast; someone might have taken it upon themselves to call hotel security about the little domestic happening on their floor. Or worse, called the police. People in London minded their own business though, or were just apathetic. Either way, he was glad of it.

Out on the fire escape, Bill held on tightly to the bundle, and moved slowly down; step by step. He used some bungee cords from his luggage to tie the thing up at both ends, and they were holding, so far. He tried not to think of the little girl inside the rolls as he made his way down. Each thud on the metal steps making him wonder was it her head or feet at the bottom of the makeshift body bag; not that it mattered. All around him, car horns blared and people's chatter floated over the air. A city getting on with its life, completely unaware of him or what he was doing. The air was crisp in his numbed nostrils. He swallowed globs of anaesthetic mucus and cursed himself for not bringing a drink. He was nearly at the bottom. The fire escape led down into a back alley, with three great industrial wheelie bins, overflowing with stinking food from the kitchens, probably teeming with vermin. The rats in London weren't as big as the ones back in New York, but that could be said about most things. There was just a short alley between him and the car. He had checked and double checked already that he remembered to bring the keys with him when he left the room, but it didn't stop him checking one more time.

They were both on their third beer, and Bob was feeling a bit tipsy now. They'd been talking about football.

'Klinsmann. We had him for a while there, at Spurs I mean. Class act he was.'

'Klinsmann, yes. You English you called him the diver, yes?'

'Hah! Yeah, liked to fall over a bit, din't he?'

'I think, well I think it was all part of the game. It is big business, football. Lot of money, even in these days.'

'Too bleedin' right. I mean that were then. Now you've got your Chelseas and your Man Citys; the whole thing's got bloody ridiculous, the money in it. It's your Arabs, innit? All that oil.'

'Yes, yes. And well, Abramovich- this is oil as well.'

'Is it?'

'Yes, yes. Siberia, this is where he brings his money from. Lot of oil in Siberia, and after Gorbachev and all of this stops; well, no one is sure who is owning anything in Russia. So the criminals and the mafia, they control all.'

'Yeah? Yeah, I suppose so. What about your lot?'

'My lot? I do not understand.'

'Yeah, the Germans. After the wall come down. Same thing, was it? In the East, I mean, mate.'

'Haha. I am not German, my friend.'

'Huh? You bloody sound German, mate. No offence.'

'Heh. I am from Austria. You know, like Schwarzenegger, yes? You know who is he? The Terminator, no?'

'Oh right, yeah. Austria. Yeah, he done some good films he did. Conan the Barbarian and that.'

Germany, Austria- pretty much the same thing, thought Bob.

'Yes. This was a good one.'

'Course, he gave all that up, didn't he? Went into politics or something?'

'For the while, yes. Until they find he has been taking the maid to bed…'

'Oh yeah! I forgot about that. The dirty bastard. She were a right old dog too, weren't she?'

'I think maybe she is not only one he takes to his bed, yes?'

'You're right there. It's never just the one. Look at Clinton.'

'Or the golfer. The negro, what is he called?'

'Golfer? Uh, Tiger Woods?'

'Yes. Yes, Woods. He is too a naughty man.'

'Haha, yep. And his missus were right gorgeous and all. Just goes to show-' He was cut off by the sound of Reinhart's mobile ringing.

'Ah, I must answer. Excuse me…

' Yes? What? Well, how long are you there? Okay. And no one has come? What about the phone; there is any calls? You don't pick them up. Okay, yes. Yes, do this. No, I will tell him when he asks me, not before. Okay. No, no. No, just… just stay. She will come, so be ready. No, plan is the same. No. No, just make sure she stays. Okay. And no mess. You have something to do it with? Good, good. Call me when it is done. Okay.' Reinhart finished call and said something under his breath that Bob couldn't hear.

'Everything all right?' He finished up the last of the Beck's. He would've liked another one, but he needed to keep sharp. There'd be plenty of time for beers once he finished, and collected the five thousand.

'Eh, yes. Just a little how do you say, hiccup?'

'Fair enough,' Bob said. Just then, the Polish girl rushed up the corridor behind them, with a look of anger on her face.

'Reinhart! I am look everywhere for you. I want go home now, yes. Where is my money? What goes on here? This is fucking no good. I want-'

'Shut up, shut up. You will not talk to me like this.' The Austrian squared up to her, towering over her.

'I talk how I like. I do job for you, where my money is? I stay longer too, I-'

'Bitch, shut up!' Reinhart grabbed her by the throat and slammed her against the wall, hitting her head hard. Bob stayed where he was, not saying anything.

'I, I, stop! Let me go!' She was trying to scream at him, but her voice was getting smaller the more he crushed her windpipe. Bob wondered quietly if he should get up and help, and which of them it was he should be helping.

'Okay. Now, be calm. I will let you go now, but only if you will be calm.' His voice quietened and lost some of its edge as he said the last part. The girl said nothing, just gave a nod. Her face was a darker shade of purple.

'Good, good. I am letting you go now.' He let go of her neck and the she fell onto the floor, gasping. Quickly, she regained her breath, and began to scream at them.

'I am wanting to go! Let me to go! I am wanting to get out of-' She didn't get to finish the sentence. The bigger man brought both fists down onto the top of her head, in a sledgehammer motion. She was unconscious before she hit the expensive flooring.

'Stupid Polish. Here, man. Help me take.' He went round by her shoulders, and pointed at her feet. Bob stood up and took the her by the ankles.

'Okay. Where to?' The girl didn't seem heavy. Bob wasn't sure if it was just because the Austrian was doing most of the lifting..

'Just follow me, bitte. I have a place for her.'

In the bathroom, Alice shut the door and sat down. She knew that he was only a few feet away; maybe even closer, listening against the door like before. She didn't care. She was overcome with a base need; something inside her was screaming for relief. She was touching herself through the underwear before she even sat down. She felt no embarrassment, or fear that anyone was listening. Still, she felt something close to guilt. Older feelings, from when she had first discovered her sexuality. Notions of sin and punishment, the remnants of a Catholic childhood. She tried thinking of Dylan. It made her raw arousal feel better; mixing it with feelings, with love. She wasn't imagining romance. She wanted it rough, violent. She thought about him in her mouth. She pictured herself, sluttish and used, on his kitchen floor; sweat dripping, mascara running.

She came, hard and suddenly, biting her lip to keep from making much noise, but that was pointless. He must have heard her. She didn't care. She sat there for a while, unable to form any thoughts. She felt her sweat turn cold as is trickled down the small of her back. She pulled herself together and tried to stand. The room swayed, and she felt herself fall back onto the seat again.

'Jesus. So she was just like- it's the music or me?' Dylan was feeling the cold. The booze had helped, but they'd finished the sherry now.

'Something like that, yeah. It's just- I dunno, mate. Women- it don't matter how well you treat them, they'll always find something to complain about. I were good to her; never got up to nothing behind her back; never gave her a smack. This were in the days when you could give a bird a smack, mind.'

'So what was her problem, like?'

'Same as your bird's problem, Dylan. I weren't looking after her enough.'

'But you were making money, right? From the band? They paid you for your gigs, surely.'

'Well, yes and no. Sometimes there'd be a few quid. But mostly they'd pay us in beers, you know? Rock and roll and all that.'

'Oh.'

'Yeah. You can't exactly open a savings account with six pints of bitter and a whiskey chaser, am I right? Hahahaha.' Went into his coat again, and this time pulled out a small bottle of Jameson's.

'Bloody hell, Del. It's like Narnia in that coat. What else you got in there? A talking lion?'

'Hahaha. C.S. Lewis, eh? We're back to him again.'

'It's the circle of life. See, more talking lions.'

'I don't get you.'

'Oh. It's a film. The Lion King.'

'I thought that were a show.'

'It is, as well. Anyway- your missus. What happened? Tell us.'

'Well, I didn't take it too well, mate. Never figured meself to be the needy type, but Christ- I wrote her a letter every day, phoned up her house, called round to her work. Did everything I could to get her back. Course, it's don't work like that, does it?'

'Nope.'

'Nope is right. She went off me big time. My own fault of course. I should have let her alone for a while. Let her miss me. Then she'd have remembered everything she liked about me, Dylan. Then she'd have realised that she bloody loved me, and that money or jobs or whatnot didn't matter.'

'Yeah. I suppose that's right. I guess.'

'No guessing or supposing about it, pal. It's the way it is. That's what I'm trying to tell you about Princess Alice over there. You need to stop talking to her. I know it'll tear you apart, mind. But you'll have to let it. It's for the best.'

'But, I don't want to let her go. Me and her, we could still be good. We just need to… iron out some things.'

'No, I get you. And you're probably right. It's just, she'll never come to that conclusion if you keep on telling her to, pal. You have to lay off. You have to make it so that she thinks she made the decision herself.'

'Hmmm. I guess so, but-'

'No buts, mate. It's just economics, innit?'

'What's economics?'

'Simple economics, Dylan. Supply and demand. As long as you keep being around and available and there for her, she's never going to miss you. And if she don't miss you, how is she going to start thinking she wants you back? She don't need you back, she's already got you, mate. On a silver bleedin' platter.'

'Uh-huh.'

'Supply and demand. You decrease the supply, what happens to the demand?'

'Um, it goes up?'

'Bingo. It might sound like I'm talking out my arse, and you mightn't believe me straight away. But if you cut off the supply of you, she's gonna realise she misses it. And she'll want it; cos there's nothing a bird wants more than something she ain't allow to have.'

'Well, that and shoes.'

'What, mate? Shoes? Hahahaha, you're not wrong there. Birds and shoes, what are they like? You want a bit of whiskey? Help yourself there, pal.'

Harry lay in silence, next to her. He didn't know what to say. Things had got complicated, after they had got to the bedroom. The sex had been good, and she had begun to talk dirty. That wasn't unusual to him.

But, as they progressed, the dirty talk had turned to role play. She put on a little girl's voice, and called him 'Daddy'. She pretended to be coy, and afraid. She had told him to be gentle with her, because it was her first time. She told him she was ten years old.

After it was over, he couldn't look at her. He didn't have the words to say. She'd been wanton and vile; she'd said things no woman he had ever been with would have dreamed to say. She had been a hundred per cent committed to the fantasy, and had taken things further and further, the more she saw him respond. If there were lines, they had crossed them. If he had any secrets about his sexual tastes, she knew them all now. He was lying with her in front of him, in the spooning position. He had never known a woman to leave him lost for words before, but she had managed it. He stared at the back of her head, trying to think of something to say, but nothing came. After a fashion, she turned to him, smiling. Looking at her, he knew his meeting with her hadn't been as random as it seemed. If she was after something from him, he was about to hear what it was.

'Oh, Daddy. I don't want to go to bed though. It's silly. I'm not a baby!' Colleen was sitting cross-legged on the floor, not even turning her head to face him.

'I know you're not, Col. But your Mum says-'

'Mum didn't say anything though!' This time she turned to him, face like thunder.

'Mum says your bedtime is- well, your bedtime is now. Okay? You need to get some sleep, all right?' He hated having to do it. He had hated school himself; it hadn't been any use to him. There were no algebra tests at Stamford Bridge. Col was bright though; she could probably end up going to Oxford or Cambridge. They'd be able to afford it as well.

'I'm not tired though! Gah!' She had a temper on her, but it wouldn't be fair to say which of them she got it from. Tamara and he both were partial to the red mist.

'Doesn't matter, Col. It ain't me that makes the rules.'

'Fffff. Well, you should make the rules. Then I could stay up as late as I wanted to.'

'Huh? What makes you say that?'

'Because you love me!' She gave him her most angelic smile.

'Haha. Col, your Mum loves you too, she-'

'No she does not. She loves getting her nails done, and buying shoes.'

'And you.'

'Hmmmm. Whatevs. I think I should stay up for… another hour.'

'No.'

'Half an hour?'

'Nope.'

'Oh, come on!' She looked like her mother when she was cross. It was pretty sort of angry.

'You come on. Come on to bed. Now.' He raised his voice. It was rare from him, and she was visibly shaken by it. He hated this part of being a parent. He would have much rather he just got to do the messing about and the presents.

'Bugger it anyway.' She threw the remote control across the room and it landed on one of the big sofas.

'Oi! Mind your fucking language, Colleen Sykes.'

'Language? Bugger is not language! Gah! And anyway, you just said fu-' She wouldn't-

'Colleen!' He threw his hands in the air, exasperated.

'Fffff. God's sake. Okay then. I'll go. Bloody-' She was red in the face now.

'Colleen! Language!'

'What? Oh, Jes- oh, blo-. Gah. Good night then!' She got up and stormed past him, into the hallway. He did his best to keep from sniggering. She was a good child. There were worse than her, and he knew it.

'Fuck it!' Rick closed down the messenger window immediately, and the messenger itself straight after. *How could I have been so stupid?*

The conversation had been so one way, even if it hadn't seemed like it. The other man hadn't said anything provocative, on reflection. Rick had scrolled up through the whole conversation to double check. It had been a lot of dodged questions and deflection. That was what policemen did. Covered themselves, in case someone accused them of entrapment. He had led Rick on, getting him to initiate everything; making sure he only swapped legally innocuous material, until the point when Rick asked him outright for hard-core child pornography. It was a trick, a trap, a honeypot. And he had fallen straight in.

Frantically, he searched Google for what to do to cleanly erase something from a hard drive. He had read about it in the past, but all of that was rapidly falling out of his head now, in the panic. There were conflicting viewpoints, as always. Most of the forums suggested a complete formatting of the drive; wiping everything, including the operating system. There were programmes that would erase it even more securely than that; 35 passes of data rewriting, but those could take hours. He had no idea how long he had. Others suggested destroying the computer itself, or at least the hard disk. This could be done in a number of ways; most people suggested the microwave. It sounded stupid, and dangerous. But it worked, according to those people.

He opened up the cleaning software already installed on his laptop. It was the one he used to clear his browser history, search term, and any saved logins or passwords for morally dubious forums and image boards. He was sure he had seen a Format Drive option in the past. And he had; it was there. There was no hesitation on his part; he selected the most secure sort of wipe, and pushed Start. It was just a question of time after that.

He often wondered how legitimate the clearing or hiding programmes were. Or how effective they'd be against the sort of advanced software the police would have. He assumed that the authorities would know about every shady programme on the internet, or that they would purposely employ the brightest minds in tech to write super-programmes for them. But that was assuming their branch of law enforcement was exceptionally clever. It wasn't a virtue which was shared across the board, in his experience.

If they came; when they came, they usually came at dawn. But he didn't know that for certain. Dawn raids were mentioned often in the press, but perhaps other kinds were reported too, and confirmation bias prevented him noting them as much. At that moment, he was unable to think clearly about anything. His eyes were on the gradually increasing red status bar on the screen, and his mind was full of images of the front door being smashed down at any minute. Going to Harry's was looking like a good plan, once he finished with the machine.

Alice's view of bathroom began to sway and grow dim. She was drunk; that had to be it. So much brandy… But she had eaten; that should have soaked it up. Apparently not though, because her legs had gone too. There was a sound, but she wasn't sure what. From outside. *Him*. She couldn't think properly. She felt ashamed, shutting herself in like that; going at herself so frantically, like an animal. When Poppy was so far away from her still, and in so much danger. She wanted to cry. The sound was still there, only louder. It was knocking. He was knocking, and a voice.

'Are you okay in there?' was what she thought she heard him say. The sound was as uneven and confused as her vision.

'I'm… I'm fine. Won't be a minute.' She was almost sure that she had said it aloud, but she might have been mistaken. He was still knocking and calling her name, so maybe she had just imagined it.

'Alice! I said, are you okay in there?' He sounded more irritated than worried about her, she thought. Not that it mattered. She didn't know who he was. Or where she was. The strange feeling was starting to return to her belly and her loins, in spite of herself. It wasn't drink. It felt more chemical, narcotic.

The door buckled with a crashing sound. Confused, she started backwards in her seat; banging her back against the cistern. Again, the wood moved inward with the force of someone's body. His body. The lock wasn't a key and handle affair, just a bolt that had been added. It was almost off, only one of the screws still intact. One more barge of his shoulder, and the whole door came crashing inwards. Alice looked at him, stunned.

'You're okay!'

'Of course I'm okay. I said I was okay, didn't I? What the hell di-'

'You didn't say anything! I asked and I asked! You didn't say anything at all. So I...'

'So you just-' she couldn't finish the sentence. The dizziness came over her quite suddenly, and she was glad she was already sitting down. Her head felt light and her body heavy. She lolled forward, her neck going slack. He moved quickly to stop her from falling. She felt his arms around her. He smelt clean; expensive aftershave and freshly laundered cotton.

'Come on. Let's get you lying down,' was the last thing Alice heard, before everything went dark. Outside, she thought she heard a car beeping, and someone shouting. But it might have been part of some dream.

Seventeen

The house was enormous, it seemed to Bob, as he helped Reinhart bring the unconscious Polish woman down yet another corridor. She hadn't open her eyes or stirred since the bigger man had pummelled her to the floor. He had said nothing to Bob since, save the odd grunt to let him know which way to turn. The place was a maze of corridors and closed doors. It would probably be difficult to get back to the room where the girl was, unless the Austrian came back with him, Bob thought, as they turned another corner. There was just one door ahead, a dead end. He felt the other man slow down, and then come to a halt.

'In here,' he said, without looking back. Bob looked toward him, looking for a sign as to whether they were going to drop her, or keep going. Reinhart turned to face him, without letting go of the women, and motioned at Bob to put her on the floor.

'What's in there?' He watched as the other man rifled through a chain of silver and gold keys.

'In here? In here is rubbish.' He found the key he wanted, and opened the green wooden door. A smell of rotting food and disinfectant hit Bob's nostrils as the room beyond was revealed. It was dark, save for a small yellow light in the corner. Large, blue plastic, industrial sized wheeled bins flanked both sides of the narrow, windowless space. At the far end there was a wide, corrugated iron garage door.

'Lift again?'

'Pffft. No need. Is trash. Here is where trash belongs.' Reinhart grabbed the woman's collar and dragged her along the floor and into the dark room. Bob followed, tentatively, breathing through his mouth to avoid the stench.

'I don't know if… I mean, what if she-' Bob began, and then the woman on the floor began to stir.

'Guten morgen, cunt,' said Reinhart; and, before the woman had time to say a word, he brought his boot down on her temple, causing her to shriek in pain. Bob held his breath, unable, or unwilling, to vocalise his thoughts. The woman whimpered, and Reinhart brought his foot down again, harder this time. Bob thought he heard the bones of her skull crunch, but he had already looked away.

'Want too much, is your problem, you Polish bitch. Ask for too much, what do you get? You get this.' Again and again the Austrian slammed his heavy boot into the girl's head, splintering the bones of her face against the concrete. Bob tried to look anywhere but down. It wasn't his business. It wasn't his place to interfere, but he was still human. He could still feel something. The girl's screams went from louder to soft, then to nothing.

'Now what do you have, hey? Stupid bitch. You should keep the mouth shut, yeah. And then you get the money. But you don't. You won't.' With one last stamp, Reinhart collapsed her skull, his boot coming clean through to the floor, with a horrifying squelch of blood, brain matter and shattered bone. Bob made the mistake of looking down, and immediately sprayed the contents of his stomach on the floor beside her. The Austrian looked at him, shocked at first, then he laughed. Loudly.

'Haha! Oh, Herr Bob. You are the old hand at this, I was told? Mister with the Kray twins, no? The old school gangster. What do you do, go soft now that you are old? Hahaha.'

'Jesus Christ. No, yeah. I mean. Fuckin hell.' Bob looked into the other man's eyes. He wanted to punch him, but immediately put the thought out of his mind. The woman was nothing to him. It wasn't his problem. And he hadn't been a part of it, killing her. He needed to shut up, and let this maniac do whatever he needed to do, he told himself. He hadn't been expecting Reinhart to kill her, but it was done. All that could be done now was damage limitation.

'Let's get her wrapped up in summink, yeah?'

'Wrapped up. Yes. This is good. I think maybe I have the… how do you say? Tar-paul-een? I will see. Stay here.'

'What about the girl?'

'What girl? This bitch?'

'Uh, no. The kid.' Bob realised his mistake too late. He kept eye contact with the other man. He might be able to gloss over it, if he didn't panic.

'Oh, you know it is a girl? How do you know this? You did not speak to her, no?' Reinhart drew himself up to his full height; his face was hard, his eyes threatening.

'What? Me? No. Nah, I heard her singing is all. She were singing earlier on, like. Singing a song.' He stood firm and tried to meet the other man eye to eye, despite the difference in height. His throat felt tight. There were no real options to weigh up. Not even running. He had no idea which of the corridors would take him out of the place and away, and he was sure that the younger man would be faster.

'Singing? Hahaha, yes. Little bird, she likes to sing, in her cage. Like the canary. Stay here. I will come with the sheet.'

Dylan was on his way to Hackney. He had taken in everything the homeless man said, and he agreed with most of it. Even the part about supply and demand. And he would do it; decrease the supply of himself, so that she would appreciate him more, and miss him more. But later, after this one last time. He had too much that he wanted to say to her, and most of it was apology. He felt like he had been unfair to her, and stupid. Childish too. He had begun to see it all clearly over the course of the evening, and he needed to talk to her while it was still fresh in his mind.

He forgot to pick up a free Evening Standard at the station, and there were no stray ones on any of the seats. His eyes were having trouble focusing. The tablet was somewhere in his bag; he was amazed that he still had the bag, after all the drinking. He had lost all manner of things over the years from being drunk: hats, gloves, mobile phones. When they were gone they were gone, too. No one handed things in anymore.

It was dark outside; he had to try to keep count of the stops. There was no public address on the train; no one announcing the stations. The second last stop was his: Stratford. Then three stops on the Overground. He couldn't wait to see her. He hoped she would be in a good mood. He looked down at his phone, wondering if he should let her know he was coming. He decided against it. She might tell him not to, and he was already half way there. A small part of him was wondering what would happen if she had someone there with her; if there was someone else already; or there had been for a while. No, she wasn't the sort, he told himself. And anyway, if he had to find out about it, the quicker the better. It would break his heart though, something like that. He pushed the thoughts to the back of his mind again, and opened up a social networking app on the phone. Reading about everyone else's boring day would kill some time before the train got to London.

Harry ran his finger across the touch screen to unlock the phone. There were missed calls and messages. Don had texted, letting him know he would be there in the morning. He wasn't sure when, as there was something going on with work, but he would let him know nearer the time. Somersby had messaged him too, a few cryptic lines to say that everything was okay, and they were still on schedule.

He hadn't set a time for the thing, but everyone being there before the afternoon would be ideal. He looked back over his shoulder at Beth, who had wrapped herself back up in the duvet after their chat, and was dozing contentedly, as far as he could tell. She would be coming too. He knew who his Maybe was, at last. The woman on the internet who he had tried to pretend he wasn't falling in love with; in case it turned out that she was wasn't who she claimed to be. Or that she wasn't a she at all. That person had been Beth. He knew that for certain now.

The sex with her had been mind-blowing, eye-opening, like nothing he had ever experienced before. She had said things to him during it; vile, depraved things, and he had lapped them up willingly. She knew exactly who he was, sexually, and made sure to push every button that she needed to. She had shocked him and appalled him, and he had loved every second of it. She was like him, he thought. Or, even if she wasn't, she was okay with who he was, and willing to indulge him. When it was all over, she turned to him and said:

'So, tell me about this film project, Harry.'

'Film project? What would that be then?' He tried to act ignorant, but he already knew what she meant. How she knew was another matter.

'Oh, you know. The big one, tomorrow.' She gave him a knowing look and a wink. He was seeing a whole different person to the girl he had shared drinks with all evening, and not in a negative way, as far as he was concerned.

'I have no idea what you mean, love. I've got a lot of projects, me. Film, TV, music. Anyone who wants my money, basically. You know me, I'm a sucker for the arts.' He gave her his best poker face. It wasn't convincing enough.

'Oh, you're going to do the coy thing, are you? After what we just- Fair enough.'

'Well, I... I can't read a woman's mind, Beth. Not for the bloody want of trying, neither.' He licked his lips and swallowed. If they genuinely had been playing poker, it might have been his tell.

'Okay, big boy. Maybe I'll spell it out for you. You see, I have a lot of famous clients, yeah? Movie stars, musicians, TV show hosts; you get the picture. And you know- surprise, surprise- some of them aren't the squeaky clean, wholesome family-friendly guys and girls that I get paid to make people believe. Some of them, for the want of a better word, Harry, are right arseholes.' She smiled, adjusting the pillow under her, to support her neck and face.

'I can imagine, yeah.' He didn't need to imagine, he met types like that all the time, through club nights he ran, or card games he organised. He looked at her, remembering the things she'd cried out while he was inside her.

'Well, the guy I'm talking about, you don't need much imagination to understand... he's a friend of yours.'

'A friend of mine? I've got a lot of friends, Beth.' Very few, in truth, he thought. But lots of people who considered him one, in a business sense.

'You know, I bet that's only half true, Harry. But yeah, anyway. This one chap, he's a cut above the rest of them. Or below, if we're being accurate. American fellow, famous for God knows how long; over there and over here. Money to burn, of course. Except he prefers snorting his money, not burning it.'

'I'm listening.' He already knew where the conversation was going. Bill Hansen's sneering, bloated features appeared in his mind, as clear as day.

'Well, yeah. This one's a bloody nightmare. The things I have to do; the strings I have to pull; the money I have to spend- his money, by the way- just to keep up the public myth of who he's supposed to be… Oh, Harry. You wouldn't believe me if I told you.'

'Heh. And he's a friend of mine, yeah?'

'He'd like to think so, yeah. I think we both know who I'm talking about here.'

'I wouldn't be so sure…'

'Oh, I'm sure. So, Billy boy, he has one loose mouth when he's on the old Columbian marching powder. Like you wouldn't believe.'

'Hansen.' Harry felt his blood boil. Anger, not fear. It had been years since he had felt anything resembling fear, no matter what situation arose. He was too well-protected to feel afraid of anything, or anyone.

'Got it in one. So, a few months ago, I'm in his hotel room with him, trying to keep the bastard alive long enough until I can get him some CBS deal, and really, I probably wasn't succeeding all too well.'

'Go on.'

'… and he was gone. I mean, *two grammes in one sitting* levels of gone. Hadn't eaten in days, living on room service, dolly birds in and out of the place at all hours… he was two Red Bulls short of an exploding heart.'

'Jesus.'

'Jesus isn't the word. Anyway, so he starts to talk. I don't know if he was talking to me, or just spouting stuff. To be honest, I'm not sure he knew who I was at that point, or that I was even there. But, off he went. A whole spiel about a beautiful little girl with a famous father, and a film that was going to be made, by one of our more, let's say, notorious directors. And he, Bill, was going to be the star. Well, the poor little girl was the star. But Bill was going to have second billing. He was the best, he said. All the others who were going to have their turn were just nobodies, he said. Nothing compared to him. *The Bill Hansen*. Award winning, accomplished… you know how a coke rant goes, Harry.'

'Yeah. Yeah, I do. And he what- he told you… what exactly?'

'Pretty much everything. Or, well, everything he knew anyway. Even took his laptop out and showed me your little website- well, I'm assuming it's yours, Har. You do like to be the boss of things, right?'

'Uh-hum.' Still no fear, but anger, and lots of it.

'Now, well... I dunno about you, Harry, but I think our Bill got lucky that night, saying what he said to whom he said it. Because, well... anyone else and there might have been a whole different outcome. A lot of blue flashing lights, and banner headlines the next morning. But, it was me. Like I said, he was lucky.'

'Hmmmm.' He was non-committal, still. It all seemed too good to be true. She was naked, so he knew she wasn't wearing a wire. But the flat- the bed itself- he should tread carefully. He had been in the game too long to let a pair of breasts and a nice smile be the undoing of him. He listened on.

'So... I signed up. Paid my subs, as it were. You and me, we've had some chats; even if you didn't know it was me you were talking to.'

'We have?'

'Yeah. Liz Seventy-Seven here, Harry. Pleased to meet you. Again.'

'Jesus Christ...' She was his Maybe. He had spent hours chatting to her on the site; never sure if she was really female. There weren't a high percentage of women in their subculture. But, woman or not, she had been compelling company. He had tried to gently coerce her into taking part in the Poppy film, as she had implied she would be someone who could afford it. He had taken that with a pinch of salt, of course. People were seldom who they pretended to be on the internet. He had been smitten though, against all of his better judgement. There had been something about 'her'.

'Yes. I mean, Bill has no idea it's me either. We never spoke about it after that time. Sometimes I think he blanks it all out, the bloody coke madness. He... he's a special one, definitely.'

'That's one name for him.' Harry's mind drifted momentarily, visualising the punishments he was going to mete out to the American.

'I've heard all the others. So, it's all going ahead? Tomorrow?'

'I have no idea what you're talking about, Beth.' He glanced around the room again, pointlessly he knew. Any device would be meticulously well concealed.

'Hah! Ever careful, my Teflon Harry. You think I'm a plant? Still? After what we just- after all I-'

'I think nothing until I know something, Beth. And anyway, you've seen James Bond. All's fair...'

'So, you want a deposit, is it?'

'For what?'

'For the main event. Ian Somersby's finest film to date. Bill said as much. He said that he told you he was game, and then you turned up at his door, out of the blue.'

'That sounds like the sort of thing I'd do, if I was that way inclined.' Hansen was going to have to pay, definitely, Harry thought. And not in dollars or pounds this time.

'You're not afraid of anyone, are you?'

'Can't remember the last time I was.' He had a strange flashback to his childhood; his father looming over him, belt in hand. He stopped been afraid of Harlen Goldman Sr. when he was seventeen years old. The first time he put the old man on the floor for using his fists on Harry's mother.

'Well, if it's money you want, you can have it. I have plenty. I already told you that in one of our chats. I was hoping we could come to an arrangement, but…'

'An arrangement?' He looked her up and down. There were women in the scene, he knew that. Rare, but not impossible. It was always the girls they were into too; a prepubescent boy's body didn't seem to do it for them in the same way as it did for the pederasts. You only heard of it when the boys were teenaged, and even then they were early developers. Tall, hairy, the opposite of what the homosexual paedophile enjoyed. Usually it was with a teacher. Those were the stories the papers loved; especially if the teacher was a relatively good looking woman. It made good copy, Monty had told him that one time.

'Well, yes. Don't you get lonely, Harry?' She touched his bare thigh. He tried to keep focused.

'Lonely? Nah. I'm good company for myself.' He always had been. Growing up an only child had played no small part in it.

'Yeah? You don't sound too sure, Harry. You wouldn't want a pretty, well-to-do woman on your arm, for things like that dinner earlier?' She moved her hand higher up his leg, and he made no attempt to stop her.

'I, erm… I dunno, Beth. Maybe I could get used to it. What is this? A proposal?' His voice had started to wobble as she kissed her way down his bare chest; the smells of her hair and perfume overpowering once more.

'Of sorts. Here, let me show you my terms.' She took him in her mouth, with a mix of delicate skill and hungry need. He closed his eyes. As her tongue went to work on him again, images of Bill Hansen, screaming in pain, filled his mind.

Bill drove as quickly as he could, within the limit. A policeman wouldn't ask to see inside the boot of the car if he was stopped for speeding. But he had taken so much cocaine, and looked such a mess, they were bound to at least test his breath for alcohol. If that showed up negative, they'd know it was drugs, and then it would all start to unravel for him. It would be a matter of time before someone found what was wrapped up in the rug.

Before long, he hit a jam, and the notion of speeding became irrelevant. He had enough petrol to get him there, with plenty to spare. He had filled up at the Shell that morning. His vision was perfect; his hearing, pin sharp. Benefits of the drug- sharpness, alertness. He could ask Harry what to do about the girl. Only Harry. The less people who knew, the better. He was trying not to think about the Albanians. They had his credit card details; they knew who he was. They might be able to find his car. Organised criminals were as good as the police when it came to tracking people down; maybe even better. He couldn't run. He was relatively famous, it wouldn't be possible for him to disappear. They would have to be paid off, and given a sincere apology. It was only a question of how much, but whatever it was, it would be easier to pay it than to suffer what those people did to someone who crossed them. He had seen YouTube videos of people killed and tortured by Mexican gang lords. The Albanians wouldn't be much different in their methods, he assumed.

'Asshole!' He screamed at driver of the BMW that had cut him up. It shook him, the adrenaline screaming through him as the red brake lights disappeared into the distance. He didn't sound the horn, or race off in pursuit. It wasn't a night to be hot-headed or reckless on the road. The Sat Nav whispered instructions in a robotic, female voice. He wasn't too far from Harry's, and the traffic would quieten down once he got out of the centre.

Poppy was awake. It felt like she had slept for years. Her stomach growled, but it felt more like from sickness than hunger. There was no one else in her room, but she was scared. People had been in there with her. She couldn't remember it like it was a real memory, but there had been someone. A man. More than one man. It was a hearing memory, not a seeing one. She remembered their voices.

She had been in the room too long. Something was wrong. Alice wasn't coming for her, she could feel it. And Magda was doing something bad. She had been different when she had come to see Poppy, and different in the morning too. Poppy wasn't even sure if it had been that morning at all. It could have been the day before. She had slept so long that it could have been a week before. Her head hurt; not in a pounding way, just a pain all over. There was water at the end of the bed, but she didn't want to drink it. The bad people had been making her sleep, and they had probably been doing it by putting things in her food or her water. She had to stay awake; she didn't know what was going to happen to her if she fell asleep again.

One time, a policewoman had come to her school to give a talk about keeping safe. She hadn't told them anything scary, and when she did tell them things, she said that the chances of anything terrible happening to them were very small, so they shouldn't worry themselves about it, or have nightmares. She told them that sometimes bad people used the internet to talk to children, and those bad people sometimes pretended to be children themselves, so they had to be careful when using the computer, and that they should tell a parent or an adult if anything strange happened. She also told them about the dangers of talking to strangers in real life, or of getting into strange cars. Poppy hadn't got into any cars, or if she had, she couldn't remember it. She couldn't remember a lot of the day, if it even was just one day. She had slept so much, and there were no windows in the room, so she couldn't tell when it was day and when it was night.

She wasn't somewhere safe. She wasn't in the house of someone she knew, or who her mother or father knew. She had been taken away by someone. That was why she was in the room, and that was why the door was locked. She wasn't okay. It was called kidnapping, and the money was called a ransom. The policewoman hadn't said anything about kidnapping or ransoms, but Poppy had seen it plenty of times, in films which she probably shouldn't have been watching. The man outside the door with the Cockney voice was a kidnapper, even though he sounded nice. Magda might be a kidnapper too, because Magda knew she was here, and she wasn't doing anything to help her get away. She felt extremely sad, all of a sudden. She hadn't known Magda as long as she had Alice, but she still liked her a lot. She had been good to Poppy, and was always kind. But now she was helping bad people to take her away from Dad and from Alice, so Poppy couldn't like her anymore. She thought about her father, and if he knew she was gone. He must have known, because that was how the kidnappers did things, she knew. They snatched the child, then they sent a message to the parent, saying to pay them money or they'd never see their little girl or boy again. Her father would definitely pay the money, but she was still there, so she didn't understand. He was away on a job though; on an oil rig in the middle of the sea. They had a phone there, because she had spoken to him on the Tuesday before last. But maybe there had been a storm, and the aerial for the phones had broken. She hoped that someone would fix it soon, because she was scared, and she wanted to go home to her own house, and her own bed. She was on the floor now, with her back to the bed. She hugged her knees tight, because it always made her feel better and less frightened.

Tamara was in their bedroom when Paul found her. He said nothing at first; just stood in the doorway, watching her. She was beautiful, and not in some cheap way that wouldn't last. She would be stunning long into her older years. It was the genes; good breeding. He hoped the girls would get most of everything from her. His family were several generations of council estate underachievers. His father was bald by thirty, and neither parent had aged well. He didn't want that for the children. His career had given them everything they'd ever need in the material sense. Tamara's genetic heritage would give them even more, if they took after her.

She was brushing her hair, in front of the mirror; humming softly to herself. The angle was such that she hadn't seen him yet. He didn't want to either, so he kept silent and still as he watched her drag the ivory handled brush through her perfect blonde locks. It was her best feature, people told him. He would have nominated a few other things before it, but he wasn't as sophisticated as most. His eyes moved down her body, taking in the expensive lingerie, and the way it clung to her perfect shape. She was as well preserved as the day he married her; it was her business to be. That was her job. She would tell him sometimes that it was her job too to keep herself beautiful for him, and whichever was the actual motivation, she certainly put the work in. Yoga classes, weights, the latest diet- he heard about them all over breakfast every day, and sometimes he even listened.

He loved her, as much as he understood the word, or the concept. There had never been any others since he met her. And, in his line of work, that was a rare thing. She was enough for him, he thought. Apart from the other thing. He didn't seem to have any control over the other thing though. He wished he did. He wished all the time that he could just walk away from the feelings; from the compulsion, the need. Every time he swore off it though, he somehow ended up back where he started. And every time, he felt less of a human being for it. She must have felt him staring, because she turned around with a start.

'Jesus, Paul! What are you trying to do, give me a heart attack?'

'What? No, haha. Just, erm. Just watching.'

'Watching? Watching what, you creep.' She giggled and threw the brush at him. He caught it, and feigned a powerful overhand return, which made her curl up on the chair and cower behind her hands. It was all play-acting though. He would never harm a hair; he wasn't one of those men, even if he did know a few.

'Jesus! You prick! I honestly thought you were going to, there. I did!'

'You didn't, you mong.' He walked toward her, a warm flush on his face, his heart thumping.

'Oh, Paul. Don't say that word.'

'What, mong?'

'Yes! You know I do that thing... the charity thing. For the...'

'For the mongs?' He squatted down so he was face to face with her.

'I hate you.'

'Nah, you love me.' He took her face in his hand, and kissed her. Firmly, with lips closed, for longer than would be considered a friendly peck. He felt her body relax and lean into him. She exhaled slowly.

'Mmmmm. Where did that come from?'

'What? Ain't I allowed to kiss me own wife now?'

'Of course you are. I hope you're not going to start something you can't finish though.' She reached down and rubbed him through his trousers. He kissed her again; rougher this time, his lips pushing hers apart. She inhaled deeply, turning the chair around so that she could press herself against him.

'Oh, I'll be finishing this one all right, love.' He lifter her out of her seat, wrapping her thighs around his waist. She was tall, but there was nothing of her. He could have been lifting a child. He shook the thought from his mind, and walked her the few feet to the enormous bed.

'Mmmmm, Mister Paul is horny tonight, huh?' She held on around his neck, looking at him with perfectly shadowed blue eyes, fluttering her lashes for effect. He pushed her down onto the silk covers, grinding himself between her thighs.

'Fucking yeah. Just a bit.'

'Oooh. Well… me love you short time or long time, Mister Paul?' She used her calves and feet to pull him closer, her fingers clumsily undoing the buckle of his belt.

'Long time, baby. Long time.' He moved her hand out of the way, it would be quicker if he opened it himself. She rubbed him again though the material of his trousers, her eyes widening at how aroused he was. His own breathing became quick and shallow. He needed her. He wanted to be inside her. He needed to feel some normality after what had happened with the girl. He didn't want to make love tonight, he wanted to fuck her, he thought. Hard, rough and to the point where she begged him for more, or she begged him to stop. He didn't want soft kisses or slow, sensual massages. That was never how either of them enjoyed it. Their tastes were in perfect symmetry, and had been since day one. That was why it had never got tired or tedious, even after two children. He needed to feel like a man, not like what he was before, with Charmaine. He wanted it all out of his head. He ripped her underwear off in one quick motion, and buried his face between her thighs. She arched her back in the way she always did, and made the noises that told him he was doing it right.

Somersby flicked through the cameras on his computer screen, holding his breath. The girl was up and about. That wasn't supposed to happen. It was coming up to ten o'clock. Reinhart had said that the drugs would make her sleep through the night. She didn't look happy either, as far as he could make out in the dark. He pulled up a sidebar menu and switched all the views to a night vision setting. The screen flashed white-green at first, before it settled down to a vague looking monochromatic scene; nothing moving but the girl, who was rocking gently back and forth with her hands hugging her knees. He couldn't see her face, and the microphones weren't picking up any sound. He switched to the nearest camera to her, the one in the lamp, and maximised it. He could call the Austrian on his mobile; he would know what to do. The other man was supposed to be on the door; the one Harry had called 'Bob'. Somersby didn't know the story behind him, but he seemed to be general muscle, albeit getting on in his years. Goldman had said something along the lines of 'diamond geezer' and 'a bloke who knows how to keep his mouth shut'. He still seemed an odd choice, but it wasn't his place to tell Harry how to do his job. Reinhart had implied that the old man wasn't clued in about what was going to go down the next day, so no one should mention it around him. That also seemed strange. He would be gone before the main event, by all accounts, so it didn't matter that much.

He switched the view to the cameras in the hallway outside, to see if Bob was at his post. The chair and table were empty. Just an ashtray and a packet of cigarettes. He wondered if the old boy had gone home for the night. He scrolled through the address book on his mobile, stopping at the Rs. The phone rang on the other end, but there was no answer. He switched the cameras back to the room, and almost jumped out of his seat with fright. The window with the view from the lamp camera was entirely dominated by Poppy's face. Her skin was deathly green from the low light filter and her eyes were shining like torches. Even though it was preposterous, Somersby felt like she was looking straight at him, and he physically moved the chair back from the monitor, shivering in spite of himself. On the screen, he saw the girl's mouth open and close, as if she was speaking. Tentatively, he reached for the volume on the speakers. Softly, and slightly out of synch with the visual feed, came the sound of Poppy singing. He didn't recognise the tune at first, and he couldn't make out any words. After a fashion though, and with another twist of the volume knob, it came out clearly:

'... *hanging out the clothes. When, a-lo-ong came a bla-ackbird and pecked off her nose...* '

Somersby grabbed the phone again and hammered on the redial key. In the little room, Poppy started her song over again, from the top.

It was dark. Alice wasn't sure where she was, or how she had got there. She was on her back, on something soft. She felt around behind her- silk, or satin. It was bedcovers. She was in a bed, or at least on one. She tried to make her eyes adjust to the blackness, but she wasn't anywhere she had ever been when it was light, so her brain was unable to fill in the blanks. He had brought her in, from the bathroom. Her chest filled with guilt. Had he caught her? In the act? No, she thought. She had been finished. She had sorted herself out before he came in. *The door*. He had broken it. He said she hadn't answered him. She had answered him though; she was sure of it. She felt down her body, with tired hands. Her clothes were gone; she was just in her underwear. She didn't remember undressing. She wondered if he had done it.

He wasn't with her. There were voices coming from outside the room, or maybe one voice. She wasn't entirely sure that she was awake yet. Pools of indeterminate colour floated in front of her eyes in the pitch blackness. That was the sort of thing which happened to her before she nodded off, not when she woke up. She was confused. Her eyes began to close again; there was nothing she could do to stop them. The voices outside were still going. One voice or two; she still couldn't tell.

It was night, but she didn't know the time. He had taken her phone, it seemed. There were heavy drapes over the window, letting nothing through. The door to the room was closed, and she had the sudden urge to check if it had been locked from the outside. Her body felt like it weighed several tonnes. She couldn't sit up, let alone get out of bed. She felt incredibly tired, but also alert. It had probably been all the alcohol. She had lost count how many drinks she had, but it wouldn't have been the first time she passed out from it. She had felt something else too, though. That feeling hadn't been a drunken one. It was somewhere between blissful, and incredibly down. Someone had described their experience of taking heroin to her before. It had sounded similar to how she had felt in the bathroom. But there had been another feeling too. Shamed washed over her again, along with something else which should couldn't quite recognise. Her eyes were shut, but the darkness inside them seemed to go bright for a few seconds, and then back to black. She wasn't proud of what she'd done in the bathroom. But it had been completely out of character. She had been animalistic, feral. And all while Poppy was still in danger.

The realisation hit her like a kick in the chest. How could she have forgotten Poppy? What was the situation now? How much time had passed? Was she okay? The fear and dread ripped through her, momentarily pulling her out of the stupor, and sobering her from the strange, almost narcotic haze. In her mind, she sat bolt upright and vaulted off the bed. It took several seconds for her to realise that it hadn't happened in reality. She was still flat on her back. Not paralysed, just unable communicate with her limbs. The warm feeling was back too, rolling over her stomach and down between her thighs. It was unwelcome and inappropriate, yet she found herself holding her eyes shut, squirming with a hot pleasure. Purple and green shapes floated across her mind's eye, under closed lids- manifesting into things that weren't any object in particular, and melting into the dark, to be replaced by others. She felt her fingers rubbing between her legs, gently, then rough. She knew, without looking, that it was an illusion. Her hands were by her side, unable to move now. The tired feeling had intensified to the point of an inability to move. All of her felt heavy; pushed down, yet not uncomfortably so. Hues from a blackened rainbow continued to dance in front of her closed eyes, while the phantom fingers indulged the base needs that flowed through her. Frank, Poppy and Tom all became impossible concepts as she drifted over the edge of conscious thought and into a mixture of ecstasy and confusion. The voices outside had stopped. She thought she heard another voice, nearer, in the room with her. Her skin felt white hot and her breath like ice. Another sound from the room, but she was already gone. There was no sounds, and no room, and no her. Completely at the mercy of a touch that couldn't be hers, she melted into a universe too impossible to be real.

Rick stood in the kitchen, trembling, in front of the oversized, stainless steel microwave oven. He had used his phone's internet to Google the solution; even then he felt waves of paranoia. There was nothing anonymous about searching that way. Still, it was just a search. Without the evidence, that would be all they had- a search. He wondered about the modem- was there a possibility to wipe that? Did it record every site he had been on? It must have done. On the other side- the servers of his ISP- they'd have records. But again, that was all they'd be- records of internet activity- no way to prove that it had been he who had been using it. It was all circumstantial. No one went to jail for circumstantial, he told himself. It was the evidence they wanted. It was possession. If he didn't possess anything incriminating, they couldn't touch him.

He prayed, of course. He never went a day without talking to God or Jesus. Even in the days leading up to the filming, he was not duplicitous in his devotion. God knew all about the plan with Poppy, and Rick had made his peace. He had pleaded forgiveness from the Holy Father, and he had received it. God had made everything and everyone, Rick knew; Poppy Riley was just another of his beautiful gifts, and he knew his God would want him to enjoy a creation as perfect and beautiful as her. There were no rules or laws besides the ones which had been made by the Almighty. In years past, girls even younger than her had been given as brides. In his opinion, God didn't care about modern ideas of morality. He was one of the Lord's special creations himself, and he had been devout since his conversion. He had lived a good life, and hurt no one. The sacrifices he had made; the vices he had abandoned: those were all beautiful gifts which he had presented to God. The Lord who loved and protected him wouldn't think it a sin to enjoy Poppy like he was going to. He was surer of that than he was of anything.

The hard drive in his hands would be the only thing that they could use against him. And he had wiped it. It had taken the best part an hour. The program would have deleted and copied over the files, many times. An endless string of ones and zeros, erasing everything that had existed on there. Still, he thought: they must have programs themselves that can recover anything. The technology the authorities possessed had to be more complex than any offered by internet firms who purported to hide someone's identity or erase their tracks.

The answers on the internet were inconclusive to say the least. Some told that obliterating the drive via microwaves was the only sure way; others screamed warnings that doing something like that would cause a minor explosion. The latter seemed more likely, given his basic understanding of science. If the oven couldn't handle aluminium foil or plates with a gold edge, a laptop HDD would more than likely combust in a matter of seconds, maybe even harming the person who had put it inside. People had suggested taking a hammer to the thing, or unscrewing it, and burying the parts in far flung locations. His mind was a mess of conflicting options. He stared at the glass door of the oven again, hearing the ticking of an imaginary clock in his head, counting down the seconds. He had to act.

The sentences for possession were notoriously soft, according to the outraged headlines in the popular press. But it wasn't prison which was the real punishment. A reputation would be wiped out in an instant; a future destroyed by a lifetime on the register, and the constant fear of discovery, no matter where one moved to after release. For someone like him; a minor celebrity now, a major one in times past; the situation was even grimmer. Once a newspaper decided that he was a cause celebre (or its antithesis), there would be no let-up. No rest, hounded until he was dead. Thinking about it, he knew that death was preferable to that. He may have no longer been universally loved, but he had been- at one time. It was a high that was hard to get over once he had drifted into relative mediocrity as far as the public were concerned. If he were to become a national hate figure, for what was considered the most heinous of acts, he was almost certain that he would be responsible for his own death. Maybe even before there was a trial. Outside, a siren blared. Not anywhere near where he was, but his paranoia amplified it tenfold. The seconds before the noise faded away felt like years to him. A pressure pushed down on his shoulders, not unlike the feeling he used to get when having the first drink of the evening, years ago. He caught sight of himself in the glass- wide eyed, unkempt, and terrified. He pulled the door open and thrust the metal and plastic device inside onto the revolving plate. Slamming it shut, he selected 'Max', and held down the 'Up' button until the display read '5.00'. Taking a breath and holding it, he hit the start button, and turned quickly out of the room. It couldn't have been more than a minute before he heard the first sounds, other than the whirring of the machine itself. Kneeling on the back of the living room sofa, he peered through the serving hatch at the fire blazing behind the quickly blackening glass. When it was over, the kitchen was thick with black smoke, and the air smelled like tyres on a bonfire. It was a smell which evoked pleasant memories of his childhood; warm, unadulterated happiness, in a Sheffield which seemed a million miles away to him now. He used oven gloves to take out what was left of the drive, and put it in an old cloth rucksack. He needed to get out. He had Harry's address jotted down somewhere. The taxi firm took cards over the phone.

Eighteen

The walk back from the rubbish room was silent and tense, until Reinhart's mobile rang.

'Hallo? What is it?'

They kept walking, Bob's eyes straight ahead.

'Awake? Oh. Yes, she will be. The woman; the Polish. She is supposed to bring food- to wake the girl and give her this last dose.' A pause while he listened to the caller.

Bob had no idea which way to go, so he was hoping the Austrian was talking them in the right direction. He couldn't make out the words on the other end of the line, nor had he any desire to. He felt like he was done. The morning couldn't come soon enough.

'Well, yes. I mean, no- she can't be wake all the night. Let me… Let me think. I will think of something.'

Bob had gone from liking him to hating him again in less than an hour. He wasn't squeamish. He had seen things over the years that would make a mortician ill, but that wasn't the point. The woman had done relatively nothing wrong. There had been no need for her to die. He hated the sort of men who thought it was all right to hit a woman. Especially, like in Reinhart's case, ones who were physically huge. It was a coward's game, as far as Bob was concerned. He didn't hurt women or children. Everyone else could take their chances.

'Okay, left here,' said Reinhart, without looking at him.

'Rightio.'

'No. Left.'

'What? Oh I, never mind.'

They were back in the corridor where the girl's room was. There was someone else there. A younger man, dressed in what Bob would call an arty way. He had small round glasses, and was staring at the screen of a smartphone.

'Somersby…' Reinhart began.

'No names, pal,' said the new man, almost whispering, but angry with it.

'Pffft. It's too late for this. We are all friends here, am I right, my friend?' The question was directed at Bob, who gave a shrug of his shoulders, followed by a nod at Somersby.

'Fine.' Somersby took out a long cigarette from a silver case. White filter, probably menthol, Bob thought.

'What is going on then? With the madch- with the girl?' Reinhart motioned toward the locked door behind the younger man.

'Well, the long and the short of it… she's awake. She's very awake. Walking around, singing, creeping me out.'

'Creeping you? How is this?'

'She just… I don't know, man. She was looking into the camera. Like she knew it was there.'

'Which camera?'

'Ehhh, the lamp.'

'The light? Was the light on?'

'Er, no, actually. No, it wasn't.'

'Maybe she is just looking how to turn it on. What about the ceiling light? Why is this not on?'

'I, ah, turned it off a while ago. While she was sleeping.'

'I see. Okay, okay. We need again to give her the dose, yes? She is not to wake all night. She will not be good in the morning if this is. She will be not any use, no. To them. To you; you understand?'

Bob was listening while trying to appear uninterested. He hadn't wanted to know this Somersby's name; the less he knew about any of these people the better. He wondered what the Austrian meant. What were they going to do in the morning, he asked himself. It could be the drop off. That made him happy. The child would be away from all of this soon, and back with the people she loved. So would he, he reminded himself. It still didn't explain who the Somersby man was though, or what he had to do with it all. He continued listening.

'I get you. So, you gonna get the Polish girl to do it?'

Bob watched the Austrian carefully, wondering what would happen next.

'Ah, yes. Yes, this is a problem. She is… gone.'

'She went home? Before she finished the job? Jesus Christ. Har- the boss isn't going to like that.'

'Something like this, yes. No, no he will not. What do you think?'

'About what?'

'About what it is we will do?'

'I don't know, man. I mean… we can't let her see us, right?'

'No.'

Bob had a thought.

'What about the blue light? When she goes to the bog- to the loo?' That had been the plan when he got there.

'Yes! My mind is full of holes sometimes. The blue light, yes. I will go and get the food and a drink for her. You stay here.'

Somersby looked at him, surprised.

'What? Me too?'

'No. No, you go and see- you go and do your job, yeah?'

'Fair enough.' He gave a nod, and headed off in the opposite direction to the way they had come. Bob had no idea what the new man's job might be.

'I'll keep an eye,' he said, reaching towards the box of cigarettes.

'Good. I will be a short time,' said Reinhart, hurrying off toward wherever the food was.

Inside the pink room, Poppy stepped back from the door, rubbing her ear, which was sore from pressing it against the wood. The kidnappers had been outside, talking about her. And about Magda, she thought. *It must have been Magda; they said 'the Polish girl'*. Poppy's heart had sank when the foreign-sounding man had said Magda was gone. Then she reminded herself that maybe Magda wasn't one of the good people, and she felt a little better.

A lot of what they'd said had made little or no sense to her. Some of it scared her. Most of it scared her, but she was trying not to be scared. She had been singing old songs; ones she learned in nursery. They were the songs Alice sang with her when she woke up with nightmares. They made her feel okay then, and they seemed to be doing the same now. *Only for a little while though.* She didn't feel okay. She was afraid; more than she had ever been before.

They said there was a camera, and that it was in the lamp. She hadn't known anything about a camera. She had gone over to the lamp to turn it on, because the room had been dark, and she couldn't find a switch on the wall. When she was next to it, the lamp started making a strange noise. She stopped singing so she could hear it. Then she started again, because the noise had scared her. She didn't know why anyone would put a camera in a lamp. She didn't like thinking that people could see her; people from outside; kidnappers. That must have been the sort of camera the man meant, she reckoned. A video camera, but not like the one her father had-more like the ones at the house, that the security guards looked through, to see if there were burglars. There had been a mad woman once, but they had caught her and called the police.

She knew what a 'dose' meant. It was either when someone got sick, like 'a dose of the flu', or when they wanted to get well, 'a dose of Calpol'. She didn't think the men wanted her to be well. She wasn't even sick. A dose was drugs, and not all drugs were meant to good things. Her father took tablets sometimes to help him sleep. The dose the men wanted to give her would probably be like those tablets, she thought. They had been talking about her being awake. They wanted her to sleep. She wasn't going to take tablets for anyone. They couldn't make her. She had a plan.

Hansen looked at the fuel gauge again. He had miscalculated how much petrol there was in the tank, he told himself. There might have been enough in the tank to get him there, but after that, he wasn't sure. The Satnav told him he was close enough, but there was a filling station between where he was and Harry's place, and it was only a short detour from his route. He didn't know if it was intuition or paranoia, but the thought crossed his mind that he might need a full tank the next day, in order to get away from the place without having to stop. The inkling grew to a nagging feeling and then finally he stopped believing there was a choice in the matter. He ignored the voice from the box, telling him he had turned in the wrong direction, and in a minute or so, he was parked at the pumps of a small Shell garage.

Standing by the meter as the Mercedes drank its fill of premium unleaded, he looked across at the lit windows of the place where he would have to go and pay. There was no queue; just a few people idly picking out chocolate bars or crisps as they waited to be served. He was glad of that. He didn't like to stand around waiting for long in any circumstances, let alone ones where he had snorted the best part of two grammes, and had a dead child prostitute in the boot. He smirked at the ridiculousness of it all. The car was full, and he replaced the nozzle with some small difficulty. The simplest things sometimes seemed insanely complicated when he was in any sort of state, he found.

Inside, the boy on the till had paid him barely any notice, something for which he was again grateful. He spied some multipacks of gum on the counter, and thought of buying some, but decided against it when it felt like he would have to say any more words than:

'Number three, please.'

The boy gave him the smallest of looks then, probably because of the accent, but then returned to his apathetic chewing while he slid the PIN machine over to Bill. A panic came over him when he realised that he would have to recall the four digit number, and he took what seemed like ages to punch in the first number, which he knew without a doubt to be a seven. Pangs of relief seemed to pound in his chest when the display flashed the words 'PIN OK' at him, and asked him to remove his card.

Back on the road, he took it easier than before, aware that his destination was just minutes away. If what Harry had told him was correct, there would be two stages to getting in. The first was an automatic barrier, for which he had been given a key card. He assumed the rest of them had too. He was to leave the Mercedes in Goldman's private car park, then make his way on foot to the gate, which had a videophone that was manned by someone on the inside. A name would get him through, he had been told; Harry had given him a pseudonym which the guard would have on a list of people allowed access.

He left the car, somewhat reluctantly, in the underground brick bunker full of Bentleys, Rolls Royces and other luxury motors, most of which he assumed belonged to Goldman. He told himself that it would be safe from theft at least, if Harry was comfortable leaving his personal fleet there. Having it stolen would have been disastrous, he knew. Even the most unscrupulous thief might develop a conscience on discovering its awful cargo. He had unrolled her from the rug as he put her in. Then he laid it over her, and closed the boot. He pictured her face then, pretty and serene. Eyes shut as if she was merely napping. He had kept the coloured contact lens with him.

'Yeah? Who is it?' The voice on the other end was crackly. It was a one way system. Bill couldn't see the guard, but there were clear instructions on the wall for visitors to stand in front of the lens.

'Alan Marsdale.' Bill wondered where the name had come from. It seemed arbitrary, and probably was. He heard the camera whirr, and had a sudden panic about being recognised by the man on the other end. And also about being recorded. The latter seemed futile to worry about; Harry had his insurance policies, it seemed. There was a silence on the other end for a long time, which sent him into a paranoid panic about police, double-crossing, and every other possible worst case scenario, but eventually the gates buzzed open, and he was in.

The Harry Goldman he had dealings with did not seem like the man about whom he had heard so many tales from various mutual acquaintances. That Harry was a crime kingpin. An untouchable, who ran his empire in an organised, methodical fashion. The rumour was that none of his employees ever met him, save a handful of trusted ones at the top. And that, most of the time, the men who robbed banks, smuggled heroin, or extorted money from local businesses, had no idea that they were part of his organisation. That had been why it was impossible to pin anything on him; that, and the fact that he was known to have half of London's police and judges taking regular payments. That was the myth of Harry Goldman. A person didn't have to be that connected to have heard it.

The Harry Goldman he had encountered in the lead up to the Poppy Riley business couldn't have been more different. He made a personal visit to Bill's flat, before any of the fee had changed hands. Before that, everything had taken place online, via the secure site. Hansen's blood had run cold when the man and his two burly associates had turned up at the door. Harry hadn't discussed anything in front of the bodyguards, of course. Once alone, he told Bill that there was simply no other way to do it. He was asking for an enormous sum of money, and he knew that Bill or the others would never just wire it to his account without knowing whom they were dealing with. And it was true. Hansen had been excited about the idea when it was first suggested in the chat room, and when he discussed the plans in depth, most of him wanted to believe that it was real, and that it was possible. But it hadn't been until Harry Goldman had walked through his door that morning, that he stopped thinking the whole business was some high level police sting. Harry Goldman didn't do cameo appearances for the good guys, Bill knew. He owned the police, not the other way around.

Bill walked through the empty, high ceilinged hallway, his footsteps echoing. There was another door at the end, between two marble pillars. The place smelt more of money than taste, in his opinion. Alone, he felt suddenly nervous. He dipped into the small plastic bag which was open in his inside pocket, and rubbed a fingertip's worth of powder onto his gums. Ahead of him, the big engraved doors looked solid and immovable. He wonder if someone was going to come to meet him, and if so, when.

Rick had sat in the back of the taxi; he always used black cabs, and usually the same company. He never had the desire to swap small talk with the people whose job it was to ferry him about, and he wasn't about to break the habit of a lifetime. The drivers from this firm never attempted to strike up a conversation anyway; it was a classier outfit than most. They were used to celebrities, and they acted as such.

He had the rucksack with him; it had felt safer to take it. If the police were truly going to come for him, they would come to the house first, so he hadn't dared to leave it there. The rest of the laptop he had taken down to the basement and hidden beneath various boxes. That had been unnecessary, he supposed, because they were sure to search the whole place if they came. It would be useless to them without the drive, he thought. But he had stashed it anyway, regardless of the logic. The drive was still warm, and smelled bad, even through the thick cloth of the bag. He didn't have a plan for what to do with it, but he felt it was safer on his person than not.

He had given the driver the postcode, and the man hadn't so much as batted an eyelid. The part of Hampstead Heath that Harry Goldman lived in might have been exclusive in the eyes of someone who drove a minicab or worked in a supermarket, but it was probably a regular destination for the man in the front seat. TV stars, Hollywood actors, and rock stars were commonplace in that area. Rick had rented a spread there himself at one point, but that was in the eighties, before Harry Goldman would have been high enough up the ladder of organised crime to be able to afford it.

Harry had given them the option of coming in the morning or the evening before. It had seemed a strange addendum to the plan, but he explained that ideally, he wanted them all there on the Monday evening, in case the plans had to change suddenly, but one or two had said no, for reasons he hadn't revealed. There was relaxed element to the entire arrangement which made it seem slightly surreal, in Jarvis' opinion. What they were going to do was momentous and abhorrent in its nature; but at times it had felt like they were organising a fishing trip, or a stag weekend. The events of the past few hours had made him consider backing out, but he knew there would be no such option. They had all committed, and they knew too much. He had met Goldman, face to face. Rick assumed that whoever the others were, they'd had the same courtesy paid to them. It was less a courtesy and more insurance, he thought. Once he had known who he was dealing with, and everyone in London knew who Harry was, he knew he was in deep, and there would be no backing out. If the whispers were to be believed, Goldman didn't leave loose ends untied, and his attitude to liabilities was to deal with them in a swift and terminal manner, putting it politely. Jarvis shuddered, remembering a story he had heard about an incident which had been widely believed, although never proven, to be Goldman's doing. A low level employee of Harry's had somehow found out that the blackmail job he had been entrusted with- extortion of money from a secretly homosexual bishop- was at the behest of Goldman. Armed with this knowledge, the man had managed to contact Harry, and demand a large sum, in return for his not turning Supergrass for Scotland Yard. It was an astonishing display of naivety on his part. A few days after, police had found the blackmailer dead at his house, along with his wife and their four children. The pathologist's report showed that the children had died before the adults, in the same location. Each of the boys and girls had been subjected to horrific sexual assaults, along with torture that included cigarette burns to the eyes, castration, and acid burns. Harry had had someone rape and torture the children in front of their parents, before giving them a similar fate. The assailants had been found, weeks later; but, as was always the case, there was nothing to tie Goldman to it, besides hearsay and supposition. The only reason Jarvis knew the part about the bishop and the blackmail was because Harry had filled him in on those extra details, the day he came to his house.

The taxi stopped outside an enormous brick wall, with a reinforced steel barrier in its middle. Behind it, modern looking building rose up, most of it in darkness. Jarvis made the sign of the cross with his fingers.

'This is the place, sir. Are they expecting you, or do you want to use my phone?'

Paul settled back onto the pillows, the hair at the back of his neck wet with sweat. Tamara's head rested blissfully on his chest; never heavy, always fitting just right. The room smelt of them, and what they'd just done. He moved his fingers through her soft, golden hair, breathing in all of her different scents. He often forgot how perfect they could be together- how much he adored her, or how much he wanted her, in the moment. She had been perfect, whether taking the initiative or giving him the submission he craved from her. They never needed to talk during; so informed were they of each other's every want and desire. It had been like that from the start, but it had also grown better with the years. He could never imagine life without her, though they had their rows and fallings out. That was just marriage, he thought. Familiarity bred contempt as much as absence made the heart grow fonder. What mattered was how they were in moments like this. Moments when the rest of the world ceased to be.

He didn't want to go through with it. He hadn't known it before, but after what they had just done, there was no desire left in him for the following day. He didn't want to be what he had become. What he had with them, with her, was what was important. The other feelings could be bottled up; they could be extinguished, even. He had never harmed a child. If there was a God, and he was to die and be judged, his crimes would surely be forgiven, because they were crimes only in his mind. It was never too late to stop; everyone could be saved. That was what they had told him as a boy in church, before he had grown bored and left all of that behind.

He had to call Harry. The money wasn't a problem. It was already spent, as far as he was concerned. There would be no asking for a refund. Harry would understand; he might understand. All Paul would have to do was bring up the girls. Harry had children too; or a child. He never heard him talk about the boy, but he knew there was one. *More of a man now, but still his flesh and blood.* Harry could keep his money, and he and the others could do what they had planned to do, without Paul. Ideally, he would have liked to be able to stop it, but he told himself to be realistic. He had money, but power was another thing; Harry had all of that. No, he thought; the film would still be made, and the little girl's life would be ruined. But he wasn't going to be a part of it. It was time to draw a line under things and start again.

He looked down at his beautiful wife, and around at their perfect home. A happy life, a happy wife, and two amazing children. It was enough for anyone. He didn't need anything else, least of all what he had been about to do in Hampstead Heath the following day. He would make the call later. Not too late, but after Tamara had gone to sleep. Harry would understand. He would have to; there was no other choice for Paul.

Don cursed and put the phone down on the living room table. He is wife looked up from her crossword and gave him a look of concern.

'Is everything okay, love?'

He turned to her with anger still in his face, but softened immediately when he saw her expression.

'What? Oh, no it's fine. Just… work. Something at work. I'm fine.'

'You don't sound fine, love. Bloody work. You're supposed to be off, remember? I've a good mind to take that thing and hide it away.' She nodded at the mobile, smiling.

'Yeah. Yeah, I've have a mind to let you. Never mind, eh? Can't be helped.'

'Do you want to talk about it?'

'What? Oh, no. No, it's fine, love. Storm in a teacup, probably. Don't you worry. Listen, you still going to Martha's tomorrow? In the afternoon, I mean.'

'Ooh, yes. I am that. Looking forward to seeing her. Been ages since we had a good old catch up. You know me.'

'I do, I do. Good stuff. I've a few things to do meself anyway.' It had been nowhere near ages since she had seen the sister. It couldn't have been more than a fortnight, he thought. He didn't say as much; there was no point. Let her have her fun; it got her out of the house for a while, and it made her happy.

'Oh yeah? Anything interesting? Got yerself a fancywoman is it?'

'Hehe. You know I only have eyes for you, Princess.' He kissed her on top of the head. He had a lot of time for her, but he was glad she never wanted anything physical from him anymore. It had been years since he had felt anything in that way for her. That was marriage though, he thought. That was how it went.

'You old charmer, you. Watch your programme now. Unless you want to help me with 18 across?'

'What's the clue?'

'It's a cryptic one- "Exclaim at males, a sign of things to come?"- four letters. Second letter is M.' She looked hopefully at him, then back at the page, scrunching her forehead.

'Hmmmm. Ah, it's "Omen". Exclaim at males, right? That's "Oh men!" And an omen is a sign of things to come, isn't it? A good omen. Or a bad one.'

'You're too good at that, Don. I always said you were a genius, didn't I?'

'Did you?'

'I dunno. Maybe I did. I think I've called you a lot of things, in fairness.' She smiled, the crow's feet around her eyes making her look every day of her sixty three years.

'And I only deserved about half of them.' He looked down at the mobile as another text buzzed through.

'Make it three quarters and you'd be closer to the truth, my sweet.'

'Guilty as charged.'

'Go on with you. And leave that mobile alone. Take a night off, for once.'

'I will, I will. I promise. Just got to check this last one, okay?'

'Fine. Yeah, Omen is right. The O fits, cause 12 Down is "Pottering", I think.'

'Good stuff. Good stuff.' He picked up the Nokia from the table again, and tried not to look as angry as he was. They'd fluffed the sting on Jarvis. He was probably wiping everything from his computer and driving to a landfill with it as their texts went back and forth. That was the last they'd hear of him.

Something wasn't right. Alice felt something on her; someone on her. Heavy, pushing her down. It wasn't part of her dream, or vision, or whatever was happening inside her mind. She couldn't move, but she could feel, and she could smell. The beautiful warmth was gone; the invisible touch had stopped after a time, to be replaced by another feeling- a less soft, more intrusive one. She went from rolling through imaginary valleys of pleasure to feeling entered, and violated. That was the word for it- violation. Something was inside her, rough and probing. More than one thing; it felt like fingers as well, but there was no tenderness to their touch.

Her eyes were shut, and even if she could have opened them, the outside world seemed far away. There was more space between her and what lay beyond her closed lids. It felt like her mind had taken hundreds of steps back. Like her consciousness was mile away from whatever was in the room; from whoever was in the room. She couldn't move, but she could feel. She tried to come back- to take her thoughts forward towards where her earthly body lay, so that she could interpret the vague feelings of movement into a picture that her mind might recognise. It was too hard; she was lost somewhere inside herself, while her flesh was manipulated, twisted and hurt.

The smell was not what she associated with the feelings. It wasn't a Dylan smell. Whenever she had been with him, intimately, his personal scent had been intoxicating to her. Their chemistry had been the glue which held them fast, while other parts of their relationship crumbled around them. That was what had kept them together for so long- that inherent notion of Meant To Be. That feeling that who you were with was The One. Whatever force was there with her physical form at that moment had nothing to do with that though, or with him. She tried to unravel her thoughts long enough to place a face or a name to the perfumey scent in her nostrils, but it wasn't there yet. She felt her body twist and rock, as someone pushed into her- a different feeling to hands or fingers. All at once, her mind recognised what she felt. Someone was inside her, entering her, raping her. She took all her energy and tried to focus it on moving her limbs, but they were dead. The thought crossed her mind that maybe she was dead too. Maybe the impossible landscapes of dark-coloured nothing that her mind was swooping through were the contours of some afterlife. A heaven, where the mind went after the body had stopped living. Again and again the invisible figure pushed himself into her; the physical mechanics of it the same as what she knew sex to feel like, but resembling it in no other way. She tried to scream, but nothing came out. She pulled away and scrambled to safety, but all of it remained locked inside her. In the real world, her body was being used and defiled, and she could feel every violent stroke of him. His hands crushing the flesh of her arms; his breath, close by her face. If she was dead, then this could only be hell. Alice caught the scent of him once more, and this time she recognised it fully. Expensive aftershave; citrus and sandalwood.

She felt him leave her body again, and prayed it was over. She was moving again, this time it felt like spinning. The bridge between her mind and body was getting shorter; her awareness of what was happening, less clouded. A sharp, violent pain as he forced himself into her again, but this time it seemed to hurt immeasurably more. A different, harder, dryer pain. When she realised what it was, she willed her brain to step back again, far back from the Hell that existed in the room.

Reinhart set the tray down on the table in front of Bob. Before either of them could say anything, the Austrian's mobile rang.

'Yes? What? How can that be?' His other hand gripped the edge of the table, shaking it with his anger.

'Yes. Yes, but you said that she was awake. You said she was singing songs. How could she- Uhum. Yes, well... She still has to take the dose. It is not so simple as that. No. No, this is a different dose, as well as for sleeping. It is... it does different things. I have the instructions from him. She needs this.'

Bob sat, not knowing if he should be involved, or if he should ask what the problem was. He had sat patiently while the other man had gone to fetch food for the girl, which he now knew to be drugged. The blue light hadn't blinked once. He didn't know why they were drugging the child. He didn't know why the child was there in the first place. Kidnap and ransom had been his original thoughts, but no one had said anything specific. And he hadn't asked. He didn't want to ask, either. He didn't want to know.

'Well. Okay, well I will see. I will call him. I will tell you then.' Reinhart put the mobile back in his pocket, the call over. He looked at Bob, as if he was trying to decide something.

'You talked to the little girl, didn't you?'

'What? No, I never. I just-' Bob hesitated before lying himself into any more trouble. He had been stupid to answer her at the door that time, he thought. He had been told plainly what he could and couldn't do. He had messed up, clearly.

'Look, never mind what you were supposed to do. It's is fine. You did talk to her, yes? It is important. You will not be in trouble.'

Bob cleared his throat and took a deep breath. He should tell the truth, he decided, quickly. The truth might be the only thing that saved him.

'Well, yeah, okay. I did. I mean, she talked to me. I didn't say nothing about nothing, though. Just sort of... calmed her down. She was frightened, like. Least I reckoned she was. I'm sorry. I just... I didn't like her being scared. I mean, there ain't nothing bad gonna happen her. No point in terrifying the little mite, is there?'

'Yes, yes. Okay. I make this call.' He picked up the phone again, turning his back on Bob, who took another cigarette out of his box, and fumbled for his lighter with hands which were less than steady. The quiet sound of the other end ringing out went for a while, before Reinhart began to speak again.

'Hallo? Hallo, yes. It's me. Okay, no, everything is fine. There is just a small problem.' He paused while the other person spoke, then:

'No, no, no. Is nothing big. The child, she was awake. When- when he looked on the camera. Somersby, yes.

'Wide awake, walking around. Singing songs. Yes, I know.

'Well, yeah. Yeah, there was a problem with this. The Polish didn't bring.

'No, no, I know. I know, but she was-

'She was trouble. She argues about going home, and money, and I-

'Yes. Yes, I am sorry.

'Yes, yes. My fault. I just couldn't-

'Yes, well no. He looks again and now she is asleep again.

'This is what I say. No, I don't know why. She will not have this dose though. The one she needs... for tomorrow.

'But there is no one- we thought, your man here said we bring it in when she is in the toilet.

'Yes. Watch the blue light.

'No. She is asleep again.

'No. No, I don't think so.

'Him? But she will see...

'You do? Look, it is up to you. I just think-

'Yes. Understood. No, I know. You trust him. I just-

'Okay. Okay, sorry, Har- Boss.

'Okay, I will do.

'Yes. Straight away. After is done.

'I will. Okay, goodbye.'

Bob had only heard the one side, and he hadn't known who it was on the other end until Reinhart had said 'Boss'. The Austrian had turned to look at him a few times during the call, making him feel like he was being talked about, but his name hadn't been mentioned; at least, Reinhart hadn't mentioned it. The other man pulled out the second chair and sat down across from him.

'The boss, he says you will do it.' He shrugged, as if to imply that he wasn't fully behind the plan himself.

'Says I'll do what?' Bob didn't like his tone, but he couldn't work out exactly why.

'Bring the food. Wake the girl.'

'Oh, oh right. Me? Why me?' He was surprised, but not exactly flattered. It seemed like dirty work; someone else's dirty work. He should have been used to it by now, he thought, taking the balaclava down from the top of the fridge.

'He says he trusts you. No mask, though.' Reinhart put his hand on Bob's wrist.

'No mask? What bloody planet are you on, mate? I ain't letting her see me face. What do you take me for?' Bob had a sudden vision of an e-fit of his face, plastered across the front of every paper in the country.

'No mask. The boss says. Polish girl is gone. Little girl talked to you, yeah? She was okay talking to you? She liked you?'

'Well, I- I dunno if she liked me, mate. I just-'

'She didn't cry, or scream and shout? When you speak to her?'

'Well, no. No, she was all right. But I can't just go barging-'

'You'll go inside. You will be quick. The light is off, she will be just awake. She will hear your voice, you will be nice. You will tell her it is time for eating and a drink.'

'Look, mate. I weren't told nothing about anything other than guarding a door, yeah? Bring in the tray when she's locked in the bog, whatever. None about this. Let me speak to your gaffer.'

'That is not going to be possible. Look, you do this, he will be happy. What does he pay you today? Five thousand? I will talk to him. We will make it more.'

Bob stopped in his tracks. The extra money would be invaluable to him. He was still paying off loan sharks, and the rent was behind. Since he had lost the house a couple of years back, times had been tough. What did it matter if the girl saw him for a few seconds, in the dark?

'Okay. Okay, and you'll do that?' He considered demanding double, then quickly forgot the notion when he remembered what had happened to the Magda woman.

'I will. You have my promise.'

'My word.'

'What?'

'We say "You have my word", not "You have my promise".'

'I see, I see. Here, take the tray. I will open for you.'

'Who was that?' She had thrown on a silk baby doll when she had gone out to fix them more drinks. Harry hadn't moved from the bed; he was still naked.

'Business,' he said. The girl asked a lot of questions, he thought. But she had told him a lot about herself too, in the couple of hours which had passed. In addition to all of the chats they'd had online in the past.

'Well, obviously. What kind of business though, smartarse? Tomorrow business?' She came back in with fresh glasses for them, the rest of the bottle, and a miniature ice bucket.

'Tomorrow business, yep.' He looked at her as she climbed onto the mattress. He had always dreamed of finding a woman who understood his thing, and wouldn't be disgusted by it. Someone who got it, or even better, felt the same way. It had sounded like a pipe dream. He occasionally met 'women' who purported to be exactly that, on the internet. It was only the most naïve or fanciful person who would genuinely believe that those people were female though. It was all a fantasy, a role play. He had convinced himself that there were no real women who liked it; let alone a woman he would be attracted to in the flesh. Beth seemed to be all of those things. It was all he could do not to pinch himself.

'It's all still okay?'

'A few complications, but I think so, yeah.'

'The kid though, she's still okay?'

'Oh, the kid is fine. She's not the problem. Well, not really.'

'Good, good. I'm looking forward to meeting her.' She filled them both a glass with ice. The thought crossed his mind that her concern for Poppy wasn't in any way maternal or typical of a female. She wasn't worried if the child was traumatised or had been harmed. She was just checking that everything was still on schedule for the next day, with no hiccups. There was a callousness to it which might have horrified most men. Harry only found it intriguing. What else did she have up her sleeve, he wondered.

'Cheers.' He clinked his tumbler to hers and savoured the fragrance, before taking a sip.

'Who's Bob, then? And why do you trust him so much?' She slid in next to him, her proximity equal parts exciting and familiar to him.

'Jesus, Beth. You ask a lot of questions, dontcha? You sure you don't work for Scotland Yard? You have to tell me if you do, by the way. Them's the rules.'

'I'm just naturally curious, dear. And no, I'm not a police officer. Blue isn't my colour.'

'Oh, I dunno. I could see you in a lady copper's get-up, definitely.'

'Yeah. I don't think the uniform you're thinking of is regulation issue, Harry.'

'If only. I probably wouldn't mind getting nicked as much then.'

'Indeed. Bob, though. Come on, spill. You've heard my whole life story, practically. Your turn now.'

'Bob? Yeah, it's a long story.'

'I don't have anywhere to be…'

'Really? All right, fine. Bob is an old mate of mine, from back in the days. We used to be muscle for the same firm in the East End. Both worked our way up from running messages across town for Ronnie and Reggie. He was a top lad and no mistake, Bob.'

'Was?' Beth took a sip of her drink, with a slight shiver as the spirit went down.

'Well, I'm sure he still bloody is. I just meant when I knew him.'

'Wait, I don't understand. When you knew him? Don't you still know him?'

'I do. But he doesn't know that I do…'

'Okay, now you've lost me.' As she spoke, she glided her fingers absent-mindedly over the skin and hair on his thigh. It was a habit she had, he noticed.

'Yeah, like I said: it's a long story. Okay… so, as I was saying, me and Bob were tight as anything. We'd have done anything for each other, basically we were brothers. That was what it felt like anyway.'

'Uh-huh. Go on.'

'And we were like that for years. This was before I had my own firm, Beth. This was back in the-'

'Black and white days?'

'More like the Kodak days, yeah? We had a bit of pull, and we always got invited to be in on the top blags; but we weren't nobody as far as the big dogs were concerned.' He noticed his accent slipping into East London when he talked about the past like that. He never considered himself to have airs and graces until whenever he went back home.

'Sounds exciting and glamorous!'

'Pffft. Most of it wasn't. Smashing up the Penny Arcade because the gaffer wouldn't pay up, or kneecapping some Turkish boy for selling smack in the wrong part of Town. That was as glamorous as it got, sweetheart. Not quite James Bond.'

'I never liked James Bond. Scarface was my man.' She winked, giving his bare calf a squeeze.

'Good girl. Anyway, one day, I got off the wrong tube, up Elephant & Castle. Definitely not our patch, and definitely not a place I could be spotted in. I was pissed as a lord of course, reckoned I didn't give a monkey's. Anyway, long story short, I end up in a scrap with five wide boy geezers from another crew. Serious bastards, all of them. One of them reckoned I'd cut his brother a few weeks back, and he was fixing to return the favour, only in a more… intimate place.'

'Jesus Christ.'

'I know. So there's me, down a little alley behind the bingo hall of all places. Three of them holding me down, one spitting in my face, and having a few kicks. The other geezer, our boy with the brother, he's got his blade out, and he's sizing up my meat and two veg.'

'Jesus Christ, Harry! What happened then?'

'Well, and I don't know to this day how he knew to come there, I'm saying my prayers and thinking about living the rest of my life with my cock and balls in a jar, when round the corner comes a blue Escort, skidding and screeching like something out of The Sweeny. And I look up, and it's only bloody Bob, isn't it? He pushes open the door, and swings around with a sawn-off. He says a few words, and the boys do one sharpish, leaving me on the ground. Never been so happy to see his bald head, let me tell you.'

'Wow. Wow, so he saved your life? That's amazing.'

'Yeah. Yeah, my bloody angel sent from Heaven, I called him. My balls still try and climb back inside me whenever I tell the story. They remember.'

'Haha! Wait, though. I don't get it. How come you fell out? It wasn't over him coming to the rescue. It couldn't have been.'

'No. No, this was a week or so later. A week or so later, he probably wished he'd left me down the alley with those bloodthirsty pricks. Trust me. Okay, how do I put this?'

He sat and told her the story of the hit on the man who had the two daughters. The way he had taken them upstairs, pretending he was their father's friend. How he got them to undress, and to do things with him. And how, when his best friend Bob walked through the bedroom door (once again showing an uncanny knack for locating him), there had been no doubt what Harry had been up to with the children. Bob didn't say a word; he simply walked out. The next day, Harry had been unable to find a trace of him. Eventually, weeks later, someone told him that Bob had gone across Town, to join another firm. He hadn't given anyone a reason, or told any story. That was Bob all over, Harry had told her. He was no grass, and he never had been.

After a few years, Harry had lost track of his friend completely. A while back though, he had come across Bob's name, by chance, in a newspaper. It was in the court report section, although it had nothing to do with their line of work. It turned out Bob was in bad financial trouble, and had had his house repossessed. CCJ after CCJ piled on, and Harry had found out through his underworld contracts that Bob was into the loan sharks too, for stupid amounts of money, at interest rates so high, he would be dead before he paid it all off.

Harry knew Bob would never take a penny from him, and even an anonymous donation would be no good. Bob was the sort of character who, if he found cash in his letterbox or his bank account, would turn it over to the police, believing them to be the ones who put it there in the first place. He was as paranoid as he was loyal, Harry remembered. So Harry started hiring him for jobs. Small jobs, nothing dangerous, but paying well. Because of the nature of his operation, there was no chance of Bob finding out who his new boss was. It was the perfect arrangement.

He hadn't needed him for the Poppy job, but it was too good an opportunity to miss. Bob would easily accept five thousand for a kidnap job. Things had got a little complicated of course. But, if all went to plan and Bob walked into the room, showing his face, Harry could make a grand gesture and hand over ten or fifteen thousand for his extra trouble. That would write off Bob's debts with the loan sharks, the County Court; and maybe it might go some way to repaying Harry's own debt, to him.

Dylan walked quickly up the street from the train station, towards the pedestrian crossing that would take him onto Clarence Road. He had found a second wind from somewhere, when he realised he was getting near Alice's place. The drink had caught up with him on the second train, and he almost slept through his stop. It was only been the screaming of someone's baby in a buggy that made him open his eyes in time to make a dash for the closing doors.

The cafés and fruit sellers were all packed up for the night; it was late and dark. He never felt unsafe in this part of town, even though some people referred it as 'the murder mile'. There were council flats, and a lot of minorities, but he had been in much whiter parts of London and only felt half as comfortable. In the years he had been coming to see her, not one person had ever given him trouble; it didn't matter what colour they happened to be. He loved the diversity of the area: from the musical West Indian boys who hung around outside Aunty Fatty's Caribbean take-away, to the cheap and delicious Vietnamese food at the other end of town.

He had had so much time to think about her; about their thing, and what it meant to him. The talk with Derek had made him see some things from a different angle, and he had thought of some other things too, of his own volition. He had been selfish and stubborn about everything, only seeing things from his point of view. There were two of them involved, and he had to stop thinking of her as some sort of ogre. She loved him, that was never in doubt. And he loved her, but he had to think bigger than that. She had worked hard to get to where she was. He had seldom worked at all, and for that reason, had nothing to build a secure future on. He realised that it wasn't horrible or shallow of her to expect him to support himself, or to contribute to their life together. He was using words like 'love' and 'romance' to sidestep his responsibilities in life; he understood that, finally. She wasn't asking him to be a millionaire, or to buy her diamond necklaces. She just wanted to live life, and enjoy it. To travel and see the world, before she settled down to have children. All she was asking was that he make it so that he could join her; in both of those things.

He felt a little bad, but mostly he felt good. It was liberating to realise his mistakes, and to understand that it was possible to fix everything. He hadn't lost her. There was a chance. More than a chance. He just needed to see her, face to face. He would be calm, and let her talk. He would be understanding, and he wouldn't be defensive. He would be kind to her, and make her feel loved, rather than just insisting that she was, as he had done before. His heart was starting to swell, with excitement and anticipation. He had no dread in him for what was about to occur. That in itself was new.

As he came through the front gate to her block of flats, he noticed her lights were off. It was the bedroom at the front though, and she was probably still up. He tried to remember if she watched some TV programme late on a Monday, but nothing came to mind. He let himself in the front door of the flats, the outer and inner doors of where she lived. Three different keys, and he never failed to get them in the wrong order. No lights in the kitchen or the sitting room. He didn't have time to think or worry; the shot rang out from inside as he crossed the threshold into the hall. He grasped at his neck, where the pain was, before falling onto the tiles without a sound.

Nineteen

Poppy lay as still as she could under the duvet. If they thought she was asleep, they would go away, she thought. They wouldn't be outside her door, talking about her. They wouldn't be bringing her tablets, or injections. They could come in and try to wake her; she wouldn't open her eyes. They could grab her and shake her and shout her name, over and over, but they couldn't make her do things if she pretended that she was asleep. They couldn't see her anymore, because she had put the lamp into the closet. She hadn't liked the idea of them watching her like that. She didn't like people looking at her; even in school, or on the bus.

There was a noise behind her. She almost turned around, until she remembered her plan. It was the door; the one to outside, which had been locked. She had spoken to the man through it. He was nice, even though he was a kidnapper. They were all kidnappers, even Magda. She had to be, because she had been there in the room, and she hadn't looked scared, or said anything. She was one of them, a bad person. Poppy thought about Alice. She wasn't a kidnapper; that was why the kidnappers had come on a Monday. On any other day, Alice would have protected her. Magda hadn't protected her. Poppy wished her father had never got Magda to come. She wished Alice could have just kept on working Mondays, even if she did go crazy at the weekends.

The sound behind her was slow and quiet. Someone coming in, but trying not to make noise, she thought. They weren't doing a very good job. She wondered should she turn over. She could still pretend to be asleep. She could keep her eyes closed, until she was sure they weren't looking at her, then she might take a peek. She decided not to. She was too frightened. She had been frightened for a while. She had probably been frightened the first time she had woken up in the room, in the morning. Looking back, she knew that she had been. She ignored it though. She tried to take her mind off it, like Alice had taught her to. Alice showed her how to look on the bright side when she felt sad, how to make herself feel full of energy when she was tired, and how to think of other things whenever she was scared. Alice was full of things to teach her, and Poppy loved learning them. She wondered if the kidnappers had done something bad to Alice too.

Someone was near the bed. Poppy tensed up, and tried to close her eyes tighter that they already were, even though it was impossible. She heard a noise of something being put down somewhere, and the small clink of ice cubes in a glass. Footsteps on the floor, although they were getting quieter, so that meant whoever it were was going away. They were going away, which meant her plan was working. She heard them at the door again; they were leaving, and no one had tried to give her tablets. She had won. Then, she heard a voice.

'Treacle? All right, Poppy? Poppy, love. Time to wake up, yeah? Supper's there, babe. Wake up now, yeah?'

It was the cockney man. She suddenly didn't know what she should do. If she acted awake, he might try to give her the drugs. She was hungry though. But maybe it was a trick. Maybe they knew she was pretending to sleep, and the cockney man had come in to fool her into opening her eyes.

'Poppy… Poppy, you're okay, sweetheart. Eat yer food there, yeah? And have a drink. You can go have another kip then, yeah? I promise.'

She pretended to stir, and turned over in the bed to face him. She was good at acting. She went to drama classes. She had been in some adverts, and had had tiny parts in a few movies that her father had been in. She still didn't know if she should open her eyes.

'Poppy? Pop? That's it girl. Wake up now. Wake up and have yer grub, there's a good girl…'

She opened one eye, quickly, to see could she see him without him seeing her. He was looking straight at her though; she was caught in the act, as Alice would say.

'Oh, hello, love. Just brought ya some food. It's pasta and that. Smells delicious. I'll stick the light on for you. Where's yer lamp, eh?'

She didn't want to answer him. She didn't want to tell him where she had put it. She didn't want to tell him anything. She knew that in the films, people who had been kidnapped would scream and shout and ask where their husband was, or their mother and father. She was cleverer than that though. She didn't want them to know that she knew. If they didn't think she knew they were kidnappers, it would be easier for her to escape, she thought. If they thought she was afraid, or wanting to run, they would guard her even more closely. She was a smart girl. Hopefully she could be smarter than them. She would wait until she got her chance, and then she would take it.

'Not chatty any more, eh? That's all right, love. You just eat yer food, yeah? Dunno where yer bloody lamp is. Here, this'll be better.'

He must have found a switch on the wall for the overhead lights; she hadn't been able to, earlier. The bulbs on the ceiling began to warm up, and she saw his face for the first time. He looked like a Granddad, not like a kidnapper she thought. He only stayed another second or two, ducking out of the door before the lights got bright enough for her to see him properly. Once she was sure he was gone, she sat up and pulled the tray over to her on the bed. She had fooled them. They hadn't been able to give her any tablets or injections, and now she had her dinner, she thought, smiling to herself. They weren't as clever as she was after all. She had won. She took a forkful of penne, and washed it down with some cold pomegranate juice.

The phone rang out on the other end, until an error noise sounded. Paul hung up and tried again. This time, Harry picked up, after three or four rings.

'Yeah? Who's this?' He sounded out of breath to Paul.

'Uh, yeah, Harry mate? It's Paul? Paul Sykes.'

'Paul? Oh right, yeah. Paul. How's tricks, pal? You all ready to go for tomorrow? You know, I said to a couple of the others: it'd be better if you could come tonight. I'd much rather have you all there at mine, so we can go at any time in the morning. Feels a bit disorganised like this, but yeah. Any chance you can get over?'

'Ah, yeah, about that, Harry.' His voice had already started to wobble, he noticed. He took a drink of beer from the glass on the kitchen side.

'What about it?'

'I… think I'm gonna have to give it a miss, mate.'

'You what?'

'The thing, mate. I think I'm gonna have to- I don't fancy it no more, Harry.'

'You don't fancy it? Is this a wind-up, son?'

'No. No, it's not a wind-up, Harry. Look, if it's the money, you can keep it, mate. I ain't gonna miss it.'

'You bet your life I'm keeping it, mate.'

'Good, good. So we good? No hard feelings and all that jazz?'

'No, we bloody aren't good, mate. What do you take me for, a mug?'

'No, I- Harry, I ain't meant nothing by it. I just- it's just that- look, I ain't got the bottle for it no more, okay? I thought I did, and I ain't. And anyway, I've got me girls, you know? Me girls is- one of 'em is nearly the same age as- as her. It don't- it don't feel right no more. You know?'

'No, mate. I don't know. Now, listen here. You paid your money, right. And you made a deal. A commitment. To me, in good faith. So much good faith, that I came round your house and showed you my face, yeah? So, here's the thing. No one- and I mean no one, is backing out of this thing. When you're in, you're in. And that's the end of it. You know me, you know this is my gig. You think I can let you walk away knowing what you know? You think I came down in the last shower?'

'Harry, no, I- I mean, you can keep the money, mate, I-'

'I DON'T GIVE A MONKEY'S ABOUT THE MONEY, PAUL. I shit two million quid. What, you think you can buy and sell me now, cos you earn a bit of fold from kicking around a ball every weekend? You go call yourself a taxi, and you get over to my gaff, sharpish. Right now even. Understood?'

'But I, I- me girl, Harry. What about me girls?'

'Your girls? Lemme tell you about your girls, mate. Pretty little Colleen, and that little cutie pie, Charmaine, is it? You are gonna make your way over to the Heath in the next hour, or God help me, I am gonna end you. In ways that so painful, your tiny little uneducated mind couldn't even dream them up. And then I'm gonna have some big black Yardie boys from the estates come round yours and put that nice little bird of yours through her paces. They'll fix her up good and proper; one after the other, two or three at a time, in every hole she has, until I tell them to stop. If I tell them to stop. And Paul?'

'…yes, Harry.'

'When that's done, your little girls are going to star in their own movie, produced by and starring yours truly. And trust me, by the time I'm done with them, the Millie Frazer film and the Poppy one will look like the Sound of fucking Music compared to the Colleen And Charmaine Show. Are we understood now, Paul?'

'I... Yeah.'

'Yeah what?'

'Yeah, we're understood.'

'Good. I'll see you in around an hour.'

Rick recognised the other man in the hall. He had seen him on the television before. An American, although the name escaped him. Neither of them moved at first, when they spotted one another. Rick hadn't expected to meet anyone when he came through the door, save for Goldman. He had known there was going to be no anonymity between the participants. That much had been outlined to them all. The same as Harry coming to meet him before he had paid up, the plan was for all of them to know who the others were, that way there was no chance of the police receiving any anonymous tips later on. Rick had thought that the same could be said for a situation where none of them knew each other, but he hadn't said anything at the time. Harry knew what he was doing, and Rick felt that no one argued with the man, if they knew what was good for them. It was the American who spoke first.

'Hey. Hey, are you here for... Jesus Christ, man. You're... Yeah, you are, aren't you? This is fucking surreal.' He sniffed hard, then swallowed with a grimace. Jarvis noticed the eyes immediately; drugs of some sort, he figured. It had been a while, but he hadn't forgotten what 'wired' looked like.

'I guess so. Yeah. Bit like Big Brother, isn't it?' Jarvis wondered if they were going to be joined by the rest soon, before Harry showed his face.

'Big Brother? Oh, yeah. Haha. Yeah, kind of like that. Bill, by the way. If you didn't already know. And you're...' He looked like he was about to offer a hand, then changed his mind, rubbing it on his trouser leg instead. That was who he was, thought Rick. Bill Hansen.

'Rick,' said Jarvis. For the first time in as long as he could remember, he wanted a drink; a strong one. He stared at the door behind the American, willing it to open. Anything to break the tension. Hansen made him nervous. There was a bad energy around the man, he thought. The sooner they were no longer alone, the better.

'Yeah. Yeah, Rick Jarvis, man. From- this is out there, man. What a trip. So, yeah... What happens now, man?' Hansen was almost smiling. His eyes were bloodshot where they should have been white, and almost black where there should have been colour.

'I ah, I don't know. I suppose we just... wait?'

'Waiting, yeah. Never liked fucking waiting, you know what I mean? Here...' Hansen took a small plastic bag out of his pocket and offered it to Rick. It was half full of a white powder.

'Ah, no. No thank you. I, well, I don't...'

'You don't?'

'I don't.'

'What, ever? I though you rock stars were-'

'Anymore. I don't... anymore.' The American definitely knew who he was. Rick could have felt flattered, but the man was the right age to remember him. That was no compliment, other than maybe to the strength of Hansen's memory.

'Ah. Clean and sober. Yeah, I've been there man. It was... well, it was-'

'Boring?'

'So fucking boring, man. But hey... good for you.'

'Heh. Yeah. Good for me.'

He watched Hansen scoop some of the powder out with an uncut fingernail, then take it all up his nostril with one snort. Immediately, he regretted declining the offer.

'I, ah, I like my drugs, man. My PA, Liz, she's always like telling me to calm it down, or to stop it, or whatever, right?'

'Right.'

'Yeah, but I mean, she's not an artiste, like us. She doesn't get it, man. She doesn't understand that it's not… it's a good thing, you know? I mean, it can be bad, and you probably know that, man. I mean, if you're clean now, and all that jazz. But me, well, I just sort of work better with my buzz on. More alert, more creative. You're creative, right? Course you are, man. I remember that shit. I had your album when I was- I mean, well now… Well, look at us now. Look at us now, man.'

'Yeah. Yeah, I guess so.' Rick wanted him to stop talking. It didn't look likely though. He was in full narcotic flow.

'No, man. It's crazy shit. I was like… I dunno what age I was, and I had that album, right. I dunno what one. There was like, you guys on the front; the original line-up, yeah? And there's like four triangles?'

'History.'

'Yeah, man. Ancient history now, but I-'

'No. No, the album is called History…'

'What? Oh. Oh! Yeah, that's it, man. Hahaha! Jesus, sorry man. I'm a bit- I, anyway, yeah I've got that album. Played it all the time that one, awesome album, man.'

'Yeah… thanks.'

'Fucking A, man. That song… the long one, with the fucking orchestra and shit? Holy… Holy War? Fuck, man. That was my tune. That was my groove. Fucking amazing. You write that?'

'Yeah. Yeah, I… I wrote all of those.'

'Jesus, man. That was like- thanks, you know? Thanks for that shit, man, cos that whole jam… all of that disc, that got me through some real shit. You know? Some bad times. And some good times too, man. So thanks. Look at us now though. Fucking crazy, man.'

'Yeah. Crazy.' Jarvis looked at the door again. He thought he heard footsteps on the other side, and hoped it wasn't just wishful thinking.

'Yeah, Don?' Harry was in the back of the car, with Beth. Terry had stayed outside her flat, waiting. She had a private parking space, so he hadn't had to worry about meters or wardens.

'Harry. What's up?'

'Yeah, listen, there might be a change of plan, about tomorrow, mate.'

'Oh yeah? Something wrong?'

'No, no. Nothing wrong. Listen, can you make it tonight, or do you still have that shit in the morning?'

'Am, tonight? No, yeah, tomorrow's gone down the tubes, now you mention it. I can… I can probably do tonight. Have to run it by the old girl, but that's not gonna be a problem. What's happened?'

'Nothing's happened, Don. We're still on track. Everything's still go. I just… well, I don't know how early we're going to do this, and I'd just like-'

'Peace of mind?'

'Peace of mind, yeah. Something like that. I've already got the rest of them coming round, it's just you.'

'Well, yeah… yeah, why not. You there now?'

'Me? No, I'm on my way. Someone will let you in at the gate. Same plan as before. Use the name on the paper. I've got someone who'll let you through.' Harry had let most of the staff have the night and the next morning off. Somersby had hooked the gate camera up to his workstation; he would be acting as impromptu door security for the evening.

'Front gates, Geoff Harding, meet you on the inside then?'

'Well, yeah. You'll meet someone anyway. Mightn't be me, but it's all kosher.' Reinhart or Somersby would let them in.

'Kosher? Harry, I thought it was just going to be you and the others, yeah? Who else is going to be there? I can't be seen to be-'

'There isn't going to be anyone there who I don't trust, Don. It's me we're talking about here, yeah? Think about it.'

'Okay. I just don't want to end up-'

'It's fine. It's good. It's all under control. You know Reinhart, yeah?'

'Yeah, of course.'

'Well then, don't worry about it. He'll take care of you. All of you. I'll be around shortly.'

'Shortly?'

'Yeah. Soon as I can. Got a little business meeting first. You lot can get to know each other.'

'Yeah. Yeah, about that: do they have to know who I am, Harry? What I do?'

'Abso-bloody-lutely, pal. That was the deal.'

'Well, yeah, you said. But I mean, I'm not in this the same as they are… I'm-'

'Yeah, you're not, mate. For one thing, they're paying for the privilege of being there. You're getting a bloody freebie. So, for all I know, you could be working the job tonight.'

'Ah, Harry. Don't be like-'

'I'm just saying, Don. I'm putting a bit of faith in you here; do the same for me. Everyone meets, everyone know who does what, and whatever. That was the plan. That way you're all in, and there's no chance of-'

'Okay. Okay, but just them and Reinhart, right? Nobody else?'

'No one you'll have to meet.' He didn't mention Bob, because ideally, Bob would be gone before anything started to happen. He didn't want the man involved any more than he already had been. It had gone far enough already. Now the girl had seen him, and he her, it was going to be his old friend's last payday, regardless. Once the story broke and Poppy's face was in the papers, Bob would know that it was no kidnap and ransom job. No one in the press would know about the film, but eventually, when the girl wasn't returned, the old man would realise that he had been part of something much more sinister than he thought. And, when that happened, Harry knew the man wouldn't work for him again.

'Good. Good, cos I don't want any complications. I'll get a cab, cos I've had a few.'

'Good thinking. You don't want to go getting arrested, do you?'

'Haha. Nope. Wouldn't be the smartest move, Harry.'

When he put the phone away, Beth was looking at him, with no particular expression on her face. He wondered to himself if it had been wise to bring her along, but he was still ripe with drink, and thinking with other things than his brain. She had changed into different clothes, but she still looked amazing. He wondered was he deluding himself, thinking someone like her was interested in an old man like him, but it wouldn't have been the first time his money or power had got him a woman who looked like her. It wasn't what she looked like which was keeping his interest though. Not by itself. He spent countless nights getting to know her before he had seen what she looked like. He had been hooked on her long before that.

'So…?' She crossed and uncrossed her legs, giving him the briefest glimpse of stocking top. He felt a stirring, the memory of their earlier antics still fresh in his mind.

'So, I think that's that sorted. That other bloke, well… he got cold feet, I think. He's come around now though. Sorry you had to hear that, by the way.'

'The guy who wanted to pull out? When you said the thing about his girls?'

'Yeah. Yeah... look, sometimes I've got to be-'

'Oh no, I liked it. You're strong, Harry. Strong, and powerful, and you get what you want. It's good. I liked it. You did what you had to do...'

'I guess, yeah. I mean, it was talk, okay? I'm not a monster, you know? It's just threats. You have to make them every once in a while.'

'And, if they ignore the threats? You have to go through with it, right?'

'Right. I mean, usually it never comes to that, Beth.'

'But, if it did, you would?'

'If there was no other option, I wouldn't have a choice. That's how they judge you- the rest of them. You can't say it and then not do it. If I got a reputation for being soft-'

'Then you wouldn't have a reputation at all, right?'

'Exactly. It doesn't matter now. He's coming.'

'He is. Because he knows you meant it.'

'Something like that.'

'So, what now?'

'What do you mean?'

'You said you had a business meeting? Was that just...'

'Oh, no. No, I do. I have to see some people. It's to do with the girl. For after she- look, I'm telling you way too much already, yeah? I dunno if it's the booze or whatever, but you have a way of getting things out of me, Beth. You'd better not be a copper, yeah? Or I'll wring your bloody neck meself, yeah?'

'Ooh, kinky.'

'You're something else, you know that?'

'Oh, I know.'

Somersby had let the first two in through the gates, but he hadn't gone to meet them. Harry's text had said that they were all coming, within an hour or two. He had sent Reinhart down to open the doors, so he could stay at his monitors and let in whoever else came. The child had woken up and had her meal. The dose would kick in soon. It was a different sort to the others. Goldman's son had been in charge of the drugs. Harry had said that the boy had two loves: computers and chemistry. When his friends had been buying dubious pills in nightclubs in their teens, he had been making his own, with varying degrees of success. Most of the grey market chemicals floating around London, and currently being demonised by the tabloid press, had their roots in his personal lab. Once a successful formula had been discovered, it quickly acquired a street name, and he used Harry's connections to push it into the pubs and clubs around the city, and even farther afield.

The boy had become a self-made man in criminal terms at a much younger age than his father; and his expertise in computers and the internet were also useful. Harry had said that the son could hack or compromise any website, without exception. That was why he had trusted him with constructing the secure underground site which had made the Poppy Riley thing possible. No law enforcement agency possessed the tools to access or spy on their affairs. The main site was difficult enough to get to, so few people had the knowledge or the means. The boy would find most of the members himself, by frequenting dubious chat rooms, and fishing for clients. There were several different ways of monetising the thing. People who were serious about joining the exclusive underground site had to pay high subscriptions. Those who decided that they didn't want to, or changed their minds after subscribing, ended up paying even more, as the boy had written scripts that could remotely access their computers, permitting him to blackmail them. Anyone he suspected of being from an enforcement agency would have their hard drives destroyed in seconds by one of his specially tailored viruses.

The private rooms within were pretty much impenetrable. You needed a personal invitation from Goldman himself, and the willingness to part with a lot of money upfront. Everyone from their private server would be there tonight. Harry had paid them all personal visits, read them the riot act; nothing had been left to chance.

The computer made a familiar pinging sound, signalling that someone was using their key card to open the outer barrier. Somersby looked at the face in the screen- a white male, with a buzz cut and visible neck tattoos. It was the football player. The one who was going to need the cover up job.

Alice lay still, wanting to cry, but daring not to move. Whatever he had given her had almost passed through her, she was sure of it. If she had wanted to, she could have moved, but it felt safer to let him think she was still immobilised. She had seen any of it. All the time he had been on her and inside her, she had kept her eyes tightly shut; feeling everything, but showing nothing of it to him, or to anyone else who might have been watching. She was sure they had been alone in the room during the assault, but given his penchant for remote surveillance, the thought had crossed her mind that her ordeal may have been videotaped, either for some sick posterity, or worse, for the entertainment of a live audience. Her plight was nothing when she compared it to Poppy's now certain fate. Frank, or whoever he was, was one of them. He had been, all along. The whole thing had been a ruse, to keep her occupied; to get Tom's money, or both. The girl was still in the room, and she was far from safe.

She didn't know how much of the tale he had spun her had been true; and although she had a faint hope that the whole story about the proposed film, and everyone involved in it, was just another lie, she knew that it was just that: a hope. The other film had been real, and he had shown her and told her too much for him to let her walk out of there alive. She knew she had limited time. He had everything he needed from her; she had become dispensable. Her arms and legs tingle, she hoped it was a sign that they were beginning to become mobile again. She would get one chance, if any at all. She had to be ready to act. He hadn't killed her yet, but that might just mean that he needed to build up the courage to do it. He hadn't struck her as the violent type, but then that had been before she had woke to find him raping her. A voice broke her train of thought.

'Alice, Alice, Alice. You know, I'm kind of sorry that it has to end this way. I was getting fond of you. Is that disgusting? Am I disgusting? I probably am. Look, really, I didn't know how this was gonna go. I mean, I knew that if I wanted to get the money, you'd know where it was; I knew that you would be the one to get it for me. My Dad- oh, my father, he had other plans for you.'

She listened, unmoving. She wondered if she should open her eyes, or if that might end his little monologue, and hasten her death.

'That's why I came and got you, see? He had one of his louts go to your house for you. That's why I got in there first. He wasn't even going to kill you, Alice. Well, not to begin with. You were going to be his… Plan B. You know, just in case something happened with Magda. He figured he could grab you, take you over to the house, and use you to keep little one happy. And, of course, if anyone at the Riley house got a bit suspicious, he could get you to tell them that everything was okay.'

It sounded to Alice like most of his earlier story had been true. Poppy was still in danger. And she didn't know where the girl was, even if she could manage to get out of the room alive. She let him continue.

'He doesn't know I have you, of course. His guy is probably still at your place. Waiting for you to arrive. A tranquiliser dart. That's what he asked me to make. How bloody Eighties is that? I mixed him up some stuff, obviously. Dad gets what he asks, you know? Don't even know if the shit works, to be honest. I don't reckon he'll get to use it anyway, since you're here and not there. I'm good with drugs, see. You probably know that already though. You've been sampling the merchandise all day, truth be told. I don't even have a name yet for the stuff that was in your brandy. It's pretty cool though. Somewhere between a love drug and a proper trip out hippy one. Of course, the paralysis thing is more of a side effect. A handy one, to be honest. Oh, was that horrible of me again? I dunno, maybe it wasn't that handy. Maybe you'd have been a better fuck if you'd been able to struggle a bit.'

He ran his fingers from her chest down her stomach, past the navel. It was all she could do not to react; to move, and strike out at him. She knew she couldn't though; she stayed stiff and still, ignoring the instinct to roll away from his touch.

'No, I'm pretty proud of this one, in fairness. When I found you in the toilet, having a go at yourself like that… well, I knew it'd done the trick. Tut, tut, Alice. Poor little Poppy, alone and scared in her little pink room, about to have God knows what happen her; and there's you, like a bitch in heat, finger-fucking yourself in a strange man's toilet, not giving a shit. Bad Alice. Naughty, naughty Alice.'

He ran his fingers over her mons pubis, in soft, circular motions. She still ached from where he had violated her, both there and elsewhere. She tried to focus her rage. He was only one man. She would have a chance. Regardless of how physically bigger he was, there was no way he would be as motivated as she was; no way he could also have the intense hate in him which would drive her. She knew in that moment that only one of them would get out of there alive, and it gave her strength, as she felt the tingling in her limbs subside, the control return. It would have to be soon. He went on.

'But, yeah, anyway. None of that matters now, honey-bun. Much as it pains me… I mean, I wouldn't say no to another- but no. No, onwards and upwards. Time to go, Alice. Can't exactly bring you over to Daddy now. Don't want him finding out about that little nest egg you gave me. Always wants his cut, does Harry. Tight bastard. Don't worry. It's not going to hurt. Just a sharp scratch, as the nurses say. Then it's sleepy time, that's all. No guns, no knives. Not my style, that sort of thing. Never has been. I'll leave that sort of shit to Harry.'

She opened her eyes just in time to see him bring the syringe down toward her neck. He paused when he saw her, his own eyes suddenly wide with shock. Before he could say anything, the mobile in his pocket began to ring, distracting him for a half a second. It was all she needed. With all the strength she could muster, she brought her knees up to her chest and kicked out at him, knocking him from the bed. He, the syringe and the still-ringing phone went in opposite directions, causing him to let go a stream of expletives. He had sworn more in the past few minutes than he had in the entire day, she found herself noting. In a second, she was off the bed and upon him; her nails clawing at his face, with her mind on the hypodermic needle to her left.

'He's not picking up.' Harry hadn't heard from Frank all day, which wouldn't have been strange on any other occasion, but given the circumstances it had been odd. Something about it gave him a bad feeling.

'Who's that?'

'Oh, no one. It doesn't matter.' He hadn't talked to her about his son. There was a protective part of him which had felt it necessary to leave the boy out of any discussion of the plan. There was no real logic to it, as he hadalready hanged himself and all the others, if it did turn out that the woman's motives were something other than he had been led to believe.

'Oh right. The cloaks and the daggers again. I getcha.'

'Shush now. We're here.'

There were two ways into to his grounds. The main gate, where he had sent all the others, and which was attached to the bulk of the property, and the back entrance, which only he and Frank could use. There was no video gate or passkeys for the latter. The boy had put chips in both Bentleys, and some of his vans, which activated the heavy steel doors. There were three buildings at the back, which were accessible by the second entrance. Frank's flat, Harry's office, and what they called the HQ. The latter was where the Riley girl was being held. Harry used it for plenty of things, among them the intimidation and torture of his rivals. His boys would arrive in the blacked out van and do their nasty work on site, never knowing their location, or for whom they were working. Reinhart's was usually the only face they saw. They'd have no idea that the man who was masterminding everything was usually a few hundred feet away, sipping fine Scotch, and running his empire over the phone. A lot of them assumed that the Austrian was the brains of the operation, which suited Harry fine.

Paul took out the piece of paper and said the name in head a few times. The instructions had been to memorise it then burn it. He hadn't paid them any attention. It was just a random name, and it had come to the door in an envelope with nothing in it. His memory was as terrible as his maths, so he wasn't going to risk forgetting the only thing that would get him through.

The cab had left him outside the front gates, the driver had given a low whistle as they'd driven up the leafy approach. Paul had never been to Goldman's house before, but there wasn't any way that he was in the wrong place. It was a palace. He had given the driver a fifty pound cash tip, even though the fare had gone on his account. It had been a peaceful journey, for which he was thankful. Most taxi drivers tended to be either star struck by him, and spend the whole cab ride gushing; or, worse, armchair pundits who decided it was their job to critique his performances. The silence had been worth every penny, he thought, as the car departed.

He used the key card to raise the barrier and made his way on foot towards the main door. The place loomed over him in dark; it was modern, and full of sharp angles. There were scores of windows, but almost all of them were unlit. He thought about his own house, so big, with just the four of them rattling around in it, as he mother had put it. Harry had an even smaller family. Just him, and a son who may or may not have lived there; Paul imagined that a grown man whose father had such considerable wealth might be living it up in a place of his own, nearer the buzz of Central London. He knew that if it were him, that would be the case.

The strip lights in the car park lit up automatically as he walked through, his footsteps echoing through the vast, concrete space. Paul had never been a petrol head, but even he could appreciate the quality of the machines surrounding him. A badly parked blue Mercedes was the only thing which looked out of place there; too modern, too lacking in class, he thought.

He made the walk to the door deliberately long; telling himself that until he was inside the building; until he was face to face with the others, or the girl, it wasn't real. Harry had him by the balls, he knew. There was no backing out, and he should have known as much. He would have to go through with the thing. The excitement and adrenaline which had been present during the planning and the lead up were gone. In their place, a sense of dread and another of hopeless resignation. The thing he was fearing most was seeing Harry himself. Goldman could be charm personified when he wanted to, thought Paul; but he could be the devil incarnate if you got on the wrong side of him. Many people had, if the stories were true, and none of them had come out of the experience unscathed.

He was at the video console. All manner of ridiculous last-minute solutions ran through his head: he could pretend to have forgotten the name they'd given him; he could feign some sort of seizure. It was no use. He had to go in, and he had to do it. His only consolation was knowing that it would be completely against his will. He would at least have that; the knowledge that his conscience was partly clear. He wouldn't allow himself to enjoy it, even if he had to put on a show for the others and Goldman. If there was a God, and he doubted that very much, he would know that Paul was only there in body. His spirit would be far away, in agony. Taking out the crumpled sheet one last time, he mouthed the name to himself, and set it alight; the smell of burning paper took him back to some childhood memory he couldn't quite place.

Poppy felt sleepy again. The food had been good, even if her juice had tasted strange. She had climbed back into bed straight after, not needing the toilet yet. Her plan had been to pretend she was asleep. They came into her when she was asleep, or when she used the toilet. She knew that, because something would have always changed whenever she came back out, or she woke up. She had remembered hearing two of them talking once, although it might have been in a dream. She hadn't felt properly awake when it was happening. There had been a clicking sound too- one she half-recognised, but she wasn't sure what it had been. She couldn't remember what part of the day it had happened at either, especially not since the sleepy feeling had come over her.

It would be no good to fall asleep for real; her plan had been to pretend, so that they might talk again, and she could figure out what they were doing with her. It wasn't much of a plan, she thought; but knowing something was always better than knowing nothing, Alice always said. And, anyway, the locked door was the only way out. If she pretended to sleep, and they came into the room, they might leave it unlocked. There might be a chance for her to run and escape. She knew that it was a dangerous idea. If they caught her, and they probably might, they would be more careful with her. They might tie her up, or worse.

The pillow felt soft against her cheek, and her shoulders seemed like they were turning into jelly. There was a strange warm feeling in her stomach, and her privates felt tingly. It was a different sort of tingly from the feeling she got when she needed the toilet, she told herself. It was a new sort of feeling. She didn't like it, but she did. She couldn't make up her mind. She felt herself drifting into dreams, as he quilt and the mattress became softer and more comfortable, over and around her. She could have a small nap, she thought; just a short snooze. She could still have her plan. She could pretend to be asleep later; after she woke up.

Twenty

Alice wasn't as strong as him, especially with the drugs in her system. They wrestled on the floor, mostly him being the one overpowering her. He wasn't very coordinated, however. Any time he tried to pin her to the floor, she was able to kick out and unbalance him. They had moved and twisted across the floor so many times that she had no bearing as to where the needle was. She knew if he got it into his hands, she was dead.

'Stay still, you fucking-' He was on her, his knees digging into her upper arms; the weight of him holding her fast to the floor. With all of her strength, she tried to move him, but he was too heavy. She saw an unpleasant smile cross his face, as he realised she was helpless.

'Yeah. Yeah, you fucking little whore. Fight it. Go on. I like it when you fight.'

She looked up at him, her face contorted with rage. He was almost laughing at her. She wanted to tear out his heart, but she couldn't even manage to lift her arms from the ground.

'What did you think you were going to do? Kill me?' He looked down at her, his eyes looked black to her; evil, she thought. He was the definition of evil. She couldn't find words to answer him.

'Nothing to say? That's a shame.' He smiled again, then drew his hand back in a fist. Her instinct to protect her face was made powerless by his immobilising her arms. The first punch didn't connect properly, scraping her cheek and hitting her on the ear. It hurt, nonetheless. The second was on target. The flesh around her eye stung, and she closed it while he flailed at her face with clenched fists. She felt her skin tear, and her cheeks begin to swell. He was relentless, raining blow after blow onto her. She felt herself slipping away, as he smashed into her. Her bottom lip split, filling her mouth with the taste of blood. He was going to kill her if he carried on, she thought. He won't need the needle.

The beating seemed to last forever. He screamed obscenities at her throughout, laughing intermittently. Then, while she was still conscious enough to understand the significance of it, she felt the pressure leave her arms, as he stood up from her. Through swollen, half-shut eyes, she saw him lift a foot, ready to come down on her already battered skull. She had told herself earlier that she would only get one chance. She grabbed the bottom of his shoe and pushed upwards with all the strength she had left. The look on his face was one of complete shock and horror, as he fell backwards, cracking his skull on the mahogany dressing table behind. He was probably out cold by the time he hit the floor, but she took no chances. In two swift movements she grabbed the hypodermic syringe from the floor behind her, and drove it into his neck. Watching his face, she pushed down on the mechanism and filled his blood with the poison which had been meant for her.

'Ah, yes. One more for the party.' The man who had introduced himself as 'Reinhart' gestured towards the door at the other end of the corridor, the one where Bill had come in himself, and he and Jarvis turned to look. An athletic looking man came in slowly, looking at them all somewhat nervously.

'I know that dude,' whispered Bill. He felt excited, a mixture of the drugs and anticipation.

'Yeah. I do too,' said Jarvis. He looked tense to Bill. Like he needed something to loosen him up. He wasn't about to offer him any of his stash. *That's mine*, he told himself, watching the other man make his way up the hall. *Asshole can get his own.*

The third man, fourth including their host, didn't make any real eye contact with the rest, nor did he acknowledge them with a nod. No one went to shake his hand, or offer their name. It wasn't that kind of thing, Bill thought.

'Okay. Okay. One more is to come, but I take you to the room now,' said Reinhart. Bill wondered what he meant by 'the room'. Were they going to the girl already? To the pink bedroom he had seen on the feed?

They followed the big man through the doors, into the main building. Bill looked around, taking everything in. From the outside, it had looked sterile, almost like a factory. The interior couldn't have been more different. The floor was marble; black and white checks, like a vast chessboard. In front of them, dominating the room, was a wide staircase, with thick handrails of polished brass. The lighting was soft, compared to the harsh glare of the corridor outside. Faux candles flickers from mounts along the walls, and above them hung enormous, antique chandeliers.

'With me, this way, please.' The European man- Bill wasn't sure what nationality he was- took them up the stairs and around the corner into another hall. Large, sombre looking portraits were hung at intervals along the passages; their frames as bright and polished as the rails on either side of the marble steps they'd come up.

'And, here.' Reinhart opened a pair of tall oak doors and led them into what looked like a small function room; the sort people hired for a modest wedding reception. In the centre was a long banquet table, covered in plates of cold meats, vegetables and desserts. At one end was an assortment of wines, beers and spirits. On the opposite side, what looked at first to be bowls of sugar, until Bill realised with some glee what their actual contents were.

'Jesus, man. Harry knows how to lay on a spread, eh?' he said, looking to others for agreement, but getting only downturned faces and averted eyes from both. Paranoia spiked in him, momentarily; he wondered if he was making a fool of himself; if these people were shunning him because he was high, and talking gibberish. It passed as soon as it came. He was fine, he told himself. He was cool. *If these assholes want to act like it's a funeral, let 'em. I paid my fucking money. I'm gonna enjoy the shit out of this.*

'Okay. You eat, you drink. Whatever you like. Be at home. Harry will be here soon. I will go and see about some things.'

With that, he was gone again, and the room filled with silence and tension. No one moved for a few minutes, then Bill muttered 'Fuck it,' under his breath, and took a chicken leg from one of the plates, gnawing hungrily on it. The man he recognised as a football player found a seat, and sat down, his eyes glued to the screen of his smartphone. Jarvis walked to the far end of the table, took a glass, and poured himself what looked to Bill like at least a triple measure of Jack Daniel's. Without looking at either of them, he crossed himself once, and then emptied the glass in one go.

'That's the spirit, Ricky. Rock and roll, man,' said Bill, receiving the weakest of smiles from Jarvis in reply.

Harry's mobile rang as he was taking Beth through into the office. He made a gesture of apology and pointed to a seat for her.

'Yeah?'

'Harry, mate. It's Max.'

'Max. Where the bloody hell have you been?' The man Reinhart had sent to Hackney to pick up the girl hadn't been heard from since. Reinhart had said is much in a text, and hour before.

'What's wrong the other fella? Why ain't he answering his phone?'

'Reinhart? Nothing, far as I know. Been talking to me just fine, I-'

'Just went straight to voicemail for me. Anyway, never mind. What's the story with the girl?'

'What do you mean? Which girl?' He raised his eyebrows at Beth, shrugging his shoulders.

'The PA. Alice. Did you pick her up?'

'What? Isn't that what you were doing? That's why I- that's why you were there. What the hell happened?'

'Christ, where do I start, mate? Absolute bloody nightmare. She didn't- she ain't turned up. All day I was in there, watching the door like a hawk. Nothing, mate.'

'She wasn't there when you got in?'

'No, mate. There were no one here.'

'What about her car?'

'Still outside. I checked again when I left.'

'For Christ's sake.'

'Yeah. So that's why I thought there'd been a change of plan, you know?'

'Well… why didn't you call? You could have asked-'

'Well, yeah. Turns out the bird's flat's a dead zone for mobiles, mate. I ain't had a bar of signal all day in there. Walls must be made of bloody lead or something.'

'And you couldn't go outside?'

'Well, yeah, I… I mean, I'd found meself a nice little corner, with a view of the front door, you know. I didn't wanna get up and have her walk in on me. You know me, Harry. I like to do things the right way.'

'And this is the right way? No girl and no idea where she is?'

'No. No, mate, I know. It's all gone pear shaped. I'm sorry.'

There had always been a chance that the girl wouldn't be at home. She hadn't been a part of the plan until well into Monday afternoon. Frank had called him and suggested that instead of just taking the child, they could buy themselves some time by having the Polish woman tell Riley's people that she was taking her somewhere afterwards. He ha said that if they could get a hold of the other child minder, it would be possible to concoct an alibi which would give them hours. If they could convince Tom Riley's security that Poppy was staying the at the girl's flat in Hackney, no one would notice anything was amiss until Tuesday afternoon, when the girl didn't come home for the second day running. It was a good plan, if a bit short notice, Harry had though. The boy had his uses sometimes. He had been the one who did the research on the comings and goings at the Riley place. He had ways of finding things out which were beyond Harry's own skills.

The call had been made, and the people at the Riley house had said it was fine, but that they would call the Alice girl later, just as a precaution. That meant she had to be taken alive. They could make sure she received the phone call and said all the necessary; people became extremely co-operative when they had a gun to their heads, Harry knew from experience. The girl was missing though, and Riley's people had probably called her already. It wouldn't be long before the police were in full swing over the thing, and the morning papers would be full of the child's face. Harry cracked his knuckles.

'Okay. Okay, well I don't know. I mean, if she's gone out for the day… maybe- Max, this is a headache I didn't need.'

'I know, Boss. I know. I'm sorry. Listen, is the other thing still on?'

'What thing?'

'The little girl. Poppy, wasn't it? You got her, right?'

'Yeah. Yeah, I do.'

'Right, well at least there's that, yeah? You gonna give 'em a call? Ask for the money?'

'Hmm, yeah. Yeah, maybe.'

'Nice one. Her old man's worth a few quid, mate. He'll pay as well. He'll be able to afford it.'

No one outside of Harry, Reinhart and people from the site knew the real reason Harry had taken the girl. Max and Bob would be the only ones outside of that group to know that he had taken her at all. He kept the details of every job confined to separate groups of people. It meant if someone wanted to turn Supergrass on him, they'd only be able to testify about a fraction of the business he did. That was why Bob and Reinhart had never met before. And why Reinhart had no idea he was in the drugs trade; or Max that he was a child pornographer.

'Yeah. Yeah, here's hoping, anyway. Right, you're not still at hers?'

'No, mate. And, listen. There's something else I gotta tell ya.'

'Something else?'

'Yeah. Someone did come to the flat, but it weren't the girl.'

Don took a minicab; he got the number from a pile of cards on the table in the hall. He had told his wife work had called- there was something they need him for, and no one else would do. He would have to cut his leave short by a couple of days. She had taken the news with a resigned sigh, and asked him if he would be home later. He told her it might end up being an all nighter; he would call her in the morning, if that was the case.

Harry had seemed on edge to him. He had plenty of reason to be, Don supposed. But if could have been much worse. The plan, or what he knew of it, had gone almost without a hitch. There had been nothing on the news, and the people on his end knew nothing yet. If they had, he would have been told.

Goldman had put a lot of money in his pockets over the past seven years. It was costing the man increasingly more for Don to turn a blind eye, as his pornography side line grew larger. The films made in Hampstead were turning up all the time during Don's investigations and raids. Harry was paying him to make sure no connection was made between them, and that it didn't become common knowledge that the films were being produced domestically. That part was easy enough, he thought; the men in the videos seldom spoke, and the girls Goldman used were of varying nationalities. To the untrained eye, the differing décor and wall paint might suggest that none of the films were made in the same location, but Don knew otherwise. He just had to inject enough disinformation and deflection into the case files to ensure no one suspected that there was a cottage industry of child pornography flourishing in the capital, and even less that the man behind it was their most sought after and elusive scalp. As time went by, the risk got greater, and Don's pay packets reflected it.

The films were never pirated or copied; each one Don had recovered from his collars had been digitally watermarked, with a copy-protection that erased the original if someone attempted to make a duplicate. Pointing a video camera at the screen was also futile; someone had encrypted the digital files so that any third party copies would come out scrambled and useless. It was incredibly high tech, Don knew, and even he didn't fully understand the process. Harry's son Frank would have been the brains behind such measures, from what he knew of the boy.

Goldman hadn't said what was going to happen to the girl after they were done. Don had tried not to think about it. He knew that the Frazer girl had never been found, and that Harry had been behind her disappearance. The police presumed her to be dead, after seven years of no leads. He was aware that the Riley girl might suffer the same fate. It was even more likely, given how high profile the case was going to be, once it broke. The manhunt would be immense. The police were supposed to be unbiased and neutral, but when a famous person's child went missing, they had no choice but to double or triple their efforts, because the eyes of the press, and everyone in the country, would be on them. Poppy Riley probably already knew too much to be allowed to live, he told himself; even with all the precautions Harry had most likely taken.

Ransoming her was still an option, he thought; but, once the girl was home, and it emerged what they had done to her, the family would want blood. The heat might be too great, even for the normally unflappable Harry Goldman. His influence rarely spread outside of the capital, and when the Scotland Yard brought in help from Interpol and the American agencies, Harry would find out that there were some lawmen who couldn't be intimidated. Or bought, at any price.

Dylan hadn't been out for long, by his own estimation. Whatever they had shot him with had stung for a second or two, then overpowered him with a thick, chemical feeling which made him want to sleep. He had come to almost right away, it felt like to him, but he had no way of checking.

He was blindfolded, and his hands and feet had been tied. He had woken up in the dark, lying on his side; so he had at least been unconscious long enough for someone to do those things, he knew. He was moving, in a vehicle. The driver, or perhaps an accomplice, had made several phone calls. As the words made their way back to him from the front of the van or car, Dylan had lain frozen with terror, unable to believe what he was hearing.

The dart hadn't been meant for him; that was clear. Whomever had tied him up had been waiting in the flat for Alice; they hadn't expected anyone else to turn up, let alone someone with a key.

Even though the story playing out made him feel sick and want to shut his ears, he knew he had to listen. He had a small advantage in that his captor or captors assumed he was unconscious, so they were speaking freely. He knew that later on, if he managed to escape, he would be asked about details- names, places, etc. Whatever he managed to retain might be the difference between life and death for someone. He had seen enough films and TV shows to know that.

They had come for Alice, but they hadn't found her. From what Dylan could make out, she was still missing; no one else had managed to locate her. That was good, he told himself; that meant she was probably still alive. He was thankful too that he didn't know where she was; because, if it came down to it, they wouldn't be able to extract that information from him, even under duress. He shuddered at the thought of what they might do to make him talk.

They had Poppy. That was the worst part, for him. Someone had taken Tom's daughter, and Magda had been part of it all, it seemed. He felt horribly betrayed. He had liked the woman; he felt like they were friends. Now, it seemed, it had been all part of some horrible plan. Just an act.

One of the men the driver spoke to was called 'Harry'. He seemed to be the one in charge, from the tone the driver used. There was talk of a ransom, which was good news, he thought. That meant that she was also still alive. Tom had money; he would pay whatever they wanted, Dylan was sure.

The boss, Harry, wanted Dylan kept alive. That was also good news, although he didn't want to imagine what they wanted with him. He was hoping that it would just be to keep Poppy calm and happy, but he knew that there were much worse options.

From the second phone call, he learned that the driver was called 'Max'. The man on the other end was 'Ryan'. 'Ryan Hart', or something which sounded similar. They had also spoken about Alice, with more confirmation that no one on their side had her, or knew where she was. Dylan hoped she was with the police already, although from what he could gather, they didn't know Poppy had disappeared. Magda had been instrumental in that. Her supposed love affair with Ted, the head of Tom's security, had been part of the plan too. He felt bad, hearing about that. Ted's wife had died three years previously, and the Magda thing had made him seem like a whole new man, Dylan thought. Alice had been happy for him, joking about wedding bells whenever they met him at the house.

Dylan's side began to ache as vehicle picked up speed; each bump on the road smashing his shoulder and thigh against the cold metal floor.

Alice looked at his body, as it began to twitch and spasm. The knock to his head had put him out cold. The poison would kill him, surely, she thought. When, she couldn't be sure. There was a pair of scissors on the bedside dresser. She looked down at her naked lower half, her heart racing. He had used them to cut away her underwear.

The rest of her clothes were in a bundle on a chair; but the knickers lay at the end of the bed, in two parts, where he had sliced them apart. She had been unable to move, and he had removed everything else, so there had been no reason for the cutting, she thought. He had done that for reasons only he would know. She wondered if there was something ritualistic to it; if he had done the same thing to countless other women in the past. Looking at his helpless, dying form, she consoled herself with the knowledge that he would never do it again.

Pulling on her trousers and t-shirt, looked around for her trainers, finding them under the bed. Tying her laces, she kept her eyes on him. He was still breathing.

I could finish him off, right now. The thought came like a voice in her head. She looked at the scissors, then back at him. It would be simple enough; she could stab him anywhere: the throat, the stomach, the heart. It wouldn't matter. Without medical attention, he would be dead in minutes, she knew. It was easier to think about it than to do it. Whatever he had done to her, and whatever was to happen to Poppy, Alice wasn't a killer. She had never been a believer in An Eye for an Eye. She would roll her eyes every time she saw someone in a newspaper or on the web talk about bringing back hanging. There were other ways to punish people, she believed. She lived in a civilised society. And yet, when handed the opportunity to dish out what the papers liked to call 'Street Justice' to someone who had wronged her so horribly and so recently, she couldn't tell herself that she wasn't tempted.

He raped you. He was going to kill you. The voice was there again. She couldn't argue with those facts. It wasn't who she was though, she thought. When people on internet threads screamed about all the barbaric and medieval methods of torture they would mete out to child molesters and rapists, she would argue with them, not join in. She had always told herself that, even if something happened to her or a child of hers, her opinion would remain the same. She looked at the scissors again, and at the face which had lost all its enigmatic charm, and was now just a thing to be hated.

She suddenly thought of Poppy, and took herself out of the bedroom, to the room where the computers were. All of the screens were on, and the large centre one still had the feed from Poppy's room. Unable to see the child at first, she gasped with relief when she realised that the shape under the duvet was Tom's little girl, and that she was still moving and alive, even if Alice had no way of knowing that she was otherwise unharmed. She looked at the box on the wall in the pink room, wondering how much of his story had been true in that respect. It didn't matter; he was practically dead, and wouldn't be able to tell her anything; truth or lies. He was part of the gang who had taken her, of that she was certain. To where they had taken her, she still had no clues. Looking up at the screen, a sense of doom came over her, as she realised she might never find out where Poppy was, and that whatever was going to happen to the child, she might end up witnessing it, while powerless to intervene.

She didn't want that. She would turn the thing off, if it came to that, she told herself. She had to get out of his flat, and find out where she was. As she deliberated over which would be the safest route: out a window or through the garage, she remembered her phone, and suddenly everything didn't seem as lost. Why she hadn't thought of it before, she didn't know. But there would be no one to stop her calling the police this time.

Food was the furthest thing from Paul's mind. He didn't want alcohol either, but he knew it was going to be essential if he was to survive the ordeal. The man who had brought them through had not come back again, and the other two men were deep in conversation without him. He had no wish to join in with their talk, but he knew that the longer he left it, the harder it would be.

He had recognised them both, although the singer had looked much older than he did on album covers or in music videos; even the more recent ones. The American looked like himself, but his personality seemed poles apart from the jovial, family-friendly person he had been whenever Paul had seen him on television. There was a surreal air to everything which made it slightly easier to cope, but Paul knew that they hadn't assembled in Harry Goldman's house for some dinner party, or male bonding session. Every time his mind wandered to the child, and what was going to happen with her, he felt a deep pain in his chest, as if he was fourteen again, with a broken heart, from some now-forgotten girl he had an unrequited love for. He had always been too sensitive; it was something he had always had to hide, growing up on a rough council estate, and doing what he did for a living.

He had changed his mind. He had done the right thing, he thought. It was never too late to change, or to start again. He had always been told that. He thought about the pictures and videos he had seen over the years; the little girls outside the school; his own little Charmaine, in her pants and socks- it all seemed alien to him. He couldn't understand how he had ever had those thoughts. It was like something had come over him and pulled all of the badness out. He was cured, he thought. He was going to be a new man, and start again, once this thing was over, he told himself. He couldn't get out of it. Harry wasn't going to let him. *After this is over though, I'm gonna change.*

He didn't want to get up from the chair. He didn't want to talk to the other two. They weren't like him, he knew. They, especially the American, were there to do what they'd paid to do. The same as he had paid. The money meant nothing to him. It didn't matter how many months or years wages it was- he was young enough to earn that amount several times over, and he already had much more in savings and property. All that mattered to him was keeping the girls safe, and Tamara. Harry Goldman didn't make idle threats, everyone knew that. He would go through with it all, Paul was sure of it.

He watched the man he knew as Bill shift manically from one foot to the other, lost in a cocaine-fuelled rant. The other man, Jarvis, was mostly listening, and downing spirits as if they were water. A drink might help, he thought. Perhaps if he drank so much that he passed out, or was rendered impotent, he might be able to avoid his fate. He was sure Harry would see through the ruse and carry out his promised punishment regardless; but he got up anyway, and made his way to the bottles of spirits. The faces of Colleen, Charmaine and Tamara floated through his mind again, and the pain in his chest returned, this time more chronic than the last.

Bob's legs felt stiff. His arthritis had got worse over the past few years, and the doctor had told him that it would never get any better. He got up and took a walk down the empty corridor; he would be all right as long as he stayed in earshot, he told himself. The girl was fine.

The place felt empty. When they had taken the Polish girl down to what had turned out to be her death, they had passed no one on the way. There had been no sounds from behind any doors, and no signs of life anywhere. It had been the same on their way back.

He had assumed that he was in someone's home, to begin with. The more he saw of it, however, he guessed it was some sort of office building. It didn't have the feel of someone's house, their home. It was detached and sterile. That was probably why it felt so empty, he thought. Offices are supposed to buzz with activity and have people milling about. When they were empty, the silence was uncomfortable, almost sinister, in his opinion.

If it was an office, then everyone had been sent home for the day, that was for sure. And probably the next day too. He wondered if any of them would ever know that the place they drank coffee and chatted around the water cooler every day had been the scene of a kidnapping. He thought about the child, and about Reinhart and Somersby. There was definitely something off about it all, he knew. He feared the big Austrian more than he did the skinny, bohemian man with his round glasses and goatee beard; but neither of them were to be trusted. He had a nose for things like that, and it had never let him down in the past.

He doubled back and returned to his chair, unsure if the stroll had done more harm than good. Taking another 7-Up from the small fridge, he thought he heard a sound from inside the child's room. Holding his breath, he listened against the door. It was there again. No talking, but singing.

'Right. Anyway, what do you want to do?'

'What do you mean?' Beth was drinking a scotch from the bottle he kept for guests and clients. He had a better sort in the decanter which was only for him. It was the same in his legitimate offices, in Tottenham Court.

'Well, I've got a meeting in a few ticks, in here, actually. So you'll probably have to make yourself scarce for that, I'm afraid. So-'

'Bit late for meetings, isn't it?'

'Yeah. Yeah, too right it is. Not my fault, though. The bastards could only give me tonight, or tomorrow afternoon. And I'm, well…'

'Otherwise engaged.'

'Exactly. So, it's now or never with these pricks, and I need to see them, so…'

'So, what will I do?'

'You're gonna come meet the rest.'

'Oh, am I now?'

'Oh, yes. No time like the present, love. And anyway, they don't know you're coming, do they? I'll have to make the... introductions.'

'I'm fairly sure I already know one of them.'

'Christ. Yeah, so you do. Jesus, I'd forgotten about that.' He thought about Hansen, and reminded himself that the man was due some harsh words and harsher accents, once everything was done. He had more than one bone to pick with him.

'Yeah. He'll be... surprised to see me, don't you think?'

'Fuck him. The prick. I've a good mind to-'

'I'd rather not fuck him, to be honest. I'd rather not fuck any of them, regardless of who they are. That's not on the cards, right, Harry? I mean, I want to be in the- I want to be involved. But they're not going to think-'

'What? Christ, no. None of them pricks are getting a look-in. Do I look like the sharing type to you, Beth?'

'Haha! No, Harry. I think you're the sort of boy who likes to keep all of his toys to himself.'

'Too bloody right I do.'

'So there'll be no trouble, from them, I mean.'

'If there is, they'll be the first blokes in history to pay two million quid to be in a fucking snuff movie.'

'Two million? I thought Bill might have been exaggerating, Harry. He usually does. Two million? Each? Listen, I don't have that sort-'

'Don't be stupid. It's on me.'

'Oh, Harry, I couldn't...'

'You could, and you will. Come here.' He pulled her close, kissing her. He felt her soft flesh sink into him as he inhaled her perfume. The embrace seemed to last several minutes, and when it was done, he found himself pondering how small a sum two million pounds was, relatively speaking.

Poppy was fighting the sleep. Her body felt soft all over, like her bones were made of rubber. She was lying down, because it was difficult to sit up. She had started another song, thinking that the singing would keep her awake. It was the Twelve Days of Christmas, even though they were in the middle of summer.

Her head felt cloudy, and when she closed her eyes, she could see colours in the dark. Colours couldn't talk, she knew that; but every time she shut her eyes, it was like something was telling her to keep them shut. Alice had told her a story once, about mermaids who lived on jagged rocks. The mermaids were evil, and they made sailors crash their ships on the rocks, so that they would sink, and their crews would drown. They were called 'Sirens', and they would sing special, magical songs, which were like spells. The sailors would hear the singing, and be unable to do anything except steer their boats toward the beautiful noise. All sailors knew the stories about Sirens, Alice had said, but it didn't stop them following the music to their deaths. Poppy knew she didn't want to sleep, but every time she closed her eyes, it seemed like the colours were calling her to come with them, and where they were seemed like a nice place. Warm, and cosy; and full of nice dreams. She knew it was a trick though; she knew something bad would happen to her if he gave in to sleep.

She had to be cleverer than the sailors in the story, she thought. She had to stay away from the rocks. Her eyelids fluttered wildly and her breaths became long and deep, as she tried to remember what it was that came after 'five gold rings'. When she finally remembered 'six lords a leaping', she had tears in her eyes. She hadn't cried once, throughout the whole day. She could hold it off no longer though, and as she sang the verse all the way back to the partridge in a pear tree, she was as much wailing uncontrollably as she was singing.

She couldn't find the mobile, nor remember when she had it last. Her thoughts were confused, more than likely by whatever he had drugged her with. It reminded her of the feelings she had after smoking cannabis when she was younger; a sort of muddled thought process, where big ideas were easy to comprehend, but simple tasks seemed beyond her. It had never been her drug of choice; there was too much chance of losing control.

She checked the kitchen first, as it was nearest. Every cupboard and drawer; the worktops, the metal racks on which he hung his pots and pans. She even checked inside the microwave and the fridge. There was no phone. Cursing under her breath, she hurried into the living room.

The scene on the monitor stayed the same; no one came in or out of Poppy's room. Alice kept half an eye on the screen as she turned the place upside down, looking for the phone in places where she was sure that it couldn't be, but had to be checked, regardless. After lifting all the cushions and pulling out the sofa and the chairs, she sank to her knees in resignation. He must have hidden it, but where? She looked at the door which led to the small corridor, and out into the garage. She could leave, she thought. There would be phones elsewhere. She might even meet someone on the way who would lend her their mobile. She stopped then, suddenly aware that she had no clue where she was, or whether that first person she met would be a friend, or someone likely to kill her. She had no information as to where he had taken her, only that it hadn't been a long drive from the station. She could take his car, she thought, and drive to get help. She needed to get help, for Poppy.

A stirring on the monitor took her thoughts momentarily away from plans of escape. The child was tossing and turning. As she squinted at the screen to try and make out more, she spotted the cordless phone in the far corner of the room. How she had missed it while looking for the mobile, she would never know. She rushed across the floor, overcome with joy, relief and hope.

'Yeah, man. This is what it's all about, right? This is what you make that cash money for. Dolla dolla bill, y'all. Can't take it with ya.' Bill was holding court, standing while the other two sat. He had been doing all the talking, which was fine by him, because he was the only one with anything interesting to say. People always listened to him, he told himself. He had a magnetism.

"Fuckin' people, man. People are always coming out with shit, like… I wanna swim with the dolphins, or I wanna jump out of a plane… Or those other assholes, buying up stocks and shit. Fucking A, man. That's not living. Might as well be dead. This shit right here, though? Little fucking Poppy Riley? Sweet little bitch like that… man, when you ever gonna get to do something like that? This is the ultimate fucking buzz man; better than any fucking blow, anywhere. You know what I mean, Ricky, man. You've been there. You've done the whole thing; women, drugs, booze. You musta had every bitch and every line from here to Bogotá, man. In the fucking eighties, for sure…'

'Well, yeah, I- I mean, I don't- I did-'

The singer seemed incredibly drunk already to Bill. He had only seen him pour a few drinks, so he guessed it was lack of practice. The man had been dry for years. He was rusty.

'Yeah, you did. Probably got some young ass back then, too. Before people started getting all shitty about that shit. I know I did. People fuck little girls all the time, man.' He remembered the girl in the trunk, and immediately tried to forget her. That was a problem for tomorrow, when it was all over, he told himself. He looked at the football player, but couldn't make out what the expression on his face was. Not that Bill cared. He went on.

'But… but this girl, man. That's the ultimate fucking- that's the- the pinnacle. I might just have to blow my fucking brains out tomorrow, guys, after we do that little slut. Because I ain't ever gonna top that, man.

None of you are. That's the fucking prime cut, right there. She's gonna fucking- I'm gonna- Jesus, man. I can't put it into words. Come on, you guys understand, right?' He looked for their approval, or for anything.

'She's... she's very beautiful,' said Jarvis, finishing off his glass of whisky.

'Beautiful? Fucking hell, man. What are you gonna do, marry her? She's hot, is what she is. A fucking hot little bitch, who's gonna look even hotter when she's got my-'

'Stop it.' It was the footballer who spoke. Bill couldn't remember if the man had said a word up until that point.

'Stop what? What's wrong, soccer guy? You pussying out on us? No fucking matter, dude. More for me and Ricky here, am I right?'

'You ain't gotta talk about her like that, okay? It ain't right. That's someone's- she's someone's little girl.' He hadn't stood up, but Bill could feel the aggression coming off him like it was heat.

'Fuck yeah, she is. She's my little girl now, man. And I'm gonna be her fucking Daddy tomorrow. Fuck yeah, I am. Little fucking bitch won't be able to walk when I'm done with her. Little fucking whore; I'm gonna show her what Daddy likes.' Bill kept eye contact with the man who he knew as Paul, the cocaine filling him with a disproportionate amount of courage. The other man stood up, his face contorted with anger.

'Fuck you.'

'Fuck me? Fuck you, asshole. I don't have to listen to your white knight shit. Why the fuck are you even here? You paid your money, right? Same as me and Ricky. You're here for the show, like we are. What the fuck is your problem?'

'You're my problem,' said the footballer, jabbing him in the chest with a finger.

'I'm your fucking problem? Huh? Huh? You want a fucking problem man, I'll give you a fucking problem.'

'You will, mate, will you? Sit down before I sit you down, you prick.' He prodded Bill in the chest a second time, almost knocking him over with the force of it.

'Okay, asshole. How about this?' Bill pulled the revolver out of his waistband and put the barrel in Paul's face. The footballer when immediately ashen, and started to step backwards slowly.

'Jesus Christ, hey. Okay, mate. Calm down.'

Bill could see him shaking. The power was exhilarating. He had brought the weapon in with him from the glove compartment, when he parked the Mercedes earlier.

'I'm calm as an ocean, baby. Now, what was that about you making me sit down?'

'Bill, Jesus Christ… put it away.' It was Jarvis who spoke, reaching a hand out towards his wrist.

'Keep out of it, asshole. This is between me and Pauly.' Bill kept the pistol trained on the other man's face, turning to look at Jarvis when he addressed him. He suddenly felt a sharp pain between his thumb and forefinger, and the gun dropped to the floor with a clatter. Before he could react, the football player had stooped to pick it up, pointing it back at him. Bill felt the contents of his stomach dive downward, and his mouth become incredibly dry.

'Right, so. Little one is here, Mum and Dad none the wiser, but no Alice?' Don and Reinhart were walking up the staircase. He had never been to Harry's home before, just to the office in town, and the ones at the back of the grounds.

'Yes, that is all of it. No girl. She was not where she is supposed to be, and now… we don't know.'

'So she's just loose? Does she know?'

'We don't know. We are looking, but-'

'But she'll probably find the cops before you find her, yeah?' Don knew that she hadn't been in contact with the police yet; someone would have told him.

'Yes. It is a small problem. Maybe they will find out sooner now. She is not most important, though. We have the child; the girl does not matter.'

'If you say so, mate.' He wondered how much of it was true, and how much was Reinhart's stubborn unwillingness to admit that he was at fault.

'I do.'

They were at the door; Reinhart opened it, and went inside first. After taking in the splendour of the room, and looking wide-eyed at the spread which had been laid on for them by Goldman, Don's looked at the three men who were already there. A premiership footballer whose name escaped him, pointing a pistol at a second man. The man in the line of fire, he recognised as the American TV presenter, Bill Hansen. The third man was backing away from the scene, towards him and Reinhart. His face wasn't visible to Don. As the Austrian rushed to intervene, the other man turned to face him; his skin pale, eyes bloodshot.

'Fucking hell, it's a small world,' said Don, quietly. Jarvis made a noise of drunken confusion by way of reply, then turned back to watch Reinhart calmly disarm the footballer, and read the riot act to the other two, the loaded pistol still in his hand.

Somersby had asked them to come to the video room, where he was remotely manning the gate, while getting on with this preparation for the following day. Harry took Beth through a side door, avoiding the side of the building where he knew Bob would be. *It'll be time to send the old boy home soon*, he thought.

'Ian.'

The room was dull, apart from the glow of several monitors. On the main screen, Poppy's sleeping form lay huddled under a duvet. Beth looked at the little girl with a smile that was anything but maternal, he noted. He wasn't quite sure how it made him feel.

'Harry. And?'

'This is… this is Beth. Beth, Ian Somersby. Our… director. For tomorrow.' He hesitated about using her real name, but then decided that she shouldn't be treated any different to the rest.

'Yeah, it is. Nice to meet you, Ian. I like your films. You have a… pretty mind. You make beautiful things.'

'Thank you… Beth. Always nice to meet a-'

'How's she been?' Harry interrupted him, remembering how little time there was before his meeting, and how many things still needed to be done.

'Poppy? Well… she ate the food, and drank the drink, but…'

'But?'

'She's not sleeping.'

'She's what? But Frank said- look, that dose should have knocked her for six, mate. That was the last one, til the morning. She should be conked.'

'I know, I know. Trust me, I know. But here, listen.' He plugged his headphones out of the jack and turned the volume knob on the external speakers. They listened, holding their breath. Someone was singing. A child's voice, delicate and soft, in between sniffles and sobs.

how I wonder what you are…

'I don't get it; is she doing it in her sleep? Singing, I mean. Frank, when he was a kid, he used to talk in his-'

up above the world so high…

'I did too. I never remembered it, but my father would tell me in the morning,' said Beth, resting her hand on his back.

like a diamond in the sky…

'No, she's not asleep. Here let me-' Somersby pushed a button on the keyboard and the camera angle changed.

twinkle twinkle, lit-tle star...

'Jesus Christ...' said Harry.

'I know,' replied Somersby, stepping back from the monitor. All three looked at the new image on screen. A close up of the child's face, from the side camera, made all the more sinister by the green glow from the night vision. Her eyes were wide and staring, their colours inverted by the low light filter. Her face was stained from tears and a running nose; her mouth moving half a second out of synch with the sound coming over the speakers.

how I. won-der. what you. are...

Twenty One

'Hello, emergency services. Which number do you require, please?'

'Oh, God. Oh, thank God. Yes. Yes, police, please. Quickly!' Alice didn't know who it was that dealt with things like kidnappings. She assumed it would be Scotland Yard, but if she was honest with herself, she didn't really know what Scotland Yard was.

'Hello, Metropolitan Police. What can I-'

'A kidnapping. There's been a kidnapping. Please. You have to help me. They have my- they have her. I don't know where they-'

'Sorry? Hello? Hello, okay. I need you to slow down for me please, madam.'

'Yes. Yes, sorry. I just- I'm sorry. I just-'

'Can I have your name please, madam?'

'My what? My name. My name, yes. Yes, it's Alice-' She struggled to remember her surname. She was on the floor. All of her was aching.

'Martin,' she said, finally.

'Okay, Alice. Thank you. We're going to do everything we can for you. I just need you to be calm for me, and to tell me everything. Okay?'

'Okay.'

'Now, your child; what is her name?'

'Poppy. Poppy Riley. I mean, she's not my child, she's-' The phone call was going differently to how she had imagined it would, although she wasn't sure how she had imagined it.

'Okay, Alice. What relation to the child are you? Aunt? Sister?'

'I'm no- I look after her. After Poppy. I'm her- I work for her father.'

'Okay. Okay, so you're the child minder; is that right?'

'Yes. I mean, no. I mean, I don't know. I work for her father- for Tom.'

'Okay, Alice. Is Tom with you? Can we speak to him?'

'No. No, he's... he's out of the country.'

'The mother?'

'I don't know.' That was the truth, she thought. The woman on the other end was wasting time. She had to make it go faster.

'Okay, okay. Now, when did you last see the child, Alice?'

'Last see... last see... what day is- Friday.'

'Friday? Three days ago? And you're just reporting her-'

'No! I mean, yes. I don't- I don't work weekends, or Mondays. I saw her on Friday, but she-'

'So, she's been missing since Friday, and-'

'No. No, she's been missing since this morning. Look, I-'

'I thought you said you saw her last on-'

'Look! I don't know how to explain it, okay. Just f- just listen to me, for two seconds. Please!' Alice thought she heard a sound somewhere; outside, or in the other room. She dismissed it.

'Okay. Okay, Alice. Talk to me.'

'Thank you! Look, I don't know where to start...'

'Start at the beginning.'

'All right. I'll try. I got... I got a phone call today, from a man. He told me that someone had Poppy, and that he was going to help get her back...'

'This man, he's the one who has the child?'

'No. I mean, maybe. He- he tricked me. Lied to me. It's not important. He's-' She paused, wondering how much she should say.

'Okay. Okay, what else did he say; this man?'

'He made me get out of the flat. And onto a train. Then he came and met me.'

'You've met the kidnapper?'

'Yes. No, I mean. I don't know if he is. Look, they still have her. I can see her.'

'You can see her?'

'I can- yes, she's not here, but I can see her. On a screen.'

'On a screen.'

'Yes. These people; the ones who have her. They are going to do something bad to her. You have to help me. I don't know where they have her- I don't even know where I am right now- I just- I need your help. Please. Please, help me.'

'Okay, Alice. Listen to me. I need to talk to my colleague, but I'm going to come straight-'

'No! No, don't put me on hold. Please! There isn't time! You have to believe me. They're going to rape-'

The woman's voice was replaced by tinny sounding classical music. She thought it might be Vivaldi. One of the Four Seasons, although she wouldn't have known which. When she looked up and saw Frank coming towards her, it almost didn't register at first. There wasn't time to scream. He sank the sharp end of the dressmaker's scissors into her eye socket, with a horrific, almost cartoonish squelching noise. She fell backwards, dropping the phone, the sound of Vivaldi becoming quieter as the handset rolled away from her across the floor.

'Gentlemen! I see you're all getting to know each other…' Harry felt the tension at once when he came through the doors into the banquet room. He looked around, and saw Don and the singer sitting at one end of the table, both silent. Opposite them, Hansen and Reinhart were deep in conversation; the American looked panicked and sweaty; the Austrian serious and intense. His hand was on Bill's shoulder in a manner which seemed less than friendly to Goldman. Seeing him, Hansen turned around excitedly.

'Harry, man! The man himself! Master of ceremonies; the head honcho; the big cheese! Liz? What the fuck?' His face lost any colour it still had when he spotted the woman to Goldman's right. Harry chuckled. He had forgotten for a second that they knew one another. It had been Hansen's loose mouth which had led Beth to the website and into Harry's life. He still wasn't sure if he should thank him for it, or have him killed.

'William. You seem… the same as ever.'

'Jeez, Liz. Good to see ya! You didn't tell me you- how do you know Harry? This is a trip, man. A fucking trip.'

'What the hell is this, Harry? Who is she? You didn't tell us anything about-' Jarvis was drunk, which surprised him. He had been reliably informed the man was teetotal, because of his new Mormon faith.

'Settle down, Rick. This is still my game. I get to decide who plays. You got a problem with that?'

'Well, no… I. I just- she's going to play? You mean-'

'Beth, this is Rick Jarvis. Rick, Beth.'

'Yes. I remember. No Escape, that was a good record.' Beth smiled at the singer. Harry noticed Reinhart get up, slap Hansen on the shoulder, and come across the room towards them.

'Thanks. Thanks… Beth. So, you're gonna be-'

'Beth will be joining us tomorrow, as long as none of you have any objections. If you do have any objections, mind, you can stick 'em. My house, my rules.' Harry took out a cigar; it seemed like it had been hours since he had smoked.

'You? You're gonna be- Poppy? Jeez, Liz. Why didn't you tell me this shit before? We could have had some awesome fun, man. Awesome fun.' Hansen dipped a wet finger into one of the bowls of power on the table, and rubbed it onto his gums.

'Heaven knows, Bill. What with you been such a discreet chap…' She leaned closer into Harry, a hand around his waist.

'What? I'm a- oh.' Hansen's eyes dropped, the realisation finally dawning that Harry knew he had been talking when he shouldn't.

'There's six of us now? Wait, seven of us, and that little- Jesus.' It was the first time Paul had spoken since they'd arrived, Harry noted. He looked crestfallen. Harry remembered their earlier conversation.

'Yeah, seven. More the merrier, right Paul?' He gave the footballer a menacing stare. Paul said nothing in reply, instead taking another gulp from the bottle of vodka. Don spoke next.

'Harry. Good to see you, mate.'

'All right, Don? Everyone, this is Don. He's the head of the child protection unit over at Scotland Yard, but don't worry- he's not here to slap the cuffs on you lot. Not if you behave yourselves, anyhow.' He noticed Don's face drop for a second, then it was gone again.

'Uh, yeah. S'pose it's only fair, if I know who you lot are, eh?'

'That's the spirit, Sergeant. Anyway, I have to go see a man about a dog. I'll leave Beth here to get acquainted with you lot. And no funny business, right? Cos I'll know. I'm looking at you, Bill. I'll know.'

'What? Aw, hell no, Harry. Liz and me, we go way back.'

'Yeah. I've heard. Anyway, help yourselves to food and drink and whatever. I'll be finished in about an hour. Then we can all have a nice chat, eh?'

They all nodded in acknowledgement, even Paul. Beth had her back to him, at the buffet table. He waited a few seconds for her to turn around, and then headed back into the house. The Albanians would be on time. He had never known them not to be.

Somersby read back through the notes he had made, wondering to himself if all of it might be for nothing. It was all very well Goldman hiring him for the job on his credentials, he thought, but he wasn't a pornographer. His films were art, not exploitation, regardless of what some critics said. Pornography was, to him, a low medium. Especially the modern sort. Perhaps if it had been the 1970s, when there was a sort of Golden Age, and people lined up outside cinemas to see films like Behind the Green Door, or Deep Throat, it might have been considered an art form. The advent of the internet and digital cameras had changed all that, in his opinion. The only thing which had improved was the standards of beauty in the girls, as social stigmas were lifted, and the cult of celebrity had become widespread. People would do anything to achieve fame nowadays, he thought, aware that one of his jobs in post production would be to ensure that none of the participants in the film could be recognised; apart from his leading lady.

On the security screen, the outer gate was opening. One black, four door car, followed by an identical one. *Harry's meeting,* he thought, forgetting his notes for a moment. He had also been told to expect a van, but Goldman hadn't said which party would arrive first. He didn't know who the people in the cars were, nor did he want to. The less he knew about Harry's affairs, the better, he thought.

Both cars found spaces among Harry's luxury fleet, and he saw the front and back doors of the first opening at the same time. Some men, dressed similarly in black leather jackets and nondescript denim, got out. The ones from the rear doors both holding the leashes of some vicious looking attack dogs. They looked like gangsters to him, and not local, at least in terms of their nationality. One man, without a dog, approached the video phone and his face appeared large on the other monitor.

'Hello?' The accent was foreign; eastern European, Somersby guessed, although he looked Turkish.

'Hello. Name?' He looked down at the list, the names on which had been almost all crossed off.

'George Ramsden,' came the heavily accented reply. The man's facial expression was constant, giving nothing away. *He looks like a killer,* Somersby thought, although he had no frame of reference for the comparison. He buzzed the gate open, and rather than coming through, the man stayed where he was; holding it open for the others.

In the main CCTV feed, something was happening. The dogs were barking and snarling at something unseen; their handlers struggling to hold onto the chains. One man shouted to the handler of the large Rottweiler, who let the leash go slack, and followed to where the big dog led. Behind them, the barrier lifted and a van came through into the garage. Black, with a dark tint over the few windows it had. *That's Max,* he thought. There was no codename protocol for the man driving the van; he had been a late addition to the plan, if he was part of it at all.

Elsewhere on the screen, the men and dogs had grouped around a blue Mercedes; Somersby knew it, it was Hansen's. He watched as passions rose; the men were shouting at one another, but he could make out no hierarchy of command. No one seemed to be in charge. The dogs were even more agitated; he could hear their growls through the video phone mic, all the way across the car park. Something was very wrong, he knew. His hand reached for the phone on the desk. The other car had emptied too, four other men joining the group, although there were no more dogs. In the background, Max's van found a space to park.

Of the men from the second car, one looked markedly different, Somersby could see. He wore an ill fitting, shiny suit, and sunglasses, despite the fact that they were indoors. This man was kneeling by the boot of the Mercedes, his ear to the door. The German Shepherd was barking and snarling, inches from his face, but he seemed not to notice. He gestured to one of the others, who went to one of the cars, coming back with what looked like a crowbar. Somersby passed the phone from hand to hand, deliberating whether or not to call Harry.

Clearly no stranger to the practice, the suited man jimmied the door of the boot open in one go, adding the shriek of the Mercedes' alarm system to the cacophony of shouts and dog noises. As the boot door rose up slowly, one of the onlookers turned away in horror, and another dropped to his knees, vomiting on the concrete. Somersby pressed the redial button, double checking the display to make sure that it had been Goldman he had called last. The shouts and screams of the men escalated, both in anger and in volume, as two of them pulled out the bloodied body of what looked to him like a teenage girl, perhaps even younger. As the man in the suit barked orders, the other rushed to their cars, and returned with several sports bags. With the ringing tone repeating in his ear, Somersby let out an audible gasp. The bags were full of guns. Pistols, Uzis, sawn-offs. He looked at the video phone feed; the first man was still holding open the door to the main hallway. A voice came on the line.

'Hello?'

'Harry? We've got a fucking problem here.'

Bob had heard her singing, and then the singing had sounded like crying, and then there was no singing, just heartfelt sobbing. Bob stood close to the door, wondering if he should speak. She had been so calm, relatively speaking, that he had almost forgotten they were keeping her against her will; alone, in a strange place, far away from anyone she knew or loved. He hadn't prepared himself for tears or hysterics; she had spoiled him, he thought.

Reinhart was gone, so it was up to him to sort it, he told himself.

'Sweetheart?' He kept his voice low so as not to alarm her, but it was too quiet for her to hear him, especially over the noise she was making herself. He tried again, slightly louder.

'Poppy? Poppy, love. It's… George. Remember me, treacle? Are you… are you all right?'

A long silence, and then:

'No.'

'Ah, okay. What's the matter, babes?' He looked over his shoulder, and around the other side; he was alone in the corridor.

'I want to go home. I want to go back home. Please. I'll be good. I want my- I want Alice. Or Daddy. Or even Mummy, I just want-'

'I know, I know, babe. Honest to goodness I do. I wanna go home meself, you know? Bloody had enough of this place for today. Won't be long though, chick. All right? Won't be too long, then we can all go home. You, me-'

'Magda?'

'Uh, yeah. Yeah, Magda too, sweetheart. All of us.'

'I don't want Magda to come home with me.'

She was still sniffly, but the crying had stopped, he noted.

'Why not, babes?'

'She's not... she's not a good person. George?'

'Yes, love?'

'Are you a kidnapper?'

He swallowed, drily, unsure of how to answer.

'What babes? A kidnapper? Course I ain't. I'm... where did you get an idea like that, Pop? I'm your friend, is what I am.'

'That's what a kidnapper would say.'

'Well, oh. I, erm...' His hands felt clammy; looking down, he noticed his nails were filthy.

'Anyway, you said you were friends with Magda, but you didn't even know her name, really. And that's- George?' She suddenly sounded lost to him; like she had forgotten herself, mid-sentence.

'Yes, babes?'

'I'm sleepy now. I'm really, really sleepy, even though I tried to- even though I didn't- they wanted me to, but I-'

'Hey, hey, hey. It's okay, treacle. If you're sleepy, why don't you have a little nap, eh? It's probably past your bedtime anyway, innit? Probably past mine. It'll all be better in the morning, love. I promise you.'

'I don't want to go to sleep though! If I go to sleep, the bad people will do bad things. I just know they will! I heard them say. I heard them-'

'There's no bad people here, Pop. Honest to God. I been here all day meself, and I ain't seen none.'

'Really?'

'Scout's honour, sweetheart. Cross me heart and hope to die.'

'I'm scared, George.'

'There's no need to be scared, babes. I know it's been a funny old day. A bit confusing, and that. I know, but if you just pop yourself to bed, and have a nice snooze, it'll all be over before you know it.'

'But what if-'

'I'm here, ain't I? And I ain't gonna let no one touch a hair on your head, right?'

'Promise?'

'On my life, babes.'

'Say "I promise on my life", or else it isn't real.'

'I promise on me life, that I won't let no one do nothing to Poppy. Okay?'

'Okay, then.'

'Goodnight, sweetheart.'

'Goodnight, George.'

He sat staring at the door for a while after she had gone. He had wanted to be in the room with her; to give her a hug, and tell her it was going to be okay. He had no idea if he would have been telling her the truth.

Dylan lay frozen on the van floor, listening to events unfold around him. Screaming, barking, the sound of car doors slamming. They had come to a halt somewhere. He wasn't sure where, but from the echoing noises, he knew they were indoors. A multi story car park was his best guess. The man he knew as Max was still inside the vehicle. He had heard no doors open.

The bonds were still as tight as they had been a half hour before. People in films seemed to be able to wriggle out of ropes or pick the locks of handcuffs at will, but the reality was more depressing, he found. He was immobile, impotent, trapped; until they decided to do whatever they had planned for him. The car alarm sound coming from outside the van stopped, suddenly. He was sure it was a van or truck, rather than a car, because he had been able to roll over several times, without hitting a seat, or anything else he would expect to find in the back of a car. They'd been stationary for some minutes, with no sign of anything happening soon. Max had made no phone calls, nor had he spoke to anyone else in the van. Dylan was also sure that he was alone with Max, and there had been no one else with them for the journey.

He heard the sound of someone keying numbers into a phone, followed by the error noise which happened when someone dialled a number which was too long; or when there was no coverage. Max cursed under his breath, and Dylan heard him try to dial out again. The dogs outside had gone quieter. Now there were only hushed voices, and loud, echoing footsteps. He listened harder, trying to make out words, but the tongue being used by the men outside was foreign.

There was a rapping sound; someone knocking on the driver's window, he assumed. He heard Max's voice; this time there was a wobble to it, he sounded afraid.

'Ah, yes, mate?'

More knocking, and an unintelligible shout.

'Yes mate? What you want, pal?'

A pause, and by way of a reply, a single gunshot rang out. It was incredibly loud; Dylan seemed to lose his hearing for a second, and when it came back, there was a loud, constant ringing. Someone at paintball had once told him that a real life gunshot was a hundred times louder than one you heard in films. He had thought the man was exaggerating at the time.

From the front of the van, he could hear a choking sound- choking, or gargling. It was disturbing; no dramatic screaming or last words, just a rasping, whistling noise as the man died in his seat. Still blindfolded, Dylan was helpless, knowing that they would check the van for others. He heard the door slide across, and there was a slight breeze on his sweating face. Someone took off the blindfold, but he kept his eyes shut, thinking he could delay the inevitable. He wouldn't even hear them cock the gun before they did it, he reminded himself. The man at paintball had explained to him that that was also something which only happened in Hollywood.

Harry came off the line with Somersby, his mind in several different places at once. He was back at the office, waiting for the Albanians to arrive. It was going to be a quick meeting, they had said. Just going over the ins and outs of him transferring Poppy over to them, and the small matter of payment. They would take her to the continent, and put her through a ruthless program of conditioning, like they had done with the Frazer girl, although Poppy was ten, not five, so it would be a harder job for them. The idea was to wash away all memories of the girls' former lives, and turn them into working girls. They would be taught a new language, and made to forget their own. Their hair would be cut and dyed, distinguishing marks disguised or removed, and their eye colour changed with the aid of contacts. He had never heard about Milly after he sold her, but he assumed that she was already on the Albanian's payroll. No age was too young, if someone was willing to pay the right price.

He needed to get Beth out safely. The rest could fend for themselves, he thought. He had their money. The Albanians might even be doing him a favour. Don might be a problem, but only if he lived.

'Reinhart? Yeah, where are you, mate?'

'Boss. Boss, I am on my way to see the girl. What is happening?'

'Forget the kid. We'll get her too. I want you to go to the main house, get Beth.'

'Beth?'

'The redhead, in the room with the others. You can't bloody miss her, she's the only bird. Get her out, safe, and bring her to the office.'

'Safe? What is the matter? Why would there be danger for her?'

'Long story mate. You got a shooter?'

'Ah, yes. Yes, actually.'

'Good, bring it with you. And not a word to those other pricks, right?' Harry pictured them in the room, oblivious to the carnage that was about to unfold. *That's life*, he told himself, grabbing the sawn-off shotgun from under his desk. *You win some, you lose some.*

'Harry, what's going on? Is it the police? If it's the police, I have to-'

'No, mate. No, not yet. Don't worry about it. Just get the bird and meet me here.'

'Okay. Okay, see you soon.'

'And you, mate.'

The car would be gone, he knew that. Terry took it home with him whenever he had a late shift, followed by an early one. The other cars were all in the front garage, which, if Somersby's tale had been accurate, was not a place he wanted to go.

Apart from Reinhart and maybe Max, if he arrived, his security was non-existent. They had been given the night off, along with the rest of the staff. He had been hesitant about it, but it had seemed like the right thing to do. He dialled Malcolm's number.

'Mal?'

'Jesus, boss. Bit fucking late, innit? I were asleep. Early ni-'

'Malcolm, get your fucking trousers on, get all the boys you can, get tooled up and get here sharpish.'

'Jesus, what? What's happened?'

'I'll explain later, Mal. Call Griff, Roycie, fucking all of them, and get here. Use the back.'

'Loud and clear, boss.'

'Nice one. And fucking hurry.'

Tentatively checking the corridor outside the office door, he dialled another number.

'Ian?'

'Boss?'

'Ian, where are you?'

'I'm in the video room, Harry. It's all gone fucking off, it's fucking-'

'Never mind that. The kid. Is she still there?'

'Of course she's- where else would she be?'

'Good. Get her. Come in through the mirror; don't let Bob hear you. Get her, get out, and get around to me. I'm next door, mate. Use the side. You got your mobile?'

'Yep.'

'Drop call me when you're outside. Oh, and Ian?'

'Yeah?'

'Fucking delete everything.'

'Already way ahead of you, Harry.'

The grounds were big. It was a long walk from the main building down to the offices, and Harry had no idea how far inside the Albanians were already. All he knew was, from what Somersby had seen them take out of the sports bags, they wouldn't be coming to him to negotiate. Whatever Hansen had done; whatever the significance of the body in his boot, they weren't likely to listen to protestations about it having nothing to do with Harry. He had two choices: run, or fight. If they reached his office before Malcolm and his boys arrived, or before Reinhart and Somersby brought the girls to him, his options would be even fewer.

Paul was getting drunk, as quickly as he could without throwing up. The incident with the gun had shaken him. The drink was helping to calm his nerves. Hansen had been lucky, he thought. Had the big Austrian not arrived when he did, there was no telling what Paul might have done. At that moment, with the loaded pistol in his grip, the options had flashed through his mind. He could have killed them both; he knew that. Then it would just have been a case of getting out of the building; using the gun on anyone who tried to stop him. He hadn't planned any further ahead than that though. It would have been suicide, and he knew it. Harry wouldn't just let him walk away from something like that. He looked over at Hansen and Jarvis, who were thick as thieves once more. The woman was with them, laughing at something the American had said. The other man, the police sergeant, was standing near them; listening, rather than participating. Either way, Paul was on his own again, isolated.

The bowls on the table had some sort of drugs in them, he knew. He had never been any sort of user, mainly because it would show up on the random drug tests he had to undergo for work. But also because, to him, drugs were a bad thing. Seedy, immoral; the sort of thing the other boys from his estate got mixed up in, while he was away at the club, cleaning the senior players' boots and generally keeping out of trouble. Football had been his saviour; he knew that all too well. Without it, he would have been just another council estate kid, with no future and no hope. Still, the idea of getting out of it for a while; losing control and absolving himself of responsibility, seemed a tempting one. He took another drink, hoping it might do something similar eventually.

The others seemed like they were in another universe to him. The policeman looked calm and content; Hansen was as high as a kite, and the other man, the singer, was sitting with a drunken smile on his face. The girl looked like she was at a society function; she was dressed to the nines, and chatting with all of them, besides him. None of them seemed tense or anxious, like he did. He wondered how he had ever come to be in their company. It had all seemed exciting when they were planning it. He had been aware of how exclusive the company he was keeping was; especially the day Harry showed up to talk to him. He became caught up in it; drunk on the power. What they were going to do was beyond any taboo he had ever considered. He would forget about it during the day; when he was training, or spending time with the girls. But at night, with a few drinks in him, and after hours trawling the net for new pictures and videos, he became someone else. He liked to tell himself that it wasn't him, but he knew it was. It was who he was inside, and he had spent most of his life trying to bottle it up, or ignore it. He felt more alive than he ever had, in those moments where he stopped fighting it, and gave into his urges. That was what he despised most; the fact that the monster was him, and not something he became. Whenever he felt like taking his own life, it was that thought which took him there, and only the girls who brought him back.

He looked around the room again. None of them were as big as him, physically. In theory, he could overpower any of them, and kill them without needing a weapon. Together though, they could probably subdue him, he knew. He closed his eyes and thought about Colleen and Charmaine, and Tamara. The younger girl had told him once that you could make anything happen if you just wished hard enough. She had believed it too, giving him several examples of how it had worked for her. The only catch, she said, was that sometimes the wish people took something from you, as payment. She had wished for sweets once, and on the same day, she couldn't find her favourite Barbie. Another day, she had wanted the sun to come out, and it did, but she lost one pound fifty from her pocket. Digging his nails into his palms, he wished for something to stop what they were going to do; he didn't care what they took, as long as it wasn't his girls. He mightn't survive, but thinking of what he felt earlier, looking at his daughter, he wondered if that would be such a bad thing. He had never touched the girls, and swore to himself that he never would. But something had changed in him. Something bad was growing inside him, and he wasn't sure he had the strength to ignore it or to stop it. He had never had the ability to walk away from the feelings he had about other little girls. He knew that, if it came down to it, he would prefer to be dead than to put his children in danger. Especially if the danger came from him. *I'm not like that, though,* he told himself, looking around the room again. *I'm not one of them.* Somewhere inside though, he knew that was a lie. Otherwise, he wouldn't have been there. Somewhere in the house, there was a loud bang. The door opened, and Reinhart came in, out of breath and sweating.

Dylan was in the hallway between the garage and the main part of the house. The men who had freed him were gone. He could see a second door, which they had opened by force. He had heard the explosion when they blew the lock. Whoever they were, they had come prepared. He could hear their shouts, so they couldn't have been much farther ahead . When they had taken him out of the van and removed his blindfold and ties, there had been a lot of screaming in broken English, and very little sense. Once they realised that he was nothing to do with whomever they had a grudge against, they had let him be, muttering curses, and words which he didn't understand . He watched them arm themselves and run into the house. The last of them had taken a gun magazine and used it to prop open the door. They had left the black sports bags on the roof of the blue Mercedes.

His first thought had been to run, but was no way out; a steel barrier door separated the place from the outside, and he had no way of raising it. Even if he could drive, the cars were useless while it stayed down. The only other option was to follow them into the house; Harry's house, he assumed, though he didn't know who Harry was. He had walked over to the blue car, it boot open. What he saw inside made him retch; the alcohol from earlier in the day coming up easily. He had never seen a dead body before; not even at a funeral. She was a child, even though she wasn't dressed like one. The eyes were closed, he was thankful for that. She was still dead though; the smell wasn't strong, but it was there.

He had looked in the bag out of curiosity more than anything; he hadn't expected there to be something in it. A pistol, and several magazines to fit it. He had never held one before. It was heavier than it looked, he noticed, and cold. He looked toward the house, and back at the steel shutters.

Poppy is in there. They have her, and those fuckers who just went in don't seem like they're the Good Guys, he told himself, pointing the gun at an imaginary enemy, touching the trigger lightly. The weight of it pained his arm.

For all you know, they have Alice too. You can't get out. You've got to go in. Even as he thought it, he knew it was madness. He had never fired a gun, and he wasn't even sure he knew how to. The ones in paintball were very different to the heavy steel thing in his hand. But he also knew he didn't have options. He could stay in the garage and wait for them to come back, if they were coming back at all, he knew that. But there was no way of guaranteeing that the next person to come through the gate would be one of them. Also, there was the chance that someone else would come through the car door; someone who worked for Harry. He had always joked with Alice that he wished he lived in the old days, when men were men, and girls needed rescuing.

'I would totally have killed a dragon for you, babe. Then it wouldn't matter if I was on Income Support, you know? They'd be all: Profession? And I'd be like: Dragonslayer, biatch.' He smiled, remembering exactly which day he had said it to her. He looked at the gun again. It couldn't be that complicated, he told himself. *They train kids in Africa to use them, for Christ's sake; how hard can it be? All you do is point... and shoot.*

He was dead. Alice had felt his neck, and his wrist. There was nothing. The pain from her eye was immense. So much so that she almost couldn't recognise it as such. Her brain must have a way of dealing with severe trauma, she thought; some sort of disassociation, as a method of survival. She touched the handle gently, wincing. She was glad there was no mirror in the room, or she might have passed out from the sight of her injury. The phone was still on the floor. She grabbed it, hoping not to hear a dead tone. There was only silence, but that was good, she thought; that meant they hadn't hung up.

'Hello?' No reply.

'Hello? Please! Someone?'

'Alice?'

'Oh, God. Thank God. Oh, I-'

'Alice, we know where you are. We're sending someone to you right now.'

'You know? How did you-'

'You're calling us from a landline, Alice. You're in Hampstead Heath. There will be someone there very soon.'

'Jesus. Okay, I… you need to send an ambulance.'

'An ambulance? Has something happened, Alice? Is your dau- is the girl there? Is she okay?'

'No. No, no, no. I don't- she's not- It's me. I've been… stabbed.' She felt the scissors again, pulling it a little, but stopping as soon as the pain ripped through her.

'Stabbed? By who?'

'A man. A man, he's… one of them. One of the kidnappers.'

'Okay. Okay, Alice. Are there others there? Is it dangerous? Are they armed? Do we need to send-'

'I don't know. I'm… I'm hurt. I'm really hurt. I don't know how to- Hello? Hello?'

The line went dead. She shook the phone, bashing the buttons, but it made no sound other than a dull, hollow hum.

'Hello? Please!' She heard only her own voice, echoing back at her. She dropped the handset. On the screen above her, something was happening. Poppy was sitting up, her hands around her knees. To her left, a large wall mirror opened as if it was a door, and a thin man, wearing glasses, walked through it. Alice sat frozen, her eye, and the woman on the phone, forgotten.

Oh no. Oh Jesus, no. Please. Not now. Oh God, no.

'You, Beth? You must come with me, please. Harry, he wants you.'

Jarvis looked at the Austrian in the doorway. The pistol Hansen had brought with him was tucked into the man's belt, next to the holder with his mobile in it.

'Me? Oh, okay. I thought he had a meeting?'

Rick turned to look at her. She was beautiful, he thought. The sort of woman a man might do stupid things over. Harry bringing her in like that had been a shock to him, but looking at her, he could understand why someone might want to do things to please her.

'Change of plan. You need to come, quickly, yes?'

He wondered what the change of plan might be. *Maybe the old fucker just wants a shag.* Jarvis couldn't blame him. She was exquisite.

'Okey doke. Sorry, boys. Duty calls.'

'Hey… Reinhart. What's the change of plan, man? Something wrong?' Rick asked it because no one else had. He didn't like the look on Reinhart's face. There was something wrong about it, he thought.

'What? No. No, all is okay. No worry. Just… stay here, I will be back later, yes? Harry too.'

Rick didn't like his tone. The man seemed insincere to him; like he was hiding something, although it could have been his own paranoia. He had drank a lot, and taken plenty of the coke that Harry had provided. It had been a long time for him, and he wasn't exactly pacing himself.

'You sure, man? You seem a bit... edgy?' said Bill. Hansen looked like hell, Rick thought. He had arrived wasted, and carried on from there.

'Edgy? Pffft.' Reinhart snorted and pointed to the pistol in his belt. Hansen's face went even redder than it had been, and he shrugged his shoulders.

'What was the bang?' It was the footballer who spoke next. He had been sitting at the opposite end of the table to the rest of them, and hadn't said a word since the thing with Hansen and the gun. Rick had forgotten he was there.

'Bang? There is no bang. Just stay here. And I will be back.'

The big man took the woman by the hand and led her through the door, closing it behind him. There was a familiar sounding noise, although Rick wasn't sure what it was. He looked down at his feet, feeling dizzy. The images shook a little at the edges, and his eyes crossed over and back again. *I'm fucked. I need to slow down.*

Hansen had run to the door and was pounding on it, while pulling the handle. It wasn't opening for him.

'What the fuck? Reinhart! REINHART! What the... he's fucking locked it, man. What the fuck is this? What are we- what the- Hey! Open the fucking door, man! Open it!' He punched and kicked the wood, but to no avail. Rick eyelids were getting heavy, the chair underneath him starting to feel extremely comfortable. The policeman, Don, was at the door now too.

'Give it here. It's probably not- Harry! Harry, what the hell is this? Harry! HARRY!'

At the other end of the table, the man called Paul stood up, a near empty bottle of something in his hand. Rick gave him a nod, which he ignored. The other man walked over to the tall window at the side of the room, and pulled the cord which worked the long, velvet drapes. As the curtains came across, Rick saw him curse under his breath at what was underneath. The window was entirely covered in steel bars. The gaps between them were so small that a child would struggle to get through. Harry Goldman obviously didn't want anyone getting into the place, he thought. *Or getting out.*

Twenty Two

Somersby found the program in a folder on the desktop. It was a one click affair. The drive and everything on it would be wiped in a matter of minutes. Harry's son Frank had written the code for it. There would be no undoing or recovery possible; he had been assured of that by Goldman. He put his finger on the touchscreen to confirm the command. Waiting a few seconds to make sure all was well, he grabbed the memory stick from its USB slot, and headed through the mirror door. The girl was awake, and sitting up.

'Hey there…' He spoke gently.

'Who are you?' She sounded scared to him. He hadn't heard her speak since they'd taken her; only the singing.

'I'm a friend of your Dad's, Poppy.'

'No you're not. Don't you come near me, or I'll scream.'

'Scream? Haha. Don't be silly, Pop. We have to go now, okay? You have to come with me.'

'No.'

'Come on now, Poppy. Daddy's waiting for us, outside.'

He saw her eyes light up, before the suspicion returned.

'He is? No. No, he isn't. You're bad, and you're going to hurt me. I will scream. I promise.'

'Come on, no need for that. Just let me-' He put a hand on her shoulder, and she flinched hard, as if he had burnt her with something.

'No! Go away! Go away! Please!' She was crying. She had struggled and got away from him. He looked at her, in her vest and knickers, and a sudden feeling of lust came over him. *No one is watching. No one knows. I paid my money. I should get something.*

'That's a pretty outfit, Poppy. You're very pretty, you know that? You're… there are a lot of people who would love to- Do you like boys, Poppy? Have you got a boyfriend?'

'Go away! Go away or I'll scream!'

His breathing grew deeper the more aroused he became. He looked at her soft skin, the golden hairs on her bare arms. His mouth felt dry. He grabbed her shoulders, pinning her to the bed.

'No! No, no, no, no!' She let out a blood curdling scream, so loud his ears rang. He put a hand over her mouth to silence her, but she moved free of it and screamed again.

'Fucking scream all you want, you little slut. No one can hear you.' He pushed her down on the bed, holding her there with his knee across her stomach. She kicked and writhed underneath him, and he leaned all of his weight on her, pushing the air out of her little lungs.

'Get off me, get off me!' She screamed again, louder. He brought his other leg up, and pinned her to the mattress. Looking down at her bare stomach and the pink waistband of her underpants, he groaned and started undoing the buckle of his belt.

'Just stay still, Poppy. Just… be good. Okay? Be a good little girl for me.' The belt open, he struggled with the buttons of his flies. His hands were sweating as much as the rest of him. When the punch came, it was so unexpected that it sent him flying, sideways, off the bed, and onto the carpeted floor. Bob was on him straight away, flailing at his face with heavy, gold-ringed fists. He only felt a few of the blows, before all the sounds from the room- the girls screams, Bob's curses, and the slap of bone against bone- faded to nothing, and the light went from his eyes.

There were three possible routes. The staircase in the middle might lead somewhere; it might take him to Poppy, but it wouldn't get him outside. Below, to either side of the steps, there were two long corridors. Dylan couldn't tell which way the others had gone, or if they had slip up into three groups. It seemed likely to him that they had. He wasn't sure if he would be safer following them, or going his own way. They didn't know he had come in after them, so they were as likely to shoot him as anyone else who might be in the place. Especially once they'd seen he had taken on of their guns.

The place was a palace, he thought. When he pictured kidnappers, they were always desperate criminal types, not wealthy millionaires who lived in mansions. He chose the right hand corridor, for no particular reason. He edged along the wall, holding the gun like he did in paintball tournaments; raised and to one side; ready to drop and fire the second he saw someone. The hallway was long. Most of the doors were open. As he passed them, he saw that they had been kicked or barged in. The gangsters had been through there before him, he thought. He slowed down, not wanting to come up behind them.

On the wall, halfway down the passage, a large plastic box had been broken open, and the wires inside ripped from their moorings. A quick glance inside it told him that it was some sort of switchboard. Possible the phone lines for the house. Up ahead, he heard voices, and the sound of more doors being forced open. He looked down at his free hand. He was shaking like a leaf. The adrenaline which was driving him forward came part and parcel with a terror greater than he had ever felt before. He tried to forget his own fears, and think about Poppy.

The chances of him being able to get to her, or to help her, were probably very slim, he thought. But to not try at all would be something for which he would never forgive himself. If they had Alice too, it was even more important that he carry on.

The hall was curved, rather than one straight line. The curve was slight, so he didn't have to worry about what lay beyond any corners; there were none to speak of. He was glad of that, but he knew that there were equally no corners for him to hide behind. If someone was to come, either behind him or ahead, it would be a case of kill them before they killed him. There would be no tactics, just quick reactions or dumb luck.

He knew that because of the curve, there would probably be no legitimate end to the passage; it more than likely joined with the other one; circling the building. Eventually though, he came to some steel double doors, with a security bar across them, and the words 'No Exit' emblazoned on some plastic tape. The men ahead of him had passed it without opening it. *They're searching the inside first*, he guessed. He gave the metal bar a kick, and the doors swung outwards, into an enormous garden. There were artificially lit trees and flowerbeds as far as he could see. Beyond the farthest of the pines, he could make out three other buildings. He took a look around for anyone else, and started towards them, the gun feeling much lighter in his hand.

'I've gotta get out. I've gotta get fucking- why's he locked us in, man? What the fuck is happened? This ain't right, man. Call Harry. Did someone call Harry? Where's my cell?' Bill didn't like locked rooms, or being kept in the dark about things.

'I've called him. He's not fucking picking up.' The policeman, Don waved a smartphone at Bill.

'Not picking up? Anyone else call him? Rick?' He looked at Jarvis, but the singer had passed out in the chair; his eyes closed, drool leaking from the side of his mouth. He looked at the footballer, but the glare he got back made him avert his eyes immediately. It dawned on him that there was still bad blood between them, and that they were now locked in a room together, with no gun, and no Reinhart to protect him. The other man was a professional athlete, he thought; and physically huge compared to himself.

'He's not answering. Doesn't matter which of us calls him. Something's gone pear shaped. He's dropped us in it, mate. That's why he got his bird out,' said Don, looking down at the handset.

'Dropped us in it? Dropped us in what, man? What the fuck is happening? How are we gonna get out?' Bill could hear his heart pounding in his chest. He had lost count of how much cocaine he had taken. He had a tolerance, but there was always a danger. There had been times in the past where he had been sure he was about to burst a valve. He put his hand to his heart, not sure what he was feeling for.

'I don't know, mate. You need to calm the fuck down. You're not helping.'

'Calm the fuck- Look… Don. You're a cop, right? Use that thing. Get us some back up, or something?'

'Back up? Back up for what, mate? What do you think is happening here? We're just locked in a bloody room. You're the only one panicking.'

'But, you said- you said he'd dropped us in it. Said it'd gone pear shaped, or something. You said that. What the fuck does that mean? What was that bang, man? That was a fucking gun, man. Something's wrong. Someone's here, fucking shooting the place up. We can't just fucking sit here- we can't just wait for them to come and kill us.' He looked imploringly at Don, unable to understand why the man didn't comprehend what he was saying; why he didn't seem bothered about what was happening.

'Kill us? Jesus Christ, mate. You've had a bit too much of the old Bolivian Marching Powder, son. There ain't no one gonna kill anyone. Except maybe me killing you, if you don't calm the fuck down. You need to-'

'The door,' said Paul. The other two looked at him; Jarvis was still snoozing in his chair.

'What about the door?' asked Don.

'We can force it. I can force it. It don't look to solid.'

Bill turned to look; it was wooden, but there were two large panels, which looked like they might be hollow.

'What, you mean kick it in?'

'Kick it, shoulder it. Whatever.' The footballer had come across the floor, and was standing next to the door, pushing against the wood, to test it.

'Okay then. Need a hand?' Don came over to join him. Bill stayed put.

'No. I'm fine.'

Taking a breath, he took a run at the door, crashing into it with his shoulder. It buckled in its frame, but remained intact. Bill sighed. Paul went again; the second time, his shoulder left a large splintered crack.

'Fucking A, man! Go Paul!' Bill's heart was racing again, but for better reasons. Still, he took some long breaths, trying to level out his pulse. Someone had taught him the trick once, on some occasion he couldn't remember.

'Try and hit the same spot, mate. If you put a hole in it, the key might still be in it, round the other side,' said Don. Paul took a longer run up. The door make an almighty cracking sound, and the panel in the middle broke through, almost to the other side.

'Fuck, yeah. One more time!' Bill was already forgetting why he had argued with the man. Paul examined the damage he had already done, and tried to push the panel through and out the other side, but it wouldn't give. Sighing, he took an even longer run up, letting out a guttural scream as he hit the thing, breaking the lock open. The door swung open, and his momentum sent him tumbling into the hallway. The others whooped and cheered, rushing over to the open door.

'Fucking yeah, Paul,' said Bill. 'You're an an-i-mal!'

The footballer turned to face them, but instead of a smile, they saw a look of abject terror on his face. Before Bill had time to process what was happening, Paul's left cheek ripped open as the bullet went through it. Shot after shot tore apart his chest, his legs, and finally the top of his skull, spraying bright red blood and orange-looking brain tissue across the wall behind him. Bill couldn't move as he watched the man fall to the floor. It was Don who reacted, screaming:

'Shut the fucking door!'

Bob held her in his arms, rocking her gently. He had got there just in time, thought. Somersby was going to the rape her. He looked down at the man; still alive, but not moving. He could finish him, he thought. And he wanted to, but not while she was there. He would get her out, and then come back. That was if he could get out. There was still Reinhart to worry about. He had suspected there was something wrong for a while. He hadn't been able to put his finger on it, but somehow he had always known that they were planning on hurting her. He didn't know what to call it, maybe a gut feeling. He didn't know if it was just Somersby, or if the Austrian was one of them too, and he didn't care, for the moment.

'Okay, babes. You're okay now. Listen… I'm gonna get you out of here, okay?'

'O…okay. You won't hurt me, will you, George?' She looked at him with wet eyes, her whole body trembling.

'Of course not, treacle. I'm gonna look after ya. Get ya home to Daddy, yeah?'

'Is my Dad at home?' She sounded surprised.

'He's ah- we'll see, okay? Let's just get you out of here, yeah?'

'Yeah. Thank you, George.'

He wanted to tell her what his real name was, but he knew that would be unnecessarily unwise. He was still likely to be implicated in the kidnap, even if he ended up being the one who got her out. It was better that she didn't know, he told himself.

The mirror on the wall turned out to be a hidden door. Beyond it was a room with a chair, a desk, and what looked like a computer screen, although he couldn't see an actual computer or a keyboard. On the screen was a red box with 'Complete' written in it. He didn't know what it meant, and carried on through. In the next room there were boxes of DVDs, stacks of magazines, but nothing useful to him. He looked at one of the grey plastic covers; it said 'Romanian, 8. O, V, A, DP'. Another said 'Ukrainian twins, 7. O, V, A'. He didn't know what any of it meant. The magazines were pornography. Foreign titles, some of them extremely old. He didn't pick any up to flick through; it felt wrong with the girl there. The next room was empty except for two chairs. At the far side was a green door, with 'Exit' written above it.

'There we go, sweetheart. Almost out of the woods, eh?'

'Are we in the woods?' She had her face buried in his neck; her breath tickled him, especially when she spoke.

'Well, no. Just figure of- it's just something people say, babes.'

The door was locked.

'I know a song about the woods?'

'Do ya?'

He spotted a bunch of keys, hanging on a nail, by the door.

'Yeah. *If you go down to the woods today...* '

The first key he tried was the right one. He carried her out onto the fire escape, joining in with her song.

'*... you're in for a big surprise.*'

'Fuck.' Harry threw the phone down onto the desk.

'What's the matter, hon?' Beth was in his swivel chair, drinking some brandy.

'Somersby. He's not picking up. If they've got him- If they've got her...'

'Who? The Albanians?' He had explained the situation to her, although not in any great detail. She didn't need to know why he was meeting them, he thought. He had told her enough about himself already. He was already regretting a lot of it, now the drink was wearing off.

'Yeah. Fuck it anyway. If they have her, then... Well-'

'What will they do with her, Harry?' He was surprised by the concern in her voice.

'Nothing worse than I was gonna, I suppose.' He had to admit it; it was true, to a point.

'Yeah. Yeah, I suppose. What about Bill though? They're going to kill him, right?'

'Maybe. Look, Mal might be here in a minute; don't forget that. For all I know, he's here already, and the whole thing's sorted. I just don't-'

'Where's the Reinhart guy gone?'

'Getting us a car.'

'You don't have yours?'

'No, it's... it's not here.'

'Oh.' She finished her glass.

'Fuck it, I'm going round myself.'

'Where? You're not leaving me here, are you?'

'It's literally next door, all right? Don't give me any more stress than I need, Beth. I'll be two seconds. I promise.'

Alice had no idea if she had watched Poppy being saved, or put into more danger. She hadn't recognised the man who burst into the room and knocked the child's attacker unconscious. He hadn't looked like a policeman, and if he had been one, the room would have been filled with other police afterwards; people collecting evidence, taking fingerprints. As it was, the bald man had just picked her up and taken her out through the same strange door that the rapist had come through. *He was a rapist*, she told herself. There was no ambiguity as to what would have happened if the other man hadn't intervened.

After it was done, she decided to take out the scissors. She remembered lots of stories and advice, where the medical people said that it was better to leave the foreign object inside the wound until you could get to a hospital, but she couldn't stand the pain anymore. She wanted it out. She knelt on the floor, bracing herself for the pain. *Don't think about it. Don't think, just do it*, she told herself, her heart racing. With no more hesitation, she gripped the thing with both hands, and pulled it from her skull. There was surprisingly little blood, but she knew she had lost a lot already. She took a thick tea towel from the counter in his kitchen and pressed it against the wound, wishing she had the courage to clean it with alcohol first.

Once she collected herself, she knew she had to get out. The door was locked, and she spent what seemed like hours searching for a key or keys. When she had given up hope, she went back out to see if the lock was weak enough to break with something heavy. She had to break into her own flat once, having locked herself out; the back door handle had come clean off when she brought the force of a breeze block down on it.

As it turned out, there wasn't a lock. Not in the conventional sense. She wondered why she hadn't noticed it when they had come in, but then she had been quite drunk, she reminded herself. It was an electronic lock; a small blue glass screen. The scanner read the fingerprint, and opened the door. It was the only way out of the flat. All the windows had bars. She knew whose fingerprint she needed. She forced herself to go back into the room, to him.

For the first time, Don allowed himself to panic. He looked at his phone. He could get SO19 there quicker than anyone just calling 999, but that would mean consequences. Even if the armed police arrived in time to save them, and that was looking unlikely, he would have to explain what he was doing there. And there was no explaining it, he thought. Not if they found the child there. Police covered for each other in most circumstances, but no one was going to turn a blind eye to something like this. He looked around at the others: the singer, still sleeping in his chair; Hansen, wild-eyed and panicking, pacing the room and talking to no one in particular.

'Fucking... Don! Don, do something! They're gonna fucking kill us.'

'They're not gonna. Here, grab the other end of this.' Don started pushing the table toward the door. It was heavy, but that was a good thing, he thought.

'What? Oh, fuck yeah. Okay, man.' The American wheeled around into position, moving the thing several feet with his first shove. Outside the door, Don heard angry shouts, in a language he couldn't understand.

'That's it. A few more pushes.' The bowls and plates on the tablecloth moved as they pushed, and several of the spirited bottles toppled and rolled off. A second or two more, and it was there. They had their makeshift barrier. Someone on the other side hammered on the door.

'Fuck! Fuck, man. It's not gonna be enough!'

'Shut up. Here, this one.' Don stooped to pick up one of the chairs, motioning to Hansen to get the other side. They lifted together and put it on top of the table, the leg jamming the door handle. He wasn't sure if that would make a difference. The shouts outside were louder.

'Fuck. Fuck! Get the other one!'

'Okay, okay.' Don helped him with the second chair, and they managed to slide one inside the other, making a solid shape.

'What do we do now? What do we-' Hansen's words were cut off by the bullet piercing the wooden panel, and both of them dropped to the floor. In the chair, Jarvis stirred, but incredibly he didn't wake.

'Just fucking... just calm down, mate. You got a mobile?' Don had several ideas, not many of them good. None of them involved using his own phone.

'A mo- a cell? Yeah, yeah man, I got a cell. Here.' Hansen slid the phone across the floor to Don. It was locked.

'Code? What's the fucking code?'

'Ah, what? Oh, oh! Ummm, 4932, man. I think. Yeah, 4-9-3-2.'

'All right.' Don punched in the numbers and the screen unlocked. He tapped three nines into the virtual keyboard, and waited for an answer.

The garden was beautiful. The trees and flowers looked nothing like anything Dylan had ever seen in London. Someone had paid a lot of money to bring in these things from all over the world. Palm trees, strange orange flowers; even the rocks looked exotic, he thought. Behind him, the main building loomed menacingly in the night. He heard what sounded like gunshots, and quickened his pace. He didn't have a plan, or know where he was going, but he had a feeling that what he wanted was ahead, not back there. The gentle sounds of water from the rock pools and mini falls lent a feeling of calm to a situation that was anything but.

Paintball and video games had taught him how to keep to the edges, in the shadows. He hoped they had also trained his reflexes, because whatever came at him out of the trees or the buildings ahead was bound to be hostile. There would be no need to check before firing. He knew that whoever came at him would be equally uncaring about which side he was on. He kept moving forward, knowing that anyone coming out of the building behind would also be an enemy, and no scruples about cutting him down.

The adrenaline was pumping through him, giving him a clarity which belied the amount of alcohol he had drank during the day, or whatever it was they had tried to sedate him with. His vision felt extra sharp; his hearing, perfect. It felt almost exactly like a video game to him, although one which would have real consequences. He had never thought about killing another human being before, but he knew it was going to be necessary for his survival. It didn't feel bad to him, when he weighed it up against the notion that his life was in genuine danger. He had already cheated death once in the past few hours; and he was doing it again. Most people didn't get a chance to decide their own fate. He was terrified and excited, not even sure that they were separate feelings anymore. The gun in his hand was no longer heavy, but it still felt strange and foreign. He knew the power of it; he knew that it held death. He was one of the good guys though, he told himself. And Poppy needed him; Alice too. He pushed all thoughts away and tried to emulate the frame of mind he had when playing Call of Duty online: no rambling inner monologues, no overthinking it. Just his eyes, a gun, and his finger on the trigger.

Ahead, the garden opened up, and the three smaller buildings came into view. There were lights on in all of them. In front, the garden had been concreted over, and gravel laid down to make a driveway. His heart leapt as he heard a door open with a click. A man came from one building, cautiously looking around, and walked over to the door of another. Still in the shadows, Dylan dropped to one knee and took aim at the man's head. Suddenly it didn't feel like a video game anymore. He had seconds to decide if he was going to end someone's life. There would be a lifetime to regret it, if he made the wrong choice.

'Where are we going, George?'

'Shush, babes. Keep your voice down, all right?' Bob took a look around, wondering what his next move would be. Poppy spoke again, whispering this time.

'Okay. It's just, will you take me home?'

'Course. Course I will, hon. We just gotta find a way out, all right? Get us a car or something.' It would be easier said than done, he thought. He had no idea where he was. There were two buildings to either side of the one they had just left, and up in front of them, what looked like a large factory, or office block. None of them looked inviting, as far as he was concerned.

'Do you have a car?'

'What? A, no, babes. No, I ain't got me car with me.'

'How did you get here then? On the bus?'

'No, treacle.'

'The tube?'

'No, I- someone drove me here. In a-' He remembered the van he had arrived in. It might still be in the garage. But that would mean going back inside, and he knew that wasn't an option. *Can't go back in,* he told himself. *That's the first place they're gonna come looking.*

They were in a sort of jungle, he thought. Between the three smaller buildings, and the big office which he assumed was part of the same property, there was a thick, leafy place, bigger than any garden he had ever been in. All around them were walls, at least twenty feet high, topped with spikes and barbed wire. It was a fortress. It would have reminded him of a prison, if it weren't for the trees and flowers. There was no getting out over those walls, regardless, he knew.

'I'm scared, George.'

'Don't be scared, Poppet. Nothing to be scared of here.' He wanted to tell her he was scared too, but it wouldn't have helped, he knew.

'It looks scary. I want to go.'

'Me too, darlin'. Working on-' Gunshots, coming from the direction of the larger building. Bob held on to her tight, and moved quickly towards the other side of the gravel drive.

'What was that?' Her voice was panicked.

'Uh, fireworks, babe. Just someone doing fireworks.' He brought them under a large palm tree by the wall, then around the back of the trunk, brushing a spider web out of the way.

'Fireworks? It's not Bonfire Night… I don't think-'

'Different fireworks, babe. Probably some other thing.' He set her down on the ground, looking back at the giant structure and listening for more shots.

'Like Diwali?'

'De-what?' He wished he had a gun with him. He wouldn't have been able to shoot his way out with her in tow, he knew, but he might have felt safer.

'Diwali. It's the Hindu festival of light. We learned all about it in RE.'

'Diwali, eh. Yeah, babes. Maybe that's what it is.'

'No.'

'No what?' Through the leaves, he saw a figure between two of the smaller buildings. He didn't recognise the man, and yet something about him looked familiar. He ducked down, even though he was sure they couldn't be seen. There was something about the way the man walked; the way he held himself. A memory from a long time ago.

'No, it's not Diwali. Diwali happens in winter. I remember now.'

'Oh? All right then. But it's probably something.' The other man let himself in the door, and Bob gave up trying to place him.

Frank was heavy. Alice had heard the phrase 'dead weight' plenty of time, but she had never associated it with trying to move a corpse. He wasn't a particularly huge man, but there was enough of him to make dragging him from one room to the next a genuine struggle. She was still weak from the drugs and the loss of blood. Defeated, she slumped on the floor beside him. Then she remembered the scissors.

It had been a stupid idea, Don knew. He hadn't thought it through. The plan had been to pretend he was a neighbour; to say that he had heard shots, and seen some suspicious characters arriving at a house across the street. He was going to destroy the SIM afterwards, and hope that it was unregistered. He hadn't asked. Even it had been registered, he didn't care about Hansen. If he had to silence him himself, he could do it. Jarvis too. If the armed response unit broke in and found him with two corpses, it would be easy to concoct a story where all three had been hostages, and their captors had killed the others. It wasn't a perfect cover. It would still be putting Harry in the frame, he thought. But Goldman had left them to stew, he thought; fair was fair. Don didn't care about him. If he had to take Harry down to save himself, he would. Any alternative would be no better or worse for him. The men outside the door had tried ramming it a few more times, but the barrier was secure for the moment. There had been a couple of more shots, but most of them had just lodged in the wood of the door.

The woman on the other end had asked him for his address, and he had frozen, cursing his own stupidity. She repeated the question a few more times, and then he hung up.

'What's happening, man? What's going on? Are they coming? Are the cops coming?' Hansen was sitting across the room, his back to the wall, between two barred windows.

'Yeah… Yeah, I hope so, mate.' Don slid the mobile back across the floor to the American. *Someone else is bound to hear the shots*, he told himself. *Someone else will call them.*

Dylan hadn't taken the shot. He had the opportunity, and his aim felt good. There hadn't been enough time to make up his mind, though. He was kicking himself. He couldn't be weak like that. Next time, he told himself, it would be someone pointing a gun at him, and they wouldn't have any hesitation in pulling the trigger. There was still time to fix it, he thought. The man still had to come out. If he used the same door, Dylan could be waiting for him. He wasn't going to screw it up a second time, he promised himself. Getting up, he looked around for anyone else, and then sprinted over to the gap between the buildings.

The door was open. There was a pack of cigarettes still on the table outside. Probably Bob's, Harry thought. Carefully, holding the shotgun out in front of him, he stepped through the door. A groan from somewhere inside make his finger jump to the trigger. There was no light, but for the glare of a computer monitor in the next room, through the open mirror-cum-door that he had fitted. The girl was gone; he knew that immediately.

'Harry?' It was Somersby's voice.

'Ian? What the fuck's happened? Where is she?' Goldman moved over to where the young director was lying on the floor; his eyes adjusting to the poor light.

'She's... the bloke- Bob, was it? He took her. He must have taken her, yeah.'

'What do you mean 'must have'? Where the fuck were you? What happed to your face?' Even in the dim, he could see that someone had worked Somersby over. There was blood all over his shirt, and his face was badly swollen.

'I... I don't know, man. I was here. And I was... I was getting her. Then, like out of fucking nowhere, the guy comes in. Hits me. I think he... I think he had a club or a cosh or something. He must have taken her, Harry. I don't know why, I just-'

'FUCK IT. Fuck, fuck, fuck... when?'

'What?'

'When the fuck did this happen? Where did he take her?'

'I don't- I mean, I don't- I have no- he just-'

'Fucking answers, Ian!'

'I don't know, Harry. I'm sorry. I'm sorry, okay? I don't know.'

'Fine. He went through there?' Harry pointed at the mirror.

'Uh, yeah. Yeah, I guess so.'

'Come on then.'

Reinhart could hear the shots from inside. The steel double doors were open. He knew what he had to do: Somehow get through the main house without being seen or confronted; get into the garage; grab one of the cars; take it out the front gate, and drive around the back to collect Harry. Part of him thought that if he got as far as getting out the front gate in a car, there would be a temptation to drive away and forget Harry; but he also knew there was a chance Harry would survive, and he didn't want to think about the sort of comeuppance he would be due if that were the case.

He was at the curve of the circular corridor that went around the building. It was a simple choice between left and right. He was only one person, even if he had the gun, so he needed to go in the opposite direction to the shots, he knew that. But from where the sounds had emanated was anyone's guess. From his position, everything was in front. He stopped hesitating, and went up the right hand passage.

It looked like someone had been through there already, he thought. Pictures had been knocked from the walls, and every other door had been kicked in or had its lock shot off. He wondered about Don and the others, in the banquet room. They were upstairs, so he wasn't going to pass them on his way to the garage. They were probably already dead. Harry might have a hard time explaining their bodies, but they might have been more trouble left alive, he knew.

More shots up ahead, but quieter. They were either coming from upstairs or out in the hall, he guessed. He was hoping it was the former. He was a good shot, but if they outnumbered him, he was only going to get one shot off, maybe two. Regardless, that would be the end of the road for him, he knew that. He was no superman. He heard voices coming near, and ducked into an open room.

He was dead. There was no doubt in Alice's mind, but as she closed the blades of the scissors over his index finger, part of her still expected him to wake up and scream. His skin felt cold and clammy to the touch. A couple of bluebottles had appeared from somewhere in the flat, and were intermittently landing on his face and hands. She shooed them away. He smelt of urine and excrement, and it was getting worse. There was another smell too, one she couldn't place. She assumed that it was the smell of death.

All she had to do was apply the pressure. There was no sawing to do. If she squeezed hard enough, the scissors could cut through the flesh, she thought. She didn't need to go through bone; she only needed the tip. She couldn't remember much from Biology class in school, but she was almost certain that there was just some sort of sinew or cartilage between joints. She took a deep breath and squeezed her hand together. Nothing happened. The blades cut through the thin skin, but there was no blood. Again, Biology class was a far off memory, but she guessed that once the heart stopped pumping, bleeding didn't happen. It made sense to her. She used two hands. The blades cut through the flesh, but there was definitely bone in the way. Her cartoon version of human anatomy wasn't entirely correct, she realised. She was going to have to use more force.

Putting Frank's hand on the floor, she held the scissors so that her hand was holding the larger handle against the ground, with the joint nearest the fingernail lying between the blades. Carefully, while keeping her balance, she pushed down with her other hand, leaning the full weight of her upper body into it, willing the metal to slice through the bone. She made some headway, but it was minimal.

Readjusting her body, she kept her bottom hand where it was, but replaced the other with her foot. Getting as much leverage as she could while still keeping her hand in the hole of the scissors handle, she stood down, and heard the bone give a crack that was equal parts satisfying and sickening. Trying not to look at him, she repeated the manoeuvre again, and a third time, until the top of Frank's finger was hanging on only by the skin. Or so she thought; because, when she gave it a final twist, the crunching sound it made told her that there had still been a little bone matter left at the end. She had her key.

Bob knew he had to move. Where to was unimportant. The other man had gone inside, and might come out again soon. He had to get the girl to a car, or to a way out.

'Come on, treacle.'

'Where are we going, George?'

'Home.'

'My home or your home?'

'We'll see, darlin'. We'll see.'

He threw her up and over his shoulder again, and came out of the bushes. The garden between the small buildings and the large on was big and well lit, but if they kept to the sides, they would be in shadow almost all the way. He didn't know what was in the larger house, or who, but it was bound to be the way out. The shots worried him, but staying where he was didn't seem much safer to him. He edged his way up along by the palm trees, cursing himself for being old and out of shape. Without being told, the child kept quiet. They passed a beautiful water feature, with a statue of a peacock. In the pond, he could see things moving; fish, he thought. He had koi carp at home in the back garden. Building the pond had been the first thing he did when he had been able to get himself a proper house. He remembered then that he wasn't going to get the five thousand, and that all of his money problems were no longer solved.

There were at least five storeys that he could make out in the big house. The architecture was square and dull, and he could see bars on most of the windows, reminding him again of prison. He had no idea where they were. The building he had come from had reminded him of an office; cold and sterile. The larger place didn't seem much different; maybe even colder. There were more shots from inside. They seemed to him to come from up high. That was a good thing, he thought. He was planning on going through the ground floor.

They were half way to the open steel doors where he planned on entering. His heart was in his throat, and it felt like minutes since he had taken a breath. He wondered if he should pray, although he never had much time for religion. Any God who would let an innocent baby like George be born the way he was… that was no God, he thought. There was no harm in trying though, he told himself. Poppy seemed to weigh a tonne on his shoulder as he tried to remember the words to the Lord's Prayer.

Rick thought he was still dreaming, when he opened his eyes. He was in a big room, but it looked different to the one in which he had passed out. The table was by the door now, and there were two big chairs piled on top. The footballer wasn't there, and the other two were sitting on the floor. Outside, he heard shouting. His head ached. He heard Hansen speak.

'Fuck, man. Where's Harry? Will I call him? Did you call him? Man, I can't take this shit. This isn't how it's supposed to go down, man. What have we fucking walked into here? A gang war? This isn't my shit, man. This ain't got nothing to do with us. I'm not getting killed for Harry's shit. I paid fucking money- I paid… Jesus, man. Paul is fucking- gah! What the fuck is going on, Don?'

Before the policeman could answer, there was another voice; outside the door. He spoke with a foreign accent, but in English. Rick blinked and rubbed his eyes, his head still pounding.

'In there. You. In there. This Hansen. He is with you.'

No one spoke. Rick looked at Bill, whose mouth was hanging open. Don looked suddenly alert. The man outside continued.

'Hansen is what we want. Open the door, give him to us. The rest of you don't get hurt. Give us Hansen. Can you hear me?'

'What the fuck?' Bill said it in a whisper, to none of them in particular. Rick's mouth was dry.

'What the hell have you done, Bill?' Don was whispering too. Outside, the foreign man raised his voice:

'I said, can you hear me in there?' A gun went off outside the door, causing all of them to jump. Rick was wondering where Paul had gone.

'Yes. Yes, give us a minute, pal,' said Don. Bill looked aghast.

'Give us a minute? What the fuck? You're not seriously thinking of- I mean, I don't know what the fuck these guys want with me. But you don't actually believe they're gonna let you fucking live, do you? The minute we open that door, we're all fucking dead, man. We're all-'

'They have no reason to kill us if it's you they want,' said Don.

'You don't fucking know that, man. You don't know that. They're like- look, I don't know what-'

He was cut off by Don, who shouted at the door:

'You. You, out there. What did he do? Hansen, what did he do?' He looked at Bill and gave a shrug. The American put his face in his hands. From outside in the hall, the voice came back:

'Mister Hansen take something that belong to us.'

'Something that belongs to you? Huh? Why didn't you fucking say, man? What was it? What is it? I'll pay you man, why didn't you just say?' Hansen was up and off the floor, and walking towards the barricaded door.

'You can't pay back. You take what is ours. And you break it.'

'Break it? What fuck was it, man? Who are you?'

'You take little girl.'

'Huh? What? Like, fucking Poppy? What the fuck, man? How was that me? How was that- dude, seriously, listen. You got the wrong fucking guy here, man. I dunno what Harry fuckin' told you, but-'

'No Poppy. No Harry. You, Hansen. You take girl tonight. She come to your hotel. You pay for her.'

Rick saw Hansen stop in his tracks, the inane grin disappearing from his face.

'I... fuck.'

'We find her in your car. The dogs, they smell her. You break what is ours.'

'I, man, Jesus, I-'

'Now we break you.'

Rick watched Bill's eyes widen in terror, then he dived for the floor as several rounds pierced the wood of the door. The singer stood up dizzily from his chair and backed away towards the opposite side of the room, knowing there was nowhere to go, but moving away from where the guns had breached the wood panelling. Don was up too, his hands held out in front of him. The door came apart with a crash, and then the table started moving. Both chairs toppled onto the floor, and in a few seconds, the men were inside. Two of them grabbed Hansen and pulled him up. The others trained their guns on all three. No one said anything for a minute, then Hansen pointed at Don.

'That one's a fucking cop. Go check his ID. You leave him alive and you're all going down.'

Twenty Three

'I sorry, Harry. I'm really- I just-' Somersby was trying to scan the man's face in order to predict what was going to happen to him, but Goldman was inscrutable at the best of times.

'Sorry's no good to me. Come on. They won't have got far.'

'Okay. Sor- Okay, Harry.'

There was no one outside. He was glad of that. If or when they caught up with Bob and the child, Harry would hear about what he had tried to do to her. It would come out. He was praying silently that they had got away clean. At least then, his only crime had been being overpowered by the old man, he thought.

'Fucking nothing. Okay, if they've gone that way, they're gonna run into Reinhart, or worse. If they've gone back the other way, well… they might get out the back gate, or they might run into Mal…' Goldman looked at his watch, shaking his head. In his other hand was a shotgun which looked like it had seen better days, Somersby noticed.

'So what do we do?'

'I've got a car coming.'

'A car?'

'Yeah. Reinhart's coming. I should fucking leave you here to rot, you know…'

'I- I know. Look, Harry, I'm so-'

'Just fucking come on. There's no time.'

They walked back around the building, away from the main house. Somersby saw the boy before Harry did. In truth, he was a grown man, but the hair, the clothes, and the nervous way he held himself, gave the impression of a teenager at first. In his hands, pointed at them, was an enormous pistol. When he spoke, he sounded even more like a child.

'Don't move. D-don't either of you fucking move, right. I'm s-serious. Fucking just- just stay there. Put that gun down, all right? I'm- I'm not joking.'

Goldman blew out softly through pursed lips, and raised his eyebrow at the youth. Somersby felt his bowels turn to water. Harry spoke.

'Dunno who you are, kid. But this ain't your fucking fight. Be a good boy and put that thing away, yeah. Put it down, walk away, and everyone goes home happy. I'll give you til three, yeah?'

Somersby watched the two of them. Harry was calm, almost smiling. The boy's hands were shaking, possibly from fear, or it could just have been the weight of the gun he was struggling to hold. He looked lost for words, and then:

'I'm not- I'm not putting anything down. I don't know who you are, but I know what you're doing. I know you have Poppy. And I want her back.'

'Poppy? Listen mate, you got the wrong geezers. I dunno nothing about no 'Poppy'. All I knows is that you're on my manor, you've a shooter in my face, and you clearly have no idea who you're fucking dealing with, yeah. I'll start the count now, okay? One-'

The boy swallowed and then tightened his grip on the pistol; his finger fumbling its way onto the trigger.

'Two…' Harry kept his gun pointed at the floor, tensing up the muscles in his other hand, so much that Somersby heard a cracking sound from his knuckles, or possibly the joint of his elbow.

'Shut up! Shut up, you don't get to count. Fucking… I have the gun on you. What the fuck do you think you can- just tell me where she is, okay? Tell me where Poppy is. And Alice. No one, two, three. Just tell me, or I'll do it.'

'Hah! Yeah. All right, fucking John Wayne. Do your worst.'

Somersby darted a glance at Goldman, panicking; then back at the boy. As if it were happening in slow motion, he saw the finger squeeze down on the trigger, and the gunman's face contort slightly in anticipation of what was about to happen. And then it didn't happen. For a second, no one moved or said anything. The boy's expression was somewhere between shock and confusion. Harry gave a horrible chuckle, then swung his own gun up to chest height, and fired it with an ear-splitting bang, sending the youth flying several feet through the air, before he hit the wall, and collapsed on the concrete.

'Fucking amateurs,' was all Harry said, as they stepped over the body and through the door to the office.

Reinhart stayed as still and silent as he could. Outside in the corridor, he heard voices. He couldn't tell how many there were. If they passed without checking the room he was in, he would have the drop on them, he thought. The noises came near and nearer, then started to fade again. They had gone past, the thought. He had to make his move. Checking to make sure the safety catch was undone, he raised the gun in front of him and swung around the door frame. There were two of them in front of him, both armed. He took the first one down with a shot to the back. The second man spun to face him, but didn't have a chance to fire. Reinhart put a bullet in his face, and then three in his chest, shooting and moving, until he stood over them both, his heart thumping. The man who had been hit first stirred and gave a groan, and Reinhart put another bullet in him; this time in the back of his head. He took the man's pistol from his hand, and rolled the other man one over. The second Albanian had been carrying an Uzi. Reinhart took the gun out of his still warm hand. In a leather bag he found two unspent magazines for the sub machine gun. He put the pistols into it, and threw it over his shoulder. Upstairs there was shouting. He would need to move fast if he wanted to reach the garage before they found him. Gripping the handle of the Uzi, he felt a glimmer of hope. The odds were beginning to turn in his favour, he thought.

'Jesus.' Bob ducked down when he heard the shots coming from inside the big house. He held the girl close as more followed.

'What's that? What's that?'

He felt her fingers digging into him with fear.

'It's- well, it's…' He couldn't think of something to reassure her.

'It's not fireworks, George. I'm scared. What is it? Is it guns?'

'I don't know, pet. I don't know.' The firing had stopped, but there was no way he was going to carry on through the door. Not without a gun of his own, and not with her on his shoulder. He would have to go back, he thought. Back to where they had been keeping her. The van might still be in the garage. And if it wasn't, there might be another van, or a car. He turned around and made his way back down the garden.

'Where- where are we going now?'

'Change of plan, treacle. Gotta go back, all right?'

'Back? But- but what about the bad man? He's back there, George, what about him?'

'Don't you worry about him, sweetheart. I didn't let him hurt you before, did I?' Bob quickened his pace. She was starting to feel too heavy.

'No. No, you didn't.'

'And I won't let him again, trust me, babes.' He stopped for a second, and put her down. 'Can you walk for me, honey?'

'Yeah. Yeah, I can. Shall we run? I'm good at running.'

'Run? Jesus- no, just walk, babes. I'm a bit old for running.' They'd reached the first of the three buildings. There were lights on inside; he wondered if he should stop and check it out. The child was several feet in front of him, moving too fast for him to catch up.

'Oi! Slow down, love. Wait for me!' He quickened his pace, watching her disappear around the corner.

Don stared across the room at Hansen, but the American wasn't looking in his direction. There hadn't been time for the men with guns to check if Bill's claim about him being a police officer was true. The majority of them had run back out into the house when there had been a barrage of shots from somewhere downstairs. They'd left one man to guard the three, but there was no chance of them overpowering him or rushing him. He had a sub machine gun resting on his hip, and from his vantage point in the doorway, he would easily cut all three down before one of them had the chance to reach him. These people weren't fools or amateurs, he told himself.

As if sensing that he was being watched, Hansen turned around and smiled at Don, his eyes looking everywhere but straight. He was high as a kite; that was clear. Jarvis looked out of it too. Don wasn't sure what was going to happen to him or Rick, but Hansen was a dead man. It was only a matter of time.

From downstairs, there were more shots. Several different types this time, he noted. The single shots of a pistol or pistols; the loud blast of a shotgun, and the rattle of an automatic weapon. He wondered who it was they were fighting. Had Harry called his armed guards back to house? Or was it Harry himself, or Reinhart. He had never known Goldman to do his own dirty work, but who knew, if the situation called for it. He knew Harry had started out as a foot soldier in the East End gangs back in the Sixties. The man probably still knew how to handle a firearm. There were more shots, and some screaming. The man who was guarding them looked more on edge as the firing went on. Don wondered if part of him was considering forgetting about them, and running while he still could. He hoped that was the case. Somewhere outside he heard a police siren, but it seemed too far away. The man in the doorway seemed to hear it too, Don noted.

Alice was through the door and into the garage. Frank's car was where they had left it, and his keys were on the driver's seat. She was almost out, she knew. There was only one problem. She couldn't open the garage door. There was no button inside, and no remote control anywhere she could see. There was a six foot gap between the car and the steel shutter. Enough to build up some speed, she thought. There was no room to turn the car around, so it would have to be reverse gear. She had no idea if it would work, but it was her only option.

She started the engine and put the gearstick into position. The car's rear hit the door with a crash, but it stayed put. Sighing, she tried again. The metal remained in place. She couldn't see if the car itself was picking up damage. She revved the engine more, pushing her back into the seat, as if it would help the Bentley do more damage. After the fourth attempt, she heard the metal at the bottom of the door screech over the concrete. Enthused, she went again and again, cursing the blacked out windows for making it impossible to see what was happening behind her. Each time she rolled back, the door made a more satisfying scraping noise. Pushing the door open, she leaned out, and with her one working eye, saw a great buckle down the centre of the slatted metal curtain. She sat back down and repeated the procedure, over and over, until the door ripped out of its moorings, and fell out onto the driveway beyond.

Reinhart had only made it as far as the bottom of the stairs when the Albanians found him. They had come from above, at least six of them, all armed and already firing. He cursed himself for not making it to the door which led into the hallway, and then the garage. Instead, he fallen back into the corridor from which he had come. He had played the waiting game, letting them empty their magazines in his direction, then he had taken a chance and leaned out, firing the Uzi in their general direction, without any real aim. He had dropped two of them, although he didn't know if their wounds were fatal. He was still battling the odds, he knew, but he also know that four to one were better odds than six to one.

The Albanians fired again, and he could tell from the trajectory that at least one of them had broken away and moved across the floor. He waited until their firing ceased, then took a gamble on where the breakaway shooter was, and was incredibly relieved when his hunch turned out to be correct. The man's expression of surprise was almost comical, before Reinhart emptied the rest of the clip into his face. *Three down, three left*, he told himself, knowing that escape was becoming ever more possible as time went by. The others hadn't returned fire, and he wondered for a moment if they might have run out of ammunition. If that was the case, he could rush them. He mightn't even have to fire. He only needed to get out, and get to the garage. He wasn't interested in killing them if he didn't have to. He wasn't even sure if he was going to go back for Harry. He would decide once he was in the car.

He thought he heard a siren outside, and for a moment his brain needed to process it, so he could tell if it was police, fire or ambulance. He had lived in England for years, but he still got the tones mixed up, because they were different to the ones he had grown up with in Austria. While he was deciding, the siren was joined by several more; all with the same sound. He never heard the young Albanian boy sneak up the corridor behind him. He was still thinking about flashing lights and loud noises when the bullet when through the back of his skull.

Harry opened the door cautiously, the shotgun cocked in front of him.

'Fucking hell, mate. Nice to see you too.'

'Mal! The rest of them here yet?' Behind him, he heard Beth let out an audible sigh of relief.

'Ah, no. First one, I think. Listen, what the fuck is-'

'No time. You got your car?'

'Well, yeah, I-'

'Good, let's go. Come on! You two as well. Go, go, go.' He signalled to the others to follow him. For the first time in his life, he didn't have a plan. Outside, instead of a car, he saw that Malcolm had brought one of the company vans. His disappointment faded in an instant when he saw the blacked out windows.

'Okay, Mal. You drive. We'll get in the back.'

'What, even you, Boss?'

'Even me, yeah.'

At first, Dylan thought it was a hallucination. Some sort of happy mirage, brought on by his impending death. He was dying, he knew that. The shotgun blast had opened his stomach, his chest, and some of his neck. He was in a pool of warm blood which wasn't showing any signs of slowing its flow. He looked up and saw Poppy come around the corner; half running, half skipping.

'Dylan!' Her voice was a mixture of happiness, surprise and horror. She rushed to him. His hand was still on the pistol; the pistol which had failed him. That old movie cliché of trying to fire with the safety off. He would have chuckled had the pain not been so excruciating.

'Poppy, I-' He struggled to speak. The breath was gone from him. He had probably punctured a lung, if not both, he thought.

'Dylan, what happened? You're bleeding. There's… blood. What happened?'

'You should see the other guy.' He half managed the smile, but the coughing fit which followed made him regret trying to speak at all.

'Oh, Dylan. I'm-' The tears came all at once, stopping her sentence mid flow. He wanted to hold her, to comfort her. But the pain was so strong, and anyway, he must have looked like something from a horror movie, he thought. Poppy fell into his lap, making the pain even worse, but he didn't move her. His arms were still okay, and he used the one which wasn't holding the gun, to hold her close. Behind her, someone spoke.

'Oi! What you think you're doing, Pal?'

In one movement, Dylan rolled her out of the way and raised the pistol. The man threw his hands in the air in protest, but there wasn't time for him to say anything. Despite only having one hand to steady his aim, the first shot from Dylan's gun was true. It tore through the bald man's throat and he dropped to his knees with a gurgling scream. Unmoved, Dylan kept aim and the second bullet took off the top of the kidnapper's skull. Poppy turned to look, but he pulled her close to him, burying her face in his chest.

'No, babe. No. Don't- you don't want to see that.'

'What did you do? What did you-' She wriggled out of his grasp and turned to look at the prone figure. She said nothing for a few seconds, then he heard her say, quietly:

'That was George. George was good. George was taking me home.'

Before he could reply, there was a screech of tyres, and a black limousine skidded to a halt, inches from them. Dylan felt more stabbing pains in his gut, and another wrenching one as he pivoted towards the headlights, raising the pistol once more.

It was a miracle, Rick told himself. God hadn't forsaken him. They had been sitting in the room, listening to the chaos all around them, watching the man who was watching them. Then there had been some commotion in the hallway outside, and someone had shouted:

'Armed police; put down your weapon!'

The Albanian did the opposite of what he was told, and was promptly cut to pieces by a hail of bullets from their unseen saviours. And then the room had been filled with officers from SO19, who had searched them for weapons, and then begun to ask questions. Hansen had said he was saying nothing until he spoke to his lawyer. Rick had quickly followed suit. Don had taken the commanding officer to one side, and spoke to in hushed tones. Rick knew that the conversation was likely to be one which incriminated him and Hansen, but he didn't care. He was alive. God had reached down and saved him from the jaws of death. He was going to change his life. He had been given a second chance. While Hansen talked manically on his phone to someone, probably his brief, Rick sat silently in his chair, a broad smile covering his face. It was the smile of the righteous, he told himself. The smile of one who has been blessed. Like the Prodigal Son. There would be plenty of time for lawyers later. Now, he needed to talk to his God.

'Was that Frank?' asked Malcolm, over his shoulder.

'Was what Frank?' Harry leaned into the small gauze covered hole which served as an intercom between driver and passengers in the vans he had had customised for privacy.

'In the Bentley, just now. Oh, sorry, Boss. Forgot you can't see nothing back there.'

'What, just now? Driving it?' He hadn't been able to reach his son on the phone, and had forgotten about him until that moment.

'Seems like it; coming out of the garage. That's still his gaff, right?'

'Yeah. Yeah, it is.' Harry had had all three back buildings built at the same time. There was only supposed to be two, but the boy had asked for a place away from the house; to give him some independence, he said. Harry knew it was more so he could bring girls home, even though he had been told that the grounds were off limits to outsiders.

'Well then, that was him.'

'What? Going the same was as us?'

'Nope. The other way, actually.'

'The other way? What the fuck would he be doing going that way?' If Frank was up to something, it wasn't anything Harry knew about. It wouldn't be the first time, of course. The boy always had some gig in the pipeline, Harry thought. Just like his father.

'Beat me, Boss. Oh, fuck.'

'What now?'

'The gate, Boss.'

'What's wrong with the gate? You got in all right, didn't you?'

Malcolm didn't answer. Harry noticed they had stopped. The driver door opened, and then closed again. Outside he heard shouting, and he thought he recognised Malcolm's voice among the others. No one in the back of the van said a word. Harry cocked the shotgun and looked at the side door of the van, waiting for the Albanians to wrench it open. When it finally slid across, and someone pointed an assault rifle through the gap, something inside told him not to fire first. When the whole door opened, he had never before been so relieved to see the word 'Police' emblazoned on a jacket. Beyond the gate, the flashing lights of some twenty or so squad cars lit up the night. He put the gun down on the floor of the van, and raised his hands.

Alice threw open the car door in shock, not sure who to go to first. Behind Poppy and Dylan, on the road, someone was lying dead; their head haemorrhaging blood onto the tarmac. She barely gave him a glance. Poppy rushed to her, tears streaming down her face, unable to articulate any words. She stooped to meet the embrace, and found herself crying too. She wanted to hold onto the child and never let go again, but she broke away and turned to Dylan. Nothing in her head made sense any more. She was escaping from the place. It was just a heads or tails decision that made her drive in their direction. The other way, and she would have never known how close they were to her.

'Baby! Why are you- how did you get- what happened?' She had too many questions.

'Me? Oh, I do this a lot.'

'What?' His voice made her want to cry even more; he sounded fragile, like a child. He was bleeding out everywhere. It didn't look good to her. She tried to stay calm.

'You know. Turning up out of the blue. When you need some space. Sorry about that, by the way. I sort of get it now. The whole space thing. What the fuck happened to you? What's with the eye? You look like Rocky.'

'Oh, baby. Oh, shush. I don't- I didn't mean to- we have to get you to a hospital.' She reached for her phone, before remembering that she didn't have it.

'Oh, you know I hate hospitals, babe. Full of fucking sick people, am I right?' He gave a half laugh, and she could see that it hurt him to do even that. His top was saturated with blood, and there was a pool of it under him; older, blackish brown blood. He must have been bleeding for a while, she thought.

'Dylan, please. I need to get you in the car, okay. We'll find a phone, or I'll drive you there myself, okay? Just- just stay with me...' It was all she could think to say; it was what people said in the movies.

'Is he going to die?' It was Poppy, standing beside them. Alice looked at her. She seemed to have aged five years since the last time she had seen her.

'Of course not, baby. Of course not. We're going to get him to a hospital. We're going to-'

'Alice?' His voice was tiny, like he was speaking from the other end of a room.

'Yes, baby?' She wondered should she get him to put pressure on the wound, but there was so much blood, she couldn't see what part was the wound and what wasn't. All of her practical sense seemed to have deserted her.

'I think- I'm not really sure that I'm gonna- you know. So I was like- well… can I say something?'

'Huh? Of course, babe. But don't say that. We're gonna-'

'Alice!'

'Sorry. Sorry, sorry, sorry.'

'Hey.' He smiled at her, and she felt her heart begin to break.

'Hey.'

'I love you, okay?'

'I- I love you too, baby. I really do, I-'

'I know. Hey! It's us, remember? We got the movie love, yeah? Like Harvey and Sabrina.' He smiled again. She couldn't look away from him. She felt like these were moments she needed to save in her head forever; but she hoped to God that it wasn't the case.'

'Harvey and Sabrina, yeah. Dylan, I-'

'I mean, yeah sometimes you're a massive twat to me…'

'I-?' She found herself laughing, in spite of everything.

'But I love you, yeah? And I know I'm a big failure, and I can't do normal stuff like normal people, but-'

'Dyl baby none of that matters, okay? Don't-'

'No, no, no, no, it does, okay. You're right. I don't take responsibility for myself, and I'm fucking awful at looking for jobs and all that shit- but, you… you do something to me, yeah?' His voice was cracking, his breathing extremely erratic. She needed to move him, but she wasn't even sure if it would make him worse.

'Dylan! We need to get you to a hospital, please! For me? I love you so much.'

'Yep. Yep, you're right, again. All I was saying was... I'm sorry, you know?'

'You don't have anything to be sorry for, baby. You don't, I promise.'

'Thanks. Oh, and when I said you looked like Rocky, I meant the boxer, yeah? Not the guy from Mask, with the freaky face. Just to clarify.'

'I know what you meant, baby. And… I don't even know who the guy from Mask is.' Somewhere behind them, there were voices, and the beams from flashlights. She ignored them and turned back to him.

'You are so shit at pop culture references.' He touched his stomach through the t-shirt, and she saw fresh blood on his hand.

'I am the worst.' She smiled at him, suddenly aware that Poppy was beside them, watching and listening. She reached for the girl's hand.

'But... seriously now. I spent so much time wanting you to accept me for who I was. But I wasn't accepting you for who you for... ugh, I, ah...'

'Huh?' She hadn't caught the last of what he said, if he had said anything at all. His eyes closed over, and his arm twitched.

The voices behind became nearer and louder. She looked up to see several policemen coming towards them, and a man and woman dressed in the green uniforms of an ambulance crew.

'Oh, Jesus Christ... Thank God you're here. Please, he's hurt!' She stood up and ran towards the crowd, dragging the female paramedic back with her by the arm.

'Okay, everybody get back. Clear a space for me,' said the woman, shining a small torch over Dylan's chest and stomach.

'All right, get that stretcher over here, Mick.'

Alice stood back and watched them tend to him, holding Poppy in her arms. She watched them give him some injections, painkillers and sedatives, she guessed. Finally, he was ready to go in the ambulance, which someone had brought around to the scene. When they asked who was coming with him, she rushed into the back of the van, taking Poppy with her. They argued a little over the rules, but eventually someone said it was okay for the child to come too. A policeman sat with them for the journey, but he didn't ask any questions. The journey to the hospital took less than fifteen minutes, she guessed. It felt like an eternity. She didn't take her eyes from him once, every fibre of her willing him to wake up again. She decided to pray to God, or to anyone who would listen. Because she didn't want the last thing she ever said to him to be 'huh?' She had told him she love him too, but it hadn't been the last thing. So, they couldn't just let him die. It wouldn't be fair.

In the weeks after, and at the funeral, she changed her mind about it. If there was some sort of afterlife, and he was looking down on her, she knew he would find it hilarious that she said 'huh?' Sometimes, on those nights where sleep wouldn't come and her thoughts refused to be quiet, she would say 'huh?' out loud in her bedroom, and she would swear it felt like he heard her.

Twenty Four

The trial was a joke; a complete whitewash, Tom had called it. First, the jury selection had been almost impossible. Of the original group, one had died in a car crash, hours after she had been chosen. Two more were found dead in the days following; both had hanged themselves, the reports said. After that, it was pandemonium. The remaining jurors tried to be excused from duty, saying they feared for their lives. The court refused, as, tragic as they had been, the three deaths were not ruled to have been the result of foul play. That was what the police had said, although Alice was sure that those were officers who were firmly in Harry Goldman's pocket. Most of the original twelve, or the nine who remained, managed to walk; doctors and psychiatrists having written heartfelt notes the court, citing mental and physical health reasons. Once they finally had their full dozen volunteers, Alice was almost convinced that every one of them was either on Goldman's payroll, or would simply turn in a Not Guilty verdict in order to preserve his or her own life.

In the end, it had been academic. Harry's solicitors had come up with a story which absolved him of all blame, placing the culpability in the hands of his dead son. The younger Goldman had organised everything- the kidnap, the video production, even extorting the ransom from Mr Riley's P.A. He had also organised a meeting with the Albanian sex traffickers who had been responsible for the siege at the Goldman mansion. The defence team said that they couldn't speculate as to what Frank was planning to do with Poppy, even though the money and safety deposit keys had been found near his body.

Harry Goldman claimed he had no knowledge the girl was being held on his property. There were many, many rooms on the premises, and he couldn't be expected to know everything that was occurring in all of them, he said; almost nonchalantly, Alice remembered thinking at the time. He had arranged an evening with some friends, the other defendants in the case, on the evening of the incident, and had been shocked and terrified when he had heard gunshots coming from the other end of the house. He had jumped in a car with Somersby, Beth and the head of his security. He felt terrible at the time for leaving the others in the house, but he had had to think quickly. He confirmed that another dead man found on the premises, a Reinhart Krostvallen, had been an employee of his. He said it was with great sadness and regret that he had to agree the man must have been involved in the kidnap plot, along with his son, the dead Polish woman, and the man who had been shot by Dylan.

Alice took the stand, in her frail condition, to tell her side of the story. The defending solicitor tore her to pieces, calling her a liar and a fantasist, and suggesting that she had been far from an innocent party in the events. He claimed that she had been co-operating with Frank Goldman, meaning to split the ransom with him after the child was returned, but that Goldman Jr. had probably meant to betray her, meaning to keep the cash while also selling the girl to the child prostitution ring. Through her vehement denials, he put it to her that her testimony was a fabrication; an act of petty vengeance against the father of the man who had double crossed her. Even Alice had to admit to herself, he was painting a believable picture for the jury.

She and Tom had deliberated about putting Poppy on the stand. She had been through enough, they both thought; but, without her words, it was just Alice's version of events against the story Goldman's brief had concocted. In the end, Poppy herself insisted on testifying. She did as well as she could, but neither Alice nor her boss was surprised when the defending solicitor ripped her to shreds under cross examination. She didn't cry, but Alice shed enough tears for the both of them that day.

The jury took no time at all to acquit, and Alice, then Tom, had to be physically restrained from attacking the freed men and woman. The jury members never looked at her, not once. In the public gallery, the people and press murmured among themselves. The defence had done such a sterling job in convincing everyone of Goldman's innocence, that the mood wasn't one of outrage or injustice. Instead, Alice felt accusing eyes on herself. It was over, in theory. But she knew it was far from that in reality.

After the trial, she and Tom were visited in an unofficial capacity by two officers from the Met. One of them was an old school friend of Tom's, the other had lost his own child in a revenge attack by a gang boss he had helped to jail for life. Alice trusted them both, almost immediately. They commiserated sincerely, but also urged Tom to do all he could to protect his daughter and Alice from the inevitable retribution that would follow. Harry Goldman was not known for letting grudges die, and they said that they could give no guarantees that the girls would be safe, even while the police were aware of the threat. Alice felt like crying with frustration. It wasn't supposed to be like that, she had told the men. The police were supposed to keep them safe. They were supposed to put men like Harry Goldman in prison, not to throw their arms up and say that there was nothing they could do. Tom listened to the men with a heavy heart, and agreed that they must do something. Poppy would be sent away, a boarding school in Switzerland, or the United States; the two men would help them to create a new identity for her. The information would not leave the room in which they sat and discussed the plans. Goldman had his people all over the Force- no one could be trusted completely.

As for Alice, she would have to disappear too. She had no real ties to the area anymore, especially since Dylan was gone. Tom insisted that he would pay for everything. The millions that would have been taken by Frank Goldman had been returned to him, intact, by the police, and he had considered the money to be a write-off, because he had got back Poppy, alive and unharmed. She could have it all, if she wanted. All he asked was that she go far away, start a new life, and try to be happy. Alice didn't want to leave him, or Poppy, but she knew there was no choice. Goldman's men had tried to kill her when she had been in the hospital after the siege; he wouldn't consider it any sort of inconvenience to keep trying, perpetually, until she was dead. Running away might seem like surrender, but she knew that living would be a victory. She had to win something. For herself, for Poppy; and for Dylan.

Epilogue

Harry looked at the newspaper that had been sitting on the desk since that morning, unread. A chill came over him as he read the headline, and he flicked quickly to the inside to read the rest. Old ghosts, coming back after all these years, to haunt him. His coffee was cold. He would ask the girl to bring him more in a bit.

A body had washed up on the banks of the Thames less than a week before. It wasn't front page news; they were always fishing corpses out of the water. Suicides, accidents- or things made to look like either. He had arranged plenty of them himself. What made the case newsworthy, especially for the sensation-hungry tabloid press, was the level of mutilation. Some papers were even making comparisons to Whitechapel; such was the horrific nature of the wounds.

Harry had first figured it for a gangland job. The Vietnamese or the Triads, he reckoned. They were the most theatrical when it came to making an example of someone who had crossed them. The body had been impossible to identify when they found it. There weren't any teeth to match with dental records. The fingertips had been sliced off too, and the eyeballs either cut out, or had decomposed while under the river. He had been weighed down with breeze blocks. They knew it was a he, even though the genitals had been cut away.

It was only now that the forensics had come up with a name, and seeing it took Harry back seven years, almost to the day. That had been the last time he had seen the young filmmaker; when the jury had come back with their verdicts. For Harry, it was the end of an era. Don didn't finger him in court, but made it clear afterwards that he was no longer going to cover for him when it came to the business of making and distributing the films. Harry had seen it as an opportunity to draw a line in the sand, and had gone back to his other business interests. He hadn't gone straight by any means, but the more distance he put between himself and those days, the more redeemed he considered his own character. He had been lucky that night, and afterwards. And he still had Beth, although she had been elusive about marriage, and still had her two flats in the City. Independent to a fault, he thought. But that was one of the reasons he loved her.

Somersby had walked, along with the rest of them, but the experience in the house that morning had left him a broken man. He hadn't worked since the trial, and had become a recluse, the paper said. That was probably why no one had reported him missing. Although it wasn't uncommon for adults to disappear and the police not be informed. People only feared the worst when a child was involved.

The report said that police had identified Somersby by a birthmark; a hammer shaped spot on the nape of his neck, under the hair- the remnant of a blemish that had been much larger when he was born. They only knew about it by sheer chance. An officer at the station had once watched an interview with the director where he had joked about it, saying he was thinking of getting a sickle tattooed next to it, to celebrate his Leftist views.

The wounds had been confirmed by the pathologist as having happened 'some hours before death'. Harry winced at the idea of it. He had watched enough men tortured to know that the best way of doing it was to do it slowly. Someone took their time with him; maybe even enjoyed it. If it was personal, they would have. And seeing as Somersby was unlikely to have become a major player in the London crime scene in under a decade, apropos of nothing, it was almost definitely personal. Harry pushed the intercom button, through to the receptionist's desk.

'Daisy? Daisy, can you fix us a brew, yeah? Good girl.'

'Yes, Mister Goldman.'

'Oh, and… am I done for the day?'

'Ah, not quite, Mister Goldman. Just one more.'

'Bollocks, really? Who is it?'

'An Amelia Barr. She's something to do with one of the big charities. She'll be here in ten. Is that okay?'

'Charities? Gah, fine. Get me some coffee, then send her in when she comes.'

Police had no leads in the case, the paper went on; Somersby had been a social pariah since his part in the famous Poppy Riley Kidnap trial seven years before, and they could find no witnesses who had seen him recently. He lived alone in a detached house with its own grounds, and had all his supplies and groceries delivered, with instructions to leave them outside the front door, without entering the premises. He had no connections with organised crime that the police were aware of. The toxicology reports had been 'inconclusive'.

Harry took a tumbler from the silver decanter tray next to his desk, and poured himself a Scotch. The coffee would still be brewing; the girl made a nice pot of black. He had found her six months before. In truth, she had found him. She somehow sneaked into The Ivy, where he was having lunch with an old face from his East End days, and dropped her CV on the table in front of him. She was dressed to impress, in a mini-skirt and heels. He thought, looking at her, she couldn't have been more than nineteen. Twenty at a push. She smiled at him and told him she heard he was looking for a new secretary. He wasn't, but he liked her, and not just for the usual reasons. She had confidence, showed a bit of initiative. And a lot of leg. He took the laminated sheets from her and told her that he would give her a ring. Within a week, she had replaced Maura on the front desk.

'There you go, sir.' She had on a black pencil skirt and a white fitted blouse, just like any other day. He liked the way it accentuated everything about her young body. And on a day as hot as it was, she wasn't shy about leaving the top two buttons undone. He looked her up and down slowly, as she put the tray down on the desk. He hadn't made any sort of move on her yet, but he was in no hurry. It could wait.

'Cheers, sweetheart. Doing anything wild at the weekend?'

'What, me? Oh, no. Nothing too crazy. Just meeting up with a friend. Yeah, probably going to be a quiet one.' She had a nice smile. Good teeth.

'Really? I thought you'd be swinging from the chandeliers, love. You're only young once, you know. Make the most of it while you can. That's what I say.'

'Yes, Mister Goldman. I'll send that lady in when she comes.'

'Thanks, doll. You're a star.'

There had been nothing on the body suggest who had done the deed; no markings, no gang calling cards. The weighting down suggested that the perpetrators had wanted the disappearance to remain secret for some time; but, when the police had searched Somersby's house, they had found no evidence of a break in, or that anyone had stolen anything. The motive remained a mystery. The intercom crackled.

'Mr Goldman? Miss Barr to see you.'

'Huh? Oh, all right. Send her in.' Harry finished the Scotch in one. He had had a couple already since the morning. The decanter had been full when he came in. The girl always topped it up before she left each evening. It was the expensive, twelve year old single malt, just for him. Guests got the cheaper one, in the bottle on the shelf. The door opened, and a tall, slim woman came through to the office. Her hair was dyed jet black, which made her face look washed out, he thought. She was wearing sunglasses, and carrying an expensive looking briefcase. Harry didn't stand up.

'Mister Goldman, I presume?' Her smile was fake, and icy. He didn't recognise anything about her in particular. They'd not met before.

'That's the one. Please, call me Harry.' He put his hand around the pot. Still hot, but about ready to pour.

'Can I get you a coffee?' He took a mug from the tray for himself, and filled it without taking his eyes off her. She didn't look like she wanted to sit.

'No, thank you. I'd rather get on with our business.' She laid the case on the chair in front of her, still wearing the opaque aviator-style lenses. Harry wondered if they were the prescription kind, or if she had some sort of condition. People who worked for charities often suffered from the afflictions of which they were trying to raise awareness.

'Right, yeah. Sorry, my memory's like a sieve these days; what was it we were going to talk about? I can't bloody remember even arranging this, Miss...' He had forgotten her name.

'Barr. Amelia Barr. Not that it matters. It's not important, that name.' She smiled again, but this time it was a different kind. Almost a sneer.

'Sorry, what do you mean?' He looked down at the case, and then back at her. He couldn't tell what was going on behind the darkened lenses, and the rest of her gave nothing away.

'My name. It's not important. It's not even my name, to be honest, Harry.'

'I... I don't know- hang on a second. Who are you?' A feeling came over him. Somewhere between apprehension and dread. His eyes drifted to the drawer on the left of his side of the desk. His stomach gave an odd rumble; not of hunger, more like he had taken one too many Alka-Seltzers.

'Right now? Right now I'm no one, Harry. I haven't been anyone for years. I definitely haven't been myself. That was down to you.' She leaned over again and popped the gold clasps on the briefcase. Harry looked at the drawer again, a single drop of sweat tricking down his temple and onto his cheek.

'Who the bloody hell are you? What are you doing here? I didn't make any appointment with you. How did you get in?' His heart wasn't racing, but the beat seemed odd; incongruous, almost. He reached for the handle of the drawer with the handgun in it.

'Oh, I wouldn't bother with that. No bullets, see. We planned ahead.' Another smile, the most genuine one since she had shown up, he thought. Harry pulled the handle to confirm what she had said. It was true. Just the gun. No magazine. Useless. Harry banged on the intercom button. His feet felt strange and numb. His fingertips were tingling too. Another rumble from his stomach.

'Daisy! Get security in here, now! Now!' There was no reply. The woman laughed.

'Oh yes, 'Daisy'. That was my idea. A flower, yeah? Clever.'

The door swung open behind the black haired woman, and in came the girl. He looked at the face. It was her all right. How could he have forgotten that face? He got up to run, but his legs didn't move.

'Feeling a little stuck, Harry? Don't worry, it's not permanent.'

'What the?' He couldn't move his feet, or his legs. His arms were by his side, and though his mind was willing them to do something, nothing happened.

'I hope you treated yourself to a few Scotches today, Harry. The more of them the better. I'd say I hope you didn't offer anyone else a glass, but I think we both know there was no chance of that. Good thing too, because otherwise they'd be feeling a little bit ill. Not like you're feeling, though. No, the second part of the dose is in that nice mug of black. Without that, the effects a bit boring. Vomiting, diarrhoea, maybe. Put the two together though, and... How are you doing? Is it in your chest yet? Or are we still at arms and legs? Good thing you're such a creature of habit, Harry. A few glasses of Scotch, every single day. Three pots of coffee, every single day. And the last pot, always at the same time.' She looked at her watch. The other girl, Daisy, or Poppy, came forward and stood beside her. She glanced down into the open suitcase and let a quite whistle escape her lips.

'What the fuck have you done to me? I'll kill you, you know that, right? You're dead, both of you are.' His legs were gone completely; the arms too, all the way up to his shoulders. He could still see his chest rise and fall as he breathed, but nothing below his neck would move for him.

'I don't think you're in any position to make threats, Harry. And anyway, you've been trying to kill me for seven years. Not very good at it, are you?' She took off the sunglasses. Harry swallowed drily when he saw the sewn up hole where her eye had been. The girl; Alice. His own son had done that to her. He should have finished the job. Harry had tried to get to her when she was in hospital before the trial, but she had been too well guarded. Police would have been easy to pay off, but Tom Riley had put his own men outside the room. After the thing was over, she had just disappeared. The child had too, evidently. Riley's people put out a release saying that it was no longer safe for her life to be documented by the popular press, and asked for her privacy to be respected. And it had been, surprisingly. Harry's men had never been able to track them down.

'Look, come on. I'm a reasonable man. And I'm worth a few bob too, in case you haven't noticed. The girl... you, Poppy. Nothing happened to you, right? It was okay in the end, wasn't it? No one laid a hand on you. We can sort something out. What do you want? Either of you. Just name it. Please.' He knew what they wanted; and it wasn't money. He thought of Somersby's body, and what must have happened to him. Harry looked down at the case, with the last bit of feeling left in his neck, and suddenly felt sick when he imagined what its contents were.

'Nothing happened?' The younger girl spoke. Seventeen was all she could be, given the dates. He had been out by a few years. 'Nothing happened, because one of those bastards ballsed up, Harry. Not because you told anyone to stop. Not because of you. Nothing happened to me? What do you think I've been doing for the past seven years? Where do you think I've been? I'll give you a clue: it wasn't Disneyworld.' She slapped him across the face, and he was somewhat surprised that he could feel it. No part of him could move any more, save for the eyes and the mouth. And they were both going, fast.

'Oh yes, I know what you're thinking, Harry.' The girl who was Alice, not Amelia, reached into the case, taking out a long, sharp implement. The surgical steel flashed under the yellow light of the ceiling bulbs. Harry tried to swallow, but his throat had stopped cooperating.

'You're thinking: how can I still feel? Well, and listen, because this is the science bit- the toxin isn't a general anaesthetic. It paralyses you, sure. But it doesn't do anything to the nerve endings. You ever heard about those people who wake up on the operating table, but they can't move, and they can't speak? And they want to shout 'Stop!', but they can't move their mouth, or their vocal cords? So they lie there, in agony, feeling every cut of the surgeon's blade. Experiencing every second of the pain. Some of them pass out from the shock, Harry. So, maybe you'll be lucky like that.' She placed the scalpel on the desk in front of him, and then took another, equally terrifying looking implement from the case. His eyelids began to flutter and droop. He was losing the power to hold them open. She went on.

'I see you read the news. Terrible stuff, yeah? I think the worst thing about it was, and Pop will back me up here, that he didn't scream. It was just so… quiet in there. I know you're about to go into the dark now, Harry. I can see your eyes starting to close, but don't worry about that. I'll show you this trick I have, later.' Harry tried to say something, but it was no use. His ability to speak was gone. One eye closed, then the other.

'Ooh, there you go. Let me tell you the rest of the story anyway. Maybe having your eyes closed will make it easier to picture it all. I'm like that, Harry. I can imagine better when I'm in the dark. So, anyway. We've been busy girls, haven't we, Pop?' He could hear the sound of plastic being moved. Like someone was rooting inside a shopping bag. A lorry passing outside sounded its horn, softened by the double glazed windows. The most ominous sound of all was the one he knew to be the steel cutting tools being placed on the table, one by one.

'Your little girlfriend, Red. She was good value. So much expression in those pretty eyes, Harry. I can see why you liked her. She should be washing up soon too. We had to weigh them down, you see. Couldn't have you realising what we were up to. You might have tried to get away.'

Inside his personal darkness, he heard his heart thundering. He had never had much luck with his health. Maybe it would give up on him now and take him before they had a chance to do what they planned. He could only hope. He wanted to talk, but he was long past being able. He wondered would the drug stop his ears from working. There must have been a muscle in the ear. He couldn't be sure.

'The others were the same. Just your lot, by the way. The Albanians… well, that isn't my fight, Harry. Or Poppy's. We got Hansen easily. All it needed was a short skirt and a low cut top from Pop here, and an 'Oh, don't I know you from somewhere? The TV, right?' The ego, that's what you go for. Especially with the men. We did him slow, Harry. Very slow. Much slower than he did that poor girl. It took him hours to die. I was almost bored by the end. I wanted to shoot him, but little one here- she wanted him to suffer. We're not bad people, Harry. I know that if you could talk right now, you'd be telling me that you aren't a bad guy either. That it was all just business. Nothing personal. But you are a bad guy, Harry. You've done bad things, to a lot of people. And now you're going to pay. Don't get me wrong, I couldn't give a shit about most of the people you've wronged. Chances are they're scum, just like you. This is just for Poppy, and for me. Your son left me with something to remember him by. You'll be sure to say hello to him for me, when you see him. I'd like to say that's going to be soon, but…'

'Tell him about Don,' said the younger girl.

'That fucker? Yeah, he was a special one, Harry. I don't know what kind of sick shit the universe was pulling when they put that man in charge of- well, he was supposed to protect them, you know? Supposed to be looking out for the kids. Instead, he was…'

Harry heard more steel scraping, and what sounded like the click of the lock on his office door. After that, something which sounded like a chair or a table being dragged. It couldn't end this way. He had men in the building. They'd come up to the office for something. One of them usually did; checking about wages, usually. Especially on a Friday. If they saw the girl was gone from her place at the front desk, they'd figure something was up. When they found his office locked, they'd shout for him. When they heard no answer, they'd kick down the door. Harry didn't know how much of him would be left by that time, but they might at least save his life. It was a chance.

'Pop? What did you tell the guards downstairs, by the way?'

'Malcolm and them? Oh, I said that Harry wanted them to leave early, but they were to keep it under their hats, you know?'

'Did they just agree?'

'Well… I sort of had to hint that he didn't- that we didn't want to be disturbed up here. And that if we were, then Harry wouldn't be too happy about it…'

'Perfect. You hear that, Harry? Your reputation precedes you, clearly.'

If he could have been capable of it, Harry might have groaned with disappointment. It had been so simple. After all the years of no one being able to get to him, a seventeen year old girl had managed to separate him from his bodyguards with a couple of sentences, and all because he was known to be a man who enjoyed the company of his female employees. Especially the younger ones. No one was coming for him. It was over.

'Am I doing this, or will you?' Daisy's voice. In his head she was still Daisy, even though the truth of the situation couldn't have been more glaring.

'I did the last one. And anyway, this one's special. You go.'

Harry wondered what was coming. There was no place for him to escape to, even in his head. The only things which calmed him were the inevitability of his fate, and the dark. He tried to control his breathing, but it had become automatic since the drug had kicked in. He heard the younger girl again.

'Okay, Mister Goldman. Time for the show…'

They hadn't lied to him. He felt every cut of the scalpel as the girl removed his eyelids. The light flooded in suddenly, blinding him. When he was able to focus again, and when she had wiped the burning blood from his eyes, he saw that it hadn't been a chair or table they were dragging. The full length antique mirror from the corner of his office was planted in front of him; his own terrified reflection staring back. He wasn't going to miss a thing.

THE END

Printed in Great Britain
by Amazon